Doors

W0010550

Doors

Colby Millsaps

Copyright © 2019 by Colby Millsaps

All rights reserved. No part of this publication may be reproduced, distributed, or transmitted in any form or by any means, including photocopying, recording, or other electronic or mechanical methods, without the prior written permission of the publisher, except in the case of brief quotations embodied in critical reviews and certain other noncommercial uses permitted by copyright law. This book is a work of fiction. All names, characters, and incidents are products of the author's imagination. Any resemblance to persons, things, living or dead is entirely coincidental.
Printed in the United States of America
First Printing, 2019
ISBN-13 978-1-7336996-0-0
ISBN-10 1-7336996-0-0

*For all the ones who fought to live for so long but
eventually couldn't fight anymore.
Most importantly, for the ones who are still fighting
today.*

Table of Contents

Colby Millsaps

Chapter One

My eye was going to swell after this one. I could already tell. I gritted my teeth and watched my fingers in the mirror as they reached up to gingerly prod the bruise that was already beginning to blossom. *Nice*, I thought sarcastically as air hissed out from between my clenched teeth at the pain my own gentle touch caused. *Real nice.* I snatched a washcloth from the closet and ran it under cold water before dabbing it along my hairline, trying to clean up the blood that was starting to clot there. This was the last time. The steely resolve that had been steadily growing in my grey eyes had finally taken over. I was done.

I grabbed my toothbrush from the holder, took the whole tube of toothpaste for good measure, and stole a towel from the closet before tiptoeing back to my bedroom. I dropped to my knees and fished under the bed for the duffle bag I kept there, even though I knew if he had ever found it, it would mean the worst punishment I had ever received. I shook myself from my memories for the moment. I didn't have time to get cold feet.

The supplies I gathered from the bathroom joined my hairbrush and most of my clothes in the bag and I spun around to take in my bedroom one last time. Not a single thing in here represented me in any way. To be honest, I had no clue what I would even put in a room if I wanted it to look like me. But the frilly, yellow curtains and matching flowered comforter on the bed definitely wouldn't be on my list. For anyone who thought they knew my mom, though, this room would make perfect sense. The bubbly, happy-go-lucky florist who always had a smile. I wanted to gag just at the thought of her like that, but the urge mingled with regret for what I was about to do.

I pulled the zipper shut on the duffle, sealing away the last eighteen years in one stroke. It was kind of sad if I stopped to think about it...the fact that a seemingly normal eighteen-year-old girl could fit her whole life in one bag. I didn't waste time on my pity party, though. I was never one to wallow. Instead, I slung the bag over my shoulder and headed out my bedroom door, not even bothering to look back. I didn't make it very far before a growl caused me to jump. My eyes swiveled to take in the door on my left and I felt the tremors starting down my arms while I looked at it, as if it could jump from the hinges and attack me. It wasn't the door that scared me, though...it was the man that hid behind it. I held my breath as I waited to hear another noise, but the only thing that came was his drunken snores. My teeth sunk into my lower lip and I hesitated again, wondering if I should try to say goodbye, at least to her. But just as I lifted one hand towards the doorknob, my eyes caught on the dent to the right of it and I froze. Just one more reminder, only this one couldn't be covered up with makeup or carefully styled hair. My gaze flicked to where my sleeve had ridden up and the bruise that wrapped around my wrist and that was enough for me to remember my time was up. Nothing behind that door could hold me here anymore.

I let my arm drop back to my side and hitched the duffle higher on my shoulder. "Bye, Mom," I whispered almost inaudibly before turning and walking from that house one last time.

~

"Blimey, Colt, where's the fire?" I skidded to a stop just before I went careening into Jeremy, who was standing at the punch machine without a care in the world. *Right*, I thought. *Not everyone ran away from home on a Wednesday morning.*

"Sorry, Jer. What's up?" I asked in an effort to appear more normal. I was fighting a losing battle, though. He pulled his timecard from the punch before grabbing mine and sliding it in. The machine made a satisfying *thunk* before ejecting it back out to me. "Thanks," I said while I took it and replaced it into the rack where we kept them because he still hadn't answered my question.

"You okay?"

I looked up to see he was studying me, even more so than usual, and I was instantly on guard. I tried to subtly fix my hair to ensure it was covering my newest cuts and bruises. "Yep," I snapped. I didn't give him time to examine me further as I took a step away from him, towards the door at my back. "Well, I better go. Chelsea needed me for something right away." That was a lie and I think we both knew it, but he thankfully let me go without another word even though I felt his eyes follow me.

"Colt, hey," I jerked my head up just in time to avoid crashing into Chelsea as I came around the first bay of stalls. *Jesus,* I internally groaned. This day was going to be a nightmare if I didn't get my shit together, and I could not afford for that to happen. No matter what was going on in my life, I always had been okay here. The barn was the only real comfort I knew and I could not mess that up on the day I had finally decided to break free from that prison. "I was just looking for you! Hey, are you okay?"

The concern for me was always present in Chelsea's eyes, but it was stronger today. Clearly, I needed to work on my *I'm fine, everything's fine* mask. "Oh, yeah, sorry. I just woke up late today so I'm a bit frazzled. No big deal," I tried to wave off. I never woke up late, but I knew she wouldn't look into my lie too much.

My words seemed to appease her and she beamed a smile at me. "Oh, okay, perfect. Well now that you're here I kind of need your help." *Of course she did,* I thought. She always did.

"What's up?" I asked, always one to please. I saw Gizmo poke his head out from his stall further down the bay at the sound of my voice and he snorted and tossed his head. After the morning I'd had, I would love nothing more than to take him out for a long ride right now. Maybe take him and never come back. But of course, Gizmo wasn't mine to take. I turned my focus back to Chelsea as her signature frantic look came back over her face.

"Well, see, the thing is, I'm pretty sure I was supposed to do this last week, but I completely forgot. So then, we rescheduled for today, except I can't make that, either. You know, with show season really kicking into gear and the training schedule changing now that it's summer, I've been a bit unorganized..." She always gave too much information, used too many words. It was part of what made her such a mess all the time. Even her *thoughts* were too much. But I didn't mind. It was such a stark contrast to my home life, where very little was ever spoken and I tried my best to have zero human interaction, that I had come to welcome her scatterbrained ways. "So anyway, I was hoping you could head over there. Just get the details down for me. Like where to park, when to be there, what they want, all that stuff. We both know you're so much better at those sorts of things than me."

"Where?" I asked.

"The vineyard!" she exclaimed, like she couldn't believe she had forgotten to mention this vital bit of information. "You know the one..." She snapped her fingers as if that would somehow jog her memory. The thing was, I did know what she was talking about. It's not like there were all that many vineyards around, and this one everyone knew. Ventrilla Vineyards was a highlight of town, far nicer than anything else around. Not that I had ever been there, but everyone knew of it and the family that ran it.

Rumors of the Ventrilla family were all over, and while I was never part of the gossip mill, even I knew them. There were apparently three children in the family, but they had all been homeschooled, so the only time people really saw them was for sports. From what little I could remember about them, I knew the oldest had already graduated from college and was being groomed to take over the family business. Which was extremely successful. The weddings they hosted alone probably brought in hundreds of thousands a year, never mind all the tours of the vineyard they gave, other functions, and the actual sale of wines. It was so much money I couldn't even wrap my head around it. And now I would get to go and see it all first-hand.

"Yeah, I can go get the details. It's for Caroline's wedding this weekend, right?"

"Yes, exactly!" She clapped her hands excitedly but then her face turned grave. "Wait, no. *This* weekend?"

"Saturday night," I specified.

"No. That can't be right. It's definitely next weekend."

I was pretty positive it was this Saturday, as in three days away, but it was best to let Chelsea come to these conclusions on her own. "Is there a problem with this Saturday?" I prompted. I knew her schedule more than anyone and I wasn't aware of anything else she had going on.

"I just got off the phone with that barn down in Kentucky. I'm supposed to go pick up that gelding I told you about this weekend. I leave Friday." She continued to shake her head, refusing to believe this new predicament. "No, this can't be right. I never would have forgotten about Caroline's wedding. It has to be next weekend. There's just no way." Except, there was a way. No matter how hard Chelsea tried to keep everything in order, there was never order here. It was just who she was. I gave her a minute to process this while I watched Derek tack up Niko, a stunning black stallion. By the time he had tightened the girth, it seemed Chelsea had come to the conclusion that she was indeed wrong. "What am I going to do?" she asked me, wide-eyed.

"Why can't Jeremy or Derek bring them? It's just getting Niko and Tierra to the vineyard, isn't it?"

"Oh…right. That's perfect! Oh, you're a genius, Colt." And this was how life at the barn went. Chelsea would manage to get herself into some predicament, she would act like it was the end of the world, I would suggest a simple solution, and then she reacted as if Albert Einstein himself had risen from the dead to solve some impossible scientific equation. At the very least, it meant there was never a dull moment around here.

"Right then…" I rocked back on my heels while I stuffed my hands into the pockets of my jeans. "When do you need me to head over there?"

"Oh!" She jumped, having already forgotten the whole point of this conversation. *And* that *is why we end up in these situations*. She glanced down at the shiny watch perched on her wrist and then bit her lip. "Uhm, right now. Yeah…I think I was supposed to be there at nine? Or maybe it was eight…huh. Oh, well. I'm sure they won't mind too much if you're a bit late."

I gave a forced smile. *We'll see about that*, I thought. "Right, I'm sure. I'll head there now," I said instead.

My hunk of metal that passed as a car sputtered to a stop in the gravel lot before the grand entrance of Ventrilla Vineyards. The rumors of this place hadn't been entirely true, I thought as I craned my head sideways so I could take in the massive function hall in front of me better. This was *way* fancier than what people made it out to be. It was the complete opposite of everything I knew. The landscaping was immaculate, all the flowerbeds overflowing with colorful blooms that would have had my mom bouncing in excitement. The thought of her caused a lump to form in my throat, so I quickly shoved it down and stepped out of my car, slamming the door shut behind me and starting towards the entrance. I stuck out like a sore thumb here. What Chelsea had said about these people not caring that she had forgotten about their meeting? Twice? Yeah, I didn't think that was going to be the case. I highly doubted a place like this would take kindly to her harebrained ways. I took a deep breath to steel myself for whatever was coming and nudged open the huge oak doors.

Cool air blasted me as soon as I stepped inside. The room before me was enormous and I scrambled to keep my jaw from dropping to the floor at the size alone. My whole *house* could fit in this room. And even though the A/C was blasting, the whole place gave off a sense of warmth, like it was homey and inviting despite being the most opulent space I had ever been in. Everything was wood, the beautiful, polished, golden kind of log cabins. Stone accented everything and capped off the perfect rustic feel with an impressive fireplace to my left. The entire back wall in front of me was glass, but upon closer inspection I realized it was really all doors, able to open onto what looked like a huge balcony. There was even a sweeping, wooden staircase on my right that led up to a loft with what looked like a hundred tiny, round tables all draped in thick, white cloth. It's like every time I turned, my eyes landed on something else that was completely stunning. Once I managed to stop gawking and accepted the grandeur of this room, I finally realized I was completely alone.

"Hello?" I called, my voice echoing in the massive, empty space. I tentatively took a couple steps further into the hall, conscious of the fact that this was no place for some dirty, hand-me-down riding boots. This floor had probably only ever been stepped on with expensive loafers and high heels. "Is anybody here?" I called out again, craning my neck to see if I had missed anyone up in the loft area.

When still no one answered, my curiosity got the best of me and I tiptoed over to the wall of glass to see what the balcony looked out at. My jaw really did drop now. Rows and rows upon grapevines as far as I could see stretched out before me in the valley. It looked like it went on for miles. I caught a flash of movement in the vines and saw there were workers there, picking their way through the grapes. I lifted my hand and pressed it to the glass longingly, wishing I could be out there with them. It looked freeing for some reason. Instead, I begrudgingly remembered why I was here and turned back to the room, trying to figure out where to go now. I spied a hidden stairwell to my right and decided to try my luck there.

Even this staircase, which was clearly not for public use, was impressive. I played a quick game of eenie-meenie-miney-moe in my head and decided to head downstairs. My foot had barely touched the landing half a flight down when I was knocked back...*hard*.

I was used to being hit, but not unexpectedly. It knocked the wind right out of me. I would have laughed at the luck I was having lately, but then I remembered how painful it was going to be when my back hit the stairs behind me, especially with my most recent wounds. I braced myself for the impact, but then it never came.

"Shit! I didn't even see you there. Shit, I'm not supposed to say shit here. Wow, I am *so* sorry." My eyes flashed open and I gasped. Except this time, it wasn't from the pain I was so used to feeling. No, it was because of the eyes that were now boring into my own. I never knew eyes could look like that. The colors within them seemed to be at war with one another, the ring of bright blue around the pupil giving way to a brilliant green that bled into a deep chocolate brown color which was probably the only thing a normal person would notice. Apparently, I had suddenly become an expert on eye color now. In my defense, I hadn't even known eyes could have all those colors in them at once.

"I'm sorry. Are you okay?" a voice was asking me now and I blinked out of the trance this person's eyes had put me in. Instantly, I felt heat seeping through the sleeves of my shirt at my elbows where his hands had been holding me and I jerked away from the touch automatically. In doing so, I managed to trip over the bottom stair that was still right behind me and lost my balance yet again. In an instant, an arm was wrapped around my waist, catching me and pulling me forward. "Careful there. You're going to crack your head open on these stairs."

I fought the person's hold on me desperately, pushing frantically against his chest that was way too close to me now. "Woah, woah. You're okay. It's okay." Whoever it was finally released me after what felt like ten years, but had probably only been a couple of seconds, and I gasped air back into my lungs. *Ten. Nine. Eight. Seven.* I tried to calm my racing heart. *Breathe,* I thought. *This person's touch had* helped *not hurt. Just breathe.* I flicked my eyes back open to finally take in whoever this was.

Oh. My. God. I struggled to remember how to breathe again, but this time for an entirely different reason. The man who was standing in front of me now was gorgeous, if that was even how you described men. I wasn't sure. I had never felt this before, but *wow.* If I had thought his eyes were special, the whole picture made them seem plain. His skin was tan, not excessively dark, but more like that was simply how it always was even when the heat of summer wasn't setting in. His hair was dark, almost pure black, and shorter on the sides but beautifully messy on top, and for some reason it seemed vaguely familiar to me, but I couldn't tell why. He was wearing a plain grey t-shirt, the sleeves stretched over his biceps perfectly, and his hands were raised up in front of his chest in a sign of surrender. He cocked his head to one side as he looked at me. "Are you okay?"

"Y-yes," I stuttered. *Screw that,* I thought. *Since when did I get affected by a guy?* I stood up straighter and braced my hands on my hips to appear more composed. "Yeah, I'm good. Great, actually."

A slow smile formed on his lips and holy shit, his lips. How had I not managed to notice those before now? "Sorry about crashing into you. I'm normally the only one who really uses this staircase…"

His sentence ended in a question, though he didn't come out to ask it. *What was I doing here?* Clearly, I didn't belong. "Sorry. I was just trying to find someone who works here. A manager or something? I'm here for a meeting?" I hated how unsure I sounded when he was standing in front of me looking like the poster boy for cool, calm, and collected.

"And you are?"

"Colt."

He crossed his arms over his chest, stretching the sleeves with his muscles. I fought the urge to stare and focused back on his face. "Colt?" he asked while he quirked one eyebrow at me.

"Jefferson. Yeah."

"Colt Jefferson? Your name is actually Colt?" he laughed.

I bristled. If there was one thing I didn't hate about myself, it was my name. I wasn't about to take any crap for it from Mr. Perfect over here. "Problem?" I snapped, matching his stance with arms crossed over my chest.

He unfolded his hands to raise them again in front of him, palms facing me, reiterating he came in peace. His smirk grew to a full-blown grin though, allowing me a glimpse of white teeth. *Of course his teeth were perfect, too*. "Alright, Colt," he drawled and I hated how my name sounded coming from his lips. It sounded good. *Too* good. He extended one of his hands for me to shake. "Nice to meet you. I'm Rainer."

I eyed his hand warily. I didn't do handshakes. I didn't do contact of any kind. But I managed to put on my mask just like I had trained myself to do years ago and gripped his hand in mine. I was expecting it to be soft, like a guy this pretty couldn't possibly have rough hands, but he did. It was clear he worked with his hands a lot if the callouses I felt were any indication. Before I could chastise myself for analyzing the feeling of his damn hand, he was already pulling it out of my grasp and tucking it into the pocket of his torn jeans. His eyes seemed to glow as he looked back at me, that ring of blue managing to shine out like he knew his touch had just flipped my stomach upside-down. And then, the next thing I knew, he was off. Taking the stairs I had just come down a moment ago two at a time in his rush to get away. *What the hell?* I thought as I stood there in shock. *What kind of person crashes into you, introduces themselves, and then runs away without a word?*

I turned on my heel, ready to storm after him and give him a piece of my mind, but then I saw he was leaning over the railing already two flights above me, looking down at me as if he was waiting for me. "Well, are you coming? I thought you wanted to see a manager or someone?" I opened my mouth to snap a retort, but then shut it and narrowed my eyes at him. I didn't know what to make of him but for some strange reason, I found myself wanting to know more.

~

By the time I got back to the barn, my stomach was growling and I had a headache. Could that headache be due to the hit I had taken this morning? Sure. But I had a feeling it had more to do with the lady I had just been forced to deal with. In her perfectly pressed blouse, pencil skirt, and five-inch heels, she had wasted absolutely no time in expressing her intense disappointment in Chelsea and the barn. I took it graciously, of course. As if I had anything to do with the missed appointment. Not that this woman had known that or cared in the least. She had no time for explanations or excuses as she stormed around the grounds far faster than I would have thought was

13

possible in those heels, pointing out exactly where the trailer would need to go and what time to be there and about a million other details that were really just common sense because clearly she thought I had none of that. I hated to admit it, but I had spent most of the tour keeping my eyes peeled for another glimpse of Rainer, though I had no such luck.

A tap on my window forced me to lift my head from my hands where I had been attempting to massage the stress from my temples. "Rough trip to the vineyard?" Jeremy asked after he had pulled open my car door for me.

I snorted. "You could say that, yeah."

"Ah, they're just a bunch of stuck up gits. Come on, I brought you pasta salad and a sub for lunch."

My feet stalled just before we entered the barn. "Jer…I told you to stop bringing me food all the time." As much as I appreciated it, I couldn't keep accepting his hand outs. It was sending the wrong message. But at the thought of his pasta salad, my mouth watered and my stomach growled loudly, reminding me I had forgotten to grab breakfast amongst the mess that had been this morning.

He laughed. "Yeah, that's what I thought. Let's eat." He made to reach for my hand, but I sidestepped him and jogged up the stairs to the breakroom before I had to see the hurt on his face from my subtle denial.

Chelsea was already seated at the table with one of the trainers she had brought up from Kentucky on her last trip down there. She might be scatterbrained, but she sure was convincing. And well-known. She used to breed horses down south for years and people would come from all

14

over to see her and the way she could ride. For whatever reason, she left that all behind to come up to New England about a decade ago. I had never asked her why. I didn't ask many questions to anyone, because if you asked then you would be expected to answer some of theirs. I never wanted to be in that position.

So, she had started this barn and people flocked to her. *I* had flocked to her. She had that way about her, like she was a light and we were all moths drawn to her. That's why so many trainers from down south would come here. Just to be around her. They never stayed for too long, because New Hampshire wasn't the horse capital of America by any means, but we always had at least two well-known trainers on our staff. And Chelsea herself. Other than that, it was Jeremy, Derek, and myself that kept this place running. Chelsea had let me stay at the barn every day since I first stumbled upon it on one of my long walks home from middle school. She never asked why I always wanted to hide out there, or where my family or friends were. She just let me stay. And then when everyone else had gone home, she would teach me. She taught me everything I knew. By the time I was fifteen, she had put me on payroll because I had become so crucial to the barn. At seventeen, she allowed me to start teaching my own lessons. A year later, I was her go-to girl for any and all things that had to do with this place.

"Colt!" she gushed now as I came in from the barn. "How was it? They weren't mad I missed it, were they?" I forced a smile and shook my head for her while I took a seat. Jeremy placed a wrapped sub and a Tupperware in front of me and I shot him a glare, but opened the container nevertheless. I really was hungry.

"You're fine," I lied. It wasn't a big deal, after all. I was used to cleaning up her little messes by now. It was kind of like cleaning up all the debris once a tornado rolled through town. "All set for Saturday. I wrote all the details down so Jeremy knows where to go."

Jeremy paused beside me, his forkful of pasta salad in the air halfway to his mouth. *Uh-oh*, I thought. "I know where to go when I get where?"

"At the vineyard," Chelsea hurried on, stabbing at her salad without a care in the world, oblivious to the new tension in the room.

Jeremy slowly lowered his fork back to his Tupperware. "What about the vineyard?"

This was another thing about Chelsea. I would come up with the simple solution to whatever problem arose, but then she failed to inform any involved parties. In this case, Jeremy. "You need to take Niko and Tierra to the vineyard for the wedding on Saturday."

I munched on my sub while I watched their exchange, happy I wasn't the one confused by Chelsea's antics for once. He raised an eyebrow at her. "Since when do we run a shuttle service for our horses?" he scoffed in his British accent.

"It's for Caroline," Chelsea amended, as if that made it acceptable.

"Bloody hell." Clearly, this did *not* make it better.

"What's wrong with Caroline?" the other trainer asked. I had forgotten she was even in the room. I hadn't talked to her much since she arrived. I think her name was Sasha. Or maybe it was Sarah. Whatever her name was, she spent all her free time at the barn ogling Jeremy, who still hadn't acknowledged her efforts in the slightest. I had once overheard her gushing to Chelsea that his accent was just the 'hottest thing ever' and that she had always wanted an English boy. I was barely able to hide my laughter from the next stall over. Jeremy ignored her yet again now, his focus solely on Chelsea. I flicked my eyes to her in time to see her face drain of color.

"Oh...right. Yeah...you probably shouldn't go."

He pursed his lips and gave a quick nod before stabbing at his pasta angrily. Curiosity was coursing through me, but again...I didn't ask questions. So instead, I just ate my food in silence, alternating looks between the two of them until that other trainer spoke up again. "What am I missing here? Who's Caroline?"

It was clear Jeremy had no intention of filling in any blanks, so Chelsea happily jumped in. "Caroline is a good friend of mine. I've known her since I moved up here. She was one of my first and best clients." I didn't remember Caroline from then, and I never really interacted with her much even now. What I did remember was that Jeremy had taken over her training when he came to the barn five years ago.

"Yeah but why can't Jer bring Niko and Tierra to her wedding?" The fact that she used my nickname for him was not lost on me. I fought the urge to roll my eyes.

"Well...Jeremy never told me. He also never knew Caroline was seeing anyone...until she showed up with an engagement ring one day."

I almost choked on the water I had just swallowed. "You're joking...You were seeing Caroline Langston?" I gasped. He didn't justify me with a response. "How long?" Again, he didn't answer. "I can't believe you didn't tell me. Wow, what else are you holding back from me?"

"Colt...piss off."

"She was like six years older than you. You were only twenty when you started training her." He snatched the Tupperware with my pasta salad away from me. "Hey, I was eating that!" I attempted to stab a noodle as he stood and brought our dishes over to the sink to rinse them out. Chelsea watched us with a bemused smile.

"Not anymore. Go tack up Vance," he grumbled.

I scowled at him. "Like I have to take orders from you." But even so, I pushed in my chair and tossed the wrapping to my sub away. I noticed the other trainer glaring at me from across the table so I quickened my pace and jogged back down to the barn. I actually did have a lesson coming up, so I really did need to tack up Vance and lunge him. I trotted down to his stall and pulled him out to the crossties. Jeremy was just stepping off the stairs into the bay when I finished.

"So?" I didn't have to ask anything else, Jeremy always overshared with me. That's why I was so shocked he hadn't told me about this before.

He rolled his eyes at me but stepped over to grab the bridle I needed and handed it to me. "What?"

"Caroline Langston...you cougar hunter, you."

"She's only six years my senior. She was no cougar. I have six years on you. You see no problem in that."

"I'm not dating you." I laughed as I tossed a saddle pad over Vance's back and Jeremy caught it and positioned it on the other side.

He caught my eye over the pad. "You could be." I immediately turned to grab the saddle, avoiding any answer. It was no secret he had feelings for me. I just could never return them. "Colt..." At least with the horse solidly between us, he couldn't invade my space. Luckily, I was spared whatever he had to say next by a kid running down the bay from the open doors.

"Colt, are you ready?" The little boy was practically humming with excitement. It was an out I was happy to take.

"Yeah, Brady. Let's go." I clipped a lead on Vance and unhooked him from my side of the crossties. I knew Jeremy enough to know he wouldn't push me further than he already had. It was further than he had ever tried before, though. For now, he unclipped Vance from his side and I turned the horse around and followed the little boy towards the riding ring.

Luckily, I had two more lessons after Brady's and Jeremy was booked for the rest of the day, so it let me go without another interaction with him. When the sky had finally turned dark and everyone else had gone home, I made my way to the grocery store to supply myself with as much microwaveable food as I could get for now. Then I drove straight back, because for the first night ever, I was homeless.

My home had never been a home, but it had been a roof over my head and a bed with warm blankets. It was a place with food in the fridge and hot water to shower. It wasn't ever something to look forward to going to, but it was a place to go. Now, the barn was the only place I had to go to. I pushed open my car door and got out to the almost deafening sound of peepers from the nearby pond. I knew a lot of people who hated the sound of the tiny frogs on summer nights, but it had always been one of my favorite sounds in the world. I used to leave my window open a crack as soon as the weather started to get warm, waiting for the first night I would hear them in spring. They signaled the time of year it was easiest to stay away from my father. When the weather was finally nice enough for me to spend time anywhere but in that place I was supposed to call home.

The sound of them now gave me a little comfort as I popped the trunk to retrieve my duffle bag and sack of groceries. Gravel crunched under my feet as I walked around to the side door and shifted my bags to one hand to fish for the key I always kept on me. When I heard the lock click, I pushed open the door with a creak. I would have liked to say this was a first for me, breaking into the barn after hours, but it wasn't. I had run here on quite a few nights, with quite a few wounds, so I knew my way around in the dark.

I locked up behind me and then pushed the inner door open to the first bay of stalls while my eyes adjusted to the gloom. My feet were halfway to the stairs that led up to the lunch room and office, the room I would be staying in for the foreseeable future, when a soft nicker made me pause. I turned to see the silhouette of Gizmo's head peeking out at me and a smile tugged at my lips. My bags dropped to my feet and I grabbed one of the apples I had just bought, taking a bite out of it before walking over to him.

"Hey, Buddy." I reached out to stroke his nose and he nuzzled into me, his breath hot on my palm when he sniffed me. "Not surprised to see me, are you?" He nudged his head towards the apple in my other hand and I chuckled softly. I took one more bite before holding it out to him; he knew I had bought it for him anyway. My hand absentmindedly stroked up and down his nose while he chewed and I took a deep breath in.

"Happy birthday to me," I sighed.

Chapter Two

"What do you mean you can't do it?" I asked as I trailed after Derek Saturday afternoon.

"I mean, I can't do it, Colt. You have to bring them." He hung his helmet on a peg and raked his hands through his hair as if *I* was inconveniencing *him*.

"Chelsea said you would take care of it because she didn't want Jeremy going there and ruining the whole wedding." I explained for what had to be the third time and yet he still wasn't understanding.

"Yes, but she never asked me to do it and I have plans tonight."

Of course she never asked him, I thought. I threw my hands up in frustration. "Well reschedule them, because we need two horses at Ventrilla Vineyards within two hours."

"I'm not rescheduling because Chelsea made yet another error. She needs to learn from her mistakes."

"Derek, come *on*," I pleaded. I never pleaded. But I hadn't spoken to Jeremy since our conversation over Vance on Wednesday. He had been here this morning to give a couple lessons, but other than that it was just me and Derek at the barn today. If he didn't bring Niko and Tierra, there was no one else to do it.

He turned to face me and casually leaned into one of the wood beams at the end of a row of stalls. "Look, Colt, I can't do it. I don't know what you want me to say. I'll help you hook up the trailer but then I really have to go. You're going to have to bring them."

"You'll...I'm...what?" I sputtered. He couldn't be serious. "You do know I've never trailered...anything."

He made a face at me. "Well, that's not ideal. But it's not too bad. Just go slow."

"Just go slow?" I gasped, but he was already striding away from me, grabbing the truck keys on his way out the main doors.

~

Sweat dripped from my forehead as I finally pulled into the assigned parking area at Ventrilla Vineyards two hours later. I put the truck in park and attempted to unfurl my fingers from their death grip around the wheel. *Just go slow*, I thought sardonically. As if that had been good advice at all. Half the drive I had spent looking in the rearview, wondering if and when the trailer would go flying off or somehow swing out and crash into another car. I was going to *kill* Derek for this. And Chelsea. And Jeremy. No one was safe from me after this debacle. I stomped my way to the back of the trailer and went about pulling out everything I needed to tack up the horses for their photoshoot. This was ridiculous. Who needed horses at a wedding anyway?

"Do you always look so stressed and out of place?" I whipped around so fast at the sound of that low, hypnotic voice that I almost lost my balance. "Woah, there. You're okay." A tanned arm came out to steady me, but I quickly backed out of reach. What was it about this guy that set me so off balance?

"Rainer." I nodded curtly, as if seeing him now hadn't just sent my heart into overdrive. His smile grew to show off his straight teeth. They looked especially white in the last light of day and I hated how I noticed these things. Hated how just seeing him again gave me this weird feeling in the pit of my stomach paired with a strange calm, as if I had somehow known him before.

"You remembered my name." He said it like this simple fact pleased him for some reason.

I refused to read into that at all. "I'm good with names," I snapped before turning back to lead Niko out of the trailer. I could still feel him watching me even after I had brought Tierra out and began to brush her down.

"I didn't realize you were coming back," he finally said.

I didn't turn when I replied. "Neither did I."

I heard Rainer's throaty chuckle from behind me and it caused goosebumps to erupt along my arms. *Pull it together, Colt*, I internally scolded myself. "You weren't supposed to be here?"

"No. The guy who was supposed to bring them bailed, so here I am." I slipped Tierra's golden bridle over her face and adjusted the bit before clipping it in place. We had been instructed exactly what equipment to bring for the wedding pictures and everything had to be perfect.

"Do you want help?"

I quirked an eyebrow at him, finally taking the opportunity to properly look him over tonight. He was dressed in a crisp, white dress shirt with the sleeves rolled up to his elbows to expose his perfectly tanned biceps that were corded with muscle. Black slacks that hung from his hips perfectly. Shiny shoes. There was no way he would go near a horse in that. "Do you even know how to tack up a horse?" I chose to ask instead.

"Well, no..." He gave me an impish grin that finally caused my defenses to crack just a bit and I smiled back at him. "But I'm willing to learn."

I narrowed my eyes at him wondering how he was yet again the picture of confidence even though he was so clearly out of his element. There were about a hundred ways I could tell him to get lost. Half of them I could use and not even come across as a complete bitch. Any other scenario, that's exactly what I would have done. But there was something about this guy that I couldn't quite place. I found that I didn't mind his company. In fact, I actually wanted it. "Alright, let's see what you've got."

"You really didn't know I'd be here?" he questioned after I had told him as much just moments ago. I rolled my eyes.

"No. I told you, I just got roped into doing this today." His strides were longer than mine but he slowed to match my pace as we trudged up the sloping lawn towards the wedding party that was waiting for us. Well, not us exactly. Just the beasts we were leading behind us.

"Huh. And here I could have sworn you made sure you were the one to bring the horses so you could have a chance to see me again." I gasped at his brazen attitude and turned my head to find him smirking at my expense. I wanted to hate that smirk, but I couldn't.

Instead, I shook my head and laughed. "Wow. Humble, aren't you?"

"You know, I actually am."

I snorted. "Right, I'm sure." He didn't get a chance to argue because we had made it up to the wedding party and Caroline was already bouncing over to meet me.

"Colt! I had no idea it was you bringing them! I feel like I haven't seen you in ages!" The one thing I did remember about Caroline was her excessive energy. On a just-married high, it was clear she had taken it to a new level. She was mere inches away from tackling me in a hug before she managed to come to a grinding halt. "Oh, sorry, right. I almost forgot. You don't do hugs."

I forced a smile for her even though I could feel Rainer's questioning stare on me. Before now, I had been a normal girl in his eyes. Maybe a little clumsy, but nothing too strange. I kind of wanted to keep that charade going. "Hey, Caroline. Stuff came up with the others, so you get me. Hope that's okay. Congratulations on all this by the way." I waved my hand around at the scene in front of us, groomsmen and bridesmaids and photographers. Seemed like a bit much if you asked me, but to each their own.

"Thank you! And thank you so much for bringing my baby." She reached out and took Tierra's lead from me. The horse's whole demeanor seemed to shift and she quickly stepped up to nuzzle Caroline's hair, causing her to giggle. Tierra had been hers since she was just a filly and the two of them were incredibly bonded. She was essentially a bitch to anyone but Caroline, but she was the sweetest thing ever when they were together. I would find it amusing if she wasn't such a pain in my ass almost every day.

"Let's go people! This sunset isn't going to wait for us! Let's move!" The midget of a man who stood behind the camera started ordering people into position, so I was luckily spared from any more awkward small talk. I gave Caroline a boost up and then stood back to wait. It really was a pretty view. A pretty sunset. It was nice to remember there were still pretty things in the world even if I never was a part of them.

"Rainer, darling, I've been looking everywhere for you. Have you been out here the whole time?"

I had almost forgotten he was there, less than a foot away from me, until I heard his name called. I turned my head to see an older woman walking towards us in a beautiful, maroon dress. She had a warm, welcoming face despite having an air of importance, and she was looking at Rainer as if he was the most perfect thing she had ever laid eyes on. *Honestly, lady, I kind of think the same.* I wanted to smack myself for my errant thoughts, but I was too interested in seeing who this woman was.

"Hey, Mom," Rainer said easily as she got closer. *Mom,* I thought. I could see it now. It was no wonder he had this permanent confidence about him. He had to have gotten it from her, because it was clear to see she commanded this whole place without needing to say a word. She just had that energy. And yet, she seemed so *nice.* Control and kindness rarely went together in my world.

"You missed the whole ceremony, dear. I was looking for you. Are you going to come inside?"

I surreptitiously watched them, interested to get a glimpse further into who Rainer was. "You know I hate weddings. I still don't see why I have to be here."

She reached up to casually smooth some of his unruly hair back into place and he kiddingly shoved her arm away, causing her to laugh. A pang of longing went through me. I wondered what it was like to have that kind of relationship with a mother. "Yeah, I know. But this one isn't bad. You may actually have fun. You could even meet someone." She waggled her eyebrows up and down at him and I saw him roll his eyes in response.

"Ah, yes, the twenty business partners you want me to talk to. What a catch," he joked back.

"Rainer," she warned, but even her warning was gentle. Unfortunately, I didn't get to hear the rest of their discussion because Caroline and her husband were walking back to me at that time.

"Did you want to stay for the reception, Colt? We have plenty of extra food, I'm sure. I kind of went overboard on the whole planning thing," she giggled and gave her husband a sheepish grin. I reached out and took Tierra's lead from her.

"Oh, no, I couldn't," I said, gesturing down at my barn clothes. It was an easy excuse to make and I jumped on it. "Thank you, though."

"No, thank you. It meant a lot for Caroline to have Tierra here," her husband said now while she looked up at him all starry-eyed. I wondered if I'd ever look at a guy like that. I coughed to cover up the laugh that bubbled out of me at that thought. *Yeah, right. Definitely not.*

"Enjoy your night, guys. Congratulations again." I gave a little bow since my hands were now full with Tierra and Niko's leads and because I was the most awkward human in social situations. If they noticed, they spared me and didn't laugh, only wished me a good night while I turned to head back to the trailer.

"Colt!" I heard Rainer's voice call out to me on my way back down the hill, but I pretended not to. It was blatantly obvious our worlds did not mix. I may not have learned too much about him from eavesdropping on his conversation, but I had learned enough. He had a family who loved him, a mom who was trying to set him up with some probably beautiful girl in that fancy wedding venue, and so much confidence I didn't even know how to handle him. I was the complete opposite of the people in his world. I hadn't been expecting to ever see him again after our run-in the other day. Tonight was just another chance meeting, but I couldn't allow myself to hope for more. Hope was ugly.

"Colt, wait up." He wasn't even out of breath when he finally reached me, though it was clear he had just jogged to catch up. "Hey, I'm sorry about my mom."

"Sorry?" I asked, finally turning my head to look at him and being shocked yet again by how good-looking he was. I wondered if everyone felt this starstruck around him or if it was just me. "Why would you be sorry?"

"She interrupted us. It's just, she always likes me to come to these so that the people at them see me. She's always on me to stop hiding out in the fields, get more on the business side of things, but..." he trailed off with a shrug.

I made a face and nodded, as if I actually understood whatever it was he was saying. "Sure, sure. Makes sense."

"Sometimes I think she cares too much about appearances," he admitted after we had finally reached the trailer and I pulled the saddle off of Niko.

"Is she the wedding planner or something? Is that why the wedding was here? Because you work here?" I asked while I worked.

Rainer chuckled like my questions were silly, but I didn't take them back. I didn't see anything amusing in them. It was clear from the other day that he was a worker here; he had said as much just now when he mentioned spending time in the fields. And it was clear she was running the show tonight. It made sense that she was the wedding planner.

When it became apparent I wasn't laughing along with him, his laughter slowed and he looked at me closely. For a brief moment, I saw that flash of blue and green in his eyes again that caused my head to spin. I looked away and finished putting Niko's gear back in the trailer.

"No, my mother isn't the wedding planner. She owns this."

I gave him a questioning look as I stepped back down from the trailer and went to work on Tierra. "What do you mean, she 'owns this'?" I made air quotes as I repeated his words.

"Well, technically she married into it. But honestly, it's her that made this place what it is now. My father was just like me. He would have been content to just work in the fields all day. She's the one that turned this place into a destination."

I gave myself a minute to comprehend what he was saying as I folded Tierra's saddle pad and tucked it away. No way. Rainer was just a farm hand here. That was clear from his dirty hands and jeans the first day I had met him. Sure, he cleaned up nice, even though I had been fighting the urge to fully check him out all night. And yeah, he had the overwhelming confidence and charm...but no. He couldn't be...I paused and looked up at him again after stepping back out of the trailer. He saw the question in my eyes and his megawatt smile appeared again.

"I'm Rainer Ventrilla."

Chapter Three

Monday morning, I woke up before the sun did. I had to if I wanted to pull this whole living arrangement off. Besides, I hadn't been able to sleep much since Saturday night. After Rainer had told me he was a Ventrilla, I completely shut down. Not only was he *a* Ventrilla, he was *the* Ventrilla. He was the oldest son being groomed to take over the business. Which meant I had been very wrong when I said he wasn't a humble person. He was apparently *extremely* humble. If I had thought our worlds were different before, knowing this about him meant we were living in completely different galaxies.

I tried to force this from my mind as I shut off the water to the outdoor shower we only used on extremely hot days. The water might only run cold, but I wasn't exactly in a position to complain. I was lucky enough there was a shower here for me to use at all. I wrapped the one towel I had around myself and snatched up my shampoo and body wash so no one would assume I was using this every day and then headed back to what had become my living space. Luckily, Chelsea rarely used her office and yet still had a couch in there. The barn really was the perfect place to crash. As long as I was in and out before everyone arrived for the day, no one suspected a thing.

I pushed open the door to the breakroom and made to cross it to get to the office, but I had barely made it a quarter of the way through the room when a voice stopped me in my tracks. "Colt? What are you…?"

I whipped my head around to see Jeremy standing by the counter, the coffee pot poised in one hand, his mug forgotten beside him. I frantically clutched the towel tighter around myself and stared back at him while my mind raced to come up with some excuse I could possibly have for using the barn's outdoor shower at five in the morning. *Yeah,* I thought. *There weren't any.* My best course of action was to simply pretend this was normal and hope he somehow went along with it. "Morning, Jeremy," I chirped at him before turning to hurry towards the office.

"Bloody hell," I heard him curse from behind me and I froze. Clearly, that had been the wrong move. *Right. My back. Bad idea.* I turned back around to face him as quick as I could, but the damage was done.

It's not like I could see my back without a mirror, so I never knew the extent of the scarring and bruises there. Regardless, I knew it was the worst part of my entire body all thanks to a night I refused to acknowledge. It was never a problem to hide it from the world, except for just now when my towel only covered up to my shoulder blades.

"Jeremy…" I started, not sure where I was even going with this. How was I supposed to explain this?

He took a step towards me in concern, but I immediately mirrored him by taking a step back. He caught the movement and while he had always shown concern for me, this was the first time I saw fear in his eyes when they looked at me. Only, I couldn't be sure if he was scared *of* me or scared *for* me.

"Who did this to you?" he asked in a low voice that caused a lump to form in my throat.

I shook my head, half turning away from him so I didn't have to see the new pity in his eyes. "No one did this to me," I snapped angrily. "You know I'm a clumsy person."

He barked a humorless laugh. "That's not clumsy. That's bloody torture, mate."

I shook my head again and continued to avoid his eyes, but then I felt his hand touch my shoulder in an effort to turn me back to face him. I jerked out of his grasp and stumbled back away from him. "Don't touch me," I practically growled.

I saw the understanding dawn on his face. "This is why you never like anyone touching you. Why you never let people hug you. This is why…isn't it?" I didn't bother responding. There was nothing I could say. Instead, I backed the last couple of steps to the door that led to Chelsea's office. I half-expected him to try to stop me. Try to reach out and hold me here and demand answers. When he didn't, I realized it was because he no longer *wanted* to touch me. I had become something breakable in his eyes. Something to pity.

I gritted my teeth and slammed the office door between us. I didn't need his pity and I sure as hell didn't want it. I could barely hold back the tears that threatened to fall as I dropped to my knees to dig out my duffle bag I kept buried in the closet that Chelsea never remembered was here. After all these years of hiding it and pretending I was fine, that everything was fine, and I finally manage to escape…this is what I got? Not even a week on my own and already I had messed up. Jeremy would never look at me the same again.

Ten. Nine. Eight. Seven. Six. I took a deep breath in. Maybe this was okay. Maybe it had just been a gut reaction and Jeremy would forget about it, take my word for it that I was fine, and everything would be normal. *Five. Four. Three.* I tugged a new long-sleeve shirt over my head, making sure any and all bruises or scars were covered, and then pushed open the door to the breakroom again.

Jeremy immediately jumped to his feet and I inwardly groaned. *So much for forgetting all about it.* I eyed the cup of coffee he extended to me warily and he sighed. "Just take the coffee, Colt. I know you want it." I rolled my eyes and reluctantly took the mug from him. He was right, I did want it. "I'm not going to hurt you," he said softly.

I bristled at his words before I could even take a sip. They were meant to make me feel better, but they did the exact opposite. "I never said you were," I snapped. I had known him for five years now; I knew he wouldn't hurt me. All of a sudden, he felt the need to say it like I was some kicked puppy? Not that I hadn't been kicked before, but I was stronger than that. I could take care of myself. I had been for years.

He scrubbed a hand down his jaw at my hostile attitude and leaned heavily against the counter. "Can't you just tell me what happened to you? I just want to help you," he pleaded.

"I told you, I fell," I gritted out through my clenched teeth. "That's all there is to it, so just drop it."

He opened his mouth to say something else, but never got the chance. At that moment, Sasha/Sarah flounced her way into the breakroom, way too chipper for this early in the morning. It was the first time I had ever been genuinely excited to see her. Her feet stuttered to a stop once she realized she wasn't the only one here. I watched as her eyes flicked from Jeremy, then to me, and back to Jeremy who didn't so much as look at her. His eyes were locked firmly on me.

"I'm sorry...am I interrupting something?" Her jealous tone made it clear she wasn't happy to find me here alone with Jeremy. *You can have him,* I thought bitterly.

Instead of saying that, I plastered on my fake smile and put down my untouched cup of coffee he had given me. "Not at all," I said in my overly-sweet voice. "I was just heading down to take care of the morning duties."

"Colt..." Jeremy warned, begging me not to walk away like this, to not run away from this conversation, but I knew it was an empty threat. He was never one to fight. So I ran.

~

By Thursday, I was sure my shirts had a hole burned through the back of them by how many times I had felt Jeremy's eyes following me, begging me to talk to him. He still hadn't succeeded in cornering me and although it was a lot more work, I managed to get my routine at the barn down enough so that he would never be suspicious of me living there. It meant I barely slept at all, but that was something I was used to from home. On top of the annoying concern in his eyes, Sasha/Sarah was also keeping tabs on me this whole week. I'm sure she assumed me and Jeremy were having some steamy love affair and were currently in a lovers' spat, but that was so far from the truth it was laughable. Even if I did find her jealousy slightly amusing, the constant staring was getting on my nerves so much that I was snapping at almost everyone.

"Colt," Chelsea called out to me as I walked through the stalls in the afternoon.

"What?" I spat and turned to look at her.

"Jeez, what's gotten into you?" Her eyes were wide as she walked up to meet me.

I pinched the bridge of my nose and exhaled loudly. "Sorry, Chels. I guess I'm just not in the best mood this week."

"I've noticed. Hey, can we talk in my office real quick?"

Uh-oh, I thought. Part of what made living here so perfect was that Chelsea barely ever used her office. She was always on the go so much that the idea of sitting still in an office to have a conversation just seemed absurd to her. She also was pretty oblivious to minor details, so I never had to worry about making sure everything was in the exact right place when I left each morning. Now, I braced myself for her questions, figuring she had found out I had been staying here. I wondered if she would just let me stay. It's not like I was hurting anything. In fact, I had even cleaned the place up quite a bit. I was small; I didn't take up much room. Heck, I was willing to pay rent if she wanted me to. She could just take some money out of my paycheck each week. By the time I sat down in the chair in front of her desk, I had a solid argument rehearsed in my head of why she should allow me to stay.

"So your mom called me…" Part of me lit up inside, as much as I hated to admit it. *She missed me, she really had missed me.* But a part of me was bracing myself for her wanting me to come back to that place. "I missed the call actually, because well you know how bad I am at answering the phone. Honestly, people use phones way too much in my opinion and too many people call me. I really don't have the time for all that. You would think they would understand that, but no. I still get yelled at for not getting back to them in a certain amount of time. Oh, but that's not what I wanted to talk to you about." She waved her hand as if she could bat away all her errant thoughts to focus on what she had called me up here for. "Anyway, I missed your mom's call, but she left me a message. Nice lady, your mom."

"Mmm," I mumbled an agreement. Sure, my mom was nice. But my mom didn't stop what happened to us almost every night. My mom didn't stand up for me. My mom didn't even stand up for herself. If that's where niceness got her, I wasn't so sure I wanted to be nice. "What did she say?" I prompted Chelsea. If she could get to the point of this sometime within the next half hour, that would be great. Did my mom want me back? Was she worried about me?

"She wanted to invite me to the charity banquet the fire department is putting on in a couple weeks. Why didn't you tell me it was already coming up?" she gushed.

My face froze in its smiling mask, but inside my blood boiled. *Really? That's* what my mom called about? Nothing about her only daughter who ran away from home over a week ago without a word? She didn't wonder what happened to me? She didn't ask Chelsea if she had seen me? Made sure I was okay?

"Must have slipped my mind," I said through gritted teeth. To be completely honest, it *had* slipped my mind, though I don't know how that was possible. It was the one time my family appeared all together, all of us putting on the perfect act. The really fun part of the torture I called my life was that on my father's days off from drinking, he was a lieutenant for the fire department. Everyone in town loved him. The men in the police department were some of his best friends, which ensured any accusation I would have thought of making would only be laughed at as childish. They all knew Lieutenant Jefferson would never hurt a fly. What no one knew was that they only ever saw his public face. They didn't get to see him at night, when he didn't bother to hide the reek of booze on him like his own personal cologne. They didn't know what he turned into.

Every year, the fire department put on a banquet as part of the kick-off to summer and Fourth of July celebrations. It was a big to-do for our town and my parents were at the center of it all. Most specifically, my father was. More than anything, it was his banquet and the town knew it and loved him for it. When I was little, I loved it. It was one day when my father would love me. He'd smile at me and introduce me to people. Except as time went on, I learned to hate it. Learned to hate the fake act he put on. It never failed to become my least favorite time of the year. I started to see how the added stress of putting it all together made my father drink even more than usual, if that was at all possible. My mom's planning of it was never good enough for him.

It only made sense he would take his stress out on us; would punish her for not being the perfect wife she always pretended to be. And then, the big day would come. We would put on our best clothes, cover our cuts and bruises with makeup and fancy cloth, and we'd be paraded around as if we were the perfect family. Everyone's favorite firefighter, his perfect florist wife, and the quiet daughter. It made me sick. I'm sure my father was missing his favorite punching bag now as the weeks before the event dwindled down.

"Nothing ever slips your mind," Chelsea laughed. "You're going, right? I mean of course you are, you go every year. Your family is the star of the show."

"No. I'm not going this year."

She gave me a shocked look. "Why not?"

"I'm busy that day," I deadpanned.

If she could tell I was lying, she didn't call me out on it. She knew I was never busy unless I had something to do for her. It was no secret that the only life I had was related to this barn. "Huh, well alright then. I just wanted to call you up here to ask if you or your mom needed me for anything for the event. I'm always available to help you guys!"

I forced a smile, more than familiar with Chelsea's idea of helping. She always meant well, but her idea of help never seemed to *actually* help. "No that's fine, just show up. You know that's all my mom ever asks for."

"Wonderful! You know I always love that event! Well, that's all I wanted to chat about. She sounded good by the way, your mom. Happy." She smiled at me like this was supposed to make me happy, too. In another situation, it would have. Now, it fell like a punch to my gut. It hurt more than any hit I had taken from my father.

"That's awesome," I told her as I turned to walk out of her office, pretending yet again everything was fine.

She was happy? She wasn't concerned where I was at all? She was simply relieved I was gone? I always thought of us as a team. We took it together. Me more than her, but still. She was the one person in the world who knew. Who understood what it was like every single day. Who knew what went on behind the doors of our house that had never ever been a home.

"Colt, we need to talk."

I jumped at the sound of Jeremy's voice. I was so lost in my own hurt that I hadn't even realized he was in the breakroom when I went to walk through it. "Jesus, Jeremy. Don't scare me like that."

"I'm sorry, but I can't keep having you run away from me." He was right; I had been keeping my distance lately. Ever since our run-in the other morning in the breakroom, I was avoiding him at all costs. Running and hiding were two things I had become skilled in over the years. Now, he tried to take a couple steps towards me but I quickly stepped around him on my way to the stairs that led down to the barn. I did not need to add this on top of what I already was feeling today.

"I've got a lesson."

"No, you don't. Just let me talk to you." He was begging at this point and instead of softening my resolve, it only increased my anger.

"Not now. I'm not in the mood today." I didn't wait to hear his reaction, just pushed out of the room and took the stairs two at a time in my rush to escape him. I nearly crashed into a guy with dark hair and olive skin at the bottom of the stairs. It seemed like I was always crashing into someone these days. I scrubbed a hand down my face in frustration. "I'm sorry, I wasn't paying attention."

"It's fine," the guy chuckled. "Hey, you're Colt, right?"

I really looked at him now and the smaller girl next to him that had to be his sister. They had the same unique skin tone and dark, dark eyes. She took lessons here with Derek and I couldn't remember her first name, but I sure as hell knew their last name. They were Rhymes, the family of boys notorious for throwing the bonfires that I used to frequent years ago. He was the youngest of the boys and had been in my class, one of the star baseball players, but I had never really talked to him. I knew his older brother better. All I knew of Nate was that he had been really good friends with this girl that had died last month in a car accident. Funny how the brain only seems to remember tragic things.

"Yeah. We had calculus together last year," I managed to recall instead of his recent dead friend.

"And bio sophomore year." He smiled and it was the type of smile that was infectious. It was no wonder he had been one of the most popular guys in school. I was surprised he remembered that we had had a class together sophomore year, let alone that he knew my name.

"Yeah, that's right," I nodded. "Well, it was good to see you."

"You, too." His little sister tugged on his hand, urging him to go, but he turned back to me before they had made it to the exit.

"Hey, Colt?" I turned back around to face him. "If you're not doing anything Saturday night, we're having a big bonfire out at Baker's Field. A bunch of kids from our class are going, probably some other people, too. If you wanted to swing by, that would be cool." He smiled at me again and I found myself smiling back and even nodding, though my mind was already racing.

"Yeah, that could be fun."

"Awesome." His grin grew. "Hopefully I'll see you."

Chapter Four

I sat in my car facing the field I hadn't been to in years. There was a time when I had thought this place might save me. How stupid could I have been?

I looked back down at my fingers which were clutching my steering wheel even though I was parked and I could see the tremors starting in them already. I couldn't stop my mind from racing to the first night I had ever come here.

The nights were just starting to get a chill in them, the sun starting to set earlier and earlier every day so that by the time I had walked from the barn back home, it was pitch black. But I didn't mind. I wasn't afraid of the dark. There were more real things to be afraid of than simply darkness. I still had over a mile to go before I'd be home, but I was fine with taking my time. And then I heard something other than the hoots of owls and scuttling of squirrels in the trees. What sounded like voices, laughter even, was coming from the woods to my right. A couple steps later, I saw for the first time a dirt path that turned off from the main road. It was mostly overgrown, just another logging road I had never bothered to pay attention to until now. The laughter was coming from somewhere down it. I couldn't remember the last time I had laughed.

What fifteen-year-old girl doesn't spend half the time giggling? This one. I looked forward towards the dark road that I took to get home every night, then looked to my right again at this new road. It only took a second for me to decide I was going to find out where this path led. Maybe my life up until that point should have molded me into a scared child who didn't do anything out of the norm. Instead, it made me more reckless.

The further my feet scuffed down the dirt, the louder the voices got. Girls squealing, a guy's deep laughter, and then a glowing light. When the woods opened up to a grassy field, I could see flames of a bonfire licking the dark sky, sparks flying up until they finally burnt out and disappeared. Cars were parked haphazardly in front of me and feet dangled from truck tailgates while some people lounged on the grass like they had no care in the world. My feet only hesitated a minute before I found myself walking straight into a group of unknown people. It didn't take them long to realize someone else had shown up and whispers to start.

"You look a bit young to be out so late," a deep voice broke through the whispers as I came closer to the main group by the flames. I turned to see a boy with deep olive skin looking at me with a warm smile, his head cocked to one side. He didn't seem angry that I was there, so I took that as a good sign. He was simply curious, something I could understand.

I shrugged my shoulders and told the truth, but laced it with a laugh to make it seem like it wasn't a concern. "Beats being stuck at home."

A couple people in the group chuckled and one girl raised a cup. "I can drink to that," she said before downing whatever had been in the solo cup. The boy next to her scoffed and elbowed her in the ribs.

"You can drink to anything, Nina," he muttered.

The first boy who had spoken was still watching me with bemused eyes, trying to get a read on me. It didn't take much to know he was the unspoken leader here. "What's your name, kid?"

"Colt." I shoved my fists into the pockets of my torn jeans and tried to stand up straighter, appear like I was older, that I belonged here.

"Odd name." The boy turned to look at a guy I hadn't noticed before to his left, giving him a questioning look. "What do you think?"

This boy wasn't paying much attention to me, he had his hands full with the girl who was wrapped around him, but now he turned to face me and I was able to make him out in the light of the flames. He was handsome, I could tell that even in the flickering light, and he seemed to give off even more warmth than the flames he was standing next to. He smiled at me as I looked at him, his teeth shining in the darkness and lighting up his strong features. "You look like a wild child," he said, then he laughed as if he had made a joke in his head. "Hey, you remember that show that was on when we were kids?" he asked the group at large, but his eyes were still fixed on me. I felt like he was only speaking to me even though there were almost twenty other people in the area. "*The Wild Thornberries*! That's what it was. You remember?"

A bunch of people laughed and agreed they remembered it. Some girls even screeched how much they had *loved* that show. I had no idea what they were talking about. I couldn't remember a time in my life that

I had ever watched TV, but I nodded at this mystery boy anyway. I didn't want to let him down. His grin grew when I nodded. "The wild child they took in, what was his name? Manny? Danny?"

"Donnie?" the leader of the group added from his right.

"Donnie! Yeah! I'm gonna call you Donnie. That sound good, wild child?"

This time there was no doubt his question was directed at me and me alone. I found myself smiling for the first time in weeks then. "Yeah. Yeah, sounds good to me," I grinned.

"Colt Jefferson, I'll be damned." I shook myself out of my memories and turned to see Marcus Turner leaning into my open window. He must have come over to see what odd person pulled up to the bonfire and then never got out of the car. I took a deep breath, reminding myself this was a different time. That had been the past. Marcus didn't know the me that used to hide out here. He only knew the façade I was for everyone else.

I had been in Marcus's English class every single year in high school and I guess if I had to choose someone, he would have been the closest thing I had to a friend in school. Not that it meant much. Friends weren't really a thing in my world. Not when you could never invite them to your house or ever have them around your family. Not when the one person who I truly thought was a friend I had found in this very field. But he had abandoned me. I shook myself again and focused on Marcus and the person he knew me to be. Cool and indifferent. It was one of the masks I wore well.

"Hey, Marcus. You going to get me a cup of that, or are you just going to stand there looking pretty?" I nodded toward the cup in his hand as I stood from my car and started to walk towards the keg. He laughed loudly and stretched his legs to keep pace with me.

"So the truth comes out after all these years. You did have a crush on me." He ambled towards the keg and grabbed a cup to fill it, flashing a too-white smile over his shoulder at me.

I smirked up at him. "You wish, Golden Boy." I had started calling him that our sophomore year, because he really was a golden boy. Between his blonde hair, blue eyes, and perpetually tanned skin, he looked like he belonged in southern California, not New England. Pair all that with the fact that he was one of the star athletes and biggest class clown of the school, the title fit him perfectly. It also reiterated just how different we were.

He chuckled and passed me the almost overflowing solo cup. When I took it, I noticed my fingers still shook from my memories so I forced a big gulp down to calm myself. Marcus walked next to me as we made our way towards the blaze and I scanned the people spread out on the logs and overturned buckets. Funny how things could change. I hadn't been back here in so long, close to two years had passed, and the faces around me now were very different from then. "Haven't seen you around in a while, Jefferson. You should come by more often."

I rolled my eyes at him and stood off to the edge of the fire, happy to watch all the conversations instead of joining in on any. "School's over. Why would you see me?"

"We do these pretty often. Figured you knew about them." He turned to see me studying the crowd and then surveyed it himself. It was clear some people had started the party early by how they were stumbling around or the raucous laughter that would erupt from a group. "Nate's oldest brother Brent is home this summer for the first time in a while so I think a few of his friends are around here, but other than that it's the normal crowd."

I nodded, not really caring but trying to appear normal. I had no idea what that meant; had no clue what the normal crowd was anymore. I hadn't realized how quickly I was drinking until I went to take another sip, but there was nothing in my cup to drink. Marcus chuckled at me. "Looks like someone needed a drink, bad. I'll go fill you up." He took my cup from my hand when I gave him a sheepish grin and disappeared back into the gloom in the direction of the keg.

I forgot how much enjoyment I got out of people watching at these parties. Seeing the different girls in their skimpy outfits growing more sloppy as the night went on. The guys reveling in the attention said girls paid them. It never failed to make me chuckle. I couldn't imagine being one of those girls; the ones who threw themselves at guys. What did they get out of that? A night of sloppy sex and then awkward interactions for the rest of the year at school? Didn't seem like much fun to me. Then again, there had only ever been one person to catch my attention at one of these parties and still I never threw myself at him. I had no desire to throw myself at any guy.

I would much rather stay far, far away from men. Especially when they had been drinking.

"I heard you needed a refill." The voice that spoke directly into my ear caused goosebumps to erupt on my neck. When I turned to face him, I'm sure my wide eyes did nothing to hide my shock at seeing him here. He took a step back so he was no longer completely invading my personal space and extended a red solo cup to me with what I had already learned was his trademark smirk. I hesitated to take it. "I didn't lace it, if that's what you're thinking. But I know, I know. Your dad probably taught you to never take drinks from a man unless you watched him pour it. Don't you trust me, though?"

I eyed him warily, taking in his mussed-up hair and white t-shirt paired with faded jeans. He looked good. Then I quickly became frustrated at myself for even thinking of how good he looked. I huffed and snatched the cup out of his hand, downing half of it before choosing to respond to him. When I did, I turned back to face the fire so I didn't get lost in those stupid, amazing eyes of his. "No, my father didn't teach me much of anything except how to take a hit. And no, I don't trust you." I tossed him a glare out of the corner of my eye. "I just really needed a drink tonight."

If the comment about my father fazed him at all, he didn't show it. I was thankful for that, because I was shocked I even said it. I hadn't drank much in the past year or so and it was clear drinking that beer so fast was already getting in the way of my normally guarded demeanor. I saw him clutch at his heart as if he was in pain. "Ouch, harsh words, Colt. *I* trust *you*."

I snorted and turned my head to look at him. "Well, you shouldn't."

Rainer eyed me for a second, trying to read into my words, but he didn't get a chance to question them. "Sorry, he said he knew you. I hope you don't mind I let him take it, I had to catch up with someone."

I smoothed my face back into a smile for Marcus as he came back to stand beside me. "It's okay. I forgive you."

"I didn't know you guys knew each other," Marcus mused.

"We don't," I deadpanned. For some reason, it caused Rainer's grin to grow.

"We met a couple weeks ago at the vineyard. Then she came back again last weekend, stalking me. She just couldn't stay away."

"God, what is it with you? I was *not* stalking you. Someone needs to knock down your huge ego a few pegs." I swallowed down some more beer as Rainer burst out in laughter.

Marcus laughed at my hostility. "Nice to know she tolerates you even less than she tolerates me."

Well, it was good to hear I kept my inner feelings about Rainer a secret. I thought it had been written all over my face just how affected I was by this guy. "Eh, it's okay. She'll love me one day."

I almost choked on the beer I had just swallowed and Marcus barked a laugh. "Good luck with that, Rainer." I didn't wait to hear how he would respond, just shook my head and made to walk away.

"Woah, wait up." Footsteps quickly followed me and a hand wrapped around my elbow. I jerked out of his grip immediately. It was easy to play it off as simply annoyance from his last comment and not from the crushing weight of fear that came over me as soon as any hand touched me. "I'm sorry." His smile seemed to say otherwise though and I scowled in return. "I would say I didn't mean it, but I did."

My mouth opened, but then closed again. I had nothing to say to that. I wasn't going to fall in love with this guy, so I didn't know what he was playing at. Sure, I found him insanely attractive, more so than any other person I'd ever met. And sure, when he touched me the fear I always had was somewhat less than normal, as if my desire to be touched by him combatted the general anxiety connected with touch. And maybe I had thought about what his lips would feel like against mine, but maybe that had more to do with the two cups of beer I had downed than any rational thought. But he didn't know any of that, and he never would. Love? Love was out of the question. I had already learned what getting close to someone could do to you.

When it was clear he wasn't going to just leave me alone, I sighed and crossed my arms over my chest. "What do you want?"

"To know you."

"You do know me. Colt Jefferson, remember? Pretty sure you made fun of my name nine days ago."

"So you've been counting the days since we first met." I didn't think it was possible, but his grin grew even larger. I brought a hand up to cover my eyes and groaned. I tossed my empty solo cup in the fire and watched it melt before I turned and headed back towards the keg. I didn't even need to turn my head to know he was following. "No response to that?"

"I've found it best to just ignore your ignorant comments. I was hoping it would prompt you to leave me alone."

"Mmm, not a chance." The little mumbling sound he had made as if he was thinking about it made my knees weak. I didn't even know that was a real thing until this moment. *Damn him.*

"What are you even doing here?" I filled up another cup and brought it to my lips as I turned to face him. His eyes squinted at me, casually calculating my alcohol intake. I pretended like I didn't notice his scrutiny.

"Hanging out at a bonfire. What are you doing here?"

"I mean, aren't you a little old for this crowd? Why are you here?"

He didn't get a chance to answer me because Nate came up behind him and clapped him on the shoulder at that point. "Rainer, I haven't seen you in years. I'm surprised you're here."

I watched a flash of something dark cross over Rainer's face, but then his overconfident grin was back full force and he playfully ruffled Nate's hair. "Hey, buddy. You've grown since I last saw you."

Nate rolled his eyes at Rainer's comment and attempted to swat his hand. "Dude, stop acting like you're so much older. You and Brent are both annoying as shit with that." Brent was Nate's oldest brother according to what Marcus had said earlier. I never knew him. He had already left for college when I first showed up to the bonfires at Baker's Field. So that meant Rainer must have been friends with Brent, making him at least five years older than me. Even though I wouldn't admit it, my heart sank at the age gap as I added it to my mental checklist of reasons why we could never ever work. Not that I had even thought about it. Definitely not.

"And that's why we will keep acting like that. Because it annoys you so much, little man." Nate just shook his head in defeat and turned his attention towards me.

"You made it!" His always welcoming personality was back in the blink of an eye. I smiled in return.

"Yep, free booze. How could I say no?" I raised my cup to him and he chuckled.

"I see how it is," he slurred, enough to make me realize he, too had been drinking plenty tonight.

"Nate, man you gotta come over here." Some guy I recognized from Nate's group of friends came up and interrupted us then.

"Why, what's up?"

"It's Samantha, dude. She's not okay." A pained expression immediately took over Nate's previously infectious smile. He scrubbed a hand down his face and nodded at the guy before turning back to Rainer and I with a smile again, though I could see through it. His eyes were sad now, his whole posture seeming defeated.

"Hey, it was nice to see you guys. Colt, you should come around more often. We do these all the time now that summer's here." I nodded but couldn't see myself coming back all that often. My days of frequenting this field were long gone. He turned to Rainer and his voice dropped, changing to something almost somber. "It's good to see you finally came back."

Rainer's throat bobbed as he swallowed hard and gave Nate a nod and I wondered what the hell that was all about. He tossed us both one more half-hearted smile and then turned to follow his friend back towards where the cars were parked. I was so focused on watching them leave and trying to figure out what just happened between him and Rainer that when Rainer spoke next, it caused me to flinch. "What was that about?"

I turned my attention on him. "What?" I had a feeling he was deflecting, making sure I didn't ask him any questions about Nate's comment. It was a tactic I knew well.

"Who's Samantha? It seemed like that was a big deal."

Part of me wanted to ignore his questions and ask my own. I had never had that urge before. I didn't care to ask more about people. But his face was back into its relaxed smile and I knew my chance to ask was long gone. Instead, I just shrugged. "Samantha's one of Nate's really good friends. Her best friend died last month and the two of them were closest to her. Mixing sadness with alcohol is never a good plan."

Rainer stuffed his hands into the pockets of his jeans and nodded like he understood. I wonder if he had ever been in the position to know. "So you're not drinking away your sorrows then?" He tilted his chin towards my half-empty cup.

Is that what I was doing? I looked up at him from under my lashes. "Nope," I replied shortly. He didn't get to know why I was drinking. No one did. His words made me realize I should probably get going, though. I wasn't one to get sloppy drunk and if I stayed here, I had a feeling I would end up that way. I quickly finished what was left in my cup and wiped my mouth with the back of my sleeve. For some reason, that simple action rewarded me with another of Rainer's smirks.

"I'm heading out. I would say it was nice to see you again, but I'm holding back my judgment of that." I stepped around him and headed towards my car, careful not to trip over any sticks out here in the long grass.

"Woah there." Of course he wasn't going to just let me go. "Where do you think you're going?"

Home, was on the tip of my tongue, but I didn't say it. I didn't have a home anymore. I'm not sure I ever really knew what a home was. "I'm leaving," I answered, not slowing my pace at all for him to catch up. Why did it feel like he was always running after me when I was ready to go?

"You're not going anywhere." His voice sounded firm now and I actually let out a humorless chuckle. He had to be joking.

"Yeah, actually, I am." I pulled my keys out from my back pocket and pressed down on the unlock button, waiting for my lights to blink their location to me. When they did, I turned and headed in that direction.

"You can't be serious."

I whipped around to face him when I finally reached my driver side door. "I don't know why you think I'm going to stay here just because you demand I do."

He chuckled as if I was something cute and ran a hand through his hair. "I'm not demanding you stay here, Colt. I'm saying you're not driving right now."

I made a face at him. "What are you talking about?"

"There's no way I'm letting you drive right now. I just watched you pound two beers and who knows what you drank before I saw you. You're not driving."

I laughed, because to me this was actually comical. Two beers was nothing. If only he knew what my father would drink in a night and somehow always manage to get his ass home. Rainer just stared back at me stoically until my laughter subsided. "You're not joking..." He shook his head and crossed his arms over his chest, drawing my attention to his very muscular biceps. I swallowed the sudden lump in my throat and refocused on his face. "I'm fine to drive, but thanks for the concern," I said coolly.

"You're not fine to drive. Give me the keys." He held one hand out, palm up, waiting for me to drop my keys into it.

"I don't know why you think you're some knight in shining armor or something, but I don't need you to save me." I turned away from him and pulled open my door. In an instant, his arm came around to slam it shut and cage me in against the car. I struggled to get my breathing under control due to his sudden closeness. For the first time, I wasn't sure why my heart was racing. I didn't think it had much to do with the fact that someone was so close to me, but more to do with the fact that it was *him*. My heart actually *wanted* him close to me.

"I'm no knight in shining armor, Colt," he practically growled in my ear. The sound of it caused me to gasp, my response to him completely out of my control. He leaned away from me, enough so that when I got a hold of myself again, I could turn around to face him. He was still entirely too close, but I couldn't help it; a part of me enjoyed it and that part was beating out terror at the moment. "Give me the keys, Colt." His voice was soft now, and so were his eyes. It was enough to make me want to melt and I found myself dropping my keys into his outstretched palm. His eyelids fluttered shut briefly, as if me handing the keys over relieved him of some immense fear. Then he walked around to my passenger door and held it open, silently waiting for me to get in.

We didn't talk at all in the car. The only time one of us spoke was when he asked where he needed to go and I directed him which turns to take. After what seemed like forever, the headlights swung into the parking lot of the barn. Rainer pulled the car all the way to the main doors and then put it in park. I unbuckled my seatbelt and went to push the door open.

"This is where you're going?" he asked.

I turned back to look at him, my eyelids heavy. In the drive over, I succumbed to how tired I truly was. I had barely slept this entire week and it was finally catching up to me. "Yeah. Thanks for the ride. Except now you're going to steal my car, aren't you?"

"I'll get it back to you." He brushed that thought off like it was no big deal. Maybe to him it wasn't a big deal, but some of us only had one car and that was our sole form of transportation. I needed this beat-up hunk of metal. If my head weren't so fuzzy, I probably would have pushed this issue. As it was, I couldn't find it in me to have a logical argument about my car right now. "This is a horse barn, Colt."

I rolled my eyes. "I'm aware of that actually. Turns out I'm really not as stupid as you seem to think I am."

"I don't think you're stupid," he sighed. "I just don't know why you brought me to a horse barn at one in the morning. I'm trying to bring you home; can't you just accept that I'm trying to be nice and let me bring you home?"

He actually thought I was messing with him right now. I suppose I could see where he would have thought that. I had been a bitch to him pretty much since I met him, but it was all in the name of self-defense. My problem now was I hadn't really thought any of this through or else I knew I never would have put myself in this position. Damn beer. Damn boy who thinks he can save me.

"I am accepting that. This is where I needed you to bring me. So thank you. You should go now." I pushed open the door fully and made to step out, but his hand found my wrist and forced me to wait.

"You needed me to bring you here? I can't just leave you outside a barn, goddammit."

I shoved a hand into the back pocket of my jeans and extracted my key before wagging it in front of him happily. "I have a key, see? Are you happy now? I can get in said barn."

He didn't say anything for a minute and I saw in his eyes that he was thinking hard, then his face grew dark. "Are you living here?" he gasped in understanding.

Not good, my fuzzy brain registered. I stood from the car and quickly walked towards the side door of the barn. "Thanks for the ride!" I tossed over my shoulder, not waiting to see if he tried to follow me. Not caring what happened with my car at this point. I just knew I needed to get away. It was my go-to tactic; just shut up and walk away.

Chapter Five

"Colt." I vaguely registered my name being called but it sounded like it was coming from far away, so I decided to ignore it. When I felt something shaking my shoulder, I had no choice but to peel my eyes open. I immediately threw one arm over my face to shield my eyes from the light streaming down on to me. It seemed to be coming from an unnatural angle, too high up to be coming through my bedroom window. Then I remembered I didn't have bedroom windows anymore. The office of the barn had no windows. So then…where was I?

I reluctantly lowered my arm and squinted my eyes. The ceiling above me was rough wood and far too high. Whatever I was sleeping on was hard, much harder than the couch I had been calling home. And then Jeremy's face came into view. "Blimey, Colt. What are you doing?"

I turned my head to the side to see the stalls beside me. I was indeed sleeping in the aisle outside of Gizmo's stall. The events from last night came flooding back. Rainer. Rainer driving me back here. Me essentially running away from his questions. Coming into the barn and hanging out with Gizmo until I apparently passed out right in the middle of the bay. Now, I sat up slowly, stretching the knots out from my back. Good thing I kept this barn in pristine condition. Even then, I couldn't believe I had slept on this floor. Jeremy's hand reached out towards my head and I jerked back. He rolled his eyes at me.

"You've got hay in your hair," he deadpanned before reaching forward and plucking out a piece of hay. I rubbed my hands down my face and then through my hair, teasing the knots from it and letting it hang down to cover part of my face. Even though I was no longer sporting a bruise on my lip and the cut through my brow had started to heal and itch, it was an old habit to always cover my face as much as I could.

"What time is it?" My voice was groggy from sleep as I finally pulled myself up. Gizmo nickered from next to me and I reached out to stroke his neck.

"Nine."

I was grateful Jeremy just left it at that instead of drilling me with questions. I took the chance to rub the sleep from my eyes and stretch my back. Even though it didn't feel like it, that was probably the most sleep I had gotten in two weeks. Jeremy still didn't speak as I walked to the feed room and started filling each of the horses' buckets with their individual concoctions. "Is Chelsea here?"

"No," he replied from his spot by the door where he was leaning to watch me.

"So why are you here?" I knew before the question was even out of my mouth that I was opening myself up to another interrogation by him, but I was genuinely curious as to why he was here. No one was supposed to be in today until noon.

"I came to check on you." I didn't even bother replying to him; there was nothing to say to that. The sound of grain hitting the plastic buckets cut through the silence. "Colt, talk to me."

"I don't know what you want me to say." I busied myself with the different feeds and medicines, making sure each horse got what they needed.

"Why don't you just start by telling me why you were sleeping on the barn floor."

"I wasn't sleeping."

"Colt, I called your name at least a dozen times before shaking you awake." I rolled my eyes and started piling the buckets back in one another to take out to the horses. "Why won't you just tell me what the hell is going on? You're showering here, you had clothes in the office to change into the other day, I find you asleep on the floor on a Saturday morning...Are you living here?"

I pushed passed him and into the first bay of stalls, unlatching a door and stepping in to take out the night feeding bucket and replace it with this morning's. I knew Jeremy had followed me out and I could feel him watching me as I made my way into each stall. When I still hadn't given him an answer after making it all the way down the bay, he growled in frustration. "You're not living here." There was no longer a question in his voice, this was a demand. I finally lifted my eyes to look at him. "I don't know what is going on with you, but if you think for one minute that I'm going to allow you to live in this barn-"

"You have no idea what you're talking about," I spat through gritted teeth.

He threw his hands in the air. "So enlighten me then! I've been trying to talk to you for a week now. You've got to give me something."

I clenched my jaw and grabbed the buckets I had prepared for the next bay of stalls. He didn't need to know my life. I didn't owe him anything. Sure, he was a nice enough guy. And sure, if things were different maybe I would have been able to return his interest in me. But that just wasn't in the cards. Him sticking his nose into my business wouldn't help anything. I was doing fine on my own. Believing someone could actually help me if I just opened up and told them what was going on had only ever hurt me.

"Fine. Don't tell me a damn thing. But I'm not allowing you to live here, Colt. You're coming home with me."

I actually laughed at his demands. He was never one to make demands. In fact, his lessons were good solely because he was a talented rider, not at all because he was tough on his students. He would let anything slide. "You've got to be kidding me."

When I finally turned to face him after exiting another stall, I could tell from his expression he was not at all kidding. "As soon as you're done here. Get your things."

"My god, you're not my father," I growled. It was just a figure of speech, though. My father was never concerned with my well-being. Clearly, since he was the one who had inflicted my current housing state.

"If you continue acting like such a child, I'm going to have to act like your father."

I couldn't help my laughter again "You're going to have to choose, Jeremy. You can't want to be my father and boyfriend all at once."

He winced from my harsh sarcasm. "Why can't you just let me care about you?"

"I don't need you to. I didn't ask you to. And for the record, I'm not acting like a child. I have *never* acted like a child." I gathered all the empty night buckets and brought them back to the grain room, then locked the door behind me. I didn't wait to see what Jeremy would do, I just pushed out the side door into the morning sun. It was already starting to get hot; today was supposed to be brutal. I had almost made it around to the front of the barn when I remembered my conversation with Rainer last night. The fact that he had my car. I had no idea when it would be returned to me.

I groaned in frustration, refusing to head back into the barn to continue my conversation with Jeremy. When I rounded the corner though, there was my car. Still looking like a beat-up hunk of metal, sitting exactly where I normally parked it. My mouth popped open in surprise, but I didn't have time to stall because I could already hear Jeremy's footsteps following behind me. I reached for the driver side door and it easily popped open, the keys dangling in the ignition. On the dash, there was a folded blue piece of paper with my name scrawled across the front of it. I quickly grabbed it and shoved it into the back pocket of my jeans before Jeremy had something else to question me about.

"Colt, wait." I didn't bother to turn and look at him, I knew him enough to know he'd continue without my prompting. "I'm going to have to tell Chelsea if you're not going to let me help you. If you're not going to tell me what's going on. I can't let you live like this."

He had hit my weak spot and he knew it. I hated him for it. "Don't." I wasn't one to beg and I didn't want to start.

"So tell me what's going on."

"Just don't tell Chelsea."

"Are you going to let me help you?"

"I don't need help," I spat.

"Then I have no choice." His eyes looked sad when he told me this, but I didn't really believe them. If he told Chelsea, she would freak out. She would call my mom. My mom who never protected me like a mother was supposed to. And I would have to go back to that place. The prospect of living with Jeremy didn't seem any more appealing. I refused to give in to his wants under the guise of helping me. I didn't need his pitying eyes on me every second of every day. I didn't have to say anything, the furious look on my face was enough to tell him he had stepped too far. The car door slammed in his face after I had thrown myself into it.

My fingers fumbled in my pocket until they latched on to paper while I drove and I pulled out Rainer's note to read, not bothering to slow down. His handwriting wasn't what I had expected. Judging from his appearance, I would have thought his letters would be precise, carefully crafted. Instead, it was a messy scrawl that filled the ripped page. For some reason, I was reminded of his words last night, spoken roughly into my ear. *I'm no knight in shining armor.*

Colt, the note read. *I'm sorry for stepping over the line last night. I wish you would forgive me, I didn't mean to make you uncomfortable. I'll be at the vineyard until eleven. If you wanted to come by. If not, I understand. But I hope you do...*

He didn't sign it. Then again, he didn't need to. I actually snorted at his idea that I would come by. Why would I go to him? We weren't friends. I didn't need him prying into my life any more than he already had. Yet in spite of that, I found my car turning off the road at the Ventrilla Vineyards sign and winding up the hill to the enormous function hall.

I parked directly in front of the hall, just as I had the first time I had come here, and I felt just as out of place as I had that day. I was starting to really question my decision to come here now. I didn't belong here. I never would. And why did I go running to Rainer Ventrilla when things got tough? Since when did I run *to* anyone? I didn't. I sighed and tilted my head to the side so I could take in all the grandeur of the function hall. I shouldn't be here.

"This was stupid," I muttered to myself and shifted my car into reverse to leave just as Rainer pushed open the front doors. His eyes landed on my car and a smile split his face.

I kept my foot on the brake as he sauntered towards me. He didn't bother to quicken his pace; he knew I wasn't going anywhere now that he was in sight. Damn him for that confidence. Damn him for always looking so good, even in his ripped and dirt-covered jeans that hung low on his hips. "I see you found my note," he drawled.

I shifted back into park discreetly. "I might have."

"And you just couldn't resist, hm?" I rolled my eyes. *Maybe I shouldn't have shifted back into park after all.* He must have seen the thought in my eyes because before I could respond, he continued. "I'm kidding. Come on." He pulled open my door and waited for me to step out, but I stayed in my seat staring at him. It was still possible to leave. I still hadn't wrapped my head around why I had driven here in the first place.

Now it was his turn to roll his eyes. "Come on, Colt. You know you came here for a reason. Get out of the car and let's go swimming."

"Swimming?" I managed to sputter.

"Yeah, it's hot as hell and I've been in the fields all morning. It's time for some fun." His grin took on a different appearance. Something close to a sexy smirk and in the very back of my mind I registered that he was attempting to flirt with me and that I did indeed feel something stirring in my stomach, but my fear overshadowed all of that. He must have finally registered the expression on my face because his smirk faltered. "You do know how to swim, don't you?"

I clung to his question because it was easier than what I was focusing on...how much skin would be exposed in a bathing suit. "I...I don't know," I admitted to him.

He cocked his head to one side in confusion. "What do you mean, you don't know? How do you not know if you can or can't swim? When was the last time you went?"

I looked away from his penetrating stare and the swirls of green and blue there. "Um...I don't know." I had a brief flash of running into a lake when I was really little. My mom was with me; I remember her laughing from the shore and there was someone else with us, too. I could remember him tossing me around in the lake. He reminded me of my father, but I was sure it wasn't him even if I couldn't fully remember the man in my memory. One thing I knew for sure was I had never laughed or had fun with my father. Ever.

"You don't remember when you went swimming last? Are you afraid of water or something?"

I shook my head, pulling myself out of my fuzzy memory. "No. It's not that."

"Then what is it?"

He got me with that one. My first instinct with him was to always tell the truth, which wasn't something I was used to. Ever. But this is where my honesty would have to end. How could I admit I hadn't gone swimming in years because that meant my skin would be visible? The cuts, bruises, countless scars, would all be on full display in a bikini. So instead of answering him, I just shrugged and stood from my car, nudging the door shut behind me.

"Is it because you don't have a suit? Because I'm sure I can find one for you. Rach must have left one out somewhere. You'd probably fit." His gaze traveled over me from head to toe and I felt myself blushing as goosebumps raised on my arms, not that he could see that beneath my long sleeves. I could feel his eyes on every inch of me, as if he was physically touching me. It wasn't a feeling I had ever felt before and I shivered involuntarily. Rainer's lips twitched up in a knowing smirk and his eyes darkened. He knew what his full body scan was capable of doing to girls. I hated that I was one of those girls. I also hated that this "Rach" person he mentioned sounded like a cute pet name for a girl named Rachel. I had no idea who she was or what she was to him, but I was stunned by my instant hatred for her. I crossed my arms over my chest and narrowed my eyes at him.

"No. I just never had an urge to swim," I lied. "Even if it was that, I wouldn't borrow your girlfriend's bikini."

My comment caused him to actually throw his head back and laugh while he stuffed his hands in his pockets and strode away from me. "Oh, so now you're laughing at me?" I growled while I hurried to catch up with his long strides. He never asked for me to follow; he just assumed I would. I hated that he was always right. I hated *him*.

"You're funny."

I glared at him out of the corner of my eye once I had caught up to him and was struggling to match his long strides. "I didn't say anything funny."

He paused and swiveled to face me as we made it to the far end of the dirt parking lot where a private lane turned off. "Rachel isn't my girlfriend," he said seriously.

"Oh." *So I was right about the cute pet name then,* I added in my head while I tightened my folded arms over my chest.

Rainer chuckled again and stepped in close to me. Way too close and my heart rate responded to that immediately. I felt his finger under my chin, tilting my face up to look him in the eye now that he was towering over me and my breathing stopped completely. "I would not have invited you here if I had a girlfriend." His eyes searched mine and paused as if he was thinking if he should say any more. Whatever he saw in me must have encouraged him to continue. "I've never invited a girl here."

His fingers left my chin and he turned to walk up the lane, leaving me behind. I gasped air into my lungs once he was no longer touching me and felt the tremors running through my body, as familiar as my own heartbeat. But there was something else this time. A warmth. I found my own fingers coming up to touch where his had branded my skin, still feeling the ghost of his touch. For the first time since I could remember, I was aching to be touched again.

~

"Mom! I'm back!" Rainer called after he had pushed open the monstrous front door to what I assumed was his house, though I'm not sure I could even call this place a house. It resembled more of a mansion and I was fighting to keep my jaw wired shut so it wouldn't hang open in awe. I didn't know much about the Ventrilla family; nobody knew much about the Ventrillas. The only thing that was common knowledge was that the Ventrillas kept to themselves. I admired that. But it also meant I had no idea what I was walking into now. That was something I did *not* like. I was always prepared; almost annoyingly so.

Surprisingly enough, it wasn't a woman's voice answering Rainer that I heard first. Instead, it was the pounding of tiny feet, then a plop, followed by more pounding, and yet another plop. I glanced at Rainer in confusion, but he wasn't paying me any attention. He still hadn't looked back at me since he had held my chin between his fingers.

"Wainer! Wainer!" A toddler came barreling towards the entryway and then suddenly tripped over absolutely nothing, falling down on her diaper-clad bottom *hard*. That would explain the random plopping noises. I chuckled to myself as she bounced back up, not seeming to be at all phased by her fall, and then careened into Rainer's shins at full speed.

"Careful, Munchkin," Rainer laughed and bent down to scoop her up in his arms, tossing her in the air lightly before cuddling her to his chest while she giggled. I didn't know babies well, had never even been around any before, but I knew this kid was small. Definitely no more than two years old, if that.

"Wain. Wawa."

Whatever she was saying, Rainer must have understood because he laughed again as he shifted her to one hip and walked further into the house. "Hmm...maybe. I told you I would later." I tiptoed after him, gawking at the intricacies of the mansion and the fact that he was so at ease with a baby in his arms.

"Rainer? That's you, right?" I heard heels clicking towards us as we made our way into an enormous kitchen. What was even the point of having a kitchen this big? You could host a whole party just in this room. And that refrigerator...I didn't even know they made refrigerators that big. My mouth watered just thinking about all the food that must be in there and my stomach growled involuntarily. I couldn't remember when I had eaten last. Between the stress with my situation at the barn and Jeremy, and then the whole night of drinking and waking up outside of Gizmo's stall, I don't think I had eaten a thing in over two days. Not that it was a huge deal to me.

I had definitely gone longer without food when I was younger and trying to avoid my father.

"Who else would it be, Mom?"

Mrs. Ventrilla entered the kitchen from another hallway holding an open folder in her hands. She looked just as stunning as she had at the wedding even though it should have been a lazy Sunday at home. It didn't look like this woman knew the meaning of that, though. "You didn't work late for once? I'm shocked." I could hear the love in her voice, even behind her teasing tone. I saw Rainer roll his eyes at her comment but he still smiled at her.

"Gammie! Wain wawa." The toddler reached out to Mrs. Ventrilla and she laughed and took her from Rainer's arms once she had put down her folder on a counter. That's when her eyes fell to me where I was still frozen in the doorway to the kitchen.

"Oh my! And you have a guest. You're just full of surprises today, Rainer. Who's this?"

I saw Rainer open his mouth to answer for me, but I could handle myself. "Colt. Colt Jefferson."

Mrs. Ventrilla smiled at me warmly. "It's a pleasure to meet you, Colt. I wish I could stay and get to know you some, but I was just about to be on my way out. I've got to meet with a potential distributor. Rachel's in her room, Rainer. She said she would watch Viviana for the afternoon."

I saw Rainer grimace and glance at me. I wasn't sure what was going on in his head, but it was clear he was having an internal debate. Then he turned away from me again to face his mom. "Nah, I've got her. I told her I'd take her swimming at some point today. Me and Colt can handle her."

My confusion was wiped away for a moment as I took in Mrs. Ventrilla's dazzling smile. That saying about a smile being able to light up an entire room? I'm pretty sure it had been made up about her. "That's wonderful! Just remember her floaties, and her hat, oh and the sunscreen, and-"

"Mom," Rainer cut her off, holding up one hand. "I know."

She chuckled, then sighed. "You're right. I trust you." For some reason, Rainer's jaw ticked when she said this. If I hadn't been watching him so closely, I never would have noticed it. "Alright, I've really got to get going. I love you," She reached up to kiss his cheek and then smiled warmly at me. "Nice to meet you, Colt. Maybe I'll see you again, soon."

Her heels clacked across the polished hardwood floors and I heard a door shut in the distance, leaving me and Rainer alone again. Well, not completely alone. There was the baby. That we were apparently watching now. Like I knew how to take care of a baby.

"She doesn't bite, you know." My gaze was drawn up from the baby's unruly curls to Rainer's face. He was watching me scrutinize her with playful eyes. "Actually, she kind of does. But it doesn't hurt." The baby giggled when Rainer tickled her sides and let out a shriek that caused me to jump. Rainer's following laughter prompted my huff of frustration as he walked closer to me.

"Do you want to hold her?" he asked.

I took a step back into the hallway, shaking my head vehemently. "No. Definitely not."

Curiosity sparked in Rainer's eyes at my adamant refusal, but he didn't push it. I didn't want to touch her. She looked so breakable. I could so easily hurt her without even trying. Something so pure, so beautiful, did not deserve to be tainted by me.

"Wain. Wawa," the little one pleaded again, smacking his chest.

"What does that even mean?" I finally asked as I crossed my arms over my chest.

"Wawa is how she says water. She wants to go swimming. So I guess you have no choice but to come with us." He flashed his dazzling smile at me, as if he thought that would get me to change my mind. It probably worked on plenty of girls. It wouldn't work on me.

"I'll watch."

"You're an odd girl, Colt Jefferson."

"Never claimed I was normal," I deadpanned. Normally, my completely closed-off nature was taken as being cold and uncaring. Yet in spite of that, Rainer laughed out loud again and the sound of it caused goosebumps to erupt all over me.

"Alright then. Let's get this one ready." Rainer brushed passed me, his arm grazing mine and sending a shiver down my spine. Again, he didn't ask me to follow but regardless, I found myself trailing behind him. I still didn't know what I was doing here. More than that, I had no clue why he wanted me here. But for some odd reason, I was actually happy to be here.

He led me up a first flight of stairs and down a hall to a white door that he gently kicked open. It looked like someone had exploded a can of pink paint in here. Multiple cans. The walls, the bean bag, the fluffy ottoman, the sheets in the crib, literally everything was pink.

"Wow," I muttered under my breath.

Rainer happened to hear it and laughed as he bent to set the little girl on a plush carpet. Of course, it was pink as well. "A bit much, right?"

I cleared my throat. I had no right to comment, but felt that overwhelming urge to always speak the truth with him. "I don't know if I've ever seen this much pink. Ever. In my entire life."

He turned from where he had pulled open a door to a walk-in closet and studied me with his head cocked to one side. "Yeah," he said slowly, his eyes traveling a path from my head to my toes. I crossed my arms over my chest again in an attempt to protect myself from his gaze and I was reminded once more just how out of place I was here, with him. "You don't strike me as a pink girl."

His words paired with that smile caused my lips to turn up just a bit. "You don't say."

"I like that about you." What little smile that had been forming on my face instantly vanished at his admission, replaced with an odd feeling of pride mixed with guilt as my cheeks heated.

I wanted to tell him he shouldn't. He shouldn't like anything about me, even if it made me happy that he did. I wasn't planning on sticking around anyone for long, so he shouldn't get attached. The baby spared me from saying anything, though as she yanked on one of my pant legs and I leaped back as if I had been shocked. I hadn't been paying attention to her crawling towards me on the rug and suddenly she was way too close. My sudden leap away from her had caused her to fall back on her bottom

75

and her face started to screw up as I stared at her. Then, out of nowhere, she started wailing. My eyes grew wide and I whipped my head back up to find Rainer already striding towards her, completely at ease, as if this sort of thing happened all the time.

"What the hell?"

Rainer laughed as he reached for her and scooped her up again. Immediately, her face smoothed out and the wailing quieted. "Don't let my mom hear you talking like that around her."

My eyebrows raised in confusion. "What the-" I stopped myself. "What just happened?"

"You startled her."

"So she cried?"

"You really know nothing about babies, do you?" He grinned over his shoulder while he laid her down on some table-like thing and began changing her into a bathing suit.

"Not at all." And I had no desire to.

"Well, for future reference, most people have fears and get scared, Colt. Not everyone is made of stone."

"I'm not made of stone," I whispered. I wished that I was. I had wished it for years. Maybe then I wouldn't hurt so much.

Rainer turned back around after pulling a floppy hat, pink *again*, low on Viviana's head and he studied me. I was realizing he did it a lot, like I was a puzzle he was trying to figure out. It shocked me that it didn't even bother me; I invited it.

He didn't pry for what I meant by that comment, but it was clear he knew there was something behind what I had said. Instead, he held out the baby to me. "Watch her while I change into my suit."

"Wh-what?"

"I've got to change to take her swimming."

"And you expect me to watch her? After all that?" I waved my hand around in the air, indicating her random bout of crying just moments ago.

Rainer laughed. "Yes, Colt. That was normal. She's a toddler."

"You trust me?"

His eyes held me frozen in place, just like they had the first time I ran into him in the stairwell. "Yes. For some reason I don't fully understand yet, I trust you."

It was clear we were talking about more than just a babysitting duty. He held my gaze a moment longer and then walked passed me down the hall. His fist knocked on a closed door further down.

"Rach, we've got Viviana. Not that you were concerned," he called on his way passed.

I was still watching him disappear down the long hallway before he turned a corner at the far end when the door he had just knocked on cracked open. A girl who looked a few years younger than me stepped out with her arms folded over her chest. I had never seen anyone with such dark hair before. It fell in soft waves all the way to her waist and was pitch black. She finally turned and saw me standing there, uncertainly holding on to Viviana, and her eyes pierced me, and not in a good way like Rainer's did. They were such a vibrant green I questioned if that was even natural. What was it with this family and eyes? Because it was clear the little spitfire before me was

Rainer's sister. There was no questioning those good looks. The resemblance was uncanny.

"Who are you?" And that was where the resemblance ended. Her voice was so icy I almost shivered.

If she thought I was one to be easily intimidated, she was in for a rude awakening. "Colt," I answered shortly. The baby squirmed in my arms and I fought to hold her still.

Rainer's sister let out a low laugh, not anything like when Rainer laughed at me good-naturedly. No, she was relishing in my obvious discomfort. "Well, Colt. Have you ever even held a baby before? Because you're doing a shit job of it." She uncrossed her arms and strode over to me, easily snatching Viviana from my grasp and holding her on a hip with one hand. Her eyes continued to scan me from head to toe, no doubt sizing me up. Probably wondering how something so dirty had ended up in her pristine world. I wanted to laugh just imagining how she would have responded if Rainer had asked her if I could borrow one of her bikinis.

"Well?" she asked. "Are you mute or something?"

"What?" I didn't realize she actually expected an answer to her question about babies. It was clear I had no idea what I was doing.

She rolled her eyes at me. "What are you even doing here?"

I fought down my initial response of *I don't know.* "I'm with Rainer."

"Obviously. What isn't obvious is why you? You're not his type."

"Obviously," I retorted, doing my best to copy her snide tone. I saw a flash of something in her shocking green eyes, almost as if she liked my response and wanted to smile, but her face remained a perfect mask.

I was curious to see what she would say next, but Rainer reemerged from down the hall at that moment, breaking up whatever it was that was going on between us. If he was aware of any tension, he didn't show it.

"Hey, Rach. I see you've met Colt. We're going to take Viviana swimming. You want to join?

She gave another of her humorless half-laughs. "No." She thrust Viviana into Rainer's arms and retreated back into her room, swiftly shutting the door behind her.

Rainer rolled his eyes and gave me a grin before leading me down the stairs. "That's my little sister, Rachel."

"Pleasant." The sarcasm wasn't hidden in my voice.

He chuckled and held open the massive oak front door for me, following me out without bothering to put on shoes. "Yeah, well…teenage girls…" He trailed off when he noticed my raised eyebrows. "She wasn't always so…"

"Bitchy?" I filled in for him. His answering laugh made me feel a little less guilty about my judgmental comment.

"Yeah, that," he chuckled while he strode across the plush lawn towards a gated-off pool area to the right. "She actually used to be pretty damn cool. Well, until Viviana. Until everything happened." His entire mood changed with that one sentence.

My curiosity got the best of me. "Everything happened?" I questioned.

He slowed his steps to match mine and opened his mouth to respond, but never got the chance to get it out.

Out of nowhere, some underground sprinkler system came on and within seconds, all three of us were drenched in icy water. Rainer's eyes found mine and I was sure his expression of pure shock matched mine as we stood in the onslaught of water. Viviana's shriek of joy broke our disbelieving stare down as she threw her little fists in the air, attempting to catch the falling droplets.

"Wain! Wain!" she squealed. I wasn't sure if she was talking to Rainer or referring to the sprinkler water as rain, but her reaction caused me to laugh. And once I started, I couldn't stop. I hadn't laughed so hard in months, *years* even. Maybe it was something about being caught completely off-guard when I always fought so hard to anticipate what was coming. Maybe it was because I had absolutely no control over this situation, and for once it wasn't even bad. Dare I say getting drenched by sprinklers was actually…fun?

Whatever it was, Rainer caught on to my maniacal laughter and Viviana's peals of joy soon joined ours when he set her down on her unsteady feet. I spread my arms wide and spun on the spot, feeling the cold water seep through my long-sleeve shirt and plaster the wisps of hair that always hung loose from my ponytail to my face. My tattered sneakers were now puddles on my feet as I spun and spun until I was as unsteady as Viviana. My eyes fell to her and I noticed she was mimicking me as best she could, but she fell on her bottom every couple of seconds.

Not fully aware of what had come over me, I ran at her with my arms outstretched like an airplane and she screeched before toddling away from me through the puddles that were already forming in the grass. She looked back at me as she ran, her little mouth open wide in delight, and I swear I had never seen so much pure joy in my life. It made me feel warm when I had only felt cold for so long. She stumbled over nothing, which I was quickly realizing was all-too-common, and I scooped her up before she could hit the ground. I spun her around in a circle in the mist of the sprinklers as she giggled and tried to catch more drops in her tiny fingers.

Finally, I caught a glimpse of Rainer as we spun and my breath caught. Water had soaked his hair, making it darker than normal but still beautifully messy. The light grey t-shirt he had thrown on with his swim trunks was now soaked onto his body as if it was a second skin, leaving nothing to the imagination. I could have counted the ridges up his stomach if I wanted to. I had never been so drawn to someone before in my life. It was terrifying. But what I saw in his eyes when they met mine unabashedly was even more frightening. He was looking at me with the same adoration I had seen him bestow upon Viviana and it caused my head to spin. He could not look at me like that. I was not pure, untouched, breathtaking, like that beautiful little girl was. He was wrong to look at me like that. But damn if I didn't wish I was worthy of it.

Chapter Six

I rested back on my elbows in the damp grass next to Rainer, getting a chance to catch my breath as we both watched Viviana continue to dance through the sprinkler spray. I didn't talk and neither did he, but it didn't feel uncomfortable. It felt...peaceful. I wasn't sure I ever fully understood what that word meant before.

"She was my brother's." Rainer finally interrupted our comfortable silence.

I turned my head to see his gaze was still fixed on Viviana and her bright pink bathing suit. His face was void of the carefree smile I had already become accustomed to. "Was?" I asked.

His eyes swiveled to capture my own and I was granted access to layers and layers of pain in them. It felt like a punch to my gut. "Yeah. Was. He's dead." His voice was mechanical, lacking all the emotion I had become so used to finding in him. Instead, he now sounded like *me*.

I didn't respond. I wasn't good with words, especially in a situation like this where no words would even be right. His eyes finally released me as he leaned forward to rest his arms on his knees. "It was my fault."

I didn't react to his admission. There was nothing to say to that. He didn't look at me still, choosing instead to keep his eyes trained on his niece. I wondered if he had ever said these words aloud, because he continued as if he needed to get this off his chest. Like his life depended on it. "I told you I was no knight in shining armor, Colt. I'm the reason my own brother is dead. I'm the reason he never got to see his baby girl take her first steps. Say her first words. I did this. I hurt everything near me. You shouldn't be around me. I know I should stay away from you, for your own safety, but I can't help it. There's something about you I need and I don't understand it. From the first time I saw you on the back stairs. There was something there." His eyes pinned me in place again and I couldn't have moved even if I wanted to. They searched my own as if he was trying to find in my gaze what it was that drew him to me. Unfortunately, I knew he wasn't going to find anything because I had been looking for the same answer in him and still didn't understand it. I felt the same thing; the same frustration of not understanding why I felt like I knew him already. Why I felt like I somehow needed him in my life. Oh yes, I knew what he was talking about. I had no control over this pull I felt to him. But it wasn't me I was worried about. I was sure I was far more dangerous than Rainer Ventrilla.

"You didn't kill him," I choked out, steering us back to the conversation at hand. I wasn't sure how I could say that with such certainty, but I knew it to be true. "You're a good man. You couldn't kill him."

I knew bad men. I knew how they hid behind a good mask. I knew when someone put on a front, and Rainer was not one of those people. He was good to the core. I knew it in my gut, even without knowing how. I knew he was good. Unlike myself. I knew what it was like to want to kill someone, because I had wanted to kill my father for years.

His eyes still hadn't left mine, only now he was looking for something else. Like he was trying to decide if I was attempting to convince him or myself. I didn't back down; I knew his truth even if he didn't. He sighed once he realized what I was thinking and then he laid back all the way, gazing up at the sky. I turned more so I was propped on one elbow, looking down at him. For the first time, I allowed myself to take him in unabashedly. My eyes trailed over his damp, dark hair that fell to his forehead. His straight nose. The strong curve of his jaw. The stubble that dotted his chin. His Adam's apple as it bobbed when he swallowed hard.

"I was the oldest, the driven one. I was always in control of everything. I had just finished my college degree and was ready to start life, and then life got fucked up. I came home to find out my brother had managed to knock up some girl from his psych class during his senior year. The family hadn't told me while I was at school because they didn't want me to drop everything to come and fix his problems. I was always cleaning up after him. He was the fun brother. The one who could make anyone, and I mean anyone, laugh. Could come out of any sticky situation smelling like roses while a mess was left behind him from his carelessness. It was no surprise he managed to get a girl pregnant.

"By the time I came home in May, the girl was starting to get round and my mom already had everything under control. She's always been the perfect planner. After she had gotten over the initial shock and disappointment, she had made sure everything would be perfect. She asked the girlfriend to move in so that they could all be together when the baby came. Ross and Lauren had already taken the guest house by May and it was baby ready even though the baby wasn't due until August. There was more than enough room for everyone here and now we would all be able to help them out. My brother would put college on hold and start working for my dad as soon as he graduated. We had a plan. It's just what we did; we helped each other. That's what families are for." My chest tightened when he said that. I'd never know that type of family.

"There were parties like the one last night every weekend at Baker's Field back then. It was where we always hung out in high school because both of us had played baseball with the Rhymes brothers. I had grown out of them, but Ross still went every weekend. Towards the end of summer, though, he started getting weird. He always asked me if I wanted to come with him quite a bit, but one night was different. For some reason, he really wanted to go that night. He was acting almost as if he *needed* to. He even begged me to go with him, telling me I hadn't seen Brent Rhymes in ages and I should go to catch up with him. But there was something else there; some reason he needed to go that night and wanted me there. I guess I'll never know what it was or why he needed me to be there, but he did.

"Something didn't seem right to me, but I humored him. I never should have done that. I should have been more on guard. I was the responsible one, I should have been paying more attention to him all night. But he took off as soon as we got there as if he was looking for someone, and I let him go. He could do what he wanted; I wasn't his keeper. So, I did what he asked me to do; I had fun with Brent and the guys. I actually enjoyed getting to catch up with old friends, joking about how we actually had real lives now. We had fun. We had *too* much fun. By the time I decided it was past time to head home, I was smashed. I could barely stand, but I knew enough to know I couldn't drive. My brother said he was completely sober, but something was off about him. I could tell even though I was hammered. And yet he insisted he was fine. He said he was totally okay to drive us home."

"Rainer..." I knew where this was going. I understood now why he had forced me to give him my keys the other night. Viviana's continued giggles from the sprinkler didn't fit anymore. The sun beating down on us didn't feel as sweltering as it had only minutes ago. I watched Rainer's throat bob as he swallowed hard and his eyelids fluttered closed.

"He didn't even die on impact. I had to sit in that crushed car with him bleeding out. Unable to stop it; unable to help him. Unable to help myself. And I did this to him. I should have been sober that night. I should have been paying attention; I knew something was different." Rainer's jaw ticked, his eyes shut tighter, as if trying to block out this next part. "He started talking to me then, but it was muffled. Blood was filling his mouth and I hated every second of it and I can't erase the sound of his voice with the blood to this day. Some stuff about a girl he was going to help. His daughter, I'm sure. He talked about her until he couldn't talk anymore. About how he'd never see her, never know her. That she wouldn't understand. That he couldn't protect her anymore. Wouldn't get to see her smile. And it was all my fault. He never said that, but it was there. I could feel it hanging in the little bit of air that was between us in that smashed scrap of metal, as thick as that damn blood that I couldn't stop from pouring out of him." His fists were clenched in the grass beside him, the muscles on his forearms bulging from the strain. I couldn't tell if the water on his cheeks was a result of the sprinkler spray or from his own tears at this point and it made my chest hurt.

"He told me he loved me. I still don't know how he said it; I hated myself at that moment. I still hate myself. He told me it would be okay; that he had to believe it would all be okay. He never said he blamed me. Not once. And when we made it to the hospital, and my parents arrived and were told he was gone, they didn't blame me, either. They sobbed and screamed and didn't understand but it was so clear to me. I was the reason. But they never said that, and they still never have. Instead, they were thankful that I was alive. They were thankful I had been there with him." His voice turned cold as ice; angry. "I should have been in charge of him, making sure he was safe. It's my fault he's dead. I wish more than anything that it was me who died that night."

His chest heaved with emotion and I didn't have to wonder anymore; the water on his face was tears. He silently sobbed, his fists still clenched in the grass, tears streaming out from behind his tightly closed eyelids. I didn't say anything. I couldn't. I thought I knew every type of pain there was to know, but I had been wrong. I didn't know Rainer's pain. I couldn't comprehend the thought of having so much guilt follow him around every single day. Couldn't imagine loving someone so much and watching them die because of something I blamed myself for.

But he was wrong. It wasn't his fault. Accidents happened. Accidents happened every single day, to every single person on this earth. This accident, this crucial lack of judgement, didn't make him the awful person he believed himself to be. The glaringly obvious fact he was overlooking was that there was a difference between intentionally hurting the ones you're supposed to love and simply making a mistake that you wish you could take back. More than that, what mattered most was how he was affected by his actions. That's how I knew what kind of person Rainer Ventrilla was. And Rainer? He was a good person.

"Sometimes, it's no one's fault," I said quietly, thinking of all the times my father had hit me over the years. What had I done wrong all those times? Nothing. I had simply been available to him. "Sometimes, things just happen. Even if we wish they never did."

His tears had stopped now and he turned his head on the wet grass to face me, the pain still clear in his eyes. He made no effort to hide it away and I wondered if I would ever have that confidence to show my emotions like he did. I doubted it.

"I don't allow anyone into my life anymore," he said. "I can't bear the thought of it. Hurting them. Having them rely on me and not being able to hold up my end of the deal. Doing what I did to my own brother. Destroying them. I just can't do it…"

I knew what he was thinking, why he was saying this, so I finished his thought for him. "And yet, here I am."

He nodded, his full lips parting as he drew in a quick breath. His soaked shirt tightened even more over his chest and my eyes were drawn to the movement. "There's something about you, Colt. I don't want to destroy you, but I can't stay away. I need more of you."

I swallowed hard, my heart hammering in my chest. I'm not sure what it was with this boy, but he messed with the emotions I had become so skilled at keeping locked away. He was chipping away at all my barriers and I had no way to stop it. Before I had even gathered my thoughts, my mouth was opening to answer him. "I'm already broken," I rasped.

I didn't see his response to my most naked truth. I was too appalled at myself for speaking those words aloud to focus, but I still heard his sharp intake of breath as I scrambled to my feet. "I...I'm sorry. I need to...I never should have...I've got to go," I stammered as I tried to regain control of my breathing.

"Wait...what?" Rainer sputtered from behind me. Whatever he had been expecting to happen between us today, just now, it wasn't me running away from him. "Colt."

I was already striding away from him, back towards the path that lead down to my car. Away from feelings and pain and uncertainty. Back to my solid ground of secrecy and denial. "Colt, wait. Where are you going?"

His words only caused me to speed up because I knew if I stayed, Rainer Ventrilla had the power to change everything.

~

The barn was quiet by the time I got back and I realized I had spent almost the whole day with Rainer. Despite his story that was still haunting me and the pain I had seen in his eyes as he blamed his brother's death on himself, I had enjoyed my time with him. I sighed to myself and shook my head at how stupid I had been. I couldn't do that again. As much as I kept the world shut out, I knew what hurt more than the ugly side of life. Hope. I had hope once before. Hope that things may work out. That there was a silver lining in this life. That everything would be okay. I had allowed myself to get close to one person, but that was years ago, and he had left me far behind wherever it was he had gone. I didn't want to be left behind by anyone else. And as Rainer had told me today, he would never be able to hold up his end of the deal.

I needed to stay far away from Rainer Ventrilla because he was offering me that same hope. That same golden idea that I could somehow be loved. But a guy like him could never want me in his life. I'd never fit in his perfect world, even if the picture he painted for me today of his world was far from perfect. Even if he and I both knew he could destroy me. My mind was still racing in circles. Maybe he wouldn't destroy me. Maybe he put on an act just as much as I did. Maybe we were more alike than I had first thought. Maybe we really could work. *Maybe* was a dangerous word. It kept very close company with Hope.

"Colt." The British accent snapped me from my dangerous thoughts. I turned to find Jeremy braced in the doorway of the stairs, his eyes probing me, taking in my still-wet clothes with curiosity. "Are you alright?" he asked.

I rolled my eyes and shoved past him, heading up to my temporary home. There was no use in hiding it from him; he knew the truth of it now. "I'm fine," I threw over my shoulder, knowing that he would be trailing after me. "God, you see a couple bruises and think I need your constant protection." I didn't have to turn around to know the pained expression that would take over his face when my biting words hit him. I was being a bitch and I knew it, but what did I care? It was hurt or be hurt in my world.

"Is that honestly a bad thing? That I want to protect you?"

I closed the door between the office and the breakroom so I could change in peace. I sighed while I ripped the dripping long-sleeve and my thin t-shirt over my head. They plopped with a wet *smack* to the office floor. "Yes," I answered Jeremy while I rummaged in my bag for a new shirt. The chill from the water had left me with goosebumps so I pulled a sweatshirt over my damp hair. Of course, it happened to be one of Jeremy's he had given me years ago when he had gotten sick of hearing my teeth chatter every winter morning we mucked the stalls. The irony wasn't lost on me that I was literally blanketing myself in his protection while being angry at him for offering it. I attempted to rein in my anger. "I didn't ask for your help." My voice had lost its bite. *There,* I thought. *That's nicer.* I shucked off my jeans next and pulled on another pair, quickly looping my belt through and cinching it as tight as it would go. I was painfully aware of my protruding hip bones accentuating the fact I had lost even more weight in the recent weeks despite having nothing to lose. If I lost any more, I'd just be a bag of skin holding the bones together.

"You never ask for help, Colt. You're a right stubborn git. But that doesn't stop me from always giving it to you. And needing you to let me give it to you now." His voice came through the door muffled, distracting me from dwelling too much on the fact that I would be needing a new hole in my belt pretty soon. I really needed to eat something.

I pulled open the office door and Jeremy was leaning against the long table we always ate at, arms crossed over his chest. I vaguely thought of how he really wasn't a bad looking guy, if I ever cared to notice that sort of thing. But he didn't hold a candle to Rainer. *Rainer.* Damn him for entering my thoughts even now. He had no place in my fucked-up world. He had enough in his own mind without adding me to it.

"Just come home with me." My eyebrows raised immediately at Jeremy's words and he ran a hand over his face in exasperation. "Christ, that's not what I meant."

Now it was my turn to cross my arms over my chest. "Oh, it wasn't?" I hummed.

"No. Definitely not. I couldn't. Not knowing, well...knowing what you're like now. How you are. I'd never..." His words struck me like a slap, the sting familiar and shameful. This was why I never let people in. This was why no one could know. Suddenly everything was different. *I* was different. Breakable. Something to be pitied. Something to be saved.

"Fuck you," I spat.

Jeremy's face drained of color. I hadn't ever spoken to him like that before. My home life had made me more of the evasive type than one to ever show any outright aggression. "Wh-what?" he sputtered.

"Fuck. You." I repeated, more defiant this time. "A couple weeks ago you were dying to get in my pants. What changed?" I was daring him to say it. *Go ahead,* I silently urged. *Man up and say it. Say what you've been scared to fully come out and say since the minute you saw my back.*

"I wasn't dying to get in your pants. That's not what I wanted, you know that. You know I wanted more than that," he groaned, avoiding the elephant in the room yet again.

I scoffed and pinned him with a glare. "Wanted. Past tense," I pointed out. "And now?"

He raked a hand over his buzzed hair and spun away from me. "Bloody hell, Colt. Now it's different. Things changed."

"Why?" I challenged, hands resting on my hips. I looked strong now. I had mastered this mode. The act of pretending not to care. Pretending that nothing could touch me, hurt me. Not words, not fists, not knives or glass.

"Because I'm scared for you, goddammit. And I'm scared of you."

My mouth fell open. I hadn't been expecting that one. "Scared *of* me?"

"Yes. Yes, of course I am. Everyone is. You've always been unreachable. Untouchable, almost. Like you don't feel anything. And now? Seeing you? Do you even feel?"

I was sure my eyes were wide as saucers as I gulped in air. In my memories, I felt cigars being stubbed out on my skin. Felt the slash of a broken bottle cut my shoulder open. Felt the lash of a belt across my back, shards of glass being pulled out of my leg and plunked into the wastebasket beside me while I held my breath to keep from crying out. I blinked back unshed tears at the pain and focused on Jeremy. "I feel."

"Do you? Because you act like these scars and bruises on your shoulders are nothing. And I'm not sure if I should be scared of that or if I should be scared of how you got them."

I held my breath. This was it. Secret's out. He was going to come out and say it. How I was abused. And how was I going to deny that? He would go to the police, try to file a report for me. Try to fix this. Only, I knew it wasn't that simple. I knew how my father had the station eating out of the palm of his hand. Police and fire; they were a family. More of a family than I would ever be to him. The report would never be taken seriously and I would be punished, far worse than ever before. It was the knowledge of what he could do if I ever tried to turn him in that kept me shackled to that house, forced to take whatever he doled out. Now, I wasn't quite sure what would happen if Jeremy tried to go to the cops. Would my father come and find me? Drag me back home and punish me?

I broke out in a cold sweat, my arms trembling. I needed to leave. Take all my stuff and go. California maybe. I wasn't sure if even that would be far enough. I should have done that right away, but my mom. I had thought she'd come for me. We could go together; make a plan. But each day that passed, I wondered if I had been wrong about her. If she truly didn't care like I thought. And the barn. Chelsea. They were the only home I'd ever had. The only peace I'd been given. I should have known I'd fuck that up, too.

"Colt, are you even hearing me?" In my panic, I had missed Jeremy finally say it. I shook my head. I didn't want to hear it. Didn't need to. "Are you in a gang or something? Owe someone money? I can lend it to you; don't worry about it. I can help you get out of it, whatever it is. Drugs. Gambling."

"What?" My brain struggled to keep up. *Drugs? Gangs?*

"I get it. It's frightening. You're here so your mum and dad don't find out, aren't you? Always handling everything on your own. But I can help."

My head spun. *What?* Of course he wouldn't possibly think my family was the problem. No, never. Not with my mom and her perfect makeup application every day and sunny florist shop. Not with my father, everyone's favorite firefighter. Of course not. It had to be me, because I was the one that never got the act fully down. I was the one that showed cracks. I was the fucked up one. I tried so hard to mask everything, black it out, blend in, but in the end, I failed. Just not in the way I thought I would. Instead, I just came off as mean and cold. The odd, small girl in oversized clothes and blank expressions. Of course it made sense that I would be in a gang feud. Messed up on drugs. Didn't my gaunt face and protruding bones just scream addict? And yet, it couldn't be further from the truth.

I fought to smooth my face back into indifference. To pretend that his words didn't hurt even though in my mind, we had come to know each other. To be friends. It was a harsh reminder that he still knew nothing. I couldn't blame him for assuming these things, it was my own fault, but it still stung. For the first time, I wasn't proud of how well I shut everyone out. I was sad. But I would have to tuck that away for now and use this to my advantage.

"I'm fine, Jeremy. I promise. I've got it under control." I willed myself to truly believe these words, even if it wasn't related to the situation Jeremy thought it was.

"Let me help you get out of it all. You need to pay someone off? You know I can cover it."

I sighed and rolled my neck out, attempting to release the tension. It didn't work. "No."

"Colt."

"I said no," I bit out. "I'm staying here and handling things on my own, got it?"

He glared back at me. "Why can't you at least stay with me? This office isn't a home."

It's more of a home than my house ever was, I thought bitterly.

If I was stuck in his warped world, I might as well use his gang theory to my advantage. "I'm not going to stay with you and have any trouble come to you and your place." Is that what gangs did? Show up to people's houses and rough them up? Sounded gang-like to me. God, I just kept digging myself into different holes.

Concern flashed in Jeremy's eyes. Before he could argue with me, I hurried on. "This is just temporary," I lied. "Please, Jer. This is how you can help me. Just don't say anything, about any of it, to anyone. Okay?" My eyes pleaded with him. *Please let this work,* I silently begged.

His expression softened. His need to do anything to help me was overpowering what was considered right in his mind. "Fine," he conceded.

My entire body uncoiled like it did when my father would finally pass out and I could hear him snoring. All the tension released and I suddenly felt like my limbs were ten-thousand pounds. "Thank you," I whispered.

"But if you still need help in two weeks, I'm taking care of it. No questions." His eyes held firm. There was no arguing it and my sudden relief was lost. Two weeks. I had two weeks to come up with some plan for my life. No problem.

Chapter Seven

Before I knew it, almost two weeks had passed, and I was no closer to finding a solution to my living arrangement. I had one day left before Jeremy's time limit would be up. Anyone else in my situation would probably be across the country by now. That's what all the movies showed, anyway. Kid runs away from home, hops on a bus, and heads to a new life. Just like that. Everything just peachy. News flash: buses cost money. A bus across the country costs *a lot* of money. Then finding a place to live isn't exactly easy, especially when you're just eighteen. While legally, eighteen may be considered adulthood, lots of leasing places won't let you rent an apartment unless you're twenty-one. Even hotels and motels have that stipulation, too. Trust me, I've done my research. While my pay at the barn allowed me enough money to buy gas for my car and get groceries, I doubted I would be able to swing the funds for a cross-country move. So basically, I was screwed.

More than the logical reasons, I knew the truth. More than the pull of the barn and not wanting to leave Chelsea, the one person who had taken me in, I knew what tethered me to this place. My mom. I couldn't leave her with him. Not when there was a chance we could both make it out and start a new life. As much as I tried to deny it, deep down I knew that's what kept me here. I loved her. Which sounds like a normal thing, for a child to love their mom, except I hated that I loved her. She didn't deserve my love. She may have never been the one to hit me, but she didn't do anything to stop it, either. She stayed with him. We could have left long ago. We *should* have left. But we didn't. *She* didn't. And even now she wouldn't. I had hoped that when she saw I finally did, she would, too. I had this stupid fantasy she would finally leave him, come find me, and we'd fix this. We'd be okay. But that was foolish.

It had been over three weeks since I left that house. My bruises had turned to a sickly shade of yellow and some had faded completely. I'm sure hers were still fresh. And still, she hadn't sought me out. I'll admit, I wasn't hard to find. She should know where I was. In fact, I'm almost certain she did. Yet she never came. Never wished me a happy birthday. Didn't wonder how I was doing. It hurt more than it should have at this point.

Instead, she was off pretending to be the perfect wife still. Planning a stupid banquet for a man who would just give her another couple of bruises for not getting the exact seating chart right. Probably even pretending her "perfect" daughter was still safe and sound in her room at home. A home that was never a home. It made me sick. It made me want to cry. So when I turned the corner of the barn and saw her standing there in the parking lot, I knew I was just imagining things. I had been obsessing over the whole situation with her so much lately I was starting to hallucinate now. I'd chalk it up to the fact that this week was stressing me out. I knew tomorrow was the banquet. That weekend after the Fourth of July would forever be ingrained in my mind. And now I was suffering the consequences.

I rubbed my eyes and looked again, but my mom was still there. I blinked some more. Still there. Only now, she had a small smile on her face. I knew that one. The one we both perfected over the years. Not too happy or friendly; not at all upset. The perfect façade.

I turned my head and spotted her car to the right. This was no mirage. This was real life. I took a deep breath. Maybe this was it. She wouldn't go through with the banquet tomorrow. She'd pack her things and we'd take off when my father was occupied with the whole town. We'd start new. For the first time in years, I allowed myself to let the hope rise up in my chest.

She took more steps towards me, that smile still in place. I wished she would let it drop. I didn't need to see her fakeness. I knew the truth. "Colt." The smile was still there. It was in her voice, too. Not warm, motherly love. Just the fake pleasure she put into all her greetings.

"Mom." I didn't want to be the one to make the first move. I was sick of always having to step up for her, to take on more than what I was supposed to. I wanted to ask her what she was doing here. If she was really here to make things right. If she was finally about to admit that what we've been through is wrong. But I shouldn't have to push her to tell me. She should be able to do it.

"How are you, honey?" she asked as if I had just gotten home from school, not as if I had been missing from her life for close to a month.

I crossed my arms over my chest, already beginning to close myself off. If only it was that easy to tamp down the hope that had flared up upon seeing her here. "How am

I?" I repeated angrily. She knew I wasn't one to be messed with. I saw her throat bob as she swallowed. Anyone else would have missed that break in her façade, but I knew it well.

"You look...good?" I didn't respond. I knew I didn't look good. But to her, good meant no visible wounds. "Look, Colt, I'm sorry, okay?"

"For what?" I waited with bated breath, though I knew outwardly I looked completely unaffected. As much as she hated to admit it, we both knew my unaffected act was always better than hers.

What was she going to apologize for? For all the years she kept us in that situation? For being married to a monster? For allowing her baby girl to be beat and mutilated for years? For not reaching out to me these past weeks? For not coming with me when I left? I wanted to hear it all, but more than that, I needed her to back it up with action.

For a second, I saw something flash in her eyes and it looked like she was having an internal debate. But what she said next was not at all what I had been expecting. "I'm sorry for coming here." Her words hit me harder than my father's belt ever had. "I'm sorry but I had to tell you...don't come tomorrow."

Don't come tomorrow? I wanted to scream at her. That's what she came here for? To tell me not to come the damn banquet?

"Don't come tomorrow and don't...don't come back, Colt."

Come back? To that house? I wanted to sputter. Gasp. Scream. Anything. For once I wanted to show that I had emotions. But I couldn't. Couldn't do anything.

"Don't come back…ever. Your father and I…we won't allow you back in our home."

I wanted to vomit. My eyes stung from tears that hadn't fallen in years. She needed to leave. I didn't want to hear any more words from her mouth. I couldn't do this. For the first time, I finally knew what giving up felt like. Because when I thought I was hopeless before, I had been wrong. This? *This* was hopeless. There was nothing left in me now.

I hadn't responded but she was still standing there in that flowery long-sleeve dress looking at me like she wanted an answer. Her mask slipped. I saw the concern in her eyes, a hint of worry for me, though that was impossible. This woman was just as much of a monster as he was. She was too weak to stand up to him. Too weak to stand up for me. And now she had the audacity to look like she may actually care for me? After shattering any scrap of hope I had ever clung to?

"Mrs. Jefferson!" Jeremy's voice floated over my head and hit my mother like a tidal wave, washing away any true emotion, splashing the mask back onto her face.

"Jeremy, dear. So nice to see you. You look great."

"Thank you, ma'am. You as well. That dress is lovely. Have you got everything ready for the big day tomorrow?" He came to stand beside me but kept his distance and I silently thanked God he did because I had no clue how I would react if anyone came too close to me right now. I was seconds away from losing it.

"You are too kind. Thank you. Actually, I do still need to get some things together so I better be going. It was nice to see you, dear." Finally, she turned back to me and her eyes, so different from my own, held mine as if they had so much to say. I was no longer interested in hearing it. That damn smile of hers was back in place, and all she said was, "Colt."

She turned to leave and was about to pull open her car door when I finally spoke. "Oh, Mother?" Her back straightened. I had only ever called her Mom before now. She turned back to face me. "A bit more concealer tomorrow." I tapped my right cheek, indicating where I had picked up on the dark tones of a blossoming bruise. Anyone else may have thought it was her natural, rosy complexion. I knew the truth. I had been taught how to cover up from the master. But even the master looked like she was showing signs of breaking.

I watched her face drain of color beneath all that makeup most people didn't even know was layered there and her throat bobbed. *Bingo,* I thought. Like I had said before, in my world it was hurt or be hurt and I was finally done with the latter.

I didn't even realize my hands were balled into fists by my sides until I felt Jeremy's fingers gently brush against them. I flinched from the touch, digging my nails into my palms. "Colt…" His voice was low, tentative. I closed my eyes slowly. *Ten. Nine. Eight. Seven. Six.* "Talk to me." My eyes flashed open before I had gotten a chance to count down to one and I started walking, bypassing my car without a second glance.

"Colt!"

"I just need to walk," I called back through gritted teeth without bothering to look back at him. He knew not to push me on this. I needed air. Space. A place to run away to. I was good at running; used to it. I was even used to the turns of the road I took without even thinking. Back to a place that used to be a solace, if only for a moment.

"Mind if I sit?" I looked up in the faint glow of the fire to see the laughing boy from my very first night here, the one who gave me the only name I went by in this place. It had been quite a few weeks since I had first stumbled onto the group and while I had gotten to know almost everyone, I still hadn't spoken to this boy. Every night I was here, so was he. And without fail, he was the center of attention. I may not have talked to him, but I had gathered quite a bit of information from watching and listening to the others. The girls wanted to get with him. The guys wanted to be his friend. His laugh was infectious; it made people feel good. For some reason, he had captured my attention even from my hidden spot in the shadows.

Except this night he had come over to me, and I realized he was actually still standing above me, waiting for my okay before he sat. "Uhm, yeah. Go ahead," I stuttered. He folded himself down on the log next to me and smiled at me. He had always had seemed larger than life from afar, but I realized with him sitting next to me now, he really wasn't all that tall or big. He still dwarfed me, though. Not that that was a hard feat as I was barely over five feet tall and pure skin and bones. But he seemed to give off a bigger presence than anyone else I had met before.

"You don't talk much, do you?" he asked after he had taken a long pull of his drink and the silence had stretched between us.

"I talk enough," I countered and it caused his smile to widen.

"Alright then. What's your story, Donnie?"

My jaw ticked and I turned away from him to face the fire ahead of us. I wasn't used to this attention. No one ever paid me any mind. Not the scrawny girl with the baggy clothes and downcast eyes. I wasn't sure how I felt about this turn of events. I especially didn't like the unsettled feeling in my stomach that I had never felt before. It was different than when I was about to be sick, but I hated it all the same. I scrunched my nose and answered his question with one of my own. "What's yours?"

He chuckled. "I don't mean to sound childish, but I asked first."

I smirked. "And yet, you still sound childish."

"I do what I have to to get what I want." He said it playfully and despite the sinister connotation, I knew he didn't mean it in that way. For some reason, I knew he was kind and that feeling I got from him was foreign to me; a feeling of safety.

"What's your name?" From all my observing, I had yet to find out this crucial fact. For some reason, I wanted to know it from him.

"What do you want it to be?"

I wrinkled my nose. "Do you always talk in riddles?"

"Do you?" His eyes flashed playfully, having fun with this unspoken game we had created. My lips tipped up just a bit and his grin grew. "Ah, a smile? I feel accomplished. Those are rare."

The hint of a smile vanished. "How would you know?" I didn't bother to argue the fact that my smiles were rare; we both knew he was right.

"You think you've got a monopoly on watching people?" He winked at me and my cheeks heated. His deep chuckle reverberated through me and warmed me even more than the fire had been. "You're different. You barely talk, yet you keep coming here. You've got to be less than sixteen years old, so that means you walk here because no sane parent would bring you here. You never smile. You seem to take in everything, your eyes never stop moving, but you're somehow more focused on me than anything else and I like it. You're interesting."

I fought down my embarrassment at being caught watching him and came back at him with my usual snappiness. "Interesting is one way to put it."

He wasn't deterred by my tone. "So tell me your story, Donnie. Why are you the way you are?"

"Life," I answered. I continued before he could ask more. "You're the life of the party. You're everyone's friend. You have a way of making everyone around you happy. You can somehow convince anyone to do whatever you say. You also drive a giant, fancy Jeep that's actually a bit too ridiculous and probably costs more than everything I own combined, which leads me to believe you're rich. You never stop smiling and yet tonight, you're over talking to me. Why are you here?"

He watched me intently while I rattled off facts about him and when I finished, he downed the rest of his drink in one go, then leaned forward to put his elbows on his knees. For the first time I had seen, his smile faltered. He reached into his back pocket and pulled out what looked like a locket, but there was no chain on it. The gold glinted in the light of the flames as he twisted it over and over in his hands. My eyes watched it slip smoothly through his fingers, like he did this often. On one turn over his fingers, I saw what looked like a "V" etched on one side, but then he closed his fist over it before I could get a closer look and turned to face me.

"And are all those things good, do you think?" he asked me, as if he genuinely wanted to know my opinion on it. I cocked my head and furrowed my brows. *Wasn't it?* I wondered. Seemed like a pretty good life from where I was sitting.

The sound of footsteps crunched through the hay that was cut short so late in the season. It was a girl with perfectly curled hair and skin-tight jeans coming towards us. I remembered her from being wrapped up in his arms my very first night here. Of course she would be coming to find him. His smile grew as he turned to look up at her.

"Hey, Babe," he said casually, but the words fell like knives in my gut. He stood from the log we shared as if that was it, like he didn't think anything of our conversation, and wrapped his arms around her like it was the most natural thing in the world. I stayed silent, trying my best not to look at them. But just as they were going to leave, he turned back to face me.

"Til next week, Donnie," he grinned.

I was surprised to think he actually wanted to talk to me again when he could have a girl like that all the time but I covered my shock and managed to lift my cup in a salute to him. It was still mostly full because I had yet to develop a taste for the beer that the others here seemed to enjoy so much. "Next week."

I wasn't expecting anyone to be here tonight, hadn't been expecting a party, but as my feet turned to take me up the familiar dirt road now, the tell-tale calls of drunken laughter and shouts pulled me from my flashback. Just like that night years ago, I kept going, curious to see who would be here, but also already knowing the answer. It would be the polished group from the other night. The band of older people I had been welcomed into even with all my oddities was long gone and I had long ago stopped wondering what had ever happened to them.

My boots scuffed the dry dirt as I picked my way through the parked cars and trucks, nearing the group with each step. My eyes burned from the dust, reminding me it hadn't rained in days and we probably needed it. Reminding me I hadn't cried in years and my body probably needed that, too since I always denied it.

"My, my...look who it is." I finally looked up from my feet and came face to face with Seymour. The same wide eyes and olive skin, but he was no longer the gangly trouble-maker I remembered from my freshman year. Now, he was corded with muscle; wide, almost intimidating. "Who invited the Thornberry kid?" he laughed over his shoulder and my stomach lurched remembering who he always directed his comments to. I braced myself to see a ghost from my past part the group of people, but only another shout came.

"No way, Donnie's here?" I glanced over to see another girl I remembered from welcoming me in all those years ago and breathed a sigh of relief. I still hadn't decided if I wanted to see *him* again or not. I was leaning towards no. But if the others were back…he was sure to be here.

Seymour stepped up to me but kept his distance. Years might have passed since we had really seen each other, but unfortunately I was still the same. Sometimes, things don't change. I could see his eyes raking up and down my body, scrutinizing me in the last light of day. "You look like shit. But better than you used to. Kind of."

For the first time that day, a corner of my mouth lifted in an attempt at a smile. Still the same Seymour. Like I said, some things don't change. I reached out and snatched his cup from his hand, taking a long pull. His eyes glinted in amusement, waiting for my shocked response to the burning liquor. This was not lukewarm beer in his cup. But the fire in my throat didn't phase me. I knew far worse pains; had been shocked much more by my mother's words today.

Seymour's eyes changed from amused to impressed. "Welcome back, Donnie," he nodded approvingly at me and then stepped to the side, sweeping his arm back just as he had so long ago, inviting me back into the fold.

It was the crowd I was used to and even though they were grown now, they were still the same. Maybe they had accepted me all those years ago because in a way, we were all similar. At the time, they were the high school's golden group. Yet beneath that, they were a group of delinquents. They put on their fake acts for their parents and the community, but on Friday nights, they came out here to be who they really were. I put on my fake act for the world, but the nights by the flames, I didn't need to act normal. They didn't care about normal here.

"How have you been?" Seymour stepped up next to me after everyone had greeted me and I was no longer on high alert. *He* wasn't here tonight. The knowledge was both calming and unsettling. I glanced over at Seymour and he grinned at me, tipping half the contents of his new cup into the one I had stolen from him. I gave him a grateful look and shrugged my shoulders at his question.

"I'm still alive."

"And graduated from barely sipping on beer, I see," he laughed, and it was true. What he had just poured into my cup was even stronger than his first drink.

"It's been a rough day."

He simply nodded and tapped his cup against mine. I itched to ask him about his best friend. The alcohol was making me bold. I wanted to know why he wasn't here tonight. When Seymour had last seen him. How he was doing. But just like long ago, I couldn't bring myself to ask; wasn't sure I wanted to know the answer. I didn't need to hear how well he was doing. How successful I knew he would be while I was still floundering. "I've got you covered. Let's just hope you can handle it." Seymour winked at me and I rolled my eyes, thinking he was being ridiculous. Of course I could handle it. Or so I thought...

"Colt." A voice jolted me and I didn't have to turn to know who it was, but I did anyway because even though I had run away from him when I had seen him last, Rainer Ventrilla drew me in like a magnet.

I wasn't sure how long it had been since I'd shown up at the fire, but a larger crowd had gathered. Seymour's older brother and his friends, people I didn't know, had shown up and I had made no effort to make new friends.

Except with Seymour's bottle of José Cuervo. José and I had gotten real close, real fast.

"Are you even hearing me?" I blinked and Rainer's demanding eyes came back into focus.

"Hm?" I mumbled. His eyes raked over me from the top of my head down to my toes, causing my skin to raise in goosebumps underneath my long sleeves. When his eyes returned to mine they were fighting amusement and annoyance.

He snatched the cup from my hand, just as I had with Seymour, only he didn't take a sip. He only sniffed it and raised his eyebrows at me. "Tequila, Colt? Really?"

I took the cup back defensively, narrowing my eyes at him. For someone who was always indifferent, Rainer had me going from hot to cold at rapid speed. It was disorienting even if I was sober. Which I definitely was not right now, but who was he to have a say in that? I didn't bother answering him, just turned my back on him.

"What? You're not going to talk to me now? Not much different from this past week. I know you've been ignoring me."

"It wasn't a secret," I snapped back at him. I knew he had come to the barn multiple times in the past week. I made sure I was hidden away each time so that Chelsea would have to tell me later that Rainer had stopped by. I wasn't entirely sure this plan was any better than actually meeting with Rainer, because Chelsea made sure to take plenty of time to tell me all about how good-looking Rainer was and how I needed to "get on that" every single time she sent him away. The fact was, I had enough going on in my life. I couldn't have an issue as stupid as a boy who tied my insides in knots to be clouding my brain.

Rainer simply grinned at my response. Seeing it only fueled my anger towards him and I gulped down more of my drink, which caused his grin to quickly transform into a glare. "That's your last one for the night," he growled.

I actually laughed in response. "Sure, Rainer. Whatever you say." I didn't wait to hear his retort, I just turned and walked away from him yet again. I could still feel his eyes on me, though. The weight of them never left me for the rest of the night. By the time the flames had died down to mere coals and many people had long ago drifted away, Rainer was still there.

When I finally lifted my eyes to meet his, he was glaring at me from across the field with his arms crossed over his broad chest. Seymour was next to him and as I watched, his glare left mine for the first time that night to turn its force on Seymour. From what I could make out, it looked like they were arguing. When I heard my name drift over from the heated conversation, my curiosity got the best of me.

"You think I don't know her? I've known her way longer than you have, Rainer. She's fine," Seymour was saying as I got closer.

"She's not fine! She's eighteen! She shouldn't even be drinking, let alone pounding tequila." Rainer's voice was icy.

"She's been drinking with us for years. This is her escape."

Rainer's hands flew into the air. "You don't even know what she's escaping from! And then what? She just leaves? And *that night* happens all over again? This was his escape, too. It's the same situation. Same age. Same stupidity. You don't *think*, do you?"

I didn't need to hear how Seymour would respond. "Rainer," I hated the slur in my voice. Hated the off-balance feeling I had now. "Stop."

He lifted a hand to rake through his hair. "You want to tell me she's fine now?" he threw at Seymour, not even looking at me.

Seymour opened his mouth to reply, but even in my current state I beat him to it. "I'm not yours to take care of."

Rainer finally turned to face me head-on and his eyes felt like they were swallowing me whole. "Yes, you are. You've been mine since the moment I saw you." He growled it as if the thought of it made him angry, and I knew from our conversation the other day that it probably did. That didn't stop me from having the wind knocked out of me upon hearing him say it. His eyes dared me to contradict him, and though everything in me was screaming that I belonged to no one but myself, I suddenly longed for someone else to share this burden with me. To want me. I was suddenly so tired. Tired of doing this...*life*...alone.

Rainer's eyes still hadn't left mine and Seymour had enough sense to stay quiet because it was only me and Rainer in this moment. He must have seen the fight leaving me because the tension slowly eased from him, his eyes melting to something softer. Finally *seeing* me and not whatever it was that had spurred this anger. "Colt," he murmured.

I shook my head, then backed away slowly. My eyes burned. My throat burned. I couldn't remember the last time I had felt this...this inability to hold back my own emotions and tuck them away. I turned my back on Rainer as fast as I could, not wanting him to see me like this. I didn't want him to see me at all, because he was beginning to see too much. I was starting to wish I could show him all of me, but that could never happen.

My foot snagged on a root in my haste to get away and then I was falling. But just like that day on the stairs, he was suddenly there, his hand wrapping around my arm to steady me. I shrugged him off immediately, stumbling forward.

"Colt, stop," he pleaded.

"Just a root," I argued, but my voice was slurred so my argument fell flat. I had never felt like this before and had no intention of feeling it again.

Rainer chuckled without humor. "There wasn't a root there."

I waved my hand at him as if I was batting away a fly at the barn, but he continued to trail close behind me while I attempted to walk away. My teeth ground together, fighting to hold everything in, but my vision blurred nevertheless. Water pooled in my eyes and I blinked desperately, but it was too late. I stumbled once more, this time pitching forward, sure to hit the ground. Before I could, Rainer's arms were around me.

"Colt." His voice was rough now, ready to reprimand me I was sure, and I simply couldn't take it anymore. The tears I'd spent years holding in finally spilled over and my knees gave out even though I had just regained my balance. Instead of cringing away from Rainer's touch, I found myself melting into it. It only took him a second to react, his hold going from firm and steadying to comforting. I didn't even have time to think of what I must look like before one of his arms swooped under my knees, cradling me to his chest as if I weighed no more than his niece.

"Shh, I got you," he murmured into my hair and I surprised myself by pressing myself closer to him, burying my face in his neck, welcoming his musky scent mixed with the sweetness that was sure to come from the grapes he spent his whole day surrounded by at the vineyard. As much as I willed myself to pull it together, I couldn't stop my tears even as he placed me into what must have been the passenger seat of his truck and buckled me in. I tucked my chin to avoid his eyes as his fingers skimmed over my waist and tightened the belt. I knew he wanted to say more, but after a minute the door closed and I curled into myself to face the window. A moment later, he slid into the driver's side and closed the door behind him. For a second, he just sat there and while I didn't look over at him, I could still feel him taking deep breaths from next to me. Finally, the key turned and he started to drive. He never asked where to turn. Didn't ask what roads to take or where I wanted to go. It made me realize I didn't care where he took me, as long as he was with me.

Dark trees blurred by outside the window and my stomach rolled. The last thing I was going to do was get sick in Rainer's truck, though. I tried to focus on the soft music coming through his speakers to distract myself. I had expected it to be the rap that was typical to so many guys. Or even country, as he used to be a baseball player and they were always known to have country blaring. Yet what came from the speakers now was neither of those things. It was a song I had never heard before. Some British man was crooning in a deep voice about laying a body six feet beneath clay. It was the complete opposite of what I had expected Rainer to be listening to. But somehow, it fit. Fit him. Fit me. Fit this moment.

"Why doesn't she love me?" I surprised myself by slurring. "Why did she pick him?" I felt Rainer's gaze on me, but he made no comment. The song continued, talking of anger but sounding so sad. I knew that feeling well. "I just don't understand. I stayed for her. I tried for her. I tried *so hard*. For *so long*. I don't want to try anymore. Why can't she love me? Why could he *never* love me?"

I turned my red eyes from the window to watch his profile while he drove. Oncoming headlights illuminated his clenched jaw, one hand tight on the wheel, the other balled in a fist resting on the console between our seats. Had my words made him angry? Did I make him angry just as I made my father angry? My eyes stayed focused on his balled fist between us and without thinking it through, I reached out to touch him. I traced over his clenched fist, wondering if he had ever used it to bruise another's skin. His eyes flicked to me, surprise clear in them, but he didn't say a word. Instead, his tanned fist opened beneath my featherlight touch and he held his hand open for me, palm up. I knew what he meant by it, and his eyes darted to meet mine again, this time in question. Would I be willing to take this leap? Take his hand and trust him? I bit my lip, tasting the salty residue of my tears lingering there. Then I folded my fingers into his hand, pale and trembling between his dark, steady ones. He pulled our clasped hands to his lips in the next second, brushing them over the back of my hand and causing breath to whoosh from my lungs.

116

As soon as he cut the engine, I was shoving the door open and falling into the grass while I proceeded to empty what little was in my stomach.

"Jesus," I vaguely heard Rainer mutter before the thud of his door and then his shoes appeared in my peripheral vision. For someone who always put on an act, I was really falling to pieces tonight. It only took a second before I felt his fingers in my hair, pulling it away from my face and I shivered involuntarily. I was about to snap at him to leave me be, but then I was bent over again, expelling every bad decision I had drank tonight. Silly me to think I could ever drink enough to forget the pain I knew.

When I was finally done, I sat back on my heels and wiped my mouth with a shaking hand, refusing to look back at him. Tears continued to leak out of the corners of my eyes and I couldn't even convince myself it was just a side effect of retching. My heart hurt. My head hurt. I shivered despite the oppressive heat even in the dead of night as his hand moved from my hair to rub circles on my back.

"Come on." Rainer's arm looped around me, offering his hand, and for a second I only stared at it; the concept was still foreign to me. Then he wiggled his fingers and I finally turned my head to meet his intense gaze and for some reason his lips were still turned up in a ghost of a smile for me. He must have read a question in my eyes because his gaze softened even more. "Come on, Colt," he repeated softly. "I'm not going anywhere."

His fingers reached out towards my face and I tracked them despite my blurry vision, bracing myself for a hurt that wouldn't come. Instead, he brushed them into the hair that was threatening to fall forward into my face. Then his palm cradled my head tentatively. I couldn't help it, my lips parted in a gasp at his soft touch. His thumb brushed by my eye, over the still healing cut that my father had given me the night before I finally left. "You're beautiful. Even now. Even as a mess," he whispered and I had to close my eyes against the intensity of his gaze. "Stop running from me. Stop hiding, Colt."

His thumb ghosted over my cheek, smearing more moisture there and I whimpered. It was a command, but it was also a question. He would never force me. I found myself nodding, my eyes still closed, and then I felt his lips press warm against my forehead and my whole body shuddered at the intimacy of it. No one had ever touched me like this before. Sobs racked through me and his hand molded around the back of my head, pulling me into his chest and gathering me in his arms completely. He stood with ease, once again carrying me as I buried my face in his shirt, soaking the soft cotton with proof of my weakness, and wound my arms around his neck.

"Thank you," he breathed against my hair, brushing a kiss there that was so soft I wasn't sure it was entirely real.

My sobs doubled as his grip tightened around me. When he finally laid me down on what felt like a bed, my eyes flew open despite drowning in tears and I blindly reached for him. "Don't leave me," I heard myself croak, though I had never spoken those words before. "Please, don't leave me."

"Shh," Rainer murmured, and then he was crawling in behind me, my back to his front while he tentatively wrapped an arm around my waist. His hesitation caused my tears to fall harder and his thumb traced patterns over my stomach in response. "Shh, I'm not going anywhere."

"I don't understand," I hiccupped. "Why can't she love me? Why could he never love me?"

"I don't know, baby," Rainer mumbled into my hair but my brain didn't even register it.

"Do you love me?" I hiccupped again and I felt Rainer's answering sigh as his chest rose and fell against my back.

"No, Colt, I don't love you. But I think I could." Those were the last words my drunken brain registered before blackness took over.

~

The faint sounds of angry voices woke me up and I immediately threw an arm over my eyes with a groan. It was way too bright for the office and the light hurt my eyes way too much. Just like that, pieces of last night started floating back to me. My mother. The bonfire. Rainer. Rainer bringing me here...wherever here was and, oh, God. I was a mess. I had to get out of here. *Now.* And never come back.

I reluctantly pulled my arm away from my eyes and sat up to take in my surroundings. The walls were dark and everything was furnished with dark wood. There was no doubt it was nice, the room was easily two times what any normal bedroom should be, but something felt wrong. Other than his scent lingering on the sheets I was currently cocooned in, there were no signs of this being Rainer's room. No pictures or trinkets, no clothes left out. It almost felt sterile.

His voice drifted up to me, reminding me what had woken me in the first place. "What was I supposed to do? She's got nowhere to go." Despite his attempt at staying quiet, I could tell he was angry. There was a bite in his voice just like he had when he was talking to Seymour last night.

"So you bring her here in that state? Where your little sister is? Where Viviana is?" Another voice answered him and I winced. They were talking about me. *I* was the danger. I didn't disagree. "I appreciate your kindness in wanting to take in a stray, but really, Rainer? You haven't done this. Ever. We don't know her. We don't know what she'll do. What she could take."

"Are you kidding me, Mom? She's not like that. She'd never steal from us. She'll barely even take a cracker from me and she's straight skin and bones. I can count every single one of her ribs." My breath caught. How could he know that? I was always hidden under the biggest clothes I could find. "Something happened. She's living in a barn. On her own. At eighteen. Something happened to her, Mom." His voice dropped on the last sentence and I could hear the heaviness of it through the door. His words landed another punch to my gut and I had to fight back tears. Apparently, once I broke the dam the tears would just keep coming. It pushed me to get out of there even faster. He couldn't save me and I refused to be a burden in their lives.

"What do you mean something happened?" The other voice, his mother I knew now, whispered back. I scrambled to free myself from his covers, my head throbbing. I didn't want to hear any more. That's when I realized I was no longer wearing my own shirt. The long-sleeve I had on was still three sizes too big, but there were no frayed sleeves on this one, no holes forming in the elbows, and it was the softest thing I had ever worn. How I hadn't noticed this before was beyond me. But that meant if I was wearing this, then...

"I don't know, Mom. Something bad. You should see her back, it's..." Rainer didn't finish his thought and bile rose in my throat again. He had seen. That's how he knew my ribs were far too visible. Had seen the white scars across my stomach. The jagged, poorly healed skin that stretched over my back. He had seen too much. I needed out. Out of this house, this shirt, this life...all *his*.

I didn't hear his mom's response. I was too busy throwing my legs over the edge of Rainer's too-big bed in a rush to get out. In my haste, I knocked something off his bedside table and it clattered on the wood floor, skittering under his bed.

"Fuck," I muttered, dropping to my hands and knees to fish under the bed for it. I would not let anything be out of place. I didn't need his mom having any valid reason to think I was a thief. My fingers fumbled blindly until they finally closed around cold metal and I pulled my hand back out. I was ready to drop whatever it was back on the table and make a break for it, but then my eyes skimmed over the engraving on one side. An elegant "V" was etched into the gold locket and my breath caught. My fingers snapped open as if the metal was burning me. It bounced on the hardwood floor again, the sound as loud as fireworks in the empty room, and it spun like a top until it came to rest with the "V" facing up. I was frozen in place, still kneeling next to Rainer's bed with my heart pounding in my ears. It was the same one, I was positive.

The same locket without a chain that I had seen slip between fingers over and over again in the light of flames. And yet here it was in Rainer's room.

Before I could think any more on it, I heard footsteps coming towards the door to Rainer's room and I panicked. In my shock of finding the locket, I missed the end of Rainer's conversation with his mother. Just as the footsteps stopped outside his door, I made a split-second decision and snatched up the locket, shoving it deep into the pocket of my jeans before hastily standing as the doorknob turned.

Chapter Eight

My heartrate was still sky high as I stood staring back at Rainer. He hadn't moved since opening his door and neither had I. In fact, I'm pretty sure he had just rendered me incapable of moving. It really wasn't fair that he could look that good, especially this morning. I swear some master sculptor had personally chiseled his face. Every feature was *that* perfect. Meanwhile, I didn't even want to know what my current state was if my fuzzy memories were any indication of how last night really went.

"Were you planning on sneaking out on me?" His voice finally interrupted our stare down. I would blame my inability to speak on my hangover, but the reality was it was him. He made me speechless. "You remember what you promised me last night?" he continued. "No more running from me."

"I don't remember making that promise," I found myself snapping. At least I could still pretend he had no effect on me, even if it wasn't the truth.

A hint of his normal smirk came and then went just as quickly. "Do you remember last night at all?" he asked seriously.

I gulped down the leftover taste of bile in my throat. "Just forget it happened." The locket weighed heavy in my jeans and I fidgeted, looking around for my own shirt in hopes to take it and get out of here.

"I don't want to forget about it."

Seeing how Rainer still hadn't moved an inch from his doorway, it looked like I was going to have to cut my losses and leave the shirt behind, wherever it was. "Well, I do," I countered, debating the best way to duck around him to make a break for it.

He finally took a step out of the doorway, except he stepped right into my own personal space so that I either had to crane my neck to look up at him or take a step back. I refused to back down from him now, though. "Well, I *can't*."

The blue rings around his eyes were so bright, holding me in place. I gritted my teeth and fought down an odd burning low in my belly. "Rainer, I-"

"No, Colt. I meant what I said last night. You're mine."

In my hungover state, his words fed my anger in a way they hadn't last night when I was too drunk to fully process them. My hands went to my hips and I stood up straighter, trying to make myself appear bigger instead of curling into myself for once. "I'm not yours," I snapped in spite of the heat racing through me. It was a different heat than anger. It wasn't one I was used to. "I'm no one's." *And wasn't that the truth*, I thought bitterly. I didn't even have a home or parents who loved me. I truly was nobody's.

His eyes flashed. "Oh yeah? And your scars, then? Did those come from No One?"

I stumbled back as if he had hit me. I wasn't prepared for that comment. He said No One like a title. There wasn't even a question of how I had earned my scars; he knew a person had inflicted them. "I...you..." My mouth fumbled open and shut before I finally masked my face back to indifference. "I don't know what you're talking about."

Rainer groaned. "Don't do that. Don't act like a brick wall. I know there are actually feelings going on in there. And I know what I saw."

"It's nothing."

Rainer's arms folded over his chest and the muscle in his jaw jumped. "Fine. You want to pull this act and shut down and then run away, be my guest. Just know you're not running far this time." He didn't even give me a chance to reply, just brushed passed me further into the room, purposefully knocking his shoulder into mine as he went, and then retreated into what I could only assume must be his own bathroom. Before the door could fall shut behind him, I heard his steps pause and I knew without looking that he had turned back to face me. I refused to turn and meet his gaze that was burning between my shoulder blades. "And Colt? It's not nothing." Again, he didn't wait to see how I'd react, he just slammed the door behind himself.

I flexed my fingers that had been digging into my palms, forming half-moon indents in the soft flesh there. Who was he to be slamming doors? If anyone had the right to slam a door right now, it was me. He wasn't the one who just had his privacy invaded, was told they were owned as if they were some slave, and then basically reprimanded for acting like a small child. He had no right. My teeth ground together and my hands balled into fists again. I had never felt this before. This fire. This urge to fight back and take action instead of just running. For a minute, I debated storming after him, but quickly decided against it. He had given me an out and years of attempting to escape had taught me to grasp any chance I got. I muttered a curse at his closed door and then slunk out, attempting to find my way through this mansion that was his house. When I finally got out the huge front door, I made sure to slam it shut behind me.

Take that, Rainer, I thought. *You don't have a monopoly on slamming doors.*

~

I was dripping sweat by the time I made it back to the barn. The sun had already reached its peak in the sky and started its descent. On the plus side, I had only thrown up two more times on my walk back and had most likely sweated out whatever other alcohol may have been left in my system.

Gizmo knickered at me as I came down the main bay of stalls and I looked at him longingly. No one else was around today; I knew where they all were and pushed the thought from my head as quickly as I could. I snatched a halter and lead from a peg before swinging open Gizmo's stall door. He nuzzled into my sweaty neck as I stepped inside, his hot breath blowing over me as I slipped the bridle over his face. His response was to nip at the shirt I was wearing and I let out a little chuckle.

"I know, buddy. It's not mine." He tugged at the hem of it again, then tossed his head with a snort of disapproval. "Yeah. I don't think I like him, either. But he does smell good, doesn't he? Come on."

I led him through the barn and out the back straight to the hose-down area which had doubled as my shower this past month. I didn't bother tethering him to the hitch here, I knew he wouldn't take off on me. The water splashed against my heated skin as I turned it on to fill Gizmo's kiddie pool. The icy stream felt so good that I grabbed a second hose for myself to wash away as much of the previous day and night as I could. The cold was shocking in the best way and once I had gotten my fill, I turned it on Gizmo as well, laughing as he threw his head back and stomped in the quickly forming puddles. His head continued to roll and I danced around him, soaking him down and reveling in the spray that ricocheted off him.

When I had found out how much Gizmo loved water back when he was just a colt, I begged Chelsea to buy a kiddie pool so I could keep it out here for him. I never asked for much, so it wasn't hard to convince her. It didn't take long to realize that we got almost as much joy from watching him play stupidly in his pool as he did from actually splashing around. I was convinced it was impossible to be in a bad mood while watching animals play like toddlers.

When his pool was finally full, I only had to give a click of my tongue before he was galloping over and splashing clumsily into the pool. I laughed and hopped over the edge to join him, which prompted him to paw the water with his hooves in excitement, drenching me in a wave. I bent down to splash more back at him and he dunked his head in before tossing it back up and spraying me in the process. Anyone who tried to say that animals couldn't understand humans clearly had it all wrong. This horse was probably the only thing on this planet that truly understood me. No matter what, he always seemed to know exactly what I needed. Today, that meant a big splash in the face.

I'm not sure how long we played like that, blocking out the real world, but I was completely numb from the icy water and soaked to the bone when my eyes finally landed on Jeremy leaning against the back barn door. I froze as he grinned at me, but Gizmo continued pawing at the water unfazed.

"How long have you been out here, mate?" He pushed off from the door and walked closer towards me, giving me the chance to register the clothes he was wearing. They were nice, nothing he would typically wear to the barn, none of his fancy riding clothes. It wasn't his casual jeans and a t-shirt, either. For a minute, the thought that he was dressed like that for the banquet flashed through my mind and briefly reminded me of the mess that was my life, but then he took another step closer and I grinned at him. Before he could react, I had bent down and sent a wave of water at him. His mouth dropped open in disbelief and he sputtered at me, which only caused me to laugh harder. I used to love cracking his prim and proper British demeanor when I was younger. It was nice to know it still gave me the same satisfaction.

"Are you mad?!" he gasped. I sent another wave of water his way and he shook himself from his initial shock to jump back out of range. Gizmo whinnied and stamped his hooves, attempting to get in on the fun.

"Good boy," I laughed, giving his rump a few pats while Jeremy schooled his face into a scowl, less than impressed with my antics. He was grumbling about the state of his fancy clothes while my mind flashed to

Rainer. I was sure he would have joined in the water fight without a second thought. He wouldn't have given a damn if his fancy clothes got ruined in the process, just as he hadn't cared that night at the wedding. I had no doubt he would have turned my playful splashes into a brutal game until we were both laughing so hard we couldn't breathe. The thought made me pause. I shouldn't have been able to know that because I didn't know *him*. And yet, for some reason I couldn't shake, it felt like I did.

"Have you tired of your fun yet?" Jeremy called with a roll of his eyes.

I matched his eye roll with one of my own and hopped out of the pool. "Sorry, I forgot you were such a bore."

He tossed a towel at my head and rewarded me with another glare. "And I forgot you can be a right prat when you're actually speaking to me."

I wrapped the towel around my shoulders and narrowed my eyes at him in a stare down until Gizmo stepped up behind me and gave a hard shove with his nose right between my shoulder blades, causing me to fall forward towards Jeremy. He immediately broke out in laughter and I whipped around to see Gizmo tossing his head again as if he was laughing, too and I couldn't hide the smile that split my face.

Just like Gizmo could so easily diffuse our standoff just now, our battles from the past weeks broke, too. I turned back to Jeremy and sighed. "I'm sorry I've been a bitch to you lately."

He unfolded his arms and his smile softened. I was reminded of the young man I had first met. The one who had become the best family I had; a brother to me. I was wrong to have shut him out these past few weeks, I knew that now. I just couldn't help it sometimes.

"I'm sorry I pushed you too hard. I should know by now that will never work with you. Let's just put it behind us, yeah? Come on, I brought you that pasta shit you love since I knew you weren't going to show today."

I felt my face light up. "Where? Where is it?"

He chuckled, giving me a full smile and exposing that endearing crooked front tooth. Then he tipped his head back, indicating in the barn, and I was off, rushing passed him without bothering to wait and put Gizmo away. I knew he would follow. Sure enough, the clatter of his hooves echoed in the barn behind me a second later. I snatched an apple from the grain room to distract him, then took the stairs to the breakroom three at a time.

"Are you just going to leave your horse out down here?" I heard Jeremy holler up the stairs. I skipped my way back down, the giant paper bowl overflowing with my mother's famous pasta salad securely in my possession. She may have been the reason for my awful bender last night and all the pain of the past twenty-four hours, but I wasn't going to pass up on this pasta. I shoved a second bite into my mouth and answered, "I'm coming right back," but it came out as more of a mumble than anything. Jeremy gave me a look of exasperation and Gizmo swung his gaze from me to him, still munching his apple in that strange way only horses had.

"What, didn't feel like changing? I know you've got all your clothes up there."

I eyed him as I swallowed my next bite, realizing just how hungry I had been, and searched his eyes for what he meant with that comment. His face remained impassive, so I only shrugged and walked by him down the bay of stalls. "I'll dry in the sun."

He fell into step beside me as I headed out the front barn doors and up a grassy knoll tucked around the corner all while Gizmo clopped along behind us. "I swear you've made that horse believe he's a dog."

I smiled when I realized we really were going to put this fighting behind us. "Shh, he can hear you," I shushed him as I threw myself down in the overgrown grass.

Jeremy took a seat beside me in a much more dignified manner than I had and chuckled while he watched Gizmo bend down to chomp at the tall stalks of grass. "Have you ever met his owner?" he asked.

"Actually, no. Never. Chelsea says he's some guy from out of state. I never really questioned it, because if I don't think about it too much I can almost pretend he's mine. I raised him. I work him. I got him to where he is now. Heck, I could compete with him and probably win with him if he really was mine. I mean, what guy buys an incredible, champion bloodline colt and then never even comes to see him? Never comes to ride him once he was old enough? I don't get it."

Jeremy's face twisted. "It doesn't make sense." As if he knew we were talking about him, Gizmo came up behind me and tried to shove his nose into the pocket of my jeans. Only today, it wasn't carrots that were hidden there.

The locket I had taken from Rainer's room suddenly burned against my thigh. I had almost forgotten I still had it. Almost forgotten the mess that was last night. I still didn't want to think about it. I was good at avoidance. Maybe Rainer was right this morning; I ran and hid and avoided anything I could. It had gotten me this far in life…alive. Wasn't that enough? He didn't understand that sometimes, that's the best I could hope for. I grumbled in response to my thoughts and stabbed angrily at my next noodles.

"Did the pasta do something wrong?" Jeremy asked from beside me.

"Hm?" I turned and found Jeremy watching me with a gaze that bordered on amusement. "Oh, no. Never. This pasta? This pasta could solve all the world's problems."

He chuckled, "You going to give me a bite?"

"Nope." I popped another forkful in and grinned around it.

"You're such a tosser."

"Call me all the stupid, British insults you want, but I'm not giving you my pasta. I'm sure you already had plenty at the oh-so-magical banquet."

He stayed quiet at that. Maybe he was smart enough to read under the sarcasm of my words and feel the pain there. I guess it didn't matter anymore; he knew my family and I weren't speaking, even if he had the reasoning all wrong. He had had front row seats to the last interaction I would probably ever have with my mother. I swallowed hard at that thought, urging my eyes not to water. "Are you going to talk about it?"

"Nope," I bit out.

"Colt…"

I swiveled to face him and placed my now-empty pasta bowl down in the grass between us. "Ah, come on, Jer. We were doing so well here. Being friends and all."

He sighed and leaned forward to rest his elbows on his knees. "Fine. I still think you need to talk about it."

"I know you do."

"I'm still worried," he added, turning his head to look at me.

"I know that, too. I appreciate your concern, I really do."

"I meant what I said before. About the living arrangements. It's been two weeks."

"Jer-"

"No, Colt. Non-negotiable. You can't live in the barn."

"I don't live in the barn," I tried to say convincingly.

"Don't lie to me, Colt. I know we haven't been on good terms lately, but we never lie to each other."

I had a brief stab of guilt because I had been lying to him the entire time I had known him. I'd been lying to everyone. But I barely got a chance to acknowledge it at all before a new voice caused me to almost jump out of my skin.

"She's not lying to you. She isn't living in there anymore." How I hadn't heard Rainer drive up to the barn and then walk up behind us was beyond me. I guess I really was into that pasta salad even more than I had thought.

"Rainer, what?" I sputtered. "What are you doing here?"

"You're the bloke who keeps coming by looking for her." Of course Jeremy had met him this past week. After all, I had been hiding from both of them. It only made sense they'd team up and corner me eventually.

"And here she is." He grinned at me as if our last interaction hadn't ended in two slammed doors and I stared back at him blankly. "Looks like I finally found her. You ready to go?"

"Go?" I asked stupidly. "Go where?"

"Home." He said it so simply, and maybe to him it was. But it wasn't that simple to me. Home would never be simple.

"Rainer, no, I-"

"You don't mind giving us some space, do you?" He wasn't even listening to me, the jerk. Instead, he had turned back to Jeremy as if the words coming out of my mouth were noiseless to him. "You got her all day, yeah? My turn to take her for the night." He said this all with a smile and an attitude like he and Jeremy were best friends. *Just how close had they gotten this past week?* I grumbled internally. The weirdest thing of all, Jeremy was falling for it. I could see him already agreeing with it.

"You're living together?" he asked, looking between the two of us with some scrap of confusion at least.

"No, definitely not. I-"

"It's new," Rainer effectively cut me off again, shoving his hands into his pockets and rocking back on his heels, that easy grin still in place. Meanwhile, I was a rubber band pulled tight and ready to snap. "She's still getting used to it, but you know her." Rainer shrugged his broad shoulders in a what-can-you-say manner and chuckled while Jeremy laughed along with him. *Seriously, what was happening here?*

There was only one other person I had ever known who could charm literally anyone, just like Rainer was now. Seeing him able to flip the switch like this was eerily similar to what I had known years ago. I dug my hand into the pocket of my jeans and felt the cool metal brush my fingers. How was it that I felt as if he was right here again? Standing right next to me?

"Well, alright then. I guess I'll head back to the banquet. I'll see you tomorrow, yeah?" Jeremy directed at me, but I only managed to blink in response. My fingers closed around the gold in my pocket. His gaze swung back to Rainer and he held out a hand. "I guess I'll see you around, mate."

Rainer's smile grew and he shook Jeremy's outstretched hand. "Definitely. I'll be around from now on. Thanks for letting me steal back our girl."

My mounting anger at his overly-friendly, calm demeanor almost boiled over at those words. Who did this guy think he was? And couldn't Jeremy see through his bullshit? Through this stupid act he was playing at? The "V" on the locket dug into my palm as my fist tightened around it even more, pressing the imprint of it into my skin. Jeremy disappeared around the side of the barn and I only had to wait a second before I heard his door slam. The engine of his car started and I rounded on Rainer.

"What the hell is wrong with you?" I growled. Gizmo snorted and tossed his head at my sudden outburst, but I didn't look at him. In this moment, I could only see Rainer. With his stupid, thick, inky hair which was carefully styled now, a far cry from the messy bedhead I had left behind this morning. He was wearing nice clothes, too. Dark jeans that fit him far too well and a button-down shirt with the sleeves rolled up to his elbows. The top button was undone, allowing me a glimpse at his tanned chest that had me gulping down unwanted feelings. His acting smile that had been in place for Jeremy transformed and I was rewarded with that infuriating smirk he reserved just for me.

"Seriously, there's something ridiculously wrong with you. You think you can just show up here, at my barn, and I'll just agree to *live* with you? Just like that? Are you *insane*? Never mind the fact that we argue every time we come within twenty feet of each other. I don't even know you!"

He didn't respond, his smirk only grew into a grin of amusement. Gizmo gave an agitated stamp of his foot in response to the anger he could feel wafting off of me and I wanted to stomp my foot, too. I probably would have if I knew it wouldn't make me look like such a child. "And what was all that just now, anyway? Who was that guy? Because that's not the Rainer I've met before. You think you can just turn on some charming demeanor and get everyone to eat out of the palm of your hand? And, oh. My. God. Stop grinning at me like that! You think you're really something special, don't you? Well, news flash! You're not! That stupid act doesn't work on me. So why don't you just stop claiming I'm yours, because it's never going to happen. Stop thinking I'm going to do whatever you say just because you say it with that annoying-as-shit grin on your stupid lips. And definitely stop thinking I'd ever come to live with you. I would much rather stay in this barn than in a place with you."

His grin had grown to a full-on smile now and my god, it was so beautiful. I growled in frustration. "Are you done?"

"Wh-what?" I sputtered.

"Are you done?" he repeated. "You got out everything you wanted to yell at me? Or did you want to add anything else? Personally, if you want to go back to talking about my lips, I'm all for it. Actually, better yet, you can get a taste of them if you really want. I'm sure you could come up with some more creative adjectives to describe them other than stupid after that."

My mouth fell open in complete shock. *The nerve of this guy.* But I couldn't stop my eyes from falling to his lips while he spoke. From the way they tipped back into that sexy smirk, I knew he was aware of the distraction he was causing in my brain. His tongue darted out to lick his lower lip and the knots in my stomach twisted tighter.

"That's what I thought. Now, where's your stuff?" He didn't wait for a response, and I don't think I was even capable of forming one right at this moment. By the time I realized he had turned and left, he was already to the barn doors, Gizmo right on his heels. *Traitor*, I growled in my head.

"You have *got* to stop doing that!" While his back was still to me, I finally stomped my foot like my inner-five-year-old had been dying to do the whole time and then stormed after him.

He was still chuckling when I finally caught up to him by the stairs. "Stop doing what?" he asked innocently.

"You just walk away and expect people to follow."

"And yet…" He looked down at me and his eyebrows raised in a challenge. Point taken, I had followed yet again. I crossed my arms over my chest and glared up at him. "Up?" he asked. I only narrowed my eyes even further, then turned to lock Gizmo back in his stall. I would *not* be helping Rainer make himself at home here.

When I turned back around, he was already disappearing up into the breakroom. "Hey!" I hustled after him, catching up as he pushed his way into the office uninvited. "Rainer, stop."

"Is this where you've been hiding each time I've come by looking for you?"

I refolded my arms over my chest and avoided his completely accurate accusation. "I'm not coming with you."

"You'd rather live here? In this office? On that ratty couch?" He looked over at the sagging, itchy couch with disdain.

"Yes," I huffed defiantly.

"Why?" he countered, as if he genuinely cared about my answer.

"Aside from the fact your mother thinks I'm a stealing whore in your bed?" I snapped. His eyebrows raised at that, surprise coloring his features at the fact that I had overheard their conversation this morning, but he didn't comment on it. He only crossed his arms over his chest and tilted his head as if to say that wasn't a good enough reason. "I don't even know you," I sighed, part of my fight leaving me as my hands slapped down to my sides.

He scoffed at that. "That's not true. Even if it was, I'll fix that for you right now. My name's Rainer Giovanni Ventrilla. Twenty-four years old. Dual degree in business management and agriculture. I love mint chocolate chip ice cream but hate chocolate, and yeah, I know that's weird so you don't need to remind me. I'm much more of a morning person than a night owl, but I've been known to sneak out a bit. I'm way too fascinated with the sky and nature, and my Mom's always telling me I need to care more about numbers and figures, but I just can't. I guess I get that trait from my dad. I used to have a need for everything to be in order, to fix everything, but then it all went to shit, as you know.

"I haven't met a girl I've liked in over three years, and even before that I kept everyone at arm's length. Since Ross died, I haven't really left the estate at all. And then you showed up. And ever since you ran into me on the stairs, it's like a drug. I can't keep you out of my head and it's becoming quite a problem. I'm really good at fixing problems, though, so I'm sorry but I'm going to have to figure this out. Which means you're stuck with me for a while, and I'm not really sure how to handle that, so maybe I'm not doing it right, but maybe you aren't, either."

My mouth fell open and then closed again as if I was a fish out of water. I had no idea how to respond to any of that and although he had said it all so calmly, I could see the rapid rise and fall of his chest under his thin dress shirt and knew it had to have had some effect on him to lay it all out there like that. He took the one step there was to take in this tiny box of a room so that he was completely invading my personal space and my head unconsciously tipped back to look up at him. His rough fingertips brushed along my jaw and I clenched it shut at the sensation, my heart beating ten times faster than his was right in front of me. "Stop running away, Colt," he said softly. "You can't erase last night. You can't erase the other day in the sprinklers. You can't erase running into me on those back stairs. I told you last night, I'm not going anywhere. You can't just push me away and hide from me like you do with that other guy out there."

"You know nothing about Jeremy," I snapped, trying to cling on to some solid bit of information that didn't involve the feelings and emotions and somersaults that were currently going on in my stomach. He laughed, but there was no humor in it and his eyes hardened. That hadn't been the response he was looking for and for a brief moment, I felt bad. Because although he wouldn't admit it, my avoidance of everything he just laid out there hurt him. His thumb and forefinger released my chin and he inched back from me.

"Don't need to. I've seen enough to know he's a pushover and you don't care about him."

"That's not true," I gasped indignantly, still trying to recover from the feel of his fingers on my skin. The feel of his heart bared wide open for me. "You're wrong. Jeremy's my best friend."

"Of course he is," he tossed over his shoulder as he pulled open the door of the closet. Even though I was relieved he had stepped away from me and I had some semblance of control back, I desperately wanted him to stay out of that closet. I reached my arm out to pull him back, but I was too scared to touch him. His eyes flicked to mine when he saw the movement and for a split second I saw pity in their depths. I quickly wrapped my arms back around my waist, effectively shutting him out and holding myself together. Just as I did that, his eyes grew distant again.

"What's that supposed to mean?" I asked.

He turned back to rummage in the closet when he realized I was too weak to stop him. "You like him because you can control him. You dictate exactly what he gets to see of you and he's so spineless, he allows it."

I gasped. Sure, Jeremy was a bit spineless, but no one actually said that. It didn't make him a bad person. It just meant he was good; kind; soft. How dare this person who didn't even know him judge him? Judge me as if I used him? And yet...wasn't he right? "I hate you."

"Sure you do," Rainer said, not the least bit concerned with the lie that just fell from my lips. I didn't hate him. Not even close. But I so wished I could.

He bent down and shoved some riding boots out of the way that Chelsea had stored in there years ago and promptly forgot about. "You like him because he doesn't even fight you. You hate me because I do."

"That's not true." My skin crawled at how close he was to unearthing my bag from the careful spot I tucked it into every day and I was powerless to stop him. "Jeremy fights with me."

I watched as his hand closed over the strap of my duffel and pulled it free of the closet, sliding it over his shoulder like it was nothing; as if everything I owned in this life wasn't now resting in his hands. "Right. That's fine. But does he fight *for* you?" His eyes met mine boldly once he had straightened back to his full height. "You might hate me right now, Colt, but I know you don't really. You just don't know what to do with someone caring about you. With someone wanting to figure you out. Figure *us* out. I'm not fighting *with* you. I'm fighting *for* you."

Chapter Nine

This was stupid. I hated him, I really did…I wished I did.

My fingers reached for the door handle but then I pulled them back. *Nope. Still a stupid idea*, I thought. My other hand reached to turn the ignition, but I couldn't bring myself to do that, either. So instead, I continued to sit in my deathtrap of a car staring up at the Ventrilla Mansion. I had already determined that would be the only way I would refer to what was about to become my prison. Home. Same thing if you asked me.

No. No, it wasn't. Because I hated Rainer and I wasn't about to take his handouts even if he gave them in that rude, confident manner that only he could make sexy. *Sexy? Did I really just think that?* My forehead dropped to the steering wheel with a groan.

"She's not here." I whipped my head up to see Rainer standing next to my car with his hands in his pockets. Instead of answering, I simply stared at him. "My mom. If that's why you aren't coming in. She isn't home. She's still at the gala schmoozing with potential clients."

"Banquet," I instinctively corrected, then slapped a hand over my mouth. Rainer raised an eyebrow at me and I slowly lowered my hand to speak with wide eyes. "He hates it when people call it a gala."

I had a flash of an open hand striking me across the face, the sting of his fingers sending fire over my cheek and instantly causing water to fill my eyes. Another hand wrapped around my tiny arm so hard I knew immediately that my bicep would have purple finger prints banded around it tomorrow.

"You stupid bitch," he breathed in my face, the stench of whiskey so strong I wanted to gag. At seven years old, I shouldn't have known what whiskey smelled like. But I did. I knew them all. Vodka. Whiskey. Tequila. Rum. I knew their stink and how they mixed with his breath once he was off-duty. I knew what one made him slap. What smell I associated with his shoves into walls and closed fists. The sharpness of tequila that meant I wouldn't have too much of a problem, but Mommy's eyes would be red tomorrow and her shirt would be a turtleneck.

Another slap rang against my cheek and his whiskey breath came again. "How many times do I have to tell you, it's not a fucking gala for rich bitches."

I dropped my eyes to the floor. I hated looking into his eyes. Hated he had given me the same flinty, grey color. *Ten. Nine. Eight. Seven...*

"Colt..." I flinched, but when I raised my gaze it wasn't my matching dead eyes I saw. It was the galaxy of colors that sucked me in. "Colt, I..."

While I had been lost in my memory, I hadn't noticed Rainer reaching in to unlock my door and pulling it open so that he was now squatting beside me, his hands casually resting against my waist in comfort. I felt the heat from his palms burning through the soft fabric of his long-sleeve I was still wearing. Felt the heavy weight start to crush my chest from anxiety, but then one of his hands lifted when I turned to meet his gaze. His fingertips brushed against my cheek, tucking hair that had fallen forward back behind my ear, tucking that rising anxiety back before it could crush me or cause me to lash out or shut down. I shuddered beneath his touch, unable to close my eyes against the intensity in his, unable to block him out.

"Colt Jefferson," he murmured. He was so close I felt his breath fall against my skin in waves, but there was no stench of alcohol tainting it. Just a sharp, fresh scent of mint. I swallowed hard, his hand still cradling my cheek, the other curved around my waist. I was so conscious of each millimeter of him pressed against me, could feel my heart pounding at the contact. "Like Lieutenant Jefferson."

I didn't confirm or deny, my eyes stayed wide and locked on him. I was sure he could read everything in them. I'm sure he could feel my heart beating out of my chest just as much as I could. I saw his jaw tick, knew he was grinding his teeth. His hand tightened around my waist and the thumb that had been absentmindedly stroking my cheek stilled. I watched his beautiful eyes frantically search mine, looking for a confirmation to a question he couldn't ask. Looking for a denial to a theory I prayed he wouldn't voice. In a second, I saw his eyes harden, and then he closed them, his dark lashes so long they touched his cheekbones once they were shut and his jaw clenched tight. Slowly, his forehead dropped the remaining inches to rest against mine and my whole body quaked at the new point of contact.

He was so still against me, if I couldn't feel his heavy exhales against my lips I would have worried he had stopped breathing altogether. Every muscle in him was pulled taut, an arrow at full draw, and being so close to someone in that state should have terrified me. I should have been running for the hills. I could feel the anger in him growing in his tense muscles, knew he could so easily break me this close to him, but I was frozen. I felt no fear. I felt something else entirely.

I lifted my hand from where it had been resting in my lap and though I could see the tremors in my fingers, I didn't stop. I reached up and ever-so-gently, I brushed my fingertips against Rainer's clenched jaw. He hissed in a breath of air through his teeth, but his eyes stayed closed, his forehead still pressed against mine. All four points of contact seared me, but I kept my fingertips against him. I moved them up, feeling his stubble scratch me, before they dipped into the thick, soft hair at his temple.

"Rainer..." I finally breathed.

His eyelids fluttered open, but I didn't remove my hand. He was so close to me, I could see every strand of green laced through the swirl of brown of his eyes. He sucked in a breath, stealing my air and making it his own. "Colt, I swear...if he did this to you..."

I whimpered, a sound I knew all too well from myself, and tried to shake my head but too many points of us were touching. One hand still cradled my neck which made it impossible for me to shake my head no. Maybe that was for the best. Maybe there was reason there.

His forehead bumped against mine, dropping in a nod to counter my shake. I didn't know it was possible to see so much emotion in someone's eyes. Mine had been dead for as long as I could remember. "Not tonight," he breathed. "but one day. One day you'll tell me your truth."

I didn't respond, but for once I knew he wasn't looking for me to. Instead, we simply stayed there just like that, pressed together but only touching at four points, and somehow it was just enough.

~

"So you know ahead is the kitchen. There's pretty much everything you could ever want in there. Mom always goes overboard. Feel free to take whatever. On the left is some weird fancy room we only ever use if we have company over, but Viviana is always trying to crawl around in there to get to my dad's office. The living room is through there, but again we don't really use that room. When you stop to think about it, this floor's pretty useless." Rainer reached up to grip the back of his neck and smiled at me sheepishly. After our moment, or whatever the hell it had been, he had stood without a word and led the way into the mansion. He had filled the silence with a mini-tour once the massive door had shut behind us, but I had yet to say anything back.

"So, yeah...let's go then." He started up the stairs now, again not waiting to see if I was following. I rolled my eyes at his back. Apparently, my words from earlier were useless.

"That's Viviana's room, the explosion of pink, remember?" He flashed his grin over his shoulder and I wrapped my arms tighter around my stomach. Stupid butterflies. They were really starting to get attached to this boy. I didn't think they'd ever get flustered by anyone else at this point. "Then Rachel's. She'll probably claw your eyes out if you ever try to go in there unannounced."

"I heard that, you dick!" The answered snap from behind the closed door startled me, but Rainer only gave a throaty chuckle. The door whipped open a second later to reveal Rachel, one hand poised on her hip, her crazy-green eyes flashing. "Just 'cause I don't want you nosing through my stuff and trying to be the overprotective big brother doesn't mean-" Her words cut off as her eyes fell to me for the first time. "What are you doing here?"

Rainer answered for me. "Colt, you remember my sister. Rachel, Colt's going to be staying with us for a while so-"

"Why?" she cut off. Her arms crossed over her chest like mine, but where my stance was to hold myself together, hers was simply a challenge.

Rainer's eyes flicked to mine apologetically, but Rachel had yet to fully look at me. It was as if I wasn't even here. He opened his mouth to answer for me; probably to make up some lie about why I was here, because that was all it could be. All I ever let it be. Lies on top of lies of what my life had been. Hadn't I just left myself wide open for him, though? Whether he had voiced it or not at my car, he knew the truth. I had seen it in his eyes. I was tired of the lies, the games, the masks I had to wear every second of every day. What if I stopped for once?

So before Rainer could try to cover for me, I forced Rachel to finally acknowledge my presence. "Because my own father beats me, my mother welcomes it, and my supposed best friend thinks I'm some drug dealer in a gang. I have nowhere else to go because the police will never believe my claim thanks to their friendship with my father and I don't exactly have the funds to support myself. So basically, I'm like one of those kicked dogs you can find at the shelter and Rainer's the lucky applicant interested in fostering me," I deadpanned.

Rainer's perpetually calm and composed face was in complete shock at my outburst. Rachel actually stumbled back a step and her arms fell limp by her sides while her wide, emerald eyes finally locked on me. I had only ever seen them narrowed and judging before. But now, she looked completely different. Vulnerable. Her mouth popped open before she could remember her manners, but I didn't give her a chance. "So that's why I'm here." I turned to Rainer, who was looking at me with a mix of what I thought might be pride, but also pain, anger, and pity. "I appreciate the tour, but I just want to be alone right now."

He nodded quickly, seeing something in me that must have told him not to push for any more right now. "Yeah, of course. Come on." I trailed after him yet again, through the door at the end of the hall. It led into another living room, though this one actually appeared to be lived-in. Then up another flight of stairs which were tucked into the corner of the room and down a smaller hallway I vaguely remembered as his from storming down it this morning. He pushed open the first door on the right, which I must have completely ignored when I was leaving earlier today, and waited for me to walk in first.

I stepped into the room and immediately felt small. It was huge, easily just as big as I remembered Rainer's being. Something about it made it feel familiar, though I couldn't place what it was. The walls were a pale blue and where Rainer's room had been all dark accents, this was light. Although just like his, this room was empty, too. As if it used to be loved and lived-in, but not anymore.

Rainer cleared his throat from behind me and I startled, then spun to find him still standing in the doorway. He wasn't looking at me, instead he seemed as intent on taking in the space as I was. "This was Ross's room."

"Your brother." My words didn't come out as a question so much as a statement, but he gave a curt nod nonetheless.

"He had moved out of it before he died, but this is still his to me. My parents still haven't touched any of his stuff in the guest house, but they don't come in here, either." His eyes finally drifted down from the enormous window on the back wall that he had been gazing out of absently to meet mine. "Today was the first time I'd come in here since…"

"Why?" I asked. I didn't have to clarify; we both knew I wasn't asking why he hadn't come in here since Ross died. I was asking why he was moving me into *this* room. I knew as well as he did there were plenty of rooms I could stay in at the Ventrilla Mansion, it didn't need to be this specific room.

"I don't know," he replied, his eyes conveying how brutally honestly that thought was. "It just felt right."

He finally took a step in from the doorway, his measured strides carrying him to stand directly in front of me. My head craned to look up at him yet again, the boy who was slowly coming to own me even if I had wanted to fight it. His hand reached up towards me, and though my eyes still followed it as if it was a knife, I didn't even flinch when his fingers finally connected with my skin this time. His hand gently wrapped around my neck and he used his thumb to tilt my chin up just a bit more. His eyes bored into my own and my heart thumped painfully in my chest.

"Thank you for giving me your truth," he breathed. Just like that, he bent and pressed his lips to my forehead. I gasped in a breath of air but didn't pull away, the feel of his lips bringing back a flash of last night and the weight of his arms around me, holding me to him in sleep. Then he was gone. The heat of his chest leaving me, the soft press of his lips disappearing. By the time I opened my eyes again, he had left the room and only the light scent of grapes lingered in his place.

My footsteps didn't make a sound over the plush carpet and I sank deep into the bed when I tried to perch myself on just the edge. My hand brushed over the soft bedspread absentmindedly and I finally allowed myself to accept this new situation, even if it was only temporary. *As temporary as a stray dog in a foster home*, I thought bitterly. My back eased into the pillows and I let my eyes wander closed once more, finally realizing why this room felt familiar. It was the color. It was the same color of *his* eyes.

"Donnie." He nodded at me and took what was quickly becoming his customary seat beside me in the shadows. For some reason, he had traded in his place as the center of attention to join me each night I was here. I didn't realize I was openly staring at him, wondering why he kept coming to sit with me, until he turned and aimed a wink in my direction. My cheeks immediately heated in the cold air and I quickly turned my gaze back to the fire in front of us. I could just barely feel its heat from where we were seated, but at least it was something. The nights were starting to get pretty cold now and I wondered how long this group would keep meeting here. All through winter? Even if it snowed? I highly doubted that. They had homes to go to. Parents that would welcome a group of friends coming over, though maybe not their beverage of choice.

"Vee," I said in as calm a voice as I could manage, finally returning his greeting.

He grinned at my name for him, though I have no idea why. Creativity had never been my strong suit and it clearly wasn't now. After our first night of banter, he had sought me out the following week to ask if I had thought of what I wanted it to be. At first, I had no clue what he was referring to; I was too shocked by the fact he had come over to me again. Then I remembered our riddle of a conversation from the week before. As if I could have ever forgotten; it had been running on a loop through my mind for six days straight. And while I hadn't been able to stop thinking about him, I still had no clue what his name was. The only thing that kept sticking out was the gold locket he had run between his fingers with the delicate "V" on it. The same locket he was toying with now.

As always, it was him who broke the silence between us. "If you could do anything in the world right now, what would it be?"

The possibilities were endless. What I said, however, was less than inspirational. "Go tip a cow."

His head whipped up from watching the locket slip through his fingers and he looked at me as if he was trying to gauge if I was being serious. I gazed back at him with a blank face and he burst out laughing. It was a sound that made my whole body feel warm despite the frosty air. "Where do you even come up with this stuff?"

I just shrugged. I had overheard some boys in my Spanish class talking about cow tipping that afternoon and it had caught my attention. I wanted to know what it was, so I had eavesdropped as they talked about their plans and who was going. I was curious about what it was like to act stupid with a group of friends like that. I wondered what having a group of friends felt like at all. But I didn't say that to Vee. We kept things light. It's why I had grown to love coming here over the past weeks. It was *fun*. So instead, I just shrugged.

His lips slipped over his red solo cup, not that I was paying any particular attention to his lips at all, and he took another drink of the lukewarm beer they always seemed to have in excess here. Somehow, he still managed to smirk at me the entire time until I finally turned away so he wouldn't catch me studying him again. It's not like I could help it, I had never seen a guy look like him before. It's like he couldn't possibly be real. "And where the hell are you planning on finding a cow to tip?" he asked once he had swallowed, easily derailing my train of thought.

I shrugged yet again and took another sip of my own beer, just to appear normal. Whenever Vee was this close to me, though, I felt anything but. "What about you? If you could do anything, what would you do?"

His face scrunched up in response, but even then, he still looked perfect. "You're terrible at this game. You can't ask me the same question. That's lame."

"You're lame," I shot back, matching his teasing tone and surprising even myself by saying it. His answering laughter was enough to make it worth it.

"Real mature, Donnie," he deadpanned.

"I never claimed to be mature," I challenged. His soft blue eyes danced with amusement before he cocked his head to the side and studied me.

"You don't have to say it. You just are."

I pulled my gaze from his to stare ahead at the bonfire and suddenly felt the chill from always staying in the shadows. He was right about me again. I was mature for a fifteen-year-old kid. It fit the whole act my family put on. Friendly, happy mom. Funny, dependable father. Quiet, mature daughter. My fingers tugged at the hem of my shirt while I thought of how wrong those assumptions were.

"Why do you still come over here?" I blurted out.

I could feel his eyes boring into the side of my head but I didn't turn. My fingers continued tugging in an effort to distract myself. "That your question?" I shrugged again, still refusing to meet his gaze. "Come on, Wild Child. Be assertive," he joked, knocking his shoulder into mine and I flinched from the contact, instinctively folding into myself and scooting away. He had no clue why I was this way. Had no clue it was the worst idea in the world to be assertive in my life. I needed to be as submissive as possible. I stood hastily and was trying to think up an excuse to sneak away for the night when that same girl came up to us.

"Babe, I've been looking all over for you," she whined, completely ignoring I was even there. "I'm cold."

Vee gave me one last concerned glance, but when he turned back to the girl, his confident grin was back in place, the one that drew everyone in. "Well I know a few ways we can fix that." He waggled his eyebrows at the girl who giggled and easily slipped under his arm once he stood. My cheeks heated at the implication he was giving her. I didn't want to think of him like that with someone else. It was gross, but I couldn't say anything. I ducked my chin as she pulled him back towards the flames but before they had made it too far, he turned with her still under his arm to look back at me.

"Donnie, this is the last night for the fall. Winter is coming," he joked. It was some quote all the guys seemed to use around school, but I had no idea what it was from. "Have a good Christmas, yeah?"

The way he was studying me, I felt like he could see right through me. I felt like he knew without me ever saying anything that I wouldn't have a good Christmas, and that made him sad. But maybe he didn't know at all. I was just a naïve kid, and he didn't have any reason to be interested in me. The tall, beautiful girl tucked under his arm was proof enough of that.

"Yeah...Merry Christmas," I whispered, but his blue eyes had already left me.

Chapter Ten

My eyes slowly peeled open to complete darkness. And silence. It was almost eerie to be so silent. No scuttling of mice from somewhere in the barn. No shuffling of hooves. No distant drunken snores I had grown up with. The soft pillows I had drifted off in as soon as I had gotten into Ross's old room still cocooned me, but I could no longer see the calming blue walls in the dark. I vaguely wondered if the rooms here were soundproof too, because it was seriously silent. My hands stretched out in front of me as I made my way towards a light I could see beneath the door and I pulled it open before glancing both ways down this shorter hallway. There was no light coming from Rainer's room, but there was a light at the other end from the stairs that led up from the smaller living room.

I padded my way down the stairs and looked around in the dim light but didn't see Rainer anywhere. The clock shining from beneath the enormous TV claimed it was two in the morning, meaning I had slept for almost six hours already. I looked back up the way I had come, knowing I should just go back to bed. I didn't know this place. I shouldn't be wandering the halls uninvited, but I was supposedly living here now. I should get to know it better. My stomach growled angrily, reminding me that the only thing I had eaten in days now was the pasta Jeremy had stolen for me from the banquet. *Rainer had said I could help myself to the fridge...* With that thought, I was off, tiptoeing my way through the door, into the hall where Rachel's room was, then down the wide, grand staircase.

Everything was huge here. Huge and silent and I felt smaller than ever. I'd spent my whole life trying to be as tiny as possible, able to be overlooked, and here now it was suddenly all I felt. Miniscule; unnoticeable. If I wanted to, I bet I could have hidden in this mansion for days without anyone knowing. Far cry from when I would huddle on the floor of my closet each time I heard my father arrive home, praying to a God I wasn't sure I believed in that he wouldn't bother to look for me that night. More often than not, my prayers went unanswered.

I let my fingers trail over the smooth walls as I went, feeling my way towards the kitchen on silent feet. I paused in the hall just before the kitchen and looked up at the wall of pictures I had somehow missed before. They were huge, covering one whole wall of the hallway, and artfully placed. My mother would have approved; she always had an eye for those sorts of things. I scanned the faces, taking in Rainer's strong jawline, always clenched tight as if he didn't know what a smile was. Rachel's piercing eyes that shone through even in photographs. Their mother, who apparently thought I was a thief, but in every picture was perfectly composed yet welcoming and at ease. Viviana in various stages of screaming infant to what she looked like now. Then someone who I had never met before who could only be Rainer's father. It was like looking at a full-grown version of him; the same inky hair, same muscular build, but where in every picture Rainer looked stoic, his father had the largest grin out of everyone. Just looking at him caused the corners of my lips to turn up infinitesimally. However, out of all these pictures, candid, professional, big, small, group shots, and individuals, not one of them showed the infamous Ross. For some reason, it bothered me. I wanted to put a face to this name I had only heard in whispers. To the brother who left Rainer with so much pain and guilt. The father who would never meet his daughter.

"What are you doing?"

I jumped almost a foot in the air and whipped around to see Rainer standing at the other end of the hall, barefoot in just his sleep pants. My eyes widened in the gloom, taking in the contours of his chest and abs as the burning grew low in my belly, the butterflies taking flight at the sight of their favorite person. I wondered how I could find something as simple as his bare feet attractive. Could feet even be attractive? Suddenly, I felt my cheeks heat knowing I had just totally checked him out and he watched me do it. My eyes returned to his face to see him grinning at me as if he had very much enjoyed knowing I had just ogled him. I had already become so accustomed to that stupid smirk, even though it seemed to be missing from every one of these photos in front of me. I wondered if I was seeing some version of Rainer that his family never had.

"Why isn't he here?" I asked, praying he would go along with my question and not point out my obvious discomfort at having just been caught practically salivating over his bare chest.

He stepped closer to me, so close I could feel the heat radiating off him, but I refused to look back at him over my shoulder while he took in the same pictures I was looking at. After a moment, he sighed and raked one hand through his hair. "My mom. She couldn't stand looking at his pictures anymore. It hurt her every day. So any one he was in, she took it down."

"That's...horrible." I finally turned around to face him and had to fight the urge to look down and count the ridges in his abs.

"Yeah. Right after it happened, she tried to be strong. Tried to pretend like she was okay. But very quickly, it got bad. She wasn't okay. Every time she passed his picture, I'd catch her breaking down. One night I found her in this same hall, ripping them all off and sobbing. It was heartbreaking. It was my fault. So I helped her do it. She was such a mess that night, she said she wanted them all gone. Destroyed. When I finally got her to calm down and head back to bed, I packed them all in boxes. I knew she didn't mean it." His hand gripped the base of his neck and he ducked his head, avoiding my eyes. "For the longest time, she even had trouble looking at us, my dad in particular. Ross took after him the most. Neither of them could ever stop smiling. They could make a joke out of anything. Put them together and you wouldn't be able to breathe because you were laughing too hard all the time. They had the same eyes, the same laugh. It was bad enough my mom had to see him every day and be reminded of Ross. She didn't want to see the pictures, too."

"I'm glad you kept them," I whispered.

His eyes lifted to meet mine and one corner of his mouth turned up. "Yeah, me too. Maybe one day I'll show you him."

"I'd like that," I promised.

A calm came back onto his face and his lips lifted in a real smile now, the heaviness of the moment dissipating as quickly as it had come. "So really, what are you doing down here?"

Before I could respond, my stomach gave a deafening growl and I clamped my hands over it, my eyes wide with shock. "Well..." I started, but Rainer was laughing too hard to even hear me and soon enough I was laughing, too. It felt good. It felt *really* good.

"Come on," he chuckled before throwing an arm over my shoulders and steering me towards the kitchen. The heat of his bare skin was pressing into me as heavy as the anxiety that normally blanketed my shoulders, and yet I allowed it. I may not have been used to it, but I allowed it without throwing him off. Because the truth was, I wanted it.

"Sit." He lifted his arm from my shoulders to point at the island and I instantly felt cold...almost empty.

"On the counter?" I asked. He shrugged his shoulders like it was nothing. "I can't," I protested.

"Do you need help?" He took a step back towards me in a prowl, but there was a playful grin on his face. I laughed and held up my hand to stop him but he just kept coming until he had backed me into the granite countertop in the center of this enormous kitchen. The only light came from above the stove and it cast odd shadows over his face, in the dips and valleys of his chest which was now directly in front of me.

"No, I don't need help," I sputtered. "I can't sit on your counters. Have you seen this place it's-" My voice cut off in a gasp. His large hands found my waist and again, he lifted me like I was nothing, seating me on the edge of the counter and then promptly stepping back and folding his arms over his broad chest. He raised one eyebrow at me, daring me to comment, that cocky grin securely in place. My heart was beating out of control; it seemed to do that any time Rainer touched me. Did he not understand that he was the first person to touch me in years? And yet, he did it without thinking. Lifted me as if it was no big deal. Yet he still backed up right away, giving me the space he understood I needed.

I narrowed my eyes and crossed my arms to match him. "I hate you," I reiterated from this afternoon, letting him know that I was aware of what he was doing. I knew he was pushing my limits to the breaking point but stopping just short of it. His grin grew in understanding.

"Oh, I'm aware."

"You know I don't like to be touched," I stated. It wasn't a secret. After tonight, he even knew why. He was only the second person to ever know why. Just the thought that I had shared my secret with him caused goosebumps to raise along my arms. Was trusting him with that information stupid?

"But you let me anyway," he replied calmly. Everything he did was calm.

"I don't know why." Again, I was shocked by my own honesty around him. There was something about this man that made it impossible to hide my truths.

Rainer's perfectly straight teeth flashed at me in the light of the stove. His smile was almost as large as his father's from the pictures. "That's okay. One day you will." He turned then and padded over to the fridge, not even allowing me to question what he meant by that. I wasn't sure I wanted to know the answer. "What do you want?" he asked with his back to me.

"Uh...what?" My brain was still fuzzy from having him so close to me and these riddles for answers he always seemed to come up with.

He smiled at me over his shoulder and pulled open a door to the refrigerator that was easily the size of my old closet. *Seriously?* I thought. *Who needed that much food?*

"Anything," I answered aloud.

"Anything?" he questioned.

I shrugged. "It really doesn't matter." And it didn't. I had been living off of microwavable goods in the barn for weeks now. I couldn't remember the last time I had eaten something that wasn't take-out food or Chef Boyardee.

He pulled a can from a shelf on the door and tossed it my way. I caught it instinctively, then looked up at him in confusion. "Whipped cream?" I asked. "What am I supposed to do with this?"

He laughed like I was joking and shuffled a few more things around in the fridge. When he straightened and turned back to see me holding out the can in question, he finally understood that I wasn't kidding. "You eat it," he laughed.

I raised my eyebrows at his form, silhouetted by the light from the industrial-sized refrigerator. His bare feet padded back over to me and he took the can from my hand, intentionally brushing his fingers against mine in the process. A shock ran up my arm and I shivered involuntarily. If he wasn't already so close to me, I never would have heard the quiet chuckle he let out at my reaction to him. Just the sound of it caused the butterflies to take flight again.

"Open your mouth." His laughing eyes held mine.

"What…"

"Colt, open your mouth," he grinned, holding the can up and at an angle.

"Why?"

"Because it reminds me of sneaking down here as a kid to do this." And he looked so much like a kid at this moment, even if I knew he was twenty-four and a death separated him from the child he had been. The boyish grin he wore now was endearing; carefree. It made me wonder if I could ever be like that. If he was able to put his guilt away and be this free, could I one day be able to put away my own problems?

"You ate whipped cream straight out of the can as a kid?" I asked, still not comfortable enough to completely let go and do as he asked.

"You didn't?"

"Uhm, no, Rainer." I didn't bother adding that I doubted we had ever even kept a can of whipped cream in the refrigerator at my house.

His eyes glinted in amusement, the boyish charm shining even brighter. "Well then, you have to now. You've got no choice. Open up." He brandished the can like a weapon, his finger poised to spray it, and I found my lips turning up at the corners, matching his childish joy despite the fact that I was shaking my head. And crazily enough, I opened my mouth for him. The can made a spritzing noise and the foam filled my mouth, the sweetness exploding on my tongue.

"It tastes better this way, right?" Rainer asked, his eyes darkening as he watched my tongue swipe across my bottom lip once I had swallowed. I shrugged, a go-to response for me, but I had to admit it did taste pretty good. As stupid as it seemed, it had a taste of freedom; rebellion. He didn't waste any time in tipping the can back and taking a mouthful himself before raising it for me again with a devilish grin. This time, he didn't even have to ask before I opened my mouth. Except instead of stopping once my mouth was full, Rainer didn't let up. I closed my mouth and swatted at his hand, but he was laughing, getting the whipped cream all over my face, in my hair, covering my clothes.

I quickly swallowed so that I could tell him how ridiculous he was being. Except, the voice that came out didn't even sound like mine. "Rainer! Stop!" I giggled as more whipped cream came at me nonstop. *Giggled? I knew how to giggle?* I sounded like those girls in school who would jokingly tell off the guys who flirted with them. I sounded like I was just another smitten high schooler.

My hands reached up to slap the can of whipped cream away from him, but he danced out of my way, still continuing to aim the stream of it over every inch of me. "Stop it," I laughed, swiping some of the sweet stuff off my cheek but also popping that finger in my mouth afterwards. It's not like I was about it waste something this delicious. Like I said, I had been living off of Chef Boyardee and this was a new delicacy. I hopped down from the counter and ran around to the other side, trying to duck behind it as cover, but he followed me and before I knew it he had grabbed me by the hips as I tried to run further away from him, easily hauling me up into his bare chest as the whipped cream canister clattered to the floor.

"Rainer!" I squealed, my feet helplessly dangling as he held me hostage. His deep laugh rumbled against my back where his chest pressed against me and I didn't even feel any of my normal anxiety. It was as if my body had already accepted that being in his arms was safe. My skin wanted to feel his on mine, even if I didn't quite know how to process that in my head yet.

His warm breath tickled against my ear and I finally stilled in his arms, though my heart continued to beat wildly. "I thought I told you. You're done running from me." Without warning, I felt a swipe of his tongue against my neck and my whole body stiffened.

"Did you...did you just..." I gasped, turning my head to find his eyes. They were darker than I had ever seen, the green a deep emerald and the blue almost navy, his pupils wide.

"Lick you?" he finished in a deep voice that had a blush rising to my cheeks and my stomach tightening in knots. I swallowed down the lump that had just formed in my throat. His eyes were challenging, daring me to say it, but I couldn't. He smirked and ducked his head again and this time his lips closed over a point on my neck that had me gasping as he sucked off the whipped cream that was there, sucked on a part of my skin. "Tastes even better off of you," he murmured against me, but I had no way of responding. I was pretty sure my entire body had just gone into shock. Seemed like a natural reaction. Watching someone die. Being in excruciating pain. Rainer Ventrilla eating whipped cream off your neck.

They all seemed like pretty good reasons for a body to go into shock if you asked me.

His forehead was still resting on my collarbone when he chuckled. "Thank you, Colt. For giving me this. You." He placed a quick kiss just under my jaw this time and then straightened up, releasing me from his hold and taking a step back while I just stayed there, unable to move. Unable to even look at him at all. "Now let's get you some real food."

~

I pulled my hair up in a knot on top of my head and then caught a peek of myself in the mirror hanging above the dresser. I almost didn't recognize the girl looking back at me. I couldn't remember the last time I had put my hair up; pulled it back from my face instead of letting it hang forward to cover a new bruise or cut. It highlighted how gaunt I had become. Or maybe I had always been this way and just never seen it. I was never one to linger long on my own reflection. Just spent enough time to know I had swiped on enough makeup to avoid any questions or concerns. For a split second, I debated taking my hair out, letting it fall back in front of my face. But then I remembered Rainer's words from last night. The emotion in his voice as he thanked me. For giving myself to him. Is that what I was doing? Giving myself over to him? That seemed like a bit of a stretch, but I *had* allowed him to break down enough of my walls to touch me. To kiss me. To freaking *lick* me. I had told him about my father, though I knew he would want more than what I had said to Rachel yesterday. Was I ready for that? No. But maybe I was ready to wear my hair up.

I hadn't gone back to sleep after my incident with Rainer in the kitchen. Instead, I found my way around the monstrous bathroom in Ross's old room and took my time washing off all the sticky residue from our whipped cream fight. I must have spent at least in hour under the stream, reveling in the feel of an actual shower with glass walls and hot water. Then I wandered back to the kitchen, though I didn't know what I was expecting to find there. For it to be empty, I suppose. I had spent my whole life hiding behind closed doors as much as possible and just assumed others did the same. Instead, Rachel was sitting on a stool by the counter, Viviana smushing some playdoh by her feet. She didn't notice me at first so I took a minute to really look at her. Despite it being so early that the sun had yet to rise, her hair was pin straight, falling like a sheet down her back. Her face almost looked like it was made of porcelain, though at the moment it was twisted in a half-scowl, half-glare that I wasn't sure she was even aware of. I followed her line of sight and watched Viviana push a blob of red playdoh through a flower form.

"Are you not a fan of playdoh or something?" I asked, figuring it was time I announced my presence before she could think I was even more of a freak than I'm sure she already did.

She whipped around on the stool to find me standing in the doorway to the hall and her startling green eyes held me in place. She didn't say anything, so I guess that was an improvement from insulting me. I took that as her idea of a warm welcome and stepped further into the kitchen. I still wasn't really hungry after the meal of chicken parmesan Rainer ended up heating up for me so late last night, but in an effort to appear as if I knew what I was doing around here, I grabbed an apple from the basket of fruit and took a bite.

Her gaze stayed on me the entire time, in the same calculating manner as always, only this time I swear I saw a little bit of human tucked away in her eyes. She didn't respond, and I wasn't about to push her to talk, so instead I leaned against the sink and took another bite of the apple, turning my own gaze on Viviana. She was wearing a frilly skirt and sparkly top, both pink of course, and her dark locks were tied up in a pink scrunchy right on top of her head so she looked like little Cindy Lou Who.

"Your dad really beat you?" Rachel's ugly words didn't seem right in the presence of something so pure. Maybe that's why I felt like I shouldn't be around Viviana, either. I would just taint her.

I finished chewing the apple that was in my mouth and looked back at Rachel who didn't look at all uncomfortable with the topic she had just so casually voiced at four in the morning. A part of me felt a little proud of her for that. For not shying away from it. Not letting the elephant in the room crush us like I hadn't dropped a huge bomb of information on them last night. Jeremy would have given me my space; not forced me to talk about anything. Maybe Rainer was right when he had said he was spineless. Obviously, Rachel wasn't one to let me off the hook so easy. I guess it was a Ventrilla thing. They clearly weren't as skilled in the deflect and run away tactic as I was. When I realized she was still waiting on my answer, I finally spoke up. "Yeah."

"Your whole life?" I nodded. "Damn."

"I thought you weren't supposed to swear in front of the kid."

She snorted before she realized she didn't like me and wasn't supposed to find anything I did or said funny. "Yeah, well, I don't really give a shit about Mom's rules regarding her."

"You don't like her," I observed. It wasn't so much of a question as it was a statement. The scowl I had seen on her face when I walked in this morning had nothing to do with the playdoh. I remembered how quick she was to shove Viviana back on Rainer the other afternoon when we watched her. I was just curious to see if she would try to deny it.

She huffed and blew a strand of black hair out of her eyes, then turned to watch the little girl whose fists were happily mushing together green and blue playdoh now. "I love her."

"But you don't *like* her," I reiterated. I saw right through her effort to get around the issue at hand. There was a big difference between like and love. Even I knew that.

Her eyes met mine and I swear I caught a glimpse of that approval I had seen the other afternoon, but just as she had then, she tucked it away quickly. "You're annoying and don't belong here."

"You're annoyed because I'm right. What's your problem with her? You think she doesn't belong here, either?"

"She doesn't," Rachel spat before she even realized what she was saying. "I didn't mean that," she tried to cover.

"But you did."

She didn't answer for a long time, instead flipping her gaze between me and the toddler as if she could somehow figure out if she could trust us. "She should be with her mother, not us."

I had been wondering about the elusive mother. Rainer said she had moved in here before the accident, but I hadn't seen her or heard of her other than that. "Where is her mom?"

"Who the fuck knows," Rachel spat and my lips tweaked at her blatant use of curse words in front of the kid. "She gave birth, stayed here for less than six months, and then gone. Nothing. No word where she went, no way to find her. Not that it mattered much. She hadn't been around Viviana even when she was here. Just slowly pushed her off on my parents. Who, of course, adore the damn kid. And why, huh?" Her eyes raised to meet mine and I had a feeling this was the first time she was ever saying this stuff to someone. She could have never let her family know she felt this way. "She doesn't even look like him...Ross," she choked on his name as if she still couldn't say it even after years.

"She doesn't look like us. And my mom loves her. My mom couldn't even look at me or my dad or my brother for weeks, but this baby? That horrible teenage mom? Those she could love. Let me know why that makes sense. I think she was *happy* when that bitch abandoned the kid to us. She *wanted* the baby, even though she didn't want us. Didn't even want to see his face. But this stranger, she wanted."

I stood frozen against the sink, unable to think of anything that would be appropriate to say to Rachel for this. I wondered what she saw in my eyes as she stared at me. At my grey eyes that looked so much like the person I hated. So dead to any emotion. I guess I would never know. But she was still waiting to see what I could possibly say to her admission now.

"Damn," I said, finally settling on the one word she had offered me earlier.

This time, her lips turned up in a smile and stayed that way. She gave a curt nod and then stood from the stool, heading towards the hall. Before she left the kitchen, she turned back to me. "Hey, you're in charge of her now. And by the way, you're not supposed to swear in front of the kid."

Chapter Eleven

"Colt." Jeremy's arm wrapped around me to snag his time card before slipping it into the machine once I had removed my own. The loud punch was as familiar to me as my own heartbeat, even if my entire world seemed to be turned upside down these past weeks. Right now, though, it felt like just another day at the barn; both of us clocking out within a minute of each other.

I had barely seen Jeremy since the day of the banquet. Summer was always busy with children coming for riding camps and older kids upping their lessons while they were on break from school. Chelsea had somehow forgotten she agreed to speak at a conference in Saratoga this past Tuesday, so she had me scrambling to get everything in order for her trip out there. Once she left for the week, Jeremy and I had to split the task of teaching her lessons on top of our own. In a way, I almost enjoyed the chaos. The barn I could handle. My own life? Not so much.

I glanced up at Jeremy after I replaced my time card in the holder and caught him scrutinizing every inch of me. My eyes rolled of their own accord. "I'm fine," I huffed.

His lips flattened, but he didn't refute my assessment. "You still living with that bloke?"

"Rainer?"

He only shrugged, though I knew he hadn't forgotten Rainer's name. As it was, Rainer swung by the barn almost every other day. I was equal parts annoyed by it and reluctantly pleased with it. He always had some excuse for his visits. One time, it was raining so he came with an extra rain jacket just in case I needed one which only caused me to laugh. I had never had a rain jacket before, so the idea of needing one was foreign to me. Another time he came with some new cookies his mom had baked and I just *had* to try one right this minute. One time it was because Viviana had specifically asked to come see Colt. That excuse I knew he made up because the kid had no idea what my name was, let alone any desire to see me. I tried to keep as much distance from her as I could.

At first, I had tried to push him away. I didn't need a raincoat. I didn't need him to bring me the lunch he carefully packed for me which I had specifically ignored when I saw it on the counter that morning. I didn't need his handouts and I didn't need him showing up to my barn at any time of the day without warning. I didn't *need* any of it. But oddly enough...I was starting to want it.

"Yes, I'm still living at the Ventrilla's."

"How do you even know him?" Jeremy held the side door open for me as we stepped out into the afternoon sunshine. He wasn't saying it rudely. He really was just curious. I hated any and all curiosity into my life, even if I had always been able to brush Jeremy's away.

"Friend of a friend," I lied. How was I supposed to explain to Jeremy that I had just barely met Rainer and yet I chose to live with him over Jeremy? Even I had enough social awareness to know that wouldn't go over well.

"Huh, I never remember you mentioning him. How long have you known him?"

"Does it matter?" I quipped. Rainer may have been softening me, but I still held on to my bite when he wasn't around. And I was right anyway; it *didn't* matter. Chelsea had once told me, in one of the rare moments where she actually made sense, that it didn't matter how long you had worked with a certain horse. What mattered was the connection you had with the animal. One rider could have been with a horse for five years and never even come close to what another jockey who had been with a horse for six months had achieved. It all came down to the connection between the two of them, not the amount of time they had known each other. It either was there or it wasn't. I was starting to think the same could be said for humans.

We paused by his car and he leaned against it to study me, but I could already see the fight leaving him. He wasn't one to fight for me. "No, I suppose it doesn't. I just worry about you."

"I know," I sighed.

"You look better. You've gotten things under control?"

It took me a minute to think of what he could mean by that. When I remembered he still assumed I was a part of some gang, I almost laughed. Somehow, I managed to school my face back into a serious expression and nodded. "Yeah, getting there." I might not have been dealing with gang business, but I was still making some progress. Kind of.

"Well remember, if you ever need anything. Seriously, anything at all, I can help. I *want* to help. It's all gonna be okay." He reached out to ruffle my hair before sliding into his car with a smile, but I was still rooted to the spot, his last words echoing in my head as he pulled down the long driveway.

I had spent years trying to forget Vee ever existed and yet this past month, suddenly I felt him everywhere. Almost every day. I watched the dust settle after Jeremy's car and my fingers slid into my pocket to grasp the locket I still kept there.

"You're alive." I couldn't help it, my lips turned up in a smile just hearing his voice after the months I had gone without seeing him. I still came back to this field each weekend, hoping the group would be out here despite the cold. I knew Vee had said it had been their last fire of the year all those weeks ago, but it wasn't like I had anywhere else to go. I'd take cold toes over a bruised ribcage any day.

"*And* smiling? Damn, Donnie, I didn't even turn on my charm yet. You're starting to make this too easy." Vee reached out and ruffled a large hand through my hair and every part of me lit on fire. My stomach got that unsettled feeling again, but it wasn't even my normal response of fear whenever someone tried to touch me. No one had ever ruffled my hair before. My cheeks heated and I ducked my head so he wouldn't see my reaction to something so simple. "I think you missed me," he singsonged as he plopped down on the log beside me before gulping down a mouthful of beer.

"You wish," I mumbled even though he was so, so right. I did miss him. Which was silly; I had never missed anyone before. I had never had a friend before. Was Vee really becoming my friend?

"Aw, come on now. You can't play hard to get when I already know the truth."

"You're delusional." I sipped from my own cup and nearly gagged. I had forgotten how bad beer was. Vee's laughter rang out across the clearing and I wondered if even the people gathered closest to the bonfire could hear it despite us staying hidden in the shadows. His hair was longer than it had been when I last saw him in December and his eyes seemed to have the faint hints of dark circles under them, but he still looked like the most beautiful boy I had ever seen.

"How was your winter?" he asked once he had finished laughing and took another drink from his beer. I shrugged and saw him immediately roll his eyes in response. "Nope, no more shrugging from you. Gotta give me something."

Now it was my turn to roll my eyes. "It was fine."

I couldn't remember a time where my family gathered around the Christmas tree and exchanged gifts. I knew my father had never gotten me a gift before. I don't think he gave my mom anything, either. It's not like we had any extended family to celebrate with. Mom's parents had both died before I was born and no one ever spoke about my father's family. I knew enough to not ask him any questions, *especially* about that. I had made that mistake only once when I was just six years old. That was the first time my mom had come to my room after he had passed out to stitch me up. It wasn't the last time, there had been many others since then, but she stopped bandaging me once I was old enough to do it on my own. Besides, stitching was only for the worst times.

"You get anything good?" he asked now. I pulled on the cuffs of my sleeves in response, thinking that a few new bruises probably wouldn't count as a suitable answer. He took my nervousness to mean something else. "What are you hiding there, Donnie? Did you go do a wild child thing?" he laughed.

I cocked my head to the side, not following his train of thought. "What do you mean?"

"You're not wearing a t-shirt today. What are you hiding?"

I chuckled and looked back to the fire ahead of us. *How could I play this off?* "I'm not hiding anything. It's cold."

"This is the warmest April we've had in years, today especially. We're all celebrating. Except for you." He wasn't wrong, everyone at the bonfire tonight was in t-shirts reveling in this crazy heat wave for New England. Some guys were even sporting shorts. I had been sweating all day in my baggy sweatshirt and cursing Mother Nature all week for taking away my happy time.

Winter was my favorite season because it was so much easier to hide then. Sweatshirts and long pants were the norm. I tried not to be too upset because this warm weather had also meant the bonfire group would return, and they had tonight. So for once, I hadn't minded losing my winter freedom from scrutiny. Until now. I felt Vee's fingers wrap around my wrist while his other hand shoved up my sleeve without warning.

"What are you doing?" I squealed, yanking away from him, but he held me firm. I tugged my arm again, my alarm growing, and he released me as if my skin burned him. I stood in a hurry and made to pull the sleeve back down, but it was too late. The damage was done.

"Donnie..." I shook my head, too numb to form a response. My arm fell limp by my side, the deep purple bruising from my father's last hold on me banded around my forearm. The circular scars from the cigars he stubbed out on my skin dotted up to my elbow. Pearly white lines marking various cuts from deep slashes to thin slices crisscrossed the flesh, all on display for the boy who used to look at me like a fun, wild child. His face was utter shock mixed with revulsion. Seeing me did that to him. Seeing who I really was.

"Don't," I pleaded.

"I didn't...I thought..."

"You thought wrong," I spat, too hurt by the horror on his face. I turned and started back down the dirt path, trying to put as much distance between myself and that field as I could.

"Donnie, stop." I was already halfway back to the main road when his running footsteps caught up to me. "Donnie!" he snapped when he finally reached my side. I didn't turn. Didn't stop. The next second, his fingers wrapped around my wrist again and he yanked me to face him. I was so shocked he would touch me after seeing the look on his face earlier that I didn't even throw a fit at the feel of his hand on mine.

"I said stop," he panted, his warm hand still on my skin. My eyes focused on that point of contact, on the permanent tan color contrasting against my pale, scarred wrist. We stood like that for a long time and I think he needed the time to collect his thoughts just as much as I did. "Look at me."

"Vee…" I warned, finally glancing up to his blue eyes. The disgust was gone from his face now and oddly enough, the corners of his lips were tilted up in the ghost of a smile.

"I thought you had gone and got a tattoo. Silly me," he joked. There was something about him, something contagious that I just couldn't explain, that had the corners of my lips lifting up, too. "Is that a smile I see? Damn, I'm getting good at this." A bubble of air escaped me at his obvious pride. *How could I seriously be almost laughing at a time like this?*

His thumb absentmindedly brushed over my wrist and my heartbeat skittered in my chest. Meanwhile, his other hand reached up to push back the new, longer strands of his hair out of his eyes. "Can I walk with you?"

"Uhm…" I sputtered. "Yeah, I guess so."

"Cool." His hand slid from my wrist to clasp my own, palm to palm, and he twined our fingers together as if it was the most natural thing in the world. I, on the other hand, was hyperventilating. We didn't speak again until we reached the main road. "Where to, Wild Child?"

I took my typical right to head home, not knowing what else to do and also not ready to break this hold he had on me. Finally, I spoke after we had gone another half mile. "Vee, what are you doing?"

"Hell, Donnie. I have no clue." He laughed then before glancing over at me and giving my hand a squeeze. "You know, my life is a shit show, too," he whispered as if this was some giant secret. In all honesty, it was. I always assumed he must live a perfect life. He had a fancy car he always came to the bonfires in. People loved him. He smiled nonstop. How could his life be a mess?

"Really?" I squeaked.

He nodded earnestly. "Oh yeah. Utter disaster. Everything down the drain in the past couple months. Do you see these dark circles under my eyes?" His free hand indicated the shadows I had noticed earlier as headlights swung over us before the oncoming car rushed passed. "Do you think I look good with dark circles? Because I don't. I just don't. How did this happen?" he fake-wailed.

I couldn't help it, I grinned at his antics. Despite knowing he was acting so ridiculous just to cheer me up, I actually felt my spirits lifting. "God, I love that smile. You know it feels like winning the lottery any time I can make you smile? That's how rare it is. Now I know why."

My grin immediately vanished and I didn't answer. Another car raced by in the dark, this one coming from behind us so that our shadows stretched out ahead of us for a brief second and I reveled in the sight of our two ghostly hands connected. For a while, the only sound was the echo of our footsteps against the pavement. "It's my father," I said, shocking myself. "He drinks. All the time." Vee's grip on my fingers tightened infinitesimally, as if he wanted me to know he was here for me but didn't want to scare me away at the same time. "I don't even remember when it started; it's all I've ever known. It's gotten worse as I get older. He does it to my mom, too, but not as much."

He waited a long time, giving me a chance to keep going, but I didn't know what else to say. "We can report him, Donnie."

I immediately shook my head. "No, we can't."

"Donnie, listen to me, I know you're scared but-"

"No, you don't understand. It's not just that. I really can't report him here. It wouldn't work."

Again, his grip flexed in mine. "What do you mean it wouldn't work?"

I shook my head, not willing to say any more. I had said enough. If I told him the real reason, who my father was, he would try to do it himself. I could see it now. Except I knew the truth. I knew my father's connections to the police force here. There was no way they'd believe me. They loved him. The only thing going to the police would accomplish would be another punishment for me. Possibly even a punishment for Vee if he had anything to do with it. I shuddered at the thought. I couldn't let that ever happen.

He blew out a puff of air like he wanted to argue me further, but when I turned I saw we had already made it to my front yard. The normally endless walk home seemed to only take seconds with Vee by my side. I stopped and he had no choice but to do the same with his hand still in mine. I almost chuckled at the thought, that being connected to someone could control how you reacted to things. I had never been connected to anyone before. My eyes focused back on our laced fingers and my stomach twisted happily at the sight of my tiny ones folded into his.

"Promise me, Vee." I finally lifted my gaze back up to meet his eyes. "You can't tell anyone. *Please*," I pleaded.

"I don't want to make that promise," he growled and my heart plummeted. He didn't understand how much damage he could do when he thought he would be helping. "But I can't force you. We'll talk more about it next week?"

"Sure," I placated him. Anything to ensure he wouldn't go running to the cops in some heroic effort to save me.

"Hey, Donnie? It's all gonna be okay." He pulled his hand from mine then and ruffled my hair just like he had at the beginning of the night, only this time it meant so much more.

~

I hadn't been able to put down the locket since Jeremy had left the barn this afternoon. For the first time in years, I allowed myself to wonder what Vee was doing now. If he ever wondered about me. Before I could think too hard on it, a knock sounded on the door. "Can I come in?"

I stuffed the locket back in my pocket before Rainer could see I had stolen it. If he'd noticed it was missing, he had yet to assume I had anything to do with it. I pulled open the door and promptly lost my breath. His hair was artfully styled, his sharp jaw free of any stubble, but it was the clothes that had me at a loss for words. The black tux had to have been custom, because there's no way any old tux could fit someone so well. From the swell of his biceps to the tapering at his waist and the way the fabric hugged his thighs, it was all too much. Like he had just stepped off some movie set.

"You're joking, right?" was the first thing to fall out of my mouth without thought.

Rainer's deep chuckle stirred my already-crazed butterflies into a frenzy. "What?"

My hand waved up and down the length of his body. "This is not real life."

"Is there something you want to say, Colt?" His smirk took on a salacious feel and my cheeks heated in response. I pursed my lips and shook my head, refusing to give in to him. "Admit it, you think I'm sexy as hell."

My eyes rolled automatically and the magical spell he had cast on me was broken with his cocky words. "And there it goes. Just when I thought it was too good to be true. What a shame," I tsked and retreated back into the room that had become mine over the past two weeks, though you would never be able to tell that. I hadn't done anything to personalize it nor did I plan to.

Rainer's full-out laughter followed me in and he took a seat on the edge of the bed without invitation. "I take it you didn't get my note?"

"What note?" I asked.

"You know, if you just had a cell phone I wouldn't have to worry about always leaving you notes," he chided. He had been trying to convince me to get a cell phone ever since he had moved me in here, but I refused. One, there was no way I would accept something so expensive from him after all he was already doing. Two, I was not going to pay for one on my own. And three, there was no one I needed to contact or who needed to contact me. Aside from Rainer apparently. I'd never admit that I actually enjoyed finding his little handwritten notes scattered throughout the day for me. I definitely did *not* have the single pocket in my duffle bag full of the folded papers that said anything from 'Spaghetti for dinner tonight. Stop hiding in your room and come eat it with me' to the very first one I had found in my car the morning after the bonfire when he drove me back. No, definitely not. That would mean I actually cared. Which I didn't. "But I'm not here to argue with you about that again. I'm here to collect you."

"Collect me?" I asked, pulled from my thoughts of his notes.

"Yeah. You're coming tonight."

"Oh, no…" I started. "No, no, no."

"Mom specifically asked."

My eyes grew wide. "Your mom asked me to come?" It had been almost two weeks since I overheard their argument about me after the night I fell apart. Two weeks of doing my best to be the perfect house guest. It was easy enough. I was used to staying holed up in my room as it was. The only difference here was the room I had now was the size of my old living room and had its own bathroom connected to it. I left early for the barn each morning and tried to slip in unnoticed in the afternoons, so I had yet to interact directly with Mr. or Mrs. Ventrilla. Rainer gave me my space as much as I assumed was possible when it came to him, but apparently my time for hiding was up.

"Yes. She is kind of curious about the girl living in her dead son's bedroom."

"Rainer!" I gasped. Did it not hurt him to say something like that? Because it hurt me just hearing it.

"I didn't mean that. Well, I did. Just not the way I said it." I could see the turmoil in his eyes as he stared down at his hands folded in his lap. There weren't many times Rainer wasn't exuding excess amounts of confidence. Right now though, he looked lost.

While I had been doing my best to stay out of the way these past weeks, that hadn't stopped me from observing what life was like within the walls of the Ventrilla Mansion. The thing about being so small and easily overlooked is that you end up overhearing a lot, and I had become well-versed in eavesdropping and analyzing others' behaviors over the years. Rainer was the rock of this household. Maybe he had been before his brother's death, but knowing his guilt behind it, I had a feeling he did everything he could in an effort to somehow make up for the loss he falsely believed he caused. If that meant watching Viviana at any given moment, or dressing nice to meet with clients for his mother even though I knew he hated that aspect of the business, or putting up with Rachel's bitchy comments with a smile even though he probably wanted to smack her, he did it all without even being asked. It was as if anything anyone needed around here, Rainer already had it done before they could realize they wanted it.

So even though there was no way in hell I wanted to go to a wedding tonight, let alone be forced to stand near Rainer and his family while they all looked like they belonged on the cover of some magazine and I looked like I belonged in an ad for supporting malnourished children, I would do it. Just like he tried so hard to make everyone else's lives easier, I could do this small thing for him to make his life easier. I suppose it wouldn't kill me to not fight him on every little thing.

"Can I wear jeans to this wedding? Because I've got to say Rain, I don't have any of those fancy clothes your mom loves so much."

He lifted his head and just like that, his smile was back. My heart kicked up a notch knowing I had done that for him. Not that I cared. Really, I didn't. I couldn't. I couldn't get attached. I was just staying here until I saved enough to get away and never look back. The fact that my body reacted to Rainer so much had absolutely no pull over what my head knew to be right. Rainer and I could never work.

"I've already got you covered." Before I could even question what he meant by that, he was striding back out of the room. I heard his door open and then close a second later from down the hall. Next thing I knew, he was standing in front of me again, holding out one of those fancy garment bags that wedding dresses came in. I eyed it dubiously, not even bothering to reach out to take it from him. "Come on, Colt. Go put it on." He shook the bag at me with a glint in his eye and after another moment of indecision, I relented and took it from him.

"I'll wait here." He grinned and resumed his post on my bed. *The* bed. *Ross's* bed. It was not *my* bed. I was not staying here. I sighed and shook my head at him, but nevertheless retreated into the enormous bathroom to go put on whatever awful thing hid in this bag.

I was still sitting on the edge of the tub staring at the offending article which I had hung on the back of the door after removing it from the bag when Rainer knocked on the door ten minutes later. "Is it on?"

"You're joking, right?"

"Colt, come on. It's not that bad."

"I can't wear that," I grumbled.

There was a thump and then a sliding sound which I could only assume meant he was now sitting on the floor with his back pressed against the bathroom door. His voice came back muffled through the wood. "Yes, you can."

I rolled my eyes at him even though he couldn't see me and looked back up at the dress angrily. The bottom half wasn't all that horrible I suppose. It was a peachy color, gradually growing darker as it draped to the floor in weightless elegance. The top, however, was another story. For one, there were no sleeves. The front was covered in a million tiny jewels, catching the light and shimmering beautifully. But the back? Well the back didn't have quite so many jewels covering the sheer bodice. "Rainer..." I started. "You know why I can't wear this."

"Please, Colt. Just try it on. For me?" I pinched the bridge of my nose. Damn him for using that tone on me. It wasn't fair.

Tentatively, I stood and made my way back across the room to where the dress hung. My fingers reached out to skim the skirt, feeling the satin slip against my skin. I didn't even want to know how much a dress like this cost. There was no way I was wearing this. But I guess it couldn't hurt to just try it on. At least then Rainer would see why I couldn't do this and hopefully leave me alone. With one final sigh, I reached out and pulled it off the hanger.

Rainer scrambled to his feet as I slowly turned the doorknob. I hadn't even bothered to look in the mirror. I didn't need a reminder of how out of place I looked. Instead, I simply pulled open the door to show Rainer so that I could take this thing off as soon as possible.

"Ho. Ly. Shit." His breath came out in a low whistle and one hand came up to grip the back of his neck as his eyes blazed a trail over every inch of overly exposed skin I had on display.

I couldn't bring myself to look at him so instead I focused on my fingers which I was incessantly twisting around one another seeing as I didn't have any sleeves to pull on at the moment. "Yeah, see, I told you. I don't know what you were thinking, I shouldn't have put it on at all, but now you know so I can go change back now and-"

I hadn't even noticed him bridge the gap between us until I felt his fingers tipping my chin up, forcing me to look at him. His eyes were as dark as they had been the other night in the kitchen, the blue almost lost now, his pupils wide. The look he gave me had my mouth snapping shut in an instant, heat pooling low in my belly. I gulped audibly.

"Colt? Stop talking."

Naturally, I opened my mouth to spew out some more word vomit, but before I could his mouth crashed down on mine and I understood his words from just a minute ago. *Ho. Ly. Shit.* His lips claimed mine, forcing me to feel what I had been trying so hard to deny between us. No other part of us touched aside from his fingertips on my chin and his lips meshed to mine. It was as if he was trying so hard to hold himself back from me because he knew I wouldn't be able to take it all, but he couldn't deny himself the need to kiss me. Because boy, was he kissing me. I had never been kissed before, so maybe I was a little biased, but this had to be the best kiss ever. His tongue traced the seam of my lips and I whimpered in response, but before he could take it any further, he pulled himself back from me with a growl.

My eyes snapped open and I saw that I wasn't alone in thinking that was the best kiss ever. Rainer's chest was heaving in front of me as if he had just run a mile and though he was trying to keep his eyes on mine, they kept falling back to my swollen lips as if he couldn't control it. "I'm sorry. I'm so, so sorry. I know I shouldn't have, but I couldn't stop and you look incredible and I know I probably just caused you to run a million miles away from me and I'm so sorry, Colt. Please, I-"

"Rainer? Stop talking." I wasn't as bold as him to forcibly stop him with a kiss, though.

"Please tell me what you're thinking right now."

I bit my lower lip unconsciously and Rainer's eyes tracked the movement, a growl coming from deep within his chest, and my eyes widened. "I…I don't know. I'm not thinking anything." And that was the truth. He had just completely wiped my brain of any logical thoughts.

He took a step back towards me, his hand coming out slowly to cup one side of my face and his thumb skimmed over my cheek. "You're not running from me?"

I shook my head infinitesimally. "Not yet."

"Oh, thank God." The relief in his voice was palpable. His forehead fell against mine and I shivered involuntarily. For the first time, the goosebumps he always caused to raise along my arms were on full display.

"Can I go change now?" I finally whispered, very aware of my bare arms and shoulders, the marred skin that was thinly veiled by the sheer fabric on my back.

"Change? Why the hell would you change?"

"Rainer!" I chided and gently shoved him away from me with a hand on his chest. "I can't wear this!"

"Why not?"

"You know why not. Look at me," I murmured even though I really didn't want him to. Logically, I knew he had seen my bare back and arms before, but that didn't change the fact that I didn't want him to see me now. I hadn't been aware of him seeing me last time. He had told me after the fact that I had somehow managed to get vomit on the shirt I was wearing that night and he had changed me out of it before we fell asleep. He promised my bra had stayed on, but what did that matter to me? He had seen more than enough. My scars were far more intimate than any breasts if you asked me.

"I am looking at you."

I huffed impatiently. "Then you know why I can't wear this."

He didn't respond then, just reached down and folded one of my hands in his, tugging me over to the floor length mirror in the corner of the room and positioning me in front of it. "Rain..." I warned, refusing to look up at the reflection in the mirror. I didn't want to see all my deformities on display.

"Just look, Colt. I need you to see what I see. Please." *Damn that tone again.*

Reluctantly, I lifted my gaze to the mirror and promptly lost my breath. The dress fit me like a glove; you couldn't even tell that beneath all those shimmering gems each of my ribs could be counted through my skin. The airy skirt fell artfully from my waist to the floor in a small puddle of dark coral satin. The neckline was high enough to hide one of my worst scars, but I could still see the others up my arms. Along my shoulders. I didn't even want to know what my back looked like, though I couldn't see that in the mirror. Instead, I saw Rainer towering behind me, his eyes taking me in as if I was the only girl he had ever seen before. I saw one of his tanned hands resting lightly on my waist and I gasped because I hadn't even realized he had been holding me this whole time, offering me his steady hand in case I needed support. I swallowed down a sudden lump of emotion that rose in my throat.

I watched in the mirror as his head dipped then, his mouth closing over a deep scar on my left shoulder. I was painfully aware of the night I had received it. The jagged glass of the whiskey bottle that had caused it. My eyes fluttered shut as I felt Rainer's tongue dart out and lick along the deep rut in my skin. And then his mouth was gone, moving to cover another scar on my back that wrapped from my left shoulder blade to the bottom of my ribs on my right side. I knew this one well. It was from my father's belt on one of the many nights he had broken my skin with it. The slashes hadn't stopped bleeding until the following evening. I had to keep changing my shirts that day and each time I pulled an old one off, it had seared as if I was ripping off another layer of skin due to the blood that had stuck to it. Now, Rainer's mouth followed along the line it had left behind five years ago, pressing the softest of kisses every inch he moved down it. I felt tears pooling under my closed lashes and it wasn't from pain. I couldn't even explain why I was crying now. I couldn't even put a name to this emotion I was feeling.

When he got to the right side of my ribs, his kisses increased, and I knew why. The scars covered my entire side, scattered, irregular. Some long gashes, others deep holes, still more just thin slices interspersed with stitching and grafts. It was from the worst night. The absolute worst night. That night he had thrown me into the glass with enough force that it had shattered, slicing my body to ribbons. I could still smell the blood that had pooled beneath me. I didn't want to relive that moment. I didn't want to think of it at all. My eyes flashed open to meet Rainer's in the mirror in front of me. Tears were pouring down my face silently and his arms wrapped fully around my stomach now, pulling me into his chest as I shook with sobs.

"You're breathtaking, Colt. Your scars don't change that." His lips pressed into my hair again and I closed my eyes at the conviction in his words. *How could he even think such a thing?*

"But I knew you wouldn't see it that way. So I got this, too." I opened my eyes again as he slowly released me and then backed away to the bed, coming back with another shimmering piece of clothing. He draped it over my shoulders as I watched in the mirror, helping one of my arms into a sleeve and then the other until I was covered again. Somehow, it matched the dress perfectly and instead of hiding it, it enhanced the beauty of the dress even more while also keeping my arms and back safely covered. I finally turned away from our reflections in the mirror to face Rainer. I knew without a doubt he had this custom made. There was no other way it would fit the dress so perfectly and not look out of place. He knew what I would need before even knowing I would agree to come.

For the first time, I initiated this touch. My hands came up to cup his jaw and I allowed myself to feel everything for once. The smoothness of his skin. The puff of air he let out as my thumb brushed over his full bottom lip. The increase in his heartbeat as it pounded in his chest. Then I reached up on my tiptoes and pressed my lips to his. He sighed into my mouth and I whimpered as his hands flexed against my hips, holding me in place but never pushing me too far. Just pushing me *enough*.

Our lips finally broke apart and his forehead rested against mine. I watched as his eyes stayed closed, his breaths falling over my lips while his breathing slowly returned to normal. Without opening his eyes, he tipped my chin down again to press his lips to my forehead before finally detangling from me. "I'll be waiting downstairs." His hands skimmed over my shoulders all the way to my fingertips with a featherlight touch before he slowly backed away, closing my bedroom door behind him.

~

"Rainer! So good to see you, son. Come grab a drink with me outside." Another older man in a suit was smiling genially at Rainer after clapping him on the shoulder.

Rainer's eyes cut to mine and he grimaced, his hand squeezing against mine. I still hadn't become used to being touched, but he had been unable to let go of my hand any time I was within reach tonight. And damn those butterflies in my stomach. They were really enjoying it. "I promise I'll be right back."

I gave him a small grin and shrugged my shoulders as his hand slipped from mine. There was really nothing else to do. This had been happening all night. Random men coming over to talk business or ask how he was doing or pull him away for some discussion. I didn't blame him for hating the business side of things. I would want to hide in the vineyards all the time, too if all these people were begging for my attention.

Once he had disappeared into the crowd, I weaved my way across the function hall and then started up the wide, curved staircase to the upper balcony. At least it was less crowded up here. I leaned against the wooden railing and watched all the people mingling and laughing below me until the DJ announced the bride and groom's first dance. A circle quickly formed around them as all their friends and family gathered to watch.

"Beautiful, isn't it?" Mrs. Ventrilla's voice was like windchimes, perfectly adding into the romantic music flowing from the speakers. I suppose I had known this was moment coming the entire night, but it didn't change the tense way I had been holding myself all evening. She had asked for me to be here tonight for a reason. If there was one thing I had learned in my observations lately, it was that Adriana Ventrilla always had a schedule. Tonight, I was on it.

I glanced to my right and took her in. Her dark hair was piled atop her head with a few curls artfully pulled loose to fall around her face. Tonight, her dress was a deep purple but when she moved, the light caught on tiny beads throughout it which gave the illusion that she was shimmering. I knew, because I had been keeping tabs on her all night, wondering when she would come and find me. In her heels, she had a good six inches on me, but I refused to cower beside her. I had done nothing wrong here.

I followed her gaze out to the dance floor where other couples were beginning to join in with the newlyweds. "Dancing?" I finally asked.

It was her turn to study me now while I kept my gaze fixed on the swirling people below us. After another minute, she made a hum in the back of her throat and looked back down to the dance floor. "Love in general." I couldn't help myself, I snorted out a derisive laugh then cleared my throat in an attempt to cover it up. She saw through it. "You don't think so?"

She gave up the guise of watching the dancers and turned to face me fully. My own eyes stayed focused on the bride, the only splotch of white twirling around the floor. "I wouldn't know."

I knew she was still studying me, waiting for me to turn to face her as well, but I refused. "Why do you say that?"

I wanted to roll my eyes because I didn't do this. I didn't deal in riddles and questions and baring your soul to someone. But this woman was allowing me to stay in her home, despite not trusting me. I could at least play along with whatever game this was. "Can't say I've ever heard the words 'I love you' spoken to me before," I muttered.

"There are a lot of ways to say I love you without saying those same words. It's as simple as saying 'I forgive you' or 'this made me think of you' or 'I thought you may need this' or 'I understand you' or 'I trust you'. Sometimes we're too blind to see it. It doesn't mean it's not there." Each word she said caused me to think of

Rainer, and I wanted so badly to force that thought from my head. Rainer didn't love me. Rainer *couldn't* love me. Apparently, she didn't think the same way. "I know you've been trying to keep your distance from us all, but I see the way he looks at you. I've never seen him look at anyone that way before. Even before the accident. I don't even recognize him anymore. He smiles again. He talks to me again. About more than just business or Viviana. He talks to me about *you*."

I finally turned to face her and her eyes were glistening with unshed tears. The clear, unhidden emotion made me uncomfortable so I forced down the lump that had formed in my throat and shook my head. "Rainer can't love me."

"You don't get to control if someone loves you or not. You can't force them to love you and you can't force them to stop. That's the beautiful thing about love; it's uncontrollable."

"I think that's the ugly part of love," I said honestly. My mind flashed to my mother. To my father. To Vee. All these people I had so badly wanted to love me. To protect me. But I could never force them to. Instead, they just destroyed me. So to answer her question from the very start, no. I did not think love was beautiful at all.

"Do you want to know the best part of love?" I didn't answer. She could say whatever she wanted; it didn't matter to me. My fingers toyed with the sleeves of the beautiful cape Rainer had given me and I avoided her eyes again. "The ones who really love us, love us in spite of all our flaws. They love us even when we don't feel very lovable at all." I hated the reaction her words caused in me. My eyes burnt with tears that I wouldn't let fall. My throat was clogged. My chest felt heavy and I wrapped both arms around myself in an effort to hold everything in.

"Rainer still hasn't told me your story. I've asked. He says it isn't his place to tell." I felt a chunk of the ice I always kept around my heart melt at that admission. To know that even when he wasn't with me, he was still protecting me. According to her, maybe even loving me. "But I think you should hear mine.

"I'm sure you know by now my son died. When he did, a part of me died with him. That night, I was so scared I had lost both my boys. When I got to the hospital and saw Rainer still alive, I had never been so happy in my life. It was the last time I felt truly happy for over a year. Two hours later, they told me my youngest son was dead. There was no one to even blame or be angry at. He hadn't been drinking, didn't even have his phone on him to have been texting. No other car was involved. He simply hadn't been paying enough attention to a curve in the road. He completely missed it and crashed into a tree. I asked God every day for months how he could be so cruel. I didn't leave the house for weeks. I couldn't even sleep in the same bed as my husband because just looking at his face hurt too much. I had two remaining children who needed me, and I couldn't find it in me to be a mother to them. How could I when I had failed already?

"And yet, they still loved me. They loved me when I was so unlovable. They understood me when I didn't deserve it. They forgave me even though I still haven't forgiven myself. How could they still love someone who couldn't love them back? Because I couldn't. I couldn't even look at my own family. But they loved me so much, it made up for where I was lacking. And eventually, I allowed myself to accept their love again. And I'm able to love them back again. So much. Because like I said, you can't control love. It just happens. It heals. Even when everything feels as if it could never heal again, love heals. You just need to let it."

Chapter Twelve

"And then I'm saying to her, is it really that hard to just keep your heels down? I mean, really. I can only do so much with stupid, ya know? That's seriously the problem with today's kids, I'm telling y'all."

Talking to Chelsea always resulted in some sort of mental whiplash no matter how much I tried to keep up. "I'm sorry, what?" Last I had checked, we had been talking about her latest rider, who if I remembered correctly was in her mid-twenties. Apparently, that was now considered today's youth to Chels. Or she had just decided to move on to another topic already. That wouldn't surprise me, knowing how she was.

"Yeah, they just think they know everything but they don't know shit. Did I tell you about the kid the other day who tried to tell me a bee wasn't an animal? He said it wasn't an animal, it was an *insect*. Newsflash pal, insects *are* animals. What did he think they were, robots? Speaking of bees, did you hear they're endangered now? They're dying at an alarming rate!"

I felt my lips turn up at the corners. Any time I smiled, I was distinctly aware of the action. They say it takes less muscles to smile than it does to frown, but I'm pretty certain I hadn't been doing much of either for so long that my face was devoid of muscles. Lately though, they had been getting a solid workout.

"You do know that's been happening for years now, right?" I chuckled. The clicking of Chelsea's boots paused against the mats of the barn.

"The bees? The bees have been dying for that long?" she gasped. "Why aren't we doing anything? We should be raising awareness. Fundraising. Something."

"I'm sure people are," I reminded her. This was just another thing she did. Causes. She would find out about some cause she wanted to support, normally months after it had been a big issue, and insist we had to raise awareness for it. More often than not, her valiant efforts would fall by the wayside within a week or so. With Chelsea, it really was just the thought that counts.

"And the plants! What about the plants? They need the bees, too. All those trees, and flowers, and fruit, and the grapes that make that sweet, sweet wine from your man."

I rolled my eyes as I grabbed an apple from the grain room and made my way towards Gizmo's stall. "Chels..." I warned.

She popped a hand on her hip and watched me offer the apple to Gizmo. "It's damn good wine."

"I don't care about your love of wine. You know he's not my man, my boy, my anything else you've tried to call him, so stop trying." My cheeks flamed just thinking of the other things she had managed to call him after I had insisted she stop telling me 'my boy' was here.

"Hey, listen, it's not my fault the guy's been here basically every day for the past month. It sure ain't me he's lookin' for. Not that I would mind if it was." She raised her eyebrows at me suggestively and I choked on the water I had just sipped from my bottle. I knew she didn't really mean it, Chelsea was completely obsessed with her husband of seven years, but I had a feeling she knew saying something like that would get me even more flustered. The past few days she had been increasingly annoying when it came to Rainer. It was as if she had finally found out there was something she could use to get me riled up and she was having her fun with it. I couldn't be mad, though. I could never be mad at Chelsea. Not when she had given me so much. Given me a life outside of pain and abuse.

Despite that, we had never truly bonded like many would have expected given the amount of time we spent together. When I first started coming here, our relationship had simply been me doing anything and everything she said until it got to the point where I knew what she needed before she even did. Since then, I've kept her on track. When she starts rambling on, I urge her back onto solid ground such as vet visits and grain orders. We didn't do the cute, girly talk and gossiping that other visiting trainers would do with her when they came around, so it wasn't often I heard her southern twang come out. That version of Chelsea was reserved for friends and fun, things I had no knowledge of.

"I will tell ya, Sharna's been tryin' to sink her claws into him." *Sharna? Really? I could have sworn her name was Sasha. Or Sarah.* Whatever her name was, that girl needed to get a hobby. Or get out of our barn. At this point, either would work for me.

"Does she even ride for us?" I snapped. I wasn't used to this feeling. Was this...jealousy? Is that what was making my blood boil right now?

Chelsea reached up to stroke Gizmo's nose from opposite me, but he took another chomp of the apple and ignored her touch. If only it was so simple to ignore her words as well. "Yeah," she chuckled. "She's giving a lesson now. What makes you ask that?"

"She just seems to spend all of her time ogling the guys of the barn and not so much time doing what she's hired to do." Aside from her ongoing infatuation with Jeremy, which still had not lessened at all in the past weeks, I had noticed her trying to catch Derek's attention as well.

Chelsea crossed her arms and leaned against the stall, smiling at me devilishly. "The guys of the barn, huh? So Rainer's one of our guys now?"

"That's not...no...you know what I meant." The barn was a family. A tight-knit group. Jeremy, Derek, Chelsea, her husband Sander who was always sweeping in unannounced and flustering Chelsea even more than she already was. I was part of that family, too, even if I had always hung in the shadows. But the rotating door of visiting trainers? Those were not part of our family. Those didn't count. Sasha/Sarah/Sharna did not count. Was Rainer really starting to count?

"Mhm..." she mumbled, but I knew she was just placating me. "Of course I do. I'll just let you go then, got another lesson to teach and all..."

"Chelsea, don't you walk away from me right now. You know I hate your stupid word games." She laughed her perfect, lilting laugh and winked at me cheekily which only caused my teeth to grind together.

"You've got a visitor," she singsonged, tipping her chin to indicate behind me, and then she turned with a swish of her ponytail and disappeared into the other bay of stalls.

I spun around immediately, expecting to see Rainer there with his stupid smirk and ripped jeans, but who I found instead shocked me.

"Rachel? I…what…I wasn't expecting you to be here," I sputtered. She was dressed casually but still impeccably. She wore a plain green, v-neck shirt but her skin-tight jeans hugged her legs until they disappeared into a beautiful pair of riding boots that probably cost more than my entire savings. Her clothes made her look like she belonged in a barn even if her demeanor said the exact opposite. Her burning green eyes met mine fearlessly as always, though, standing out even more so than normal thanks to her shirt today.

"Yeah, well, I didn't exactly expect to be here, either."

That's when my heart stopped. "Is something wrong? With Rainer? The baby?"

She let out one of her patented humorless laughs. "Rainer's always fine. And Angel Child? Nah, I'm sure she's still shitting out rainbows with Mom."

I let out a breath I hadn't realized I was holding while my heart dislodged itself from my throat and returned to its spot in my chest, which I had falsely assumed had been frozen solid. My reaction just now to thinking Rainer was in trouble clearly showed how much he had been thawing it. And to care about Viviana, too? *What was happening to me?* Gizmo nuzzled into my hair as if he could sense my unease.

"So why are you here then?"

"I don't really know, to be honest. I guess I thought we could maybe ride?" For the first time I had met her,

Rachel Ventrilla was vulnerable. She didn't have up her bitchy walls of confidence.

Being such a social, welcoming person myself, I had absolutely no clue how to react to this new side of her. "Do you even know how to ride?" *Yeah, way to go, Colt,* I internally berated myself. *Way to be warm and fuzzy.*

Rachel lifted her chin defiantly and rolled her eyes at me. "Yes, I know how to ride," she snapped in her usual tone.

After a beat of her not saying anything else, I just said, "Okay…"

Gizmo stuck his neck further out of his stall and turned to look at Rachel, then back at me. We had to be two of the most socially inept people on this planet. Even Gizmo could tell that.

"So can we go or what?"

I snorted at the return of her normal attitude. *So much for soft and vulnerable*, I thought.

"Yeah, let's go."

~

She asked to ride Tierra. *Of course* she asked to ride Tierra. The horse was a beautiful bitch; essentially the horse version of the girl who now sat astride her as we came to the pond on the far edge of the property. We had to have been riding for over an hour now, through trails and across fields out behind the barn, but we had yet to say a single word to each other. It was clear Rachel could ride. She did so effortlessly, as if Tierra was an extension of herself, and that was saying something because I knew first-hand how difficult Tierra could be. I wondered when she had learned. And where. But more than anything, I wondered why she had stopped.

She slowed Tierra down to a walk and turned her towards the pond, easily dropping down a slope to the water as if it was a simple descent when in reality it was anything but. I maneuvered Gizmo down until we came to stand beside them and both horses dipped their heads to take a well-deserved drink. I let go of the reins to pat under Gizmo's sweaty mane.

"Thanks," Rachel grumbled. I straightened up and turned in my saddle to face her.

"Thanks?" I asked.

She fidgeted, that vulnerability coming back as she pulled her hair up in a messy bun. Of course, it still looked perfect. Damn her and her brother for always looking perfect. "For letting me ride. I haven't in a long time."

I nodded in response but then added after a moment, "You're good." *There,* I thought. *That was a nice response to a vulnerable moment. A compliment. See? I could be a normal human after all.* She only shrugged a dainty shoulder at my compliment. I had expected her to bask in it; she seemed like one of those girls who did that. Or the type to just say how they already knew. Maybe I had Rachel all wrong. "Why'd you stop riding?"

"Life happened."

That was an answer I knew all too well. "Your brother?" I prodded. It seemed unfair how much their lives had all been affected by one accident. And that's what it was, an accident, no matter what Rainer may believe.

"Yep." Her small fingers toyed with the leather reins but she didn't say anything more. No wonder we had rode for so long without talking. We sucked at it.

"So why'd you come here today?"

Rachel didn't answer. Instead, she pressed her heels into Tierra and guided her further into the pond before turning to follow along the shoreline. I urged Gizmo to do the same and he looked back at me as if to ask why I was being so difficult. I was starting to see Rachel took the hard route every time and still managed to excel in it.

I shrugged back at Gizmo as if he would understand and spurred him to catch up to Rachel. "Well, I don't exactly have a ton of friends, you know."

"Really? I would have never guessed," I deadpanned with a teasing grin.

She turned to look at me with narrowed eyes, but her glare softened after a moment. "Okay, I deserved that. I know I can be a bitch sometimes."

"Sometimes?" I coughed.

For the first time, I saw Rachel's full smile and *woah*, it was breathtaking. I had thought she looked perfect when her face was in a constant scowl, but with that smile? Good luck to Rainer if he wanted to keep her away from boys until she was eighteen. She laughed and I realized it was the first time I had heard her genuine laugh, too. "Yeah, you're right. I'm a straight-up bitch."

I felt myself smiling back at her without thought. "Hey, you said it, not me."

"I don't mean to be, I swear! It just kind of happened when...well, you know."

For someone who was so blunt and could talk about my abuse over a cup of coffee, she still couldn't put this accident into words. I was reminded again of how young she still was. How hard that had to have been.

"Ross died," I supplied for her. She nodded sadly.

"Yeah. I was just so angry, you know? I was only thirteen. I spent that whole summer begging Mom to let me go to public school for high school. I didn't want to stay homeschooled the whole time like the boys had. Yeah, it made them super advanced and smart, but I just wanted to be *normal*. I wanted to eat lunch in a cafeteria with friends and go shopping and gossip and have boyfriends. I was a teenager. I just wanted to be a normal teenager.

"Ross was my biggest supporter. My best friend. I was always closer to him than Rainer, because Rainer was always yelling at me. Trying to make me do the right thing, or whatever. Ross was the one who helped me plan elaborate pranks just to annoy Rainer. He could convince anyone, anything. So with his help, we finally convinced my mom I could go to normal school. And then he...well...he *died*." She spat the word out like it was dirty. It really was. A dirty, hideous word. Dead. Dying. Died. They were ugly words, all of them.

"He just left me. He left me and I still had to go to school because Mom had already enrolled me and I couldn't bother her to take me out and homeschool me again then because she was so much of a mess. She couldn't even get out to keep taking me to my riding lessons, and I wasn't about to ask Rainer to do that. He was already doing everything else. So that's when the riding stopped. And I went to high school like I had always dreamed of to be normal, but instead I was known as the weird new girl whose brother had just died.

"Then the baby came and that's all that mattered. Everything just went to shit after that. My dad worked and kept his distance from my mom because she still couldn't look at him. My mom obsessed over the baby. Rainer held everyone and everything together with his damn order and need to solve every problem. And I became a bitch."

A part of me wanted to laugh at her words because she put it so bluntly. Who was I to judge her for being a bitch? She clearly had enough reason to be.

"I really don't mean to be, but I can't help it. And Rainer blames himself for that, too."

"What do you mean?"

"He's got this hero-complex. I don't even think he realizes it. Like he's got to keep everything in its place, make sure everything is okay, but he can't. It's so annoying. He's not God. It's not his fault I had to sell my horse because I had no one to even drive me to the barn to ride anymore, though he thinks it is. It's not his fault the baby got any and all attention that was available. It's not his fault I was the weird new girl whose brother just died. It's not his fault Ross is...dead."

I gave her a moment before speaking because I had a feeling saying that was an exorcism of sorts for her. It gave me time to think of her words, too. Rainer once told me he destroyed everything around him. I now understood he thought he destroyed Rachel as well. Gizmo plodded along beside her, a step ahead of Tierra now as I turned us back in the direction of the barn instead of continuing to run away. "It's not his fault Ross died?" I asked hesitantly. I wasn't sure how she would react to my question.

Her head whipped around to face me. "Of course not," she gasped. "Why would you even ask that?"

I shrugged my small shoulders under my long sleeves despite the temperatures being in the high eighties today. "You ever tell him that?"

"Tell him I don't think it's his fault Ross is dead?" I nodded. "Why? He knows that. That's obvious. None of us think that."

"Some things that are so obvious to us aren't always as clear to others." I thought of how the town viewed my father. I thought of all the times growing up that I prayed the police would believe me if I finally got up the courage to say anything to them.

I caught Rachel giving me an odd look out of the corner of my eye, almost as if she couldn't believe I could say something so profound. *Huh*, I thought. *Neither did I.* I guess staying in The Mansion really was messing with my brain.

"All I'm saying is we all struggle to see the truth sometimes. Like with you. As much as you'd like me to believe you're a bitch, I know you're not really. I know you don't actually hate Viviana because you know none of this is her fault at all. I know you never really hated your mom, you just didn't know what to do to help her. And I know you care about Rainer and think he's not to blame for any of this, but you've been too angry at the whole entire world to even let him know that."

By now, we had made it back to the wide lane that led out from the rear doors of the barn, so I swung down from Gizmo and flipped the reins over his head to lead him back in. After a couple of steps, I realized Rachel and

Tierra had stopped following me. I paused at the back entrance to look back at her. "What?"

She swung down off Tierra and her small feet caused a puff of dust to explode from the dirt lane. She stalked silently towards me and now that her feet were back on solid ground, she seemed to lose all the vulnerability she had shown while on horseback. If I hadn't just spent the past two hours with her, I would have sworn she didn't have a soft side at all. Only now, I knew better.

"Remember when I said you weren't Rainer's type?" That same first day I had labeled her as a bitch. "I was wrong about you."

My breath caught but I schooled my face to its usual mask of indifference so she couldn't see how much her words affected me. *She thought I was good enough for her brother? Was she insane?*

"Yeah, well, I was wrong about you, too."

She laughed, only this time it wasn't the humorless one I had grown accustomed to from her. "No, you weren't. I'm still a bitch. Just now you know why." She handed Tierra's reins to me and went to disappear around the corner of the barn, back to her car without a goodbye I'm sure, but at the last second she stopped and turned back.

"You know all that shit you were saying about stuff being obvious to others and not to us?" I nodded cautiously. *Where was she going with this?* "You can stop wearing those ugly-ass shirts and jeans, Colt. We all know you've got scars. The only one who gives a damn about them is *you*."

~

I used to love winter because it meant my sweatshirts and long-sleeve shirts were considered normal. I used to love summer because the days were longer which meant I could stay longer at the barn before the sun went down and forced me to head home. Now, however, I found myself leaving the barn whenever I finished my lessons for the day. When I got back to the Ventrilla Mansion today, the sun hadn't even begun to set. I still wasn't used to this new routine. I wasn't really used to a routine at all.

I noticed as soon as I walked into Ross's old room that someone had been in here since I left this morning. My first instinct was to be on guard, but as I stepped further into the room, I saw what had been left for me on the bed. I reached out a tentative hand to thumb through the stack of t-shirts there, all from Rachel no doubt. While they filled me with a sense of dread, I couldn't help the smile I felt on my face.

After my shower, I stood before the same enormous mirror Rainer had forced me to stand in front of just last week. The only difference was this time, I didn't have his steadying warmth at my back. I was surprised to know I actually wanted that warmth. I wished I had it now.

I was worried Rachel's shirts would be too small on me because the only things I had ever seen her wear were skin-tight. Instead, the plain black t-shirt I had slipped into draped off my shoulders, my collarbones clearly visible through my pale skin. But it wasn't the fabric I was focused on. Not even the fact that my bones were protruding that worried me. Weight could be gained. What couldn't be fixed was the crisscrossing, grotesque pattern of abuse that was so clearly visible now. The longer I stood here and analyzed myself, the more I wanted to pull one of my sweatshirts from my duffle bag I still kept packed and ready to go under the bed and hide myself in the roomy fabric. Rachel's words echoed in my head as I turned to do just that. *We all know you've got scars. The only one who gives a damn about them is* you. With a huff, I pulled my gaze from my arms in the mirror to look out the monstrous window on the back wall.

Everything in this place was huge, so it only made sense this window with such a great view would be as well. A flat roof jutted out from beneath it and there were no screens to keep out the bugs should I ever want to open it. I found that a bit odd, but also extremely convenient. Without much thought, I shoved up the massive pane of glass and ducked through, stepping down onto the shingles of the roof which were still warm from today's scorching sun. It extended further than I had been able to see through the window so I tentatively walked forward until my toes were on the edge and took in the land spread out before me. The inground pool Rainer and I never got around to swimming in was almost directly below me. Out from there, the lawn sloped down gradually, an impossibly vibrant shade of green despite the lack of rain this summer, until it eventually met a lake towards the left and thick forest to the right.

"You know if a gust of wind comes, you could fall and die?"

I whipped around at the sound of Rainer's voice, careful to not do what he just so kindly pointed out. "Jesus, Rainer. Or I could fall and die because you scared the shit out of me."

He chuckled from where he was seated with his back against the house. I hadn't even noticed him leaning there to the left of my window when I had stepped out. "What? Not afraid of heights?"

I shrugged my shoulders and took a step away from the edge; a step closer to him. How could I explain that falling from a roof seemed less terrifying to me than walking closer to him? Less terrifying than any human contact? "I guess they just never really bothered me."

"Not as much as I do?" I cursed how he could so easily read me when no one ever had before. I also cursed that damned smirk he was flashing at me again. "Come on." He nodded his head to the spot beside him between what I realized must be our two windows. "I promise I won't even kiss you again. But I definitely wouldn't be opposed to you kissing me."

He wiggled his eyebrows playfully and I gulped. We had yet to talk about the kiss. Well, kisses. I had kissed him, too. I bit my lip hesitantly, then took the two steps that separated us and sat beside him with my back pressed against the house, careful to keep almost three feet of space between us. His deep, throaty chuckle wasn't lost on me. It heated my cheeks and stirred that god-awful feeling low in my stomach.

"I don't know, though. You're wearing short sleeves tonight. You know I can't control myself with your bare arms around." I gasped and turned my head to see him with his eyebrows raised suggestively. When his eyes caught mine, he winked at me.

"You did *not* just seriously wink at me," I deadpanned.

"That depends...did it work?" he laughed back.

I shook my head and faced forward again so he couldn't see my wide smile. Lord knows, he didn't need me adding any more to his ego.

"That's what I thought." Even his voice sounded cocky. I hated it. I loved it.

He didn't speak for a couple more minutes, letting the sound of the peepers fill the silence between us. When he finally did, his voice was serious again. "It looks good. In case you were wondering."

I turned from watching the now-setting sun to face him. The late golden rays on his face made him look even more like a Greek god than he already did, softening the harsh planes of his face and his sharp jaw. "You don't mean that."

He cut me off. "Don't. Just accept that I wanted to say it. It's true. Don't try to argue with me." My jaw snapped shut as he stared at me, his intense eyes skimming over every inch of me and I felt it just as much as if his own fingers were touching me, inspecting me. I wondered what it was he saw. How he could see anything beyond the deformities that marred my skin. It looked like he was still trying to figure it out, too. I was still that puzzle to him he had yet to solve.

"Stop trying to figure me out," I snapped, folding my arms over my chest defensively.

Rainer only laughed at my childlike outburst. "Fine. For now." I breathed a sigh of relief as he leaned his head back against the siding again, stretching his long legs out in front of him.

"Ross and I used to come hangout here. It's why we never had screens on our windows. The housekeeper was always so confused how we seemed to "lose them" each year. We'd laugh about it when we snuck out here to smoke a joint."

"You smoked?" I gasped. I don't know why it was so shocking to me. Plenty of young people smoked weed. I guess I couldn't picture Rainer, the man who wore tailored suits and schmoozed with older businessmen in ballrooms, who coddled babies swathed in pink and kept everything in perfect order for his mother, who was disappointed in my excessive tequila binging, to sneak out and smoke pot.

He laughed at my surprise. "Yeah. It didn't happen often, but I could be young and stupid. Mostly at the hands of Ross. He was always egging me on to do something dumb. I never really was all that fond of smoking, though. I haven't smoked at all since he's been gone."

"I hate it," I said vehemently. I wasn't even sure where that thought came from, but I knew it to be completely true as soon as it left my lips. Rainer turned to face me when he heard the disgust in my voice.

"Why?" he asked innocently. Of course he would never just let it slide. He would always push me for more. He was the first person to ever push me to open up and I was finally accepting that from him. I would probably still run if anyone else had asked me questions like these but for Rainer, I wanted to answer honestly.

I thought about his question. It wasn't any of the typical reasons that spurred my intense dislike. It wasn't because I hated the smell, or the taste, or worried about the future of my lungs. No, those would be too normal. Too simple. Instead of verbalizing an answer, I carefully unfolded my arms from over my chest and extended one across the space between us. In the last light of day, the pearly white circles stood out in stark contrast up my arm, from my wrist all the way until they disappeared beneath the sleeve of Rachel's t-shirt I was wearing. Air hissed in through Rainer's teeth as he took in the perfect, circular scars which were each no larger than a dime. I saw his hand twitch as if he wanted to reach out and touch them, but he held back and I silently thanked him for that.

For the first time, I carefully studied them exposed in the sunlight. In a way, it was kind of like art. A sick, twisted art. "He didn't even smoke." My voice had turned back to the cold monotone that used to be all I ever knew. "Only when he came home from whatever dive he had been at, completely wasted. He'd light up a cigar. I can still smell the damn things. That sickly, sweet smell that would cling to everything. And then, no matter where I was when he was finished with one, he'd find me. I think it was one of his favorite things to do with me. A game of sorts. Some fathers enjoy playing catch in the yard. Mine liked to burn me." I chuckled darkly at that.

My eyes stayed locked on the round scars. They each had slightly jagged edges, but you could only tell that if you really stared at them hard. It was from the skin melting off in an uneven pattern. I could still feel the cigars stubbing into my skin, singeing it away as his thick fingers held me in place, always holding too tight, always leaving behind bands of bruising.

Rainer's long fingers wrapped around my wrist now, just as my father's used to, though his touch was so gentle I could barely feel it. His thumb stroked back and forth over the delicate skin there until I no longer had the phantom scent of cigars and burning skin stuck in my nose. Until I was able to finally lift my eyes to meet his.

Colby Millsaps

"He won't find you here. Okay?" His eyes, the same ones that had captured me weeks ago with their strange mixture of blues and greens and brown, held me tight now. They held promises I wanted to believe, but didn't know how. For now, I nodded and he smiled back at me in relief as if it really could be that simple.

Chapter Thirteen

"Coat."

"Colt," I corrected.

"Coat."

"No, that's what you wear in the winter. My name is Colt."

"Coat."

I slapped a hand to my forehead. Clearly, I was getting nowhere with this conversation. "Never mind," I finally sighed.

"Here." It sounded more like 'he-yuh' than 'here', but I got what she meant. Viviana's pudgy hand thrust a new tub of play-doh at me.

I looked at the cap. "You want the blue?"

"Boo." I pinched the bridge of my nose between my fingers and raised my eyebrows at her but she just stared back at me, not at all recognizing how she was butchering the English language.

"Well, what do you want me to do with it?"

"Open peas." Her little fists opened and closed, impatiently waiting for me to give her back the blue play-doh.

"Oh, you can't open this on your own? Damn, that must suck, huh? Oh shit, I'm not supposed to swear in front of you." I slapped a hand over my mouth in an effort to prevent any more profanities from slipping out.

"Sit," she giggled happily. I guess it wasn't such a bad thing she sucked at pronouncing things, after all.

Damn you, Rainer, I thought for what had to be the hundredth time in the last forty-two minutes. Not that I was counting the minutes since he had left me alone with a toddler or anything.

I had taken a rare day off from the barn, which Rainer had been thrilled about. He was going to take me out to the vineyards and into the plant to see how they made the wine. Only, his mom had gotten a call from a frantic wedding planner and had to rush off, leaving us in charge of Viviana. Which wasn't ideal, but it kept me from having to worry about what the hell Rainer and I were doing lately. At least with Viviana around, he would be focused on her and hopefully unable to twist my stomach into knots with his smirks.

We were just about to head out with the baby when someone knocked on the door saying Mr. Ventrilla needed Rainer's help as soon as possible. I could see Rainer's hesitation as he looked between me and the man who had to have been some worker from the vineyard, because his boots were covered in dirt from the fields. His need to immediately jump to the rescue for his family was battling with his knowledge that I had no idea what to do with a toddler. At the time, I had waved him off, thinking I could handle babysitting for a couple minutes. Twelve-year-olds could do it. How hard could it really be?

That was almost an hour ago.

"Here." I passed her the gob of blue play-doh after opening the tub and digging it out for her. "Have your blue play-doh since the red apparently wasn't good enough."

"Tanks!" she squealed. I grabbed another tub from the floor beside us and offered it to her.

"You want this one, too?"

"Ew." She shook her head adamantly. "No." I looked down at the color of the cap. Pink. Go figure.

"Coat, watch." She had just learned to say watch in the last week or so and was now on a roll of saying it for everything. I humored her and watched her press the blue play-doh onto some flower mold before she held it up to show me the finished product.

I squinted my eyes and even cocked my head to try to get a different angle on it, but it still looked like a blob to me. "Nice," I tried to say with enthusiasm. What else was there to say? She wasn't very good at this shit.

"You turn." She pushed some doh towards me.

"Oh, no. I'm good."

"No, you play."

There was probably some kindness rule somewhere that said you weren't supposed to deny a toddler's invitation to play, so I reluctantly grabbed a chunk of the play-doh and smushed it in my fist. She passed me a block of molds.

"Make candy! Make candy!"

Seemed simple enough. I pushed the play-doh into a candy bar mold and pulled it back out, but it looked absolutely nothing like a candy bar. Damn thing. I squished down the play-doh and tried again, realizing I needed to use less this time. It looked slightly better, but when I went to pull away the excess from the sides, my play-doh chocolate bar became more of a long ribbon.

"Fuck," I grumbled. Viviana giggled and clapped her hands at my outburst. "Oh no. No, no, no. Do not repeat that."

Her little lips started making an 'eff' sound, spittle flying everywhere as she tried to imitate my word. Without thinking, I shouted the first F-word I could think of to cut her off. "Frog!"

"Fog!" she squealed back. *Crisis averted.* "Foggie, foggie."

"Yeah?" I asked, making yet another attempt at the candy bar. "You like frogs?"

"Yeah! Foggies!"

"Of course you do. You hate pink and you like frogs. What else? You probably hate that pink bow they always put in your hair, don't you?"

"Yeah," she said seriously, though I had no idea if she even knew what I was talking about.

"Don't worry, kid. I got you." I reached forward from where I had been sitting cross-legged on the floor and carefully undid the pink bow that tied her dark curls up in a Cindy Lou Who ponytail on the top of her head. My breath caught as I felt how soft her hair was, how fragile her skull was beneath my fingertips. She grinned at me, the tiny baby teeth that had come in so far winking at me from her gums. With one hand, she grabbed a fistful of her now-loose curls. She used her free hand to point at my arm.

"You drawed on youself."

"What?" I looked to where she was pointing, but all I saw was my skin. Then I realized what she was referring to.

"Oh, no. That's not..." There was really no way to explain this to a toddler. Nor would I ever want to. "Someone else drew those," I whispered.

She wrinkled her baby face at me. "That's yucky." Her comment caused bile to rise in my throat. This is why I always wore long sleeves. This is why I never should have been left around her. She didn't need to see this. No one should have to see this. She had been blessed enough to live in a perfect bubble so far, and I was ruining that. "I fix."

Before I could see what she could possibly mean by that, I felt something press down on my forearm. When I looked to see what the hell she was doing, she had a blue marker clutched in her fist and she was tracing it over a scar that ran from the outside of my arm to my inner elbow. I remember the cut that had caused it, another souvenir from that worst night, and wanted to wince but I held perfectly still for Viviana. Her little tongue was poking out from her mouth as she focused with all her might to stay on the line of the scar. Finally, when she reached my elbow, she lifted the marker from my skin and clapped her hands together.

"Dare!" she said happily. "Pwetty now. No one draws in white. White is boring."

I gasped as I realized what she had done. She truly thought someone else had drawn on me in white ink. My father's abuse had drawn those scars, but she had turned one into art. When I looked back at her, she was staring at me as if she was waiting for a response. "Yeah," I managed to choke out. "Very pretty now." That was all the assurance she needed before pressing the marker back down on my skin.

"More, more, more!" Viviana clapped. My arms were now *covered* in marker. Burns she had decided to color in red. Thick cuts remained blue. Thin slashes she had determined would be green. My skin now looked like some odd, multicolored spiderweb.

"I don't know about more," I laughed. How I was laughing right now, I had no idea. Her tiny hands had been all over me and at first it had made my skin crawl, but now it was almost soothing. As if by coloring over the reminders of my pain, she was taking it all away. Like the antibiotic ointment I smothered over them when I had first received the wounds, her markers were taking the same sting away.

"Deys more here." Her little hands tugged down the collar of my shirt, exposing more canvas for her to explore and trace.

"Yeah…"

"Take it off! Take it off!"

I hesitated, but there was no one else around. This whole giant mansion, and it was empty. And as odd as it was to me, Viviana didn't find my marred skin revolting. She was actually *enjoying* it. So despite my hesitations, I grabbed the neck of Rachel's shirt I was wearing and tugged it over my head. Her answering squeal of delight caused me to chuckle and she wasted no time in pressing the blue along my ribs, tracing back to my spine over that same awful memory Rainer's lips had pressed against the other night. I took a deep breath in and let my eyes flutter closed.

I wasn't sure how much time had passed since she had determined she was going to be the next Picasso, but most of my upper body was covered in ink at this point. Viv's green marker was tracing along the barely-there scars of my collarbone, causing me to almost giggle as the marker tickled over my skin, and my hands were loosely holding her tiny waist to keep her steady in my lap when I heard voices coming down the hall towards us.

"It ended up being a pipe between one of the crushers and one of the vats. It took longer to find the issue than to actually fix it."

"I keep telling him we just need to replace all the pipes throughout the-" Mrs. Ventrilla's response cut off in a gasp. "Oh my God."

My back was to the hall, so I couldn't see when Rainer and Adriana came into view, but Viv's head lifted from her artwork to focus behind me. "Gammie, look! Someone drawed on Coat so I made it pwettier."

"I think I'm going to be sick."

"Hey, Viv? Why don't you get up a sec, okay?" I carefully lifted her off my lap and placed her back on the hardwood floors of this formal living room that apparently no one ever lived in until now. I quickly snatched up my shirt and shoved my head and arms back into it in an attempt to cover up as much as I could. "Mrs. Ventrilla, I…I didn't mean…I…I'm sorry. She just… and…"

Her hand was pressed over her mouth and her face was a mask of complete revulsion before her eyes overflowed with tears and they silently dripped down her face, cutting streaks through the immaculate makeup there.

"Gammie, don't cry." Viv barreled towards her, dropping her still-open markers as she went. Adriana scooped her up almost protectively and half-turned away, not able to keep her eyes on me.

"Rainer, can you...uhm...just..." She waved her hand towards the hall, up the stairs. "Help her clean...I'm going to just..." She choked out a mumble of words and then turned with Viv in her arms, her heels clacking down the hall towards the kitchen.

"Rainer...I'm so sorry," I whispered, shocked at the tears that were starting to brim in my eyes.

"Hey...shh. What are you sorry for?" He finally stepped out of the doorway and into the immaculately furnished, never used room. He only stopped when he was directly in front of me, the toes of his dusty work boots brushing my bare feet. His hands came up to cradle my face, his thumb sweeping against my cheek softly.

"This is why I shouldn't be allowed near children," I murmured, not even flinching at his soft touch now.

He grinned back at me. "You called her Viv."

I opened my mouth and then closed it again. I hadn't even realized I had given her a nickname. That insinuated a closeness. A connection. I gritted my teeth. "Yeah, well, Viviana's a mouthful. Kid probably can't even say her own name. It only makes sense to shorten it," I rationalized.

Rainer barked out a laugh and then without warning, he lowered his mouth to mine. His lips pressed against mine in a quick, hot kiss that sent me reeling. I gasped against him and my eyes flashed open to find his dancing with mirth. "Mhm...that's all. I'm sure. Come on, let's get you washed off." His hands released me and he reached down to interlock our fingers before pulling me up the grand staircase. He still hadn't changed from just expecting me to follow, only now he ensured it happened by linking us together. I guess that could be seen as somewhat of an improvement.

"I really am sorry. Your mom…she's so mad," I choked out while I let him pull me after him, feeling the zaps of electricity traveling from our laced fingers up my multicolored arm. He didn't stop until he had pulled me all the way into the bathroom that led off from his room.

"Nah, she was just…caught off-guard."

"Rainer," I whined. "She said she was about to throw up," I reminded him as he toed off his boots and reached back to tug his shirt over his head. My breath caught in my throat as I stared at the ridges and planes of his chest suddenly on full display. I had seen him shirtless before, that night in the dim light from the kitchen, but nothing like this. With the bright light of the bathroom, every inch was highlighted for my viewing pleasure. "Wh-what are you doing?" I gasped.

His answering chuckle came from deep in his chest and I felt it down to my toes as he loosened his belt and his jeans fell in a puddle around his ankles. Just like that, he was standing in front of me in nothing but his boxer briefs. My heartrate instantly spiked, blood rushing to my cheeks.

"Rainer!" I gasped, covering my eyes with a hand as soon as I had gotten over my initial shock. *What the hell was he doing?* I heard him move and a moment later the spray of his shower kicked on.

"Colt? I'm about to touch you so you may want to stop covering your eyes so you can see what I'm doing." His voice was deep and slow, soothing, as if he was talking to an animal that may bolt at any minute. I can't lie, if my legs had been able to work at this time, I was pretty sure I would have been bolting. He knew me well.

"You're...I...what?" My voice came out in a pitch I didn't know it was capable of making. However, I immediately did as he said because no way in hell was I going to let him touch me without me seeing it. I may have begun to trust him, in whatever messed up way I was able to, but not that much.

He was squatting down in front of me when I lifted my hand from my eyes. He was so perfect. Every inch of him was perfect, and not just the outside. Just looking at him had me completely frozen, unable to do anything but stare. His face was level with my belt loops but he was staring up at me as if he was waiting to see some sort of permission from me. Whatever he saw on my face must have been enough of an approval, because the next thing I knew his long fingers were unfastening my belt and popping open the button of my jeans. The sound of the zipper coming down was earsplitting in the tiled room. I could hear it over the spray of water and the pounding of my heart, which I'm sure was about to beat right out of my chest. Was it possible to have a heart attack just from someone touching you? Because I wasn't sure my heart could handle this. I wanted to tell him to stop; beg him not to do this. I couldn't stand here and be bared open to him, but for some reason I didn't open my mouth. I couldn't find the words. Instead, my tears fell noiselessly down my cheeks while I watched him in front of me.

My jeans hit the floor, falling from my hips too easily to be considered healthy. I think this pair was originally supposed to be skinny jeans, yet they still bagged off me. Rainer's fingertips grazed up the outsides of my thighs, skimming over raised scars that had been spared from Viviana's coloring extravaganza, and my tears fell harder but still I didn't stop him. He grasped the hem of my t-shirt, dragging it up my body as he rose in front of me, his knuckles brushing against my now-bare skin and setting off fireworks in my chest. I found myself hesitantly lifting my arms and he pulled until it was over my head, then discarded it in a heap in the corner of the bathroom with his.

Rainer took a step back, his eyes sweeping over everything I had hid my entire life while my chest heaved and I struggled to pull air into my lungs. *Heart attack,* I thought. *I definitely must be having a heart attack.* This wasn't okay. I wasn't ready for this. I don't think I ever would be ready. What the hell was he thinking? What the hell were we doing? How had I allowed him to undress me?

I couldn't look at him. I didn't want to see his eyes, didn't want to confirm the look of disgust in them. Instead, I kept my eyes focused over his shoulder at the ridiculous reflection in the mirror behind him. His perfectly tanned, untouched back rippling with muscle when he moved even the slightest bit did not fit at all with my pale skin with the bones poking through, covered almost completely in a child's doodles to hide the truth.

Finally, I couldn't take his silence any longer. I couldn't help myself. I dropped my eyes from our mirrored selves to meet his gaze and my breath stopped altogether. I'm pretty sure I finally understood that whole "heart skipped a beat" saying, because my heart definitely stopped for a minute there. I suppose that made sense. A natural progression from heart attack. Right on to full-out cardiac arrest.

I had never seen anything like what I saw in Rainer's eyes right now. The hunger. The need. The pure, unhidden adoration. "God, you're so fucking perfect, Colt." That was all it took. A sob broke free of my chest at the same moment he stepped back into me, pulling my lips roughly to his, fisting a hand in my hair to bring us even closer. It was almost painful but in the most amazing way. I never knew that was even possible.

I could taste my tears in our kiss but I didn't know how to stop them. I didn't even know what I was crying for. For the way he looked at me, like none of my scars could change how he saw me? For the way Viv had colored me, as if there was absolutely nothing wrong with having more scar tissue than skin? For the pain in Mrs. Ventrilla's eyes? For the pain in my life that no little girl should have ever known? Or maybe for this chance to be something new, something desired, with a man who saw all of me and accepted it.

I whimpered as one of his hands drifted down my neck, down my ribs, and squeezed my hip, bringing me flush against him. I gasped at the total contact of his bare skin on mine and his tongue took the opportunity to dive into my mouth, tangling with mine in the most delicious way. Tentatively, my arms lifted from where they had been limp at my sides in shock to wrap around his neck. I carefully threaded my fingers through the strands of hair at the base of his skull, loving the silky feel. He groaned into my mouth in response and deepened the kiss, pulling me impossibly tighter against him until I was sure I couldn't take any more. It was not possible to feel this much. There was no way this was normal.

His lips broke from mine and I sucked in as deep a breath as I could manage, attempting to clear my foggy brain, but then I felt his teeth nip my jaw before swiping his tongue over the spot and smoothing over it with another kiss. "Rainer!" I gasped. My hand fisted tighter in his hair at the new sensation he was causing in me and he groaned against me in response. I'm pretty sure the butterflies that came to life every time he walked in a room had self-combusted. They had dissolved into a puddle of desire now. Because it was high time I admitted what this was in me. The twisting stomach and sweaty palms and shaky breaths around him. There was no more denying this. I wanted Rainer Ventrilla. I had wanted him from the first day I saw him, even if I knew I had no right.

"Shh, baby," he finally murmured when his lips lifted from my neck. I hadn't realized I was still crying until he kissed away a tear that was trailing down my cheek and caught another with his thumb. His lips were salty with them as they pressed to mine again and again while he grabbed me around the waist, lifting me up and carrying me into the stream of hot water from the shower. The spray mixed with my tears until it was impossible to say what was from crying and what was from the shower as I clung to him desperately. It was as if he had peeled away far more than my clothes just now. I was raw, split wide open, and I needed something to steady me. I needed *him* to steady me.

He set me back on my feet and tried to disentangle me from him so he could finally move back a step to look at me. "You're okay, baby. You're safe here. With me." He positioned me under the water, his thumbs rubbing circles on my shoulders where he still held me. "I'm never gonna hurt you, Colt. I promise."

My tears came harder at his words, at the sincerity behind them, but the shower spray washed them away just as fast as they came. I wanted so badly to believe him. "Don't say that," I croaked.

"I mean it, I-"

"Stop." I shook my head harder to cut him off. "I don't want to remember you telling me that. I don't want any more promises that can't be kept. It hurts less if you never say it."

He hung his head at my words and I saw his shoulders rise and fall as he took a deep breath in. Then his hands left my shoulders to grab the body wash from behind me. He didn't even bother to argue with me. I was trying to swat away the tears that wouldn't stop falling when I felt his hands on me again. Lathered in soap now, they started to gently rub circles over my skin. The water turned murky with the suds, the colors from the markers mixing together before swirling down the drain. I bit my lip as I watched his hands skim over my skin, washing it all away. If only he could really wash me clean.

"It's okay if you don't believe me yet. I'm not going anywhere." I should have known better than to think he wouldn't fight with me on this. Fight *for* me, as he would put it. I stared at his face, so calm, so sure of his words, and wondered if they could ever be true. If there was a world where I could ever deserve a man like him. His hands dipped lower over me, slipping under my bra strap and then making sure it was back in place as he scrubbed down my arms, then swiped the color from my ribs and stomach while my heart hammered away in my chest. I knew he could feel it beneath his palms. I knew he was aware of how completely terrified I was right now, and yet we both simply accepted that fear and refused to let it take control of this moment. *Our* moment.

I should have been ogling him, any normal girl would be jumping at the opportunity of a nearly-naked Rainer Ventrilla in front of them in only his now-wet boxer briefs. But I couldn't take my eyes off his hands. I couldn't get over the feel of his rough palms sliding over my tainted skin so impossibly gently. Rubbing away every bad thing that had happened to me. No one had ever touched me like this before, not once. No one had ever cared like Rainer cared. I doubted there was anyone in the world who ever could.

"Okay, turn around," he said once the water eventually ran clean down my chest and arms. I finally lifted my eyes back to meet his and I knew they were as wide as saucers. "I just need to get your back and wash your hair, Colt. It's okay." His hands skated soothingly up and down my arms, but I shook my head adamantly. Even if I had somehow managed to let this all happen, I couldn't turn around. Couldn't turn my back on him here, where I was so vulnerable, where he could see all of me.

He seemed to understand this was where I drew the line and his eyes softened. "Alright, come here. I promise this won't be bad." He tugged me into his chest and rested his chin atop my head so he shielded me from the water. I wanted to stiffen in his hold, but then his hands were swirling circles over my back, washing away the color there without having me turn away from him and I sighed against him, lifting my own arms to gently rest around his waist and held myself to him. His heart picked up its pace against my ear and if I wasn't so on edge from this whole situation I would have smiled, knowing that my touch had the same effect on him as his did on me. Maybe we weren't so different after all.

I felt him reach behind us and looked up to see him squirt a sizeable amount of shampoo into his palm. "Okay?" he asked and I felt another chunk of the ice walls guarding my heart melt off at his need to know I was still okay.

"Okay," I croaked, my throat still clogged from the tears. I rested my chin on the center of his chest so my head was tilted back for him as his fingers slipped into the soaked strands of my hair. My arms tightened around his waist and I bit my lip as I watched him work.

His eyes roved over me, drinking me in with that same open adoration while I attempted to swallow the lump in my throat. "See? I kept my promise. I told you this wouldn't be bad." His boyish grin of confidence almost caused me to smile in response. "Close your eyes." He pulled the showerhead down from above him and held it out, ready to rinse my hair, but suddenly any comfort I had allowed myself to feel evaporated.

"I can't."

"I don't want to get shampoo in your eyes, baby. You've got to close them."

"Please," I begged. I couldn't. Not yet. Not even with Rainer. Closing my eyes would be giving complete control to him.

He had to have seen the intense fear flood my eyes again, because I saw his face scrunch up in pain and he didn't push the issue. Instead, he reached one hand up to create a shield over my eyes while the other raised the shower head so that water cascaded over me. I kept my eyes on him the whole time he rinsed my hair, watching the beads of water collect on his ridiculously long lashes. I would never understand why he chose me. Why he kept choosing me each time he saw more of my darkness. But maybe it was time I accepted it. Accepted that he was bringing me into the light.

"Thank you," I whispered.

~

"Mrs. Ventrilla?" My voice came out as barely a whisper as I stood in the doorway to the three-season porch she used as an office of sorts. I'd never set foot in it before. I had never sought her out.

She startled in the chaise lounge where she had been sitting, staring off at the pond in the distance. "Oh, Colt, you scared me darling."

"Sorry, I didn't mean-"

"Oh, no, no. You're fine. I should have come to you earlier but I wanted to give you some time. Please, come sit." She waved her hand at the big, padded wicker armchair beside her and I hesitated for a moment before tentatively making my way over to take a seat. I glanced around the area, but Viv was nowhere in sight. Probably down for an afternoon nap. Funny, how I was already learning these routines when I had never known what routine was before.

I tried to force down the thought that Viv was hidden away now just to keep her from me and focused on the view Mrs. Ventrilla had been looking at before I came to interrupt her. It really was gorgeous, this little corner of the world they inhabited. Gorgeous until I had come and tainted it. I made sure to put on one of my long sleeves after the shower even though Rainer had ensured there was no marker left on my body.

"I wanted to tell you how sorry I am. I'm really *so* sorry, Mrs. Ventrilla. I wasn't thinking and she was having fun, but I never should have let her see them, and I promise to always wear long sleeves again. I understand if you want me to leave, I never should have been here in the first place. Or if you just want me to stay away from Viv, I get that, too. I promise not to go near her. I know I never should have at all. And you probably want me to stay away from your son after seeing who I really am and I understand-"

She leaned forward in the chaise and her hand reached out to cover mine, giving it a squeeze. I stared at it, trying to understand what she was doing; why she was touching me. *Kindly* even. I had disgusted her. I had tainted her home and her son and her granddaughter.

"Colt." I finally tore my eyes from her hand on mine to look at her face. "Honey, *I'm* sorry."

"You're sorry?" I sputtered. "For what?"

She swung her legs over the edge of the chaise so she was facing me fully and held my hand between both of hers, forcing me to look at her. "I reacted horribly. And I am so sorry for that. I know I can't undo that initial reaction, but I'm going to do my best to try. I've wanted you to feel comfortable here. I hoped that once you were comfortable enough, you would start to open up to us. I've been trying to give you the space I thought you needed while also desperately wanting to know the girl who's stealing my son's heart. Yet the first opportunity you gave me to see who you are, I ruined it. I'm so, so sorry."

"But…" I started. What was she saying? *She* was sorry? She wanted me to be comfortable here? "But you were disgusted."

She winced at my honest words but didn't shy away. I had to admire her for that. She couldn't have wanted to have this conversation, and yet she still did. They were all so alike, this family, and they were so much stronger than I had ever been. "You're right.," she nodded. "I was disgusted. But *not* by you. Not by you at all. I don't want you to ever think that. I am disgusted by whatever sick, twisted, psychopath could have ever done that to you. I am disgusted by myself. By how I reacted to seeing it. Because I'm not as strong as you are to handle it well. But I am *not* disgusted by you."

For the second time in less than twenty-four hours, my eyes welled up with tears. These people were making me soft. But maybe there was a different strength in that. "I…Mrs. Ventrilla…I-"

"Shh, come here," she cooed, sounding so much like Rainer that I found myself drawn to her as she pulled me up by my hand that she still held in hers. "Can I hug you?" she asked. I hesitated, but then nodded numbly and her slim arms wrapped around me, pulling me into her and stroking my hair while she gently rocked us side to side. Tears poured down my cheeks silently, soaked her shoulder, and for the first time in my life I wondered if this was what a mother's love felt like.

Chapter Fourteen

"I never mentioned it at the time, but I saw you the other afternoon. With my mom."

We were sitting in what had quickly become "our spot" with our backs pressed into the siding of The Mansion, legs stretched out in front of us. It seemed each time Rainer took his position beside me on the roof, he managed to sit another inch closer. The space separating us had dwindled to barely half a foot now.

I turned my head to face him and saw him wearing a content smile this evening. His hair was still damp from the shower he had taken after coming in from the vineyard and my cheeks heated at the thought of our own shower. Nothing happened; I knew that. In the sense of a guy and a girl showering together, that is. For us though, I couldn't help but think *everything* had happened.

"I had to apologize."

"Apologize? For what?" he asked.

"For what happened with Viv the other day."

He turned his eyes with their myriad of colors on me and I saw the confusion there. "Colt, you didn't do anything wrong."

I opened my mouth to answer, but then snapped it shut. Knowing how he had grown up and being able to witness that sort of love and understanding firsthand, I don't think

I'd be able to explain it to him in a way he would ever understand. He wouldn't be able to grasp that all I ever knew was anger. That everything and anything was my fault. That no matter what I did, I was wrong and no simple sorry could fix it. With every wrong step, there was a punishment waiting for me. Rainer would never be able to comprehend the fear and anxiety that came with that, so there was no use trying to explain it.

But like it always seemed to be with Rainer, he was able to read what I was thinking just by looking at my face because his expression softened. His hand bridged those six inches between us and his long fingers brushed lightly across my brow, across the deep scar there that had still been red with dried blood that first day I ran into him.

"I told you, you're safe here." His hand left my face but just so he could wrap his fingers around my own. I stared at them. At us so casually touching when it was anything but casual to me. I couldn't help thinking of the first time I'd ever held someone's hand. That walk from the bonfire with Vee.

"You haven't been going to the bonfires," I said quietly. It wasn't like I was stalking him or anything, because I wasn't. We shared a wall. It was easy to know his comings and goings. And since it was almost August now, I knew the fires would be a weekly occurrence at this point. But Rainer's weekends had been spent here. With me. My stare was still fixed on our joined hands when his thumb swiped over mine and my breath hitched, that's how easily I was affected by him.

"Neither have you," he countered.

The fires had always been my escape. Just like the barn, they allowed me an excuse to stay away from my house as long as I could. And then they became Vee. But when Vee left, I stayed away. Until it all became so much that I needed to escape again. The thing was, these past few weeks I found there wasn't anything I was trying to escape from.

"I don't think I need to anymore," I breathed out. My eyes lifted from our hands as Rainer squeezed mine and I met his smile until he turned away to look out at the growing twilight and his expression turned serious.

"You know the first night I ran into you there was the first time I had gone back since the night Ross died," he confessed.

It was my turn to offer a squeeze of comfort to his hand and I was surprised by how naturally that response came. Like I was meant to comfort him. "What made you go?"

His head fell back against the siding and I watched his throat bob as he swallowed. I had to bite my lip as I tried to quench the now all-too-familiar desire he stirred in me. "I just had to," he replied cryptically. "And then you were there and it just seemed right. So I went back again, just to see if you'd show up. And then you did again."

I grimaced at the night he was remembering. The night I *barely* remembered. The night my mother had disowned me. His head swiveled back to face me and his eyes roved over my features in the way only he had that managed to heat every inch of me.

"Do you believe in guardian angels?" he asked seriously.

"I don't know if I believe in much of anything anymore."

He finally tore his eyes from mine, releasing me from that magnetic pull he had on me, and I sucked in a breath

I hadn't realized I was holding. "You don't believe in God?"

Why was it that we always had such heavy conversations? Was it simply because Rainer never shied away from anything, even if it was hard? Or was it because my life rarely allowed for anything outside of those hard truths?

I mimicked him and faced forward, looking out at the now pitch-black sky. The only light around came from our bedroom windows behind us. "I don't see how I ever could now." I paused and waited for Rainer's inevitable push for me to tell him more.

"Why not?"

"Because. Even if there was a God, I don't want to know him. What God allows a little girl to grow up the way I have? What God allows my father to be the monster he is? God is supposed to punish the sinners, right? My father is a sinner if I ever saw one. And yet, I get the punishment. I understand I'm no angel, but I can't believe in a God that would let that happen. He's supposed to have this great plan, right? And everything happens for a reason? Well, what's the reason in that? What could possibly be His reason for allowing that? For taking innocent people from this earth and leaving babies fatherless and allowing others to grow up with *that* as a father?"

I hadn't realized my eyes were leaking tears until I felt Rainer's hand on my cheek and he caught one with his thumb as he turned me to face him. He didn't respond to me with words. Instead, his lips closed over mine and I gave in to him. It was becoming natural for me to melt into him, allow him to catch me as I was falling apart.

His mouth finally left mine and his knuckles grazed my cheek before he stood and held out his hand to me. "Come on," he whispered even though there was no one else around who could possibly hear us out here. "It's late."

I looked at his hand, at what he was asking. For me to go with him. To not retreat back through my own window and hide like I always did. He was asking me to let him hold me, and I felt one of the final chunks of the ice around my heart break off and shatter. The now-familiar butterflies tap-danced along in my stomach as I swallowed hard and took his hand. His answering smile was all I needed to know I made the right decision. He leaned down and kissed a stray tear from my chin, effectively stealing my breath, then waited for me to climb through his bedroom window first.

He dropped to the floor beside me and turned to slide the glass back into place. Then, as if it was the most natural thing in the world, he scooped me into his arms and carried me to his bed, laying me down as gently as he would Viviana. I stayed facing the wall, my heart pounding in my chest as I tried fruitlessly to calm it, and he slid in behind me. His arm wrapped around my waist and he pulled me back into him until my back was flush against his chest and I could feel his breaths rise and fall against me.

"Okay?" he breathed in my ear. I nodded against him because I had no words for what I was feeling right now. I was terrified, but happy. I was broken, but mending. I was lost, but his arms holding me to him made it feel as though I was found. He was so still and silent for so long, I wondered if he had already fallen asleep. But then he spoke and I realized this whole time, he had just been allowing me the time I needed to get used to this. Because in those silent moments, I had unconsciously relaxed against him and I now realized one of my legs was threaded between his, my fingers were laced with his where his hand rested over my stomach, and my heart had slowed to match the rhythm of his I felt against my back. I closed my eyes and just listened to his voice. I hated to admit it, but I knew it had become my favorite sound.

"My family's always been religious," he whispered. "It was never a choice of if you believed or not, it was just a known fact to us. When Ross died, that changed. Suddenly this thing we had always known and believed in wasn't so sure anymore. I think that's only natural when tragedy happens. You wonder why. You wonder how He could do this to you? To your family? To Ross? He didn't deserve it. For a long time, I was like you. I didn't want to know a God who could do that. I was angry at Him. And then I met you, Colt." His breath tickled my ear, causing goosebumps to erupt all over my skin, and I squeezed his fingers to let him know I was still awake and listening.

"Seeing you on the stairs that day... it shouldn't have mattered. *You* shouldn't have mattered, because nothing had in a long time. But you did matter. It was like waking up. Seeing you, it was like Ross had never left. That's how light I felt. Like it had all been a bad dream and seeing you was enough to wake me up from it.

"And then the night of the bonfire. I hadn't been back since he died. The fires had stopped for a little while right after it happened and then after that, I never wanted to go there ever again. But that night, I needed to go. And you were there. And you were still that damn light. And I swear Ross was standing right there with us that night. So you may not believe in God, or guardian angels, but I want you to know I do. He's my guardian angel, Colt. I know it. And he's led me to you."

My heart was beating against my ribs almost painfully and I knew he could feel it since he was wrapped around me so completely. Then he said the words I knew could never be true, but I wanted to believe nevertheless. "I think I might need you even more than you need me."

I gritted my teeth and pulled the edge of my sweatshirt up, checking to see if I could notice anything immediately wrong. Air hissed in through my teeth as I gingerly lifted my arms and I fought to keep from crying out.

No bones were protruding from what I could see, so that was a positive. Unfortunately, I had heard a snap when the toe of his boot connected on that final kick, felt the crack vibrate through my chest. There was definitely a broken rib in there. Damn those steel-toed boots. I knew I should have burned them, but I was just too scared of what he'd do if he found out I had done it. Even if he never found out for sure, he would still blame me and punish me for losing them.

I pressed one hand against my side and whimpered, but held it in place as I reached up for the Ace wrap I hid in the back of my closet. I had bruised ribs plenty, but I don't think he'd ever actually broken one before. Not that I knew for sure, because I could never go to the hospital for x-rays, but I had never felt this much pain before. The older I got, the less gentle he became. *Yay for the teenage years*, I thought grumpily.

I was just fastening the wrapping with those stupid little metal clips when headlights swung across our front lawn and came to rest facing the house. A glance at my clock told me it was almost one in the morning. *Who would be at the house?* I wondered absently. Never mind the time, no one ever visited us here. God forbid they see my father in his natural state.

I shuffled to my window in time to see Vee step down from his fancy, lifted Jeep and slam the door. *Shit, shit, shit. He could* not *be here,* I panicked. What the hell was he doing here? I never should have let him walk me home that night. Now he knew where to find me. If my father caught him here? *Shit.*

I hobbled as quickly as my battered body would allow to my bedroom door and pulled it open again, then held my breath. It had been close to an hour since my father had finished using his favorite punching bag, so by his normal standards he should be passed out, but I never took any chances. Yet here I was, creeping my way down the hall back to the living room I had fled from.

The lamp that had crashed to the floor in tonight's scuffle was still sideways by the coffee table. The glass of the bulb spread over the hardwood floors until it disappeared under the couch. He hadn't moved from where he had collapsed after he landed that final kick to my ribs. One arm dangled to the floor, brushing against some shards of glass, his legs bent at an odd angle, and his mouth open in a snore. I looked down at him and felt my hatred rise. I hated him. I hated him so much. I hated every single thing about him. I hated his brown hair that was always just a bit too long so he somehow still looked boyish. I hated his wide, open face that everyone saw as so trustworthy and welcoming. I hated the biceps that stretched the sleeves of his t-shirt and the strength I knew they held all too well. I fought down the urge to spit on him, knowing it would do no good, and hurried to the front door on silent feet. I whipped it open just as Vee raised his fist to knock.

I flinched back at the sight of a raised fist, but quickly remembered who I was looking at. "Are you crazy?" I hissed. I snuck a glance over my shoulder to make sure I hadn't woken my father and then shooed Vee back off the top step. As gently as I could, I pulled the front door closed behind me and then leaned against it. "What are you doing here?" Damn, even talking hurt. I wrapped an arm around myself, hoping that might offer some relief to the pain.

"What am *I* doing here?" he scoffed and I could smell the beer on his breath. Not as strong as my father's, of course, but enough to know he had come straight from the bonfire. "Where have you been?"

Why couldn't he just let this go? I cursed in my head. I hadn't been back to the field since the night he had walked me home. I had been careless that night; stupid. I was better than that. I knew better than to tell him the truth. I never should have let him walk me home. He proved that as soon as he opened his mouth and tried to say we could report my father. As soon as he said it would all be okay. It wasn't ever going to be okay. And damn him for putting that thought in my head. For letting me believe he may actually be able to make my life better.

"You need to leave," I demanded.

Even though he was two steps below me on the front walk, he was still taller than me. "Hell, no. I'm not leaving until you tell me where you've been. Do you know how worried I've been about you? When you didn't show the week after I found out, I was about to drive straight here. But I knew you were probably just overwhelmed and needed your space and would hate me if I showed up, so I waited. It's been over a month, Donnie. What else was I supposed to do?"

"Keep your voice down," I hissed, quickly storming down the steps and towards his Jeep so he would follow me further away from the house. My ribs screamed in protest but I ignored it. I knew it would be even worse if Vee woke my father with his shouting.

"Are you hurt?" He must have noticed me wincing because he grabbed my shoulder to stop me before we reached the driveway. I flinched from the searing pain that shot through me at his touch. "What did he do to you?" Vee growled. I could see the battle in his blue eyes. He wanted to storm through that door and find my father. Only, he had no clue what kind of monster my father truly was.

"Nothing," I managed to grit out. "It's nothing. Listen, you can't be here. You can't come here ever again. Do you get that?"

"No. I'm not just going to stand by and let you live like this."

"I was doing fine! Until you, I was fine. Maybe not great, maybe not normal, but I accepted my fate. I knew this was my life. Then I met you and your friends and I start thinking of what it's like to have a normal life. I start seeing what it looks like to have friends, relationships, fun. You start talking to me and I want more of it. But all that? You? That can't happen. I've always known what my life is and what it isn't, but now you've got me hoping for better. You have me wishing things could be different. But they *can't*."

His face pinched in pain at my words and he ran a hand through his hair. It was even longer now and I absently wondered when the last time he got a haircut was. Actually, the more I looked at him even out here in the dark, the more changes I noticed. He was thinner, though it wasn't extremely noticeable. The only reason I could tell was because I had spent so much time studying him last fall. The dark circles I had just started to see hints of in mid-April were deep purple now. The carefree, joking manner he had was gone. He stood taller now, more commanding almost.

"Don't be like this. Things *can* be different," he said, interrupting my scrutiny.

"What happened to you?" I asked, unable to hold in my curiosity for once.

"Don't try to turn this around on me. That's not gonna work, Donnie."

"Why not? You can ask me impossible questions, but I can't ask you this? What's going on with you?"

He pulled that gold locket he always had from a pocket and flipped it over and over in his palm. "There's a lot going on right now. I told you my life went to shit. Lot of changes happening." I watched his fingers flip the gold but he still wouldn't meet my eyes.

"Like what?"

He didn't respond for a minute. "I'm graduating at the end of the month."

"The thought of graduating causes you to lose sleep and stop eating?"

He finally lifted his head and his lazy smile was back. "You're such a smartass, Donnie." I made to smile back, but my jaw was stiff from one of my father's punches and I grimaced instead. He caught it and frowned. "Fine. I hear what you're saying. I don't want to share just like you don't want to share. I won't come here anymore; I get that could make things worse for you. But you not coming to Baker's Field makes things worse for me, okay? I worry about you. And if you couldn't tell from all this?" He paused to wave his hand over his new haggard appearance. "I don't need any more worry in my life. I need to know you're okay. And I'll figure something out so we can get you out of here, okay? But you need to come so we can make a plan. I promise. Things *can* get better."

I pulled my bottom lip in between my teeth and looked up at him from under my lashes. I didn't want to agree with him. Didn't want to believe him because it was far too good to be true. But the way he said it, so sure of himself, left almost no room to doubt him. The way his eyes held mine, daring me to disagree, made it impossible to argue.

"Vee…"

"Please, Donnie? Can you just trust me? I promise I'm going to make this better."

Trust him? Could I really trust him? I barely even knew him. But I *wanted* to. "Okay," I whispered, not exactly answering what he had asked but also not saying no.

His answering smile lit up his face and I almost stumbled back from the intensity of it. One hand reached to me, but I stepped back out of reach and he winced from the denial. He masked his hurt with a grimace and a slight nod. "Get some sleep, Donnie. I'll see you next weekend. We'll make a plan."

I kept my arms hugged around me, holding my newly broken ribs in place, while he climbed up into his Jeep. "Vee?" I called just as he was about to pull the door shut. He paused and waited to see what I would say. "Whatever it is that's going on with you…you should still get a haircut. It kind of looks like shit."

He laughed, the sound mixing with the few peepers who were singing their songs of summer already and shook his head at me. "Such an asshole," I heard him mutter as he finally pulled the door shut and my lips lifted in my first smile in weeks, even if it did hurt my face.

Chapter Fifteen

"Hey, hey...you're okay. It's okay. I'm right here. You're safe." I whipped my head around to see Rainer sitting up in bed beside me. His hand was rubbing soothing circles over my back while my breathing slowly returned to normal. "It's okay. It was just a dream."

I wrapped an arm around my middle, my hand splayed against my ribs, but I felt no pain now. "Not a dream," I muttered anyway. "A memory."

I dropped my hand and stood from the bed, thankful the pain of my broken ribs was just a ghost of the past. Those had been a bitch to heal. Rainer's hand snaked around my hip before I could make it too far. I gasped as he pulled me back down to the bed and expertly rolled me under him.

My eyes were wide as he held himself above me and searched my face to make sure what he had just done was okay. I could see the question in his eyes. It was mixed with playfulness and stark desire, but his concern for me and how I would react to things was always there. I think I loved that most about him.

I gasped again, this time not from his actions but from my own thoughts. *Loved? I* loved *something about him? No. Oh, no. I don't think so.* I swore he was some sort of mind reader because his cocky smirk suddenly took over his face as if he knew exactly what I had just thought.

"I don't have work today," he whispered from above me, still bracing himself on the arms that caged in my head on his pillow. No part of him was actually touching me and I knew that was taking a lot of strength from him and I also knew it was only because he was so aware of how touch affected me. The fact that he was so conscious of that was more of a turn on than if he had pressed himself against me, and that was saying something because my friends the tap-dancing butterflies were screaming for him to press against me right now.

My heart was racing, both from our current positions and my recent epiphany, but I pretended like I was unaffected by him. "Okay?" I questioned. "Good for you?"

He dropped his face to the crook of my neck and gently ran his nose from my collarbone up to my ear. That one touch caused my entire body to ignite and my breathing sped. His lips tickled my ear as he whispered, "You should stay home with me."

Before I could respond, he pressed his mouth to mine. It started just as all his kisses to me did, soft and sweet. But then his tongue darted out to tease the seam of my lips and I willingly opened beneath him, allowing him access to explore. When he groaned into me, my hands raised of their own accord and tangled in his thick hair, pulling him closer. He caught my bottom lip between his teeth and pulled until I gasped. Then he released it to trail kisses along my jaw all the way back to my ear where he lightly bit my earlobe. I should have hated that slight sting of pain, but I couldn't help my body's reaction. I had lost that battle to Rainer Ventrilla long ago. I gasped and arched up into him, pressing our chests and hips together so that he finally sank his weight down on me and I moaned. *What was this man doing to me?*

"So is that a yes?" he whispered before sucking on the sensitive skin just below my ear.

"No," I managed to pant, but my hands in his hair told a different story as I tried to tug his mouth back to mine.

He easily broke my hold on him and pulled back from me. I whimpered at the loss, arching my hips back up into him, but he held firm even as his lips tipped into a smirk. "No?" he asked incredulously.

"Rain," I pleaded as I wriggled beneath him. I didn't know this side of me, didn't know who this girl was, but I didn't care at the moment. All I cared about was him.

He grinned at my urgings. "You just said no to me," he laughed. "Even while I was using my incredible tools of persuasion."

I huffed when I realized he wasn't about to give in and kiss me again. I trailed a hand up his chest, loving the solid feel of him against me and the twitch of his muscles as he reacted to my touch. It was still strange to me to actually want to reach out and touch someone. To feel someone's skin against mine. I never thought I would ever want that. I never believed I would get to this point. But I craved Rainer more and more every day. It was terrifying.

"If by tools of persuasion, you mean your tongue," I grumbled. At that, he ducked his head and made an exaggerated swipe of his tongue from the base of my throat, up my neck, and all the way across my cheek. I laughed and my hands went from trying to pull him closer to pushing his face away. "Ew!" I squealed. "Did you really just lick me, you freak?"

He was laughing even harder than me as he finally let me wriggle free from his bed to stand. I straightened my shirt and made a dramatic move to wipe off his slobber from my cheek before turning back to face him. He was laying flat on his back now while he watched me with his hands folded behind his head. "So you really won't skip work today?"

I braced my hands on my hips. "No. I have lessons to teach."

"Cancel them."

"You know there are little children out there who want to learn how to ride a horse? I can't just cancel on them," I laughed.

"Oh, so it's all about teaching kids, huh?"

"Yeah," I started and his mischievous grin grew. I narrowed my eyes at it, already feeling like he was up to something, but he didn't crack under my scrutiny. "Right, then. I'm gonna go…" I hitched a thumb over my shoulder at his door, then scuttled out before he could find ways of convincing me to stay.

~

"Guys, did you know that bumble bees are listed as an endangered species now? That's how fast they're dying!"

"Bloody hell," Jeremy grumbled around his bite of chicken salad.

"Not this again," Derek groaned as he came up the stairs into the breakroom.

"Okay, okay, so maybe I really am the last to find this out, but this is a big deal, guys! I've been thinking-"

"Uh-oh, that's never a good thing," Jeremy whispered from the right of me while I put the cover back on my now-empty container that had held Mrs. Ventrilla's famous shrimp carbonara. I chuckled and shook my head at him.

"What if we put on a riding camp and call it something cute like Baby Bumble Bees Bootcamp for ages six to ten or something? And then all the registration fees we can donate to the Bee Saving Fund!"

There was a solid minute of silence while everyone paused to stare at Chelsea, who of course, was unfazed by this reaction. Derek finally broke the tension. "That is the stupidest fucking thing I've ever heard."

Sharna's mouth dropped open at his blatant disregard for Chelsea and choice of words while a couple of the other visiting trainers gasped. Jeremy let out a snort and even I couldn't help but laugh out loud.

"Derek!" Chelsea snapped.

"No, it is. Baby Bumble Bees Bootcamp? You're joking, right? No way in hell am I attaching my name to that. Can you even imagine what kind of mothers would be signing their kids up for that? And the kids..." He visibly shuddered at the thought and sat down beside a new trainer who had just arrived last week and was currently looking at this whole interaction like he was a bit scared.

"You. Are. Heartless," Chelsea huffed, punctuating each word with a jab of her finger in his direction. "You, sir, are the reason the bees are dying!"

"Colt," Derek said while taking a bite of his sandwich and completely ignoring Chelsea's anger. He waved his free hand between the two of us carelessly. "Explain why this is stupid."

I bit my lip to hide my smile as I turned to face Chelsea across the table. "Well, I mean, not *all* the fees could go to the charity, of course. We'd still need to be paid for instructing at the camp."

"Oh." I watched as she visibly deflated while I walked to toss my trash away. "Right, that's true but-"

"And you'd probably need to find a legitimate organization that is working to protect bees right now to donate the money to because I doubt there's actually one called the Bee Saving Fund."

Her face changed to the look she always got when she knew I was right and she leaned back in her chair. "You make a point," she acquiesced.

"I know," I laughed. "Maybe you just need to think about it a bit more. But hey, I have a new rider now?" I asked while glancing up at the clock on the back wall.

"Oh, yeah! I can't believe I forgot about that. Got called in this morning. Yeah, they're coming at one so...well, right now."

I shook my head. She might not be able to believe that she had forgotten about it, but I sure could. "Are you coming to greet them and do all the registration stuff now?"

"Yeah, yeah. One minute, I'll be right there." She waved me off and I turned to jog my way back down to the barn. My foot stopped short of the last step when I caught sight of who was here and I eased down slowly while a smile broke across my face.

"What are you doing here?"

"Coat!" Viviana's tiny footsteps ran at me once she had broken free from Rainer's grasp and I bent down to catch her as she came crashing into me. It was crazy for me to think the first time I had ever met her, she had trouble keeping her own feet under her and now she could run the length of the barn no problem.

"Hey, Viv," I laughed as I scooped her up in my arms to walk back to Rainer. "What are you doing here?"

"Horsies!"

"Yeah, horses," I corrected lightly. I looked from her face to Rainer's as he stood with a smug grin waiting for us to get to him.

"I just so happened to have a little child who wanted to learn how to ride a horse."

My mouth popped open as I recognized my words from this morning. "You didn't...you signed Viviana up for a lesson?"

"Horsie, horsie!" She clapped her hands excitedly while I perched her higher on my hip and stopped in front of Rainer.

"You're insane, you know that? If I didn't know better, I'd think you're stalking me, Mr. Ventrilla."

"I thought it was only fair to return the favor." He grinned at me devilishly, referring to that night at the bonfire when he claimed I would love him one day. Was that really what was happening now? The thought caused my stomach to drop and my hands started to shake. I set Viv down and straightened back up, surreptitiously wiping my now-sweaty palms on my jeans.

"You know she's too young to ride."

He opened his mouth to reply, but it wasn't his voice that answered me. "On her own, of course not. But just have her ride with you." Chelsea came skipping down the stairs and flounced into the barn, the disappointment from Baby Bumble Bees Bootcamp being shot down already forgotten.

"Hey, Hot Stuff." She strode past me to lean in to give him a hug and a kiss on the cheek as if she was some sophisticated human. *Yeah, right*, I scoffed in my head. I seethed at the sight of her touching him at all and then immediately hated myself for even having such a reaction.

Rainer just went with it, ever the good sport, and chuckled. "If only I got that same greeting from my girlfriend."

He grinned at me salaciously and my jaw dropped. I swear if it wasn't connected to me by skin and bone it would have hit the dusty barn floor right then. "What did you…" I sputtered.

He stepped around Chelsea and closed the two feet of space that separated us to pull me in for a kiss before I could even try to snap my mouth shut again. Even though I knew I should fight him, remind him how ridiculous he was being for saying such a thing, tell him he had no right to make those decisions for me, I found my body melting into his. My hands coming up to steady myself against his chest and my lips melding perfectly with his.

"Kiss, kiss, kiss!" Viv chanted from somewhere around our knees and the reminder that we had an audience was enough to break me from the spell he managed to put on me. I jerked back but his hands still held my waist, keeping me close to his chest, and he dipped his head to laugh directly into my ear.

"I called you my girlfriend," he confirmed from my earlier sputtering. "I felt it was much more civilized than simply calling you 'mine' like some caveman. I had a feeling you'd prefer it."

I leaned back to look into his eyes, the blues and greens standing out now with his playfulness. He was serious. "You are such an overconfident asshole!" I grumbled. He only laughed at my anger. "I don't know how to be a girlfriend," I admitted.

His grin grew to that full smile that was so rare but so beautiful. "That's okay. I don't know how to be your boyfriend, either. It's just something we figure out as we go."

I weighed his words for a minute. Could I do this? Be Rainer Ventrilla's girlfriend? "What if I don't want to be your girlfriend?"

His smile faltered, but only for a brief second, and then he threw his head back and laughed again. Actually *laughed*, the asshole. "Well, we both know that's a lie," he finally said once he had stopped laughing. I slapped his chest and made to turn out of his arms so he couldn't see the smile I was fighting to hide. He let me go, his body still shaking in silent laughter. Now that I was out of his grasp, I could see Chelsea had joined in on his fun and was smiling at me while she twirled Viv around her finger in circles. "I told you, Colt," Rainer laughed from behind me. "You're going to fall in love with me one day."

"Fat chance." I met Chelsea's eyes, and she was looking at me like she knew more than I ever could. I shook my head at her, too. "You just going to stand there or are you going to help me tack up some horses?" I snapped at her. Just like Rainer had, she laughed at my anger.

"What are these?" I looked to see what Rainer was indicating now. He had swung himself into the saddle easily enough, but not after about a thousand questions.

"The reins, Rain," I laughed while I slipped a halter over Gizmo's head. Chelsea chuckled as she tugged on the lead line still attached to Lucy, the mare we had chosen for Rainer to ride, and she started to move down the barn.

"You really are clueless," Chelsea giggled as she turned Lucy around just outside the barn to walk back my way. I tossed the saddle up, making sure it was situated over the saddle pad just right. Gizmo pawed the ground impatiently, upset Lucy was already ahead of him.

"Listen, I wasn't intending to ride a horse today," I heard him grumble back while I peeked over the stall door where I had locked Viv in. It was probably frowned upon to lock a toddler in a horse stall, but hey, it was clean. I just needed to keep her out of the way while I finished tacking up Gizmo.

"Oh yeah? What *were* you planning on doing here in my barn, Hot Stuff?" Chelsea asked playfully as she moved Lucy into a trot. I looked up and caught a glimpse of Rainer's teasing smile. Of course the two of them together would be a nightmare.

"Well, I just so happen to know there's a couch up there…"

"Rainer!" I reprimanded, unintentionally pulling Gizmo's girth too tight in my shock at his blatant innuendo. Gizmo snorted in disgust and pawed the ground. "Sorry, buddy," I hushed and quickly loosened it again. Rainer let out a lilting laugh that echoed around the barn and had me melting despite my outrage.

"Damn, boy. You don't play around," Chelsea applauded, her southern twang slipping out.

"You are not actually going along with him right now," I gasped. Through her laughter, she tugged the lead line and then brought Lucy to a stop right beside Gizmo as I unhooked his crossties and adjusted the stirrups. Rainer was wiggling his eyebrows at me suggestively. "Knock it off or I'm sending you home," I chided.

"No way, he stays. I like him too much," Chelsea cut in happily. She reached over to open the stall door and unleash Viviana while I swung into the saddle. "And so do you," she added more quietly as she scooped Viv up and walked over to me. I narrowed my eyes at her and she laughed again. "Up you go, little one."

"Chels, I don't know," I started, but she had already swung Viv into the saddle in front of me, half on my lap. My arms immediately came to clutch her to me tighter, scared she would fall. "I don't think this is a good idea. What if she falls. Or if she starts wiggling. Or doesn't-"

"Colt?" Chelsea cut me off. I stopped midsentence and looked down at her. "Stop. Stop thinking you can't handle things. You can." She looked into my eyes, seeming to see me more than she ever had before. "I trust you. Rainer trusts you. Viviana trusts you. It's about time you start to trust yourself." Before I could answer, she gave Gizmo's rump a smack and that was all the prodding he needed to take off down the barn, Viviana's peals of joy echoing through the high ceilings.

"How do I make it turn?" Rainer finally called out from behind me after we had been riding for almost a half hour.

"First of all, it's a she. Second of all, how have you been turning this whole time?" I laughed. I tugged Viviana's left hand that she had fisted around the reins under mine and Gizmo easily turned back to face Rainer in the open field we had just stepped into.

"I don't know! It...*she*," he stressed when he saw the look I was giving him. "She just follows you."

I laughed as Lucy plodded to a stop when she saw Gizmo had turned back to face her. She really was a good horse, great for any newbies. Though our newbies tended to be fifteen years younger and probably a hundred pounds lighter than Rainer was, but Lucy was being a good sport about the change of rider. "I thought this lesson was for Viv?"

"Yeah, so did I," he grumbled, tapping his heels into Lucy who still refused to move an inch. I giggled and Viviana followed suit, though I doubt she had any idea of what she was laughing at. She was sitting half on my lap, half in the saddle in front of me, and I had gradually been able to loosen my grip around her waist. When Chelsea had first swung her up into place in front of me, I thought she was insane. There was no way I could do this. I couldn't be trusted to keep her safe. We all saw what happened the last time Rainer had trusted me with her. Yet here I was, actually enjoying myself. Feeling in control but also relaxed. I never thought those two feelings could ever go together but I was finding that I liked it.

Doors

I trotted Gizmo around Rainer in a circle just to tease him and Viv giggled excitedly. "What exactly did you think you would be doing, hm?" I asked.

He attempted to flick Lucy's reins, but she only snorted and bent her head to eat some grass. I threw my head back to laugh and he glared down at her in frustration before raising his eyes to meet mine. His lips pulled into a flirty grin that said it all. *Overconfident ass,* I thought to myself but couldn't help my smile. I raised my eyebrows at him in a challenge and then without warning, I urged Gizmo into a full gallop across the open field. He didn't need to be told twice, he had been waiting days for me to open him up like this. If there was one thing Gizmo loved, even more than water, it was to run. When he got going, it was the closest thing I could imagine to flying. Jeremy had said more than once I should get him into racing, but I just couldn't see Giz on a track. He needed wide open spaces. He needed free rein. We were alike in that way.

Now, I leaned low over the saddle, huddling Viviana closer to me to make sure she was safe, and let Gizmo do his thing. "Fly! We flying!" Viv squealed in my ear and I laughed along with her, allowing myself to feel what she was feeling as if it was my first time, too. I didn't look back once. I was starting to learn that all I really needed to do what look forward and allow myself to fly.

When I finally slowed Gizmo to a canter and then a walk, it was only done reluctantly. I had let him whip across the meadow as fast as he could before doubling back, looping Rainer as he stared at us slack-jawed. Then I had wound him through the trees lining the edge of the clearing as if they were barrels, making sure Viviana was

261

secure the whole time, before opening him up again to really hit his stride. Rainer may not have come to ride, but I sure had. It was almost *fun* to show off to him. There was a part of me, one I had never felt before, that was excited to share this thing I loved with him. To let someone see me in my element for the first time. It wasn't as if I ever shared this side of me with anyone else. Only the barn family knew this version of me. And now Rainer would, too.

My hair was in knots from the wind, but I couldn't wipe the smile off my face. This was what living really felt like. This was incredible. "Hold on," I told Viviana before swinging down to the ground. She immediately complied and I marveled again at how fast she was growing. Just a few weeks ago she would have paid no mind to anything I said, unable to wrap her little brain around simple things like that. I reached up and she easily launched herself into my waiting arms, no fear at all that I would drop her. Just pure trust. Maybe I was learning from this little thing after all. I might never trust that completely, but I could try.

I set her down on her feet and the grass here came all the way up to her chin, wildflowers and weeds weaved through it. Finally, I heard Lucy's slow steps plodding over to us. "Okay, what the hell was that?" Rainer asked in complete disbelief. I only turned once I had ensured Viviana was okay and smiled up at Rainer.

"Nice of you to finally catch up," I taunted. My eyes watched his muscles ripple beneath his clothes while he clumsily dismounted and tied Lucy's reins to the tree behind me next to Gizmo.

"Viv, stay close." I noted his use of my nickname for her and for some reason it made me warm inside. Her dark curls were already bobbing through the grass, chasing a butterfly further into the meadow. He finally turned to face me and his eyes were shining with what I could only assume was...pride? I don't think I'd ever had someone proud of me before, but there was no other word for what he was looking at me with right now.

"Colt, you're incredible. That was incredible. What the hell was that? Where did that even come from? You were *flying*. I've never seen anyone move on a horse like that before. It's like you were one person. One animal. That was *insane*."

I laughed awkwardly and avoided his wowed expression, choosing instead to watch Viv as she tried and failed to capture the elusive butterfly. "Have you ever watched anyone ride a horse before?"

"You're such a brat," he laughed. "Just take the compliment, Colt. You've got to know you're incredible. Why am I just finding this out now?"

I shrugged my shoulders as if his words didn't just build me up more than anyone else's ever had. "I guess there's just a lot I don't share with people." I turned to face him again and he was watching me with that same hint of love I had seen creep into his eyes before. Only this time, I was starting to believe I might actually deserve it. "I'm glad you came today."

His white teeth flashed at me in a full-out smile now. "I think that's the first time you've ever admitted that you're happy to see me."

I bit my lip and shook my head at him but knew he was right. I directed my words to the ground when I spoke next. "I'm always happy to see you," I mumbled.

His dirt-caked work boots stepped into my line of sight at the same second I felt one of his long fingers press under my chin to lift it up until I was looking into his eyes. "Say it again," he commanded.

I gulped at the command, given so soft and sweet it almost wasn't a command at all. For once, it was one I was willing to obey. "I'm always happy to see you, Rainer," I whispered.

His smile grew and his eyes swallowed me whole, as if I was the only thing he ever needed to see in his life. His finger left my chin so that his whole hand could cup one side of my face and he tucked my hair back behind my ear like he wanted, *needed*, to see even more of me. He never let me hide from him. "I think I might be falling in love with you, Colt Jefferson."

I was frozen at his confession but he gave me the time I needed to let it sink in. It was like he knew I wasn't able to process things like a normal human being and he was okay with it. Who did that? How did I ever find this person? Finally, I pulled myself back together enough to answer him. "You probably shouldn't do that." Anyone else would have been mad I ruined what could have been a beautiful moment. Anyone else would have given up on me right then and there. And that's what I would have wanted with anyone else. It's what I'd *always* wanted. To just be left alone. It's what I'd always known; to keep up my walls and prevent anyone from worming their way into my world. But not Rainer.

Rainer's eyelids fell shut as he chuckled, the sound washing over me in waves as he dropped his forehead down to rest against mine. My whole body quaked at the contact. *Two*, I thought in my head as I counted the places where his skin pressed into mine just as I had every time he touched me since that night in my car. He didn't open his eyes when he spoke. "You're probably right."

"How do you know?" I whispered back.

"That I'm falling in love with you?" My heart stuttered in my chest at his words and I could only nod my head as an answer, my forehead bumping against his. "I just do."

"But how?" I croaked.

His eyes finally opened again to meet mine, as if he needed me to see the complete honesty there. "Some things you can't explain. Or have a reason for. Some things you don't decide. They just happen. *You* just happened for me."

I pulled my bottom lip between my teeth and bit down on it, needing to feel some sort of pain to know this moment was actually real and not just some weird fantasy I was dreaming up. His other hand lifted and his thumb gently pulled my lip from between my teeth. "Colt?" he asked quietly, knowing his words had just rocked my entire world. I stared back into his eyes, taking the time to catalogue the bright ring of blue and the green as it swirled into deep brown and just like that, I started to feel grounded again. Just like that, Rainer gave me peace even when he set my heart on fire. My eyelids fluttered shut briefly as I sucked in a deep breath.

"You know, I haven't even accepted the fact that you think I'm your girlfriend. Now you think you might love me?" I snorted as I opened my eyes with a grin on my face. "You're pretty sure of yourself, there, aren't ya?"

His grin matched mine. "Are you trying to say I should be worried?" he quipped.

I raised an eyebrow and daintily lifted one shoulder in a shrug but then laughed. "No," I replied seriously. "I don't think you need to worry."

"Good," he breathed before pressing a quick kiss to my lips that made my knees weak. "Because you might want to hold onto that feeling once I tell you my mom wants us all at another wedding reception tonight."

As if he knew how I would react to that fun bit of information, he immediately was dancing out of my reach. But not before I caught his chest with a smack. "Rainer!" I tried to scold, but it came out more as a laugh.

"Tag! We play tag! Wain is it!" Viviana giggled from beside us, and I realized she must have given up on her pursuit of the butterfly and come back to get us. I laughed at her interpretation of my playful smack to him but he was already running with it.

"Not if I get you next, Munchkin! You better watch out!" And just like that, they were off, Viviana toddling through the grasses that were as tall as her and the man I thought I just may be falling in love with, too chasing after her.

Chapter Sixteen

"No." My foot froze mid-step and I swiveled my eyes to where the bored voice had come from. "Yeah, it's me. Get in here. Now." I turned around before I could reach the top of the stairs and saw that Rachel's door was half-propped open and I could see her sitting in front of a huge vanity mirror in her room. I think this was the first time I'd ever seen her door open. I had grown so used to it being shut tight each time I walked down the hall that I hadn't even thought to look at it as I passed.

I took two steps back and poked my head through her door. "What?"

She lifted her eyes to meet mine in the mirror. "You're not wearing that."

I glanced down at what I had on because I still wasn't used to anything this nice being on my body. The other afternoon, I had come back to The Mansion to see the closet door in Ross's old room had been left open. I had never opened it before, my stuff was still carefully tucked into my duffle under the bed, so I knew it hadn't been me to leave the door open.

I had cautiously tiptoed over and looked in. It was huge, easily the size of my old bedroom at my house, and mostly bare. But not completely. There were at least a dozen dresses hung on the rack to the right, some floor length, some shorter, all impossibly gorgeous. And on the shelf directly in front of me had been clothes I recognized. My own clothes. Carefully folded and neatly stacked. Altogether, they didn't even fill one shelf. A note had been left on them. In perfect, loopy cursive it had read, "You belong here."

That was it. Just three words and I had been reduced to a crying mess on the plush carpet of that walk-in closet. It wasn't the fact that Mrs. Ventrilla had said I belonged, when I had never belonged anywhere before. It had nothing to do with the fancy dresses I knew cost a small fortune that she had to have bought specifically for me because I had already noted how most of them had sleeves. It was knowing that she had come in and done this. In this room that she hadn't been in since her son had died. And she had done it for *me*.

"Your mom got me this dress," I said now to Rachel as I leaned against the doorjamb of her room. She finally swiveled from the mirror to face me and looked me over from head to toe in that scathing way she had, though I knew her enough by now to know she didn't mean it.

"Right… And who would you trust to dress you more? Me? Or my mother?"

"Uhm, neither?" I tried. Her eyes rolled so hard in her head at my answer that I was sure it had to be painful. She strutted over to her closet and disappeared inside where I heard hangers clicking together as she shuffled through things. A minute later, she came back out with what I assumed was something she thought I would wear tonight.

"Here." She thrust it towards me.

"What is that?" I folded my arms over my chest, the flowy sleeves of the dress I was wearing bunching together on my arms.

She shook the dress in question and I recognized it as lace despite the dark navy color. "This is the dress you're wearing tonight."

"*That* is not a dress. That is a scrap of fabric."

"Oh, I'm sorry. They must have missed the memo for ratty sleeves when they made this one," she simpered while slapping a hand to her forehead dramatically. I narrowed my eyes at her and snatched the dress from her hand, finally stepping in from the hallway.

"You really are a bitch," I grumbled half-heartedly.

Her smile blinded me. She must have got that from her mom. "Oh, I know. Bathroom's there. Hurry up, Mom wanted us there five minutes ago, so you don't have any time to be a chicken shit about it." She didn't wait to see me go, just turned back to her mirror and picked up a tube of mascara she had abandoned when I had walked by.

Her bathroom door clicked behind me and I slipped off the dress I had been wearing. It was a yellow, airy thing with sleeves that flared out around my wrists. My mother would have loved it. It was innocent. Pretty. Fancy. Girly. Everything I was not. It reminded me of my old room that had never reflected who I really was.

I didn't stop to look at the dress Rachel had given me before pulling it over my head. I knew if I did I would never walk out of this bathroom. I would end up being a "chicken shit" in Rachel's words. The material clung to me like nothing I had ever worn before, stretching over breasts I never even knew I had, hugging my hips and staying tight until just a little before mid-thigh where it abruptly cut off. I felt naked. Exposed. I had never shown this much skin in public. I had never willingly shown this much skin...ever. Regardless, I took a deep breath and pushed open the bathroom door.

"Now *that* is how you wear a dress." Rachel pushed off from her vanity and stalked towards me, circling around behind me to see how I looked from all angles. I forced myself to roll my eyes and appear bored by her antics, but my body was on high alert. "Damn, I'm good. It's like this dress was made for you. Okay, sit real quick."

"Rach, I don't think I can in this thing," I said honestly, wondering how girls ever did it in such tight, short clothing.

Her hands reached forward to push me towards the stool in front of her mirror and I surprised myself by letting her. "Oh, hush. I need to fix you." I gulped at those words, wishing she actually could, and looked down at my lap as I sat so that I didn't have to see my own reflection.

Rachel grabbed a palette of eyeshadow, something I never bothered with in all the years I had been using makeup to cover up my bruises, and went to work. "Close," she demanded. I gritted my teeth and breathed deep through my nose. *Five. Four. Three. Two.* I let my eyes fall shut. *One.* I felt the brush as she dabbed it along my lids. *This was fine. I was fine*, I tried to tell myself, but my heart was beating almost too loud to hear my own voice in my head. My hands trembled in my lap and I clutched them together to stop the shaking. It was one thing for Rainer to know just how messed up I was.

Rachel didn't need to know I was such a freak that I didn't trust anyone enough to close my eyes around them.

"Devin's going to be there tonight. It's his sister getting married. That's why Mom wants everyone to be there. She didn't even have the nanny watch Viviana tonight. It's like we're actually guests for once. She wasn't super uptight about it, either. Said it was okay if we didn't make it to the actual wedding as long as we were all at the reception. I haven't seen her this laid back in years. If only I could feel the same way about having to see Devin," Rachel chattered on while I tried to focus on taking deep, calming breaths. I felt her finger smudging the shadow over my eyelids to how she wanted it.

I forced myself to keep my eyes shut and attempted to turn my focus to what she was saying. She was giving me another one of her vulnerable moments. I could tell from the tone of her voice. "Who's Devin?" I managed to ask in a passably calm voice.

"A guy." I heard her tapping off the excess powder from a brush before it dipped to my other eyelid. I waited a beat but she didn't continue.

"Huh. Riveting," I said dryly. I could feel her answering eyeroll even if I couldn't see it and my lips twitched into a small smile.

"His family is friends of the family, so I've known him my whole life. Perks of being homeschooled forever; I barely knew anyone. When I started going to public school, he was like, the only person I knew. And then, this winter, we kind of became more. Well, I thought we were seeing each other. We talked all the time, hung out, kissed, you know…" She trailed off, leaving me to fill in the blanks. Only, I *didn't* know. I had never done any of that. Had never been "seeing" anyone. Until now. Rainer's words from this afternoon rang in my head. *My girlfriend. I think I might be falling in love with you.* Were we "seeing" each other, as Rachel put it? I had a feeling my relationship with Rainer wasn't exactly typical by any means, so maybe not. I guess I still couldn't relate.

"Open." My eyes flicked open to see her face inches from mine and I wanted to flinch back, but she was looking at me as if she was studying a painting in a museum, not actually seeing me. "Okay, look up." The mascara wand swiped over my lashes.

"So then at the beginning of the summer he just randomly says to me, 'Hey, this has been fun but I'm not looking for a relationship right now.' Like, what does that even mean? And then we just kind of stopped talking. Isn't that ridiculous?" she grumbled. I wasn't sure if she actually wanted an answer or not, so I just stayed silent as she moved on to my other eye. "I mean, really? Like, I'm not looking for a million bucks, either, but if I randomly found it on the ground I wouldn't be like, 'oh, I'm sorry, but I actually wasn't looking for you right now.' Okay, you're done."

I couldn't help it, I doubled over in laughter. "Did you really just compare yourself to a million dollars?"

She stood from in front of me and tossed her long, black hair over her shoulder dramatically. In all honesty, she looked like a million bucks. Especially now with her short emerald dress that matched her eyes so well it was almost eerie and her hair curled in perfect waves. "You're right," she said seriously as she looked at her reflection in the mirror. "I'm definitely worth more." I laughed even harder as I stood and faced her.

"Aren't you going to look?" she asked, looking down at me since she towered over me in the heels she had on.

"I'm sure it looks great," I tried to wave off.

"God, you're such a bitch. It's why we make such good friends." I was too stunned by her claim of our friendship to protest when she grabbed my shoulders and spun me around to face the mirror. "See? Definitely worth more than a million bucks."

Again with that confidence. I wondered if she and Rainer were simply born with it. They had to have been. But when I finally looked in the mirror, I hardly recognized the girl staring back at me. I wasn't seeing scars and bruises that I wanted to cover. Instead, I was focused on how big and bold my eyes looked with the perfect smoky shadow she had applied. How my normally dull, grey eyes looked like they were shining and I could even see hints of blue swimming in them. I was seeing the intricate lace pattern and the edgy cuffs that just barely covered my shoulders and laid across the tops of my thighs.

And there was Rachel, leaning casually against me with her arm resting on one of my shoulders. We were night and day. Her with her dark tan and midnight locks brushing against my impossibly pale skin, yet we were both smirking. It was unconscious for the first time, my lips twitching up at the corner just like hers.

"Told ya," she sang. "Million. Bucks. Now let's go show Devin just how stupid he was to pass up on this." She waved a hand up and down her body and I shook my head while I laughed at her antics. "And make my brother

lose his mind. But please, spare me the details on that."
My laughter doubled and she smiled back at me, taking
my hand to pull me out of the room with her.

"You're late," Mrs. Ventrilla scolded as we tried to
sneak in from the side stairwell I had first run into Rainer
on so many weeks ago. My stomach twisted in knots. I
told Rachel this wasn't going to be good. Mrs. Ventrilla
was a stickler for being on time and I had never been one
to disappoint. Until now. She was going to be so mad.
And here she was...mad.

I opened my mouth to apologize as quick as I could
and hopefully smooth this over. "Mrs. Ventrilla, I'm-"

"How are we late when you said we only had to be at
the reception?" Rachel cut me off before I could even get
out my apology. I swiveled my head to look at her with
wide eyes. Was she crazy? Rule number one of diffusing
tension: never talk back.

"Because your brother has been here the whole time
and you even missed dinner. They've already had the first
dance."

"Yes, but Rainer actually was friends with Tia
growing up. *I* was not. Besides, I had to make sure I
looked presentable. You wouldn't want me coming and
looking like a troll now would you?"

Mrs. Ventrilla rolled her eyes at that comment and I
had to fight back my laughter because she looked so much
like her daughter when she did that. But then she turned
her attention to me and I remembered this was no
laughing matter. We were still late and therefore in
trouble. "What dress is that?" she asked.

Uh-oh, I thought. And I hadn't even worn one of the dresses she had been so nice to go out of her way to get for me. I was literally the worst person when she had been nothing but nice to me. How could I have been so stupid? This was such a mistake. I deserved whatever she was about to do to me.

"I'm so-"

"It's one I bought a while ago but never wore. Isn't it perfect on her?" Rachel cut in, yet again talking over any apology I could make.

"Stunning! I wouldn't have ever picked it myself, but it suits you so well, Colt!"

Wait...what? I stared back at her in confusion, my brain still trying to catch up to what was going on here. *She wasn't mad at me?*

"I'm sorry we're late but you had her dressed up like a butterfly."

"I did not!" Mrs. Ventrilla laughed back at Rachel. She was...laughing? This was okay?

"You so did! She literally had wings! Yellow, puffy wings! I couldn't let her out like that."

"Oh, stop. I thought that dress was so cute! It had sleeves. Colt loves sleeves. Don't you, darling?"

"Wait...you're not mad?" I had to clarify. I still wasn't entirely sure what was going on right now.

"Mad? Of course I'm not mad you wanted to wear a different dress. I wouldn't have thought you would show so much skin, just because of what you always wear around the house, but this looks amazing on you." She turned her smiling gaze from me to Rachel and squinted her eyes. "Though it wouldn't hurt to have a bit more fabric on the things you wear."

Rachel rolled her eyes dramatically. "Oh, please. You're just jealous because you know I have way better style than you do."

"You are so full of yourself," Mrs. Ventrilla laughed at her.

"I learn from the best," Rachel quipped, popping a hand on her hip and I couldn't help it, I was laughing along with them. When just moments ago I was terrified of what might happen to me, here I was laughing.

"Coat!" I looked up to see Viviana coming towards us from the dance floor, trying desperately to break free from her grandfather's hold on her little hand. Once they had gotten close enough, he unleashed the beast and she came barreling directly to me.

"What am I? Chopped liver?" Mrs. Ventrilla scoffed in mock disgust once I had lifted Viv into my arms in her poofy pink dress.

"Hi, Gammie."

"Pink? Really?" I asked as I tried and failed to smooth down the mass of pink tulle in my arms.

Rachel laughed at the comment I hadn't even thought through before making. I wanted to slap a hand over my mouth because I had essentially just questioned Mrs. Adriana's decisions but before I could take it back, Mr. Ventrilla was laughing as he came to stand next to his wife. I had seen him in passing plenty of times and even at some of the dinners I had started to join the family at, but this was my first time seeing him all dressed up and not stressed about work things.

"Right? I swear that kid doesn't own a single thing that isn't pink." He leaned in to give Mrs. Ventrilla a kiss on the cheek and she melted into his touch, fitting under his arm like a puzzle piece made just for him as he pulled her in close. I wondered if this was how parents were supposed to look together. Happy. In love. I liked that idea. Even at the banquets when my family tried to put on the perfect show, my mother and father never looked like this.

She smiled up at him after smacking his chest lightly. "Not you, too! My goodness, everyone is attacking my fashion choices today!"

Mr. Ventrilla threw his head back to laugh and for some reason it was extremely familiar to me. It had to have been just because he was Rainer's father, but it reminded me of something else I couldn't quite place. "I think you look stunning, sweetheart. So stunning, I just had to come over and ask you for a dance."

"Oh, Matt, I don't know. I really should-"

"You really should dance with your husband." He smiled down at her and I knew she didn't stand a chance. Sure enough, she turned back to us quickly.

"Girls, you don't mind just watching Viviana for a moment, do you?"

"Go, go! Have fun!" Rachel shooed them off, literally waving her hands behind them until Mr. Ventrilla had pulled her to the center of the dance floor and began twirling them around flawlessly. I stood with Rachel just watching the two of them silently while Viviana tugged absentmindedly on the loose strands of my hair that were closest to her.

"I couldn't tell you the last time I saw them dance," Rachel finally said. I looked over to see her eyes firmly on her parents. Mr. Ventrilla dipped her mom low before pulling her back into his chest and spinning them again and Mrs. Ventrilla threw her head back to laugh. Other couples around them were watching as they seamlessly moved across the floor, that's how perfect they looked together. Like they were made to dance with each other.

"Really?" I asked. I found that hard to believe from the show they were putting on, though it seemed they were oblivious to all the attention they were garnering.

"Yeah. My mom used to *love* to dance. It's actually how they met, right here on this dance floor. Her dancing out there. My dad watching her like a lovesick puppy."

"No way," I laughed.

Rachel smiled at me wistfully. "That's what she always told us. I believe her. She used to have Daddy wrapped around her finger just as much as I did. They met at a wedding here, back when Gram and Gramps still ran the place. That was before Mom made it look like this of course. The rest is history.

"She was always dancing. Here. In the house. Every single wedding we came to...and we came to a lot." Rachel eyed me to make sure I got her point. I only laughed and hitched Viv higher on my hip. "She was always dragging my dad onto the dance floor with her. At home, she would beg the boys to dance with her, even if it was just around the kitchen. I think they both knew how to dance before they knew how to walk. That's what Daddy says at least."

"So why haven't you seen her dance in so long then?" I asked, but I had a feeling I already knew the answer.

I saw Rachel's smile falter out of the corner of my eye, but she didn't let it fall. It was nice to see her with something other than her permanent scowl. "Ross. When she went into those Dark Days, as I like to call them. She didn't even come to the weddings for a long time and then once she did, all she did was work. That's why I avoid them at all costs now. She's a monster at them, always forcing me to be a perfect, angel child. As if."

I forced back a laugh trying to picture Rachel as anything close to an angel child. Definitely not even possible. "She doesn't seem to be a monster now," I observed.

"No." She cocked her head to one side and continued to study her parents. They were seriously the life of the party out there. "She's been different ever since you've been around."

I turned to face her, finally taking my eyes off of Mr. and Mrs. Ventrilla. "What do you mean, since I've been around?"

She turned to face me as well and reached out to tickle Viv's side so that she squealed and tried to hide behind my hair. "I think you finally snapped her out of it. Or maybe the timing was just a coincidence and it was time she realized she still needed to live a life. But she's been different ever since you moved in."

"Oh, no. No, no. I haven't moved in. I'm just staying there temporarily. It's not like I'm going to be-"

"Uh-huh," she cut me off with a smirk that was far too similar to Rainer's. "Right. Just temporary. Try telling that to lover boy, here." Then, without another word she reached over and pried Viviana from my arms before waltzing out onto the dance floor and spinning the toddler around in circles.

"I'm sorry...did my sister just voluntarily take Viv from you and is now *dancing* with her?" Rainer's deep voice spoke directly into my ear and sent shivers down my spine.

"I think I'm just as confused as you right now." I cocked my head to one side, watching Rachel actually *smile* in public. With Viviana. What kind of apocalypse was this?

I felt his answering chuckle against my back as he came up behind me and gently rested a hand on my hip. My first reaction was to stiffen and pull away but before I could, I felt his lips brush against my neck. "You look beautiful," he mumbled against my skin before closing his lips over the spot. Instead of pulling away, I found myself relaxing into him and his hand on my hip tugged gently so that I was flush against him.

I leaned my head back against his shoulder so I could look up at him. "You'll have to thank your sister for that."

"Hmm?" he mumbled, more interested in trailing kisses from my collarbone up to my ear instead of listening to me.

"Rainer," I chided, but then his lips found mine and I lost any argument I meant to have. His hand on my hip spun me so that we were chest to chest and he moved his other hand up to cup my cheek while he deepened the kiss. Just when I had lost all sense of where we were and how I should be acting, he pulled away and rested his forehead against mine. The blue ring around his eyes was bright and his lips were swollen as they tipped into a knowing smile. He knew exactly what his kisses did to me.

"Dance with me."

I chuckled against him and made to pull away, but his hands tightened around my waist. A wave of panic washed through me before I remembered it was Rainer who held me now. I *wanted* to be held by him. As much as I had tried to fight it, I knew it was true. I was done fighting him. I took a deep breath and shook my head so he couldn't see my moment of weakness. "That didn't sound like much of a question."

"That's because I already knew your answer would be yes." He started pulling my towards the dance floor effortlessly and I let him.

"Oh really? And how could you possibly know that?" My laugh was cut short by a gasp as he pulled me flush against him and wound one arm around my back and lifted my hand with the other. I knew I looked ridiculous staring up at him with wide eyes, my mouth hanging open, but he was breathtaking right now. A few strands of his dark hair fell forward into his eyes as he stared down at me with his lips turned up at just the corner, the top two buttons of his white dress shirt popped open just inches in front of me showing off his flawless, tanned skin. I swear he wasn't real. There was no way this could be real.

His chuckle rumbled through me from where we were pressed together and he started to move us around the dance floor with ease. His head dipped so that his lips were at my ear again. "Because I used my wonderful tools of persuasion. You can't resist me." His lips gently closed over the sensitive skin just below my ear and I melted into him even more, if that was at all possible. I couldn't even keep a count on how many places he was touching me right now because I was pretty sure he had taken over my entire body.

"You're such an overconfident ass," I managed to mutter even as his lips were making a sweep across my jaw towards my mouth now. Just before he got to my lips he pulled back again to look down at me, his eyes dancing in laughter.

"Yeah, well I guess that's okay for me because I know you love it." He didn't give me a chance to respond before his lips pressed to mine again and then we were spinning out around the dance floor and all I could do was let him lead.

Chapter Seventeen

"Stupidest thing you've ever done?"

"I don't do stupid things," I quipped from my spot on the edge of the dock.

"Oh, please. You have to have done something really dumb in your life." He let the stone he had been flipping in his hand fly. It skimmed through the air before dropping to the water where it skipped along five times before sinking.

"Again, again!" Viv clapped from next to him.

"I need another rock, Munchkin." A minute later she came hustling back with a handful of stones, none of them flat or good for skipping but Rainer praised her for them all the same. He plucked out a small one from the pile she had given him and whipped it out over the water. It skipped twice before dropping under the surface even though it was the lumpiest rock I had ever seen. Was there anything this man couldn't do?

I shook my head and trailed my feet back and forth through the cool water of the lake at the edge of the Ventrilla's backyard. It was the first time I had ever worn shorts and the feeling of sun and the warmed planks of the dock on my bare thighs wasn't something I was used to. Rachel had dragged me out shopping with her the other day. Apparently she needed a new outfit because she was going out with some kid she had met at the wedding the other night. I asked if it was that Devin guy she had been talking about, but she said it was one of his friends, even though she didn't like him. She was only going out with him to make Devin mad. It made zero sense to me whatsoever, nor did I understand why I had been dragged along to shop for a new outfit, but off to the mall we went.

I had never actually been to the mall before, so it was kind of interesting. Though the sheer amount of people there who had no concept of personal space as they rushed passed me had been a bit unnerving. Rachel ended up spending more time picking out clothes for me than for herself. She then insisted on buying everything I had tried on for me and nothing I had said could change her mind. Eventually I just refused to try anything else on. In the end, I came home with three new pairs of riding pants, five t-shirts, and four pairs of shorts. None of which I had even touched. Until today.

"So are you going to give me an answer or what?" Rainer called as he sent another stone flying and Viviana jumped up and down excitedly. She was wearing an army green dress I had found at the mall for her. The only purchases *I* had made were four new outfits, size 2T. I had learned that's how they sized kids' clothes; by age. So now they hung in Viv's closet like blinking lights, clearly standing out from the abundance of pink. Green and blue and black, though Mrs. Ventrilla had yet to dress her in that one. I guess black wasn't exactly a baby color. Whatever that meant.

"I told you," I laughed. "I never did stupid things. What's the stupidest thing *you've* ever done?"

"You're not supposed to ask me the same question. That's cheating." I swallowed down the nauseous feeling his words caused. They were so similar to ones Vee had said to me years ago, but he couldn't know that.

"Oh, I'm sorry. Is that Mr. Perfect not wanting to show he actually can have a flaw?"

"So you think I'm flawless, do you now?" he prodded. I rolled my eyes and used my feet to kick a plume of water his direction. "Fine, I'll go first since I'm clearly the adult here. Then it's your turn."

"Whatever you say, Rain," I laughed because he may have at least six years on me, but I think it was pretty clear to both of us who the adult was in our relationship.

His eyes stayed on Viviana where she was wandering the edge of the lake trying to find more skipping stones for him as he took a seat beside me on the edge of the dock. I looked down at the space he had left between us and grinned. Two inches. Pretty soon there would be none. "Man, there are quite a few. And you know, they all include Ross."

My eyes flicked to his face to try to catch any sadness at the mention of his brother, but he was only smiling. "Yeah? He was the wild child?" I hadn't even thought of it before speaking, but as soon as those words left my mouth it was like a punch to the gut. I hadn't heard them since I had last seen Vee. *I* had been *his* wild child.

Rainer didn't notice my change in demeanor. He only laughed and nodded before leaning back on his palms against the warm dock. "Yeah, you could say that. You think *I'm* an overconfident asshole? You should have met my brother. He was the master of charm. We were always doing stupid shit together, but eventually I grew out of it. I guess the worst one would have to be the roof incident."

"Roof incident?" I asked, trying my best to focus on his words and forget Vee, though for some reason that had been impossible these past few months.

Rainer chuckled. "Oh, yeah. I had to have only been fourteen so that made Ross, what? Ten? Anyway, at that age we were always making up these stupid dares for each other. So he dared me to jump off the roof."

"You're kidding me, right?" I gasped, looking back up at the roof of The Mansion. That thing was five stories in places.

"It was just from the roof outside our windows," he said, as if that somehow made it better. That was still at least twenty feet up. Maybe twenty-five.

"You did not jump that."

"There was snow on the ground," he tried to rationalize, as if that made it better.

"So? I wouldn't have jumped that even if there was water underneath it! You could have died!"

He only laughed harder at my outrage. "But I didn't."

"You brother sounds like an idiot," I said calmly and then smacked a hand over my mouth and turned to look at Rainer in apology. "I am so sorry. I shouldn't have said that. I didn't mean it like that."

But Rainer wasn't hearing my apology. He was doubled over in laughter while I sat there shocked at my own stupidity. "No, he really was. He was the stupidest shit I ever knew. Damn, I miss him." Finally he straightened back up and swiped away a lone tear that I wasn't sure was from laughing so hard or from missing his only brother. "You know it's going to be two years next Saturday."

I bridged the two inches of space between us and folded my hand into his and he squeezed back. "I'm sorry," I whispered.

"You know...I don't want people to be sorry anymore."

"What do you mean?"

"It's been two years. I'm tired of pretending like it didn't happen. I'm tired of tiptoeing around everything that had to do with him. Hell, I've got his pictures still hidden away in my closet. It's like he never even lived. But he lived the most out of everyone in our family. Out of all his friends. And no one even talks about that anymore. I've talked about him more to you in the past two months than I've talked about him in the past two years that he's been gone." I stayed silent, not knowing what to say. I knew what it was like to want things to just be normal. I had firsthand experience with wanting to avoid any pity from people. I could only imagine what it had been like for Rainer the past two years.

He lifted his head from watching where our feet were dangling above the water and focused on Viviana who was doing her best to skip rocks from the shore, but each time she tried to toss one it only made it about a foot before hitting the water and sinking beneath the surface. "She doesn't even know what her dad looked like," he croaked. "I don't want her to grow up not knowing who he was."

"So don't let her," I said simply. He turned his attention from her head of dark curls to look at me.

"What do you mean?"

"Don't let her grow up not knowing who her father was. Thinking that he didn't love her. She should be able to see his picture and know who he was and talk about him without feeling bad."

"I don't know how to do that," he admitted, for once not looking like the picture of confidence.

I took a deep breath and scooted closer to him, laying my head against his shoulder as he wrapped his arm around me, completely eliminating those two inches that had separated us. His lips found the top of my head and he pressed a kiss into my hair as I tried to think of what I wanted to say.

"You know when you get a really deep cut? Like so deep that it doesn't even bleed right away? You look and it feels like you can see all the way down to the bone for that split second before the blood comes rushing in? And you think, oh shit. This is bad. This is really bad. This is never going to heal."

"Uhm, I guess?" he asked from above me and I gave a sad smile that he didn't see. Maybe he didn't get it like I did. I guess it wasn't the best analogy, but it was one I knew well.

"Well, the thing is, you're right in a way. It's bad. It's really bad. And it's just this gaping hole for those few seconds. But eventually the blood comes, and finally it starts to heal, and you can keep it covered with a Band-Aid for a while, but there comes a time where you need to let it breathe. It might never be the same again, but it's healed. You just have to let it."

"You think it's time for us to take off the Band-Aid?"

I turned my head on his shoulder to look up at him and gave him a smile. Of course he had somehow understood me. For some reason, he always did. "I think it's time you guys let it breathe."

For the first night in weeks, I didn't want to come. I knew Vee would take one look at me and be able to tell. Even with the layer of makeup I had meticulously applied, the bruising was clear. Things had been going well the past few weeks, surprisingly enough. Jeremy had been nice enough to bring me car shopping with him a couple weeks ago where I emptied out almost all of my savings from the past two years of working at the barn to buy the most beat-up old clunker in the lot. I loved that thing no matter how much he made fun of it because it was the closest I had ever gotten to feeling free. I had been able to stay away from the house so much, I had rarely even seen my father in the past two months. So although Vee still asked about him every weekend, I didn't have to completely lie to him. Things really *had* been fine. Until this week.

"Donnie!" I whipped my head up at the sound of his voice and instantly winced. My vision swam but I could still see Vee hurrying to squat down in front of me, his hands raised like he wanted to reach out to me but couldn't. I wouldn't let him.

I gritted my teeth and forced a smile. "I'm good. It's good. Just looked up too fast."

I watched as his eyes flicked over every inch of me he could see. It was something he had taken to doing since the night he had shown up at my house, only this time he was actually seeing bruises. "What did he do?" he growled.

"Nothing. I told you, it's fine."

"Don't try to put on an act for me, Donnie. It's too late for that. Jesus, your eye." I saw him lift a hand as if he wanted to touch the black and blue that was surrounding my left eye but he hesitated.

I turned to look away, but the pain from the back of my skull shot through me again and I winced. If I had doubted it was a concussion before, I was pretty sure I had my answer now. "I fell a couple nights ago. Bashed my head on the coffee table on the way down. Not a big deal," I said through gritted teeth. Vee's long lashes fluttered closed at my admission and he ran a hand through his hair. "You got a haircut," I commented. He hadn't cut it in months even though I ragged on him every chance I got. I think he had been putting it off just to spite me.

Without thinking, I reached out to him just inches in front of me and ran my fingers through his shorter hair. His jaw ticked under my touch but he didn't open his eyes and for that I was grateful. I had never touched anyone before. Not like this, where I reached out and initiated it. I wasn't even scared. I could see his thin t-shirt rising and falling as he tried to slow his breathing down and I wondered if there was something he was scared of right now, because his heart seemed to be pounding even more than mine was. Finally, his eyelids lifted and his blue eyes met mine with tears pooled in them.

"Do you trust me?" he croaked.

My eyes widened and my hand dropped from where it had been running through his hair but he caught it in his own before I could pull away. "Donnie...do you trust me?"

I wanted to shake my head no but I knew if I did the pain would be excruciating. Did I trust him? No. I don't know. Maybe. Is this what trust was? I didn't even know him. Did I? Hadn't we spent every Saturday night together for the last eight weeks? Each weekend he spent almost the whole night in the shadows with me. I hadn't seen that girl who had always been begging him to come back to the group since last winter. I wondered what happened to her, actually. Why did she stop coming to these weekends of free beer and laughter?

Vee's hands finally reached up to cup my face and I flinched, but he didn't back away. "Listen to me. You are not living in that house anymore. You are not living with that monster anymore. Do you hear me? I am getting you out of there, okay?"

My heart was pounding and I think I was on the brink of some sort of anxiety attack because I could hardly catch my breath. He was too close. He was touching me. He was saying words I wanted to hear but couldn't believe. How could he somehow save me? He was just a boy.

"I want you to pack a bag, okay? Pack a bag with anything you need. Next Saturday, I want you to bring it with you. Just come to the bonfire like you always do, it's no different. Only this time you'll bring your stuff. I promise you, it'll be okay. Just one more week and then you're never going back to that place. He's not going to touch you again, okay? Do you hear me? I promise I will take you out of that place." He must have seen me struggling to take in a deep breath. "Hey, hey. Shh. Breathe. Just breathe. Just count down from ten, yeah?

And take deep breaths. It's going to be okay. Ten. Nine. Eight. Seven."

I sucked air in and breathed out in time with his slow counting until he finally got back to one and I opened my eyes again to look at him. He hadn't moved this whole time, still crouched down in front of me, his palms warm and soft against my bruised skin, the raging bonfire lighting him up from behind. For a second, I stupidly thought that's what angels must look like silhouetted with the bright light behind him.

"Okay?" he asked now. "Whenever things are overwhelming just do that. Count back from ten and just breathe." A voice called out from near where everyone parked and he winced but kept his eyes on me. "Listen, I need to go now. I don't want to, but I have to. I know you're probably mad, but it's complicated. You know how I said stuff was changing?" he chuckled darkly. He may have gotten a haircut, but there were still hints of dark circles under his eyes that had been there for weeks. Whatever was going on with him was still affecting him and yet he was focusing on me. "I'll explain everything next week, okay? I just need you to trust me. Saturday night. It'll all be okay, Donnie."

For some reason, I wasn't sure if he was trying to convince me or himself in that moment. Whoever had called him just now had clearly shaken the calm he had been trying to give me. He straightened up from in front of me and went to turn towards the cars, but I called out to him one last time. "Hey, Vee?" Immediately, he turned back around to face me. "Breathe," I reminded him. The answering smile he gave was enough to get me through this next week. I could trust him. All I had to do was trust him. It was all going to be okay.

Ten. Nine. Eight. Seven. Six. Five. Four. Three.

Breathe, the thought repeated in my head as I tugged on my ponytail yet again and looked over myself in the mirror, anything to put off going downstairs. I plucked at my t-shirt, thinking of how it had been getting tighter over the past few weeks. Tighter as in I no longer looked like an advert for hungry children of America. I had Mrs. Ventrilla's various pasta dishes to thank for that. It hadn't taken her long to realize I was a sucker for anything pasta, and being the wonderful Italian goddess that she is, she took it upon herself to become something of a personal chef for me. She decided it was her new goal in life to fatten me up and I wasn't about to complain. I was the only teenage girl I knew who was excited to get fat.

"You're such a chicken shit."

I turned from the mirror to find Rachel leaning against my door with a smirk. I wasn't surprised to see her here. Somewhere over the last month, she had determined I was her new best friend. I didn't point out that I was pretty sure I was her *only* friend. Regardless, over the past weeks she had transitioned from spending all her free time locked away behind her closed door to now lounging in my room. *Lucky me*, I thought sardonically.

It had been a bit weird at first, neither of us exactly excelled in the friend department, but she had been completely unfazed by my lack of enthusiasm for her visits. Instead, she took it upon herself to talk enough for the both of us. I had learned her entire history with that Devin boy, who was now talking to her yet again despite me telling her she was too good for him. I also learned about endless drama that I had absolutely no interest in about the queen bees of her grade. At this point, I'm not sure who was more nervous for her to start her junior year next week, me or her. I was starting to think it was me.

"I was just…"

Rachel raised an eyebrow at me and crossed her arms over her chest in disapproval. "Even my mom is down there laughing. I mean, don't get me wrong, there are lots of tears, but good tears. So if she can do it, you can. Stop hiding up here."

"I'm not hiding," I muttered, turning away from her and tugging on my t-shirt again. I saw her patented eyeroll in the mirror behind me.

"Right, of course not. And Rainer hasn't been glancing at the stairs every two minutes, wondering where you are and worrying about you instead of enjoying the fact that he pulled this together and it's amazing."

I narrowed my eyes at her, letting her know I was aware of what she was doing. She only smiled back at me sweetly, as if she was innocent. It's not like I had any reason to be nervous. I had been to plenty of weddings this summer, so it wasn't the amount of people around that was a problem. I had even gotten used to my scars being on display in my t-shirts, even if it still did feel a bit strange. I was growing more confident, more alive. I had no connection to Ross, so it's not like today would be hard for me like it would be for the rest of the Ventrilla family and the countless friends Rainer had reached out to for this so-called "celebration of life". It was a happy event. Heck, I was the one to encourage him to put it all together. And yet for some reason, I had been hiding upstairs since I first heard the doorbell ring over an hour ago.

"You're right," I sighed, turning back around to find Rachel had made herself comfortable on the bed. "I'm hiding."

She popped up at my admission like she was some porcelain jack-in-the-box. "Damn right you are. Now let's go celebrate my dead brother." She clapped happily before grasping my hand and tugging me forward, as if that had been a completely normal sentence to come out of her mouth. There were definitely a few screws loose in that pretty head of hers.

I dragged my feet as she skipped her way down the first set of stairs and across to the other hallway without a care in the world. The laughter that had been muffled in my room was louder here, easily drifting up into the loft area. With my free hand that wasn't currently locked in Rachel's grasp, I reached into the pocket of my jeans and felt the cool gold brush against my fingers. The feel of it was enough to calm me and I could hear Vee's words repeating in my head as we finally reached the bottom of the grand staircase. *Five. Four. Three. Two...*

Rachel's hand jerked me to a stop and I was forced to look up from where I had been watching my own feet cross over the shiny wood floors. "Guys, there's someone I want you to meet," she started and I inwardly groaned. Of all the times for her to remember the good manners her mom was constantly trying to drill into her, it had to be when it would make me uncomfortable. "This is Colt. She's Rainer's-"

"Ah, gang's all here," a deep voice cut her off before she could finish introducing me as Rainer's…whatever. Girlfriend still seemed too weird to me. "I was wondering if we'd see you here. You never did come to the funeral, did you?"

My eyes finally found who was speaking. He was perched on the arm of one of the fancy couches in the formal living room dressed so impeccably that the only recognizable thing about him was the red solo cup currently dangling from his fingers.

"Seymour?" I asked. There was no doubt it was him. Same unique olive skin. Same commanding presence like even here in a completely different setting from the open field in the woods, he was still in charge. I quickly took in the others in the room who were lounging on the fancy furniture without a care in the world and standing cluttered around new picture frames on the back wall. Sure enough, I knew them all. The bonfire group was back, only this time they were dressed to the nines and wandering around The Mansion like they had grown up here. Suddenly I realized they probably had. Had Ross been part of this group the whole time? Had he been one of the many who gathered around the flames each weekend that I had spent watching from the shadows?

"Who else would it be? You know I'd never miss an opportunity to shit on Ross, even if he is six feet under," Seymour laughed.

"You're such a dick," one of the girls spread out across an armchair called out. If I remembered correctly, her name was Nina. "Hey, Don," she added and I waved stupidly.

Seymour shrugged at her insult and took another sip from his cup. "I don't change," he replied. "Unlike you. I don't think I've ever seen you in a t-shirt before, Donnie. You look good."

"Wait a minute, you guys know each other?" I hadn't realized I had been clutching Rachel's hand for dear life still until she finally ripped it from my grasp. I crossed my arms over my chest, hating the sudden attention that was now on me.

Seymour chuckled good-naturedly. "Of course we do. Her and Ross were practically glued at the hip those last weeks before…" My eyebrows furrowed. What was he talking about? I wasn't glued to anyone, ever, except…

"What are you talking about? You've known Ross this whole time? And you never said anything?" I whipped around at the sound of Rainer's voice. I had never heard it sound like that before. *Betrayed.*

I was already shaking my head adamantly. "No. I didn't. I don't know what Seymour's talking about," I promised. But just then, my eyes landed on a new picture that was hung on the wall right next to where Rainer was now standing. I felt all the blood drain from my face. Felt my knees start to shake even as I forced myself forward so I was directly in front of this frame.

I would have recognized him anywhere. I could even tell exactly when this picture had been taken. Late spring two years ago, when his hair was too long, curling over his ears just as it had been the night he had showed up on my doorstep. The photographer had obviously tried to cover up the dark circles under his eyes, but I knew they were there. My fingers reached out and pressed against the cold glass, tracing over the bluish tint there that anyone else would have missed.

"No," I sobbed, finally putting together what I had refused to see for months now. "No!" I screamed, knowing I was making a scene but not giving a damn. "No, no, no."

"Colt, what's going on?" I heard Rainer ask from next to me but he felt a million miles away. The only thing I could see right now was Vee's face right in front of me. I couldn't think of anything but that final smile he had tossed me over his shoulder when he walked back towards his Jeep that last night.

"Shit, Donnie. You never knew, did you?" I knew Seymour had stood from the couch and came to join me by Vee's picture, but I couldn't look at him, either. I was breaking. I was shattering right here in front of everyone. "I had no idea. He told me you didn't call him Ross but...fuck," he breathed out. "You never knew who he was, did you?" When I still didn't answer, he tried to pull me into a hug and that's when I finally snapped.

"No!" I screeched, not even recognizing the sound that tore from my throat. "No, this isn't true. This can't be right. *No.*" I was still shaking my head violently, as if by doing so I could somehow erase the truth, because that's what it was. The truth. I knew it as soon as I saw the picture. I think I had known all along, but my brain had been trying to protect me. I didn't *want* to know. But I had known since the first morning I woke up in Rainer's bed and found the locket.

Rainer. I finally turned and found his eyes on me, looking at me like he no longer knew me. I didn't blame him. "Colt..."

I shook my head, tears finally brimming over my lashes and pouring down my cheeks unchecked. "I'm so sorry," I sobbed. Then I was pushing past him, shoving my way through people gathered in the hall looking at all the new picture frames hung up. I didn't want to see them. Didn't want to see Vee in his baseball uniform, leaning against that stupid lifted Jeep I had always given him shit for, laughing with his arm thrown over Seymour's shoulders, posed nicely between a younger Rachel and Rainer. I didn't want to see any of them, but I did.

My stomach twisted and I felt like I was about to be sick. I could hardly see through my tears now. I had never cried this hard before; I could barely catch my breath. I couldn't even feel the people I was shoving out of the way in my haste to get out. I just needed to get out of here. Run. *Breathe.*

"Oh, good, Colt! You finally came down. Have you had a chance to meet Mrs. Rhymes? I was just telling her how much you work down at the stables and she was saying her daughter is learning to ride there! Isn't that such a coincidence? What a small world, right?" I caught a glimpse of Mrs. Ventrilla seated at the counter beside a woman who could only be Seymour and Nate's mother. "Oh, Colt, what's wrong?" she asked as soon as she caught a glimpse of my tear-soaked face. Immediately, she was on her feet and making her way towards me, her concern clear to see. I didn't deserve it.

"I'm sorry," I croaked before turning to bolt out the back door. I could hear her still calling my name but I didn't stop. I just kept running. And running. And running. I didn't even know where I was going, just knew I had to go.

I ran until I couldn't anymore. Until my legs were shaking and my chest was heaving and my lungs were screaming and I. Still. Could. Not. *Breathe.*

My legs gave out and suddenly I was kneeling in the dirt gasping for air through my sobs because no matter how far I ran, I couldn't escape from this. I couldn't escape what I had done. Rainer was wrong. He hadn't been the reason his brother died. *I* was.

Chapter Eighteen

"Colt!" I heard my name being called but still I didn't move. I hadn't moved since I collapsed into the dirt here hours ago. The sun had almost set but in the last golden rays filtering through the grapevines surrounding me, the locket glinted as I flipped it over and over in my palm.

"Colt, please," the voice pleaded. It was Rainer. Of course it was Rainer. My eyes squeezed shut and I half-heartedly hoped he wouldn't find me. I didn't want to face him. It was weak, I knew that, but I didn't want to see the pain I caused him. I didn't want to see him look at me with hatred instead of love. It was what I deserved, but I wasn't ready to see it.

"Colt, please, baby. You promised you wouldn't run from me anymore. Please don't run from me now."

I thought I couldn't possibly cry anymore, but at the sound of his broken voice, another sob ripped its way out of me and I hunched over in the dirt. "Hey, hey, shh...I'm here. I'm right here. I'm not going anywhere." I could hear Rainer's running footsteps and the next thing I knew his arms were around me, scooping me up into his lap and pressing his lips into my hair that had fallen from its ponytail.

I fought against his hold. I didn't deserve his touch now. I didn't deserve his care or his love. "Don't say that," I growled, but he was too strong for me and for once he wasn't letting go as soon as I showed any signs of discomfort. Instead, he held on tighter.

"I promised," he said simply but firmly.

"I told you not to. You didn't know what you were saying then. You didn't know *me*. I'm a monster. I'm just like him." I continued to fight him, thrashing in his arms until I simply had no strength left and sobs took over. "I don't want to be just like him. I don't want to be like him."

"Shh, you're not your father. You're nothing like your father. It's okay. I'm right here. It's all going to be okay." His words, so much like his brother's from years ago, ripped me open so that I was completely falling apart in his arms.

"Vee," I hiccupped. "He promised the same thing."

"Vee? You mean Ross?" I nodded and shook my head at the same time, burying myself deeper into his chest. "That's why you don't trust anyone, isn't it? Why you won't let me promise you anything. You thought he broke his promises." I nodded against him as realization colored his words. My tears were soaking his shirt, plastering it to his chest, but I couldn't get myself to stop. For once, I had no control over my emotions. I struggled to remember how my voice worked to give him an explanation. He deserved an explanation, but I didn't know if I was even strong enough to give one.

"Seymour told me as much as he knew. How you showed up one night at the bonfire out of the blue looking like a drowned rat," his chest rumbled against me in laughter but I couldn't find any humor here. "He told me how Ross had become your friend, even though he always gave him shit for it because you were some scrawny kid who barely ever talked. But Ross wouldn't hear it. He kept hanging out with you every weekend." I was waiting to hear the inevitable anger in his voice, betrayal, frustration, but it never came. I pulled back to look at his face in the growing twilight and my breath caught. Even now, with his face lined with worry and pain, he was still the most handsome man I had ever seen.

He smiled at me softly and leaned in to brush a soft kiss against my lips but I was too numb to kiss him back. When he pulled away, his hands came up to cradle my face and he tried in vain to catch all my falling tears.

"I'm so sorry. I'm so, so sorry Rainer," I sobbed.

He shook his head, dipping to kiss me again. "You never did anything wrong. There's nothing to be sorry for."

I focused on a spot in the vines over his shoulder, unable to look at him now. He didn't understand. He still didn't see that it was my fault his brother was dead. "He was weird that night you said?" My voice held no emotion. I had resorted back to that dark place in my mind where I hid and locked away any and all feelings. I didn't want to say this. I didn't want to hurt Rainer any more than he already had been. But I had no choice.

He didn't need to ask what night. We both knew the night I was talking about. "Yeah…"

I nodded, still focused over his shoulder. "He was distracted when you left the fire? Something wasn't right?"

"Right…"

I finally dropped my gaze to Rainer's eyes. Even though it was about to be completely dark, I was still able to pick out the ring of blue and flecks of emerald. "Where did you crash?"

"What?" he asked, confused by my question and sudden need to know.

"Where, Rainer? Where did Ross forget to turn because he was too lost in his own thoughts? Where did you go off the road?"

I wanted to be wrong. God, I had never wanted to be wrong so badly. *Please*, just let me be wrong.

"About a mile and a half down Bay Road." The ice I had built up around my heart had been completely melted over the past months so when my heart shattered at his words, I felt every single crack. "Hey, woah, Colt, you're scaring me. What does it matter? Why does it matter?"

He was so shocked by my sudden burst of hysteria that I was finally able to stand from his lap. The locket I had forgotten I still had went tumbling to the dirt and I watched numbly as he reached forward to grab it. "You had it this whole time? I thought I had lost it."

I nodded and crossed my arms over my chest while I fought fruitlessly to hold myself together. "Why were you on Bay Road? Did you never wonder why you were in a crash headed the opposite direction from where you lived?" I cried. Rainer was still kneeling in the dirt in front of me, that all-too-familiar locket in his open palm, confusion coloring his perfect face.

He never did abandon me. All this time, I thought Vee had simply headed off to college and never looked back. I thought he never cared about me. I had been wrong. He had cared about me *too* much. He had cared so much he had gotten himself killed for it. He had died on his way to try to save me.

"He was coming to get me. He died because he didn't know that road well, didn't know the turn there, and was distracted because he was worried about why I had bailed on our plan. He died because of me," I whispered so softly I didn't even know if Rainer would be able to hear me, but it was the only way I would be able to say it. If I said it any louder, it would destroy me.

I knew I was right. I knew how worked up Vee could get. I knew how worried he must have been when I didn't show up like I was supposed to that night. He had crashed less than two miles from my house and I never knew.

"I don't understand," Rainer murmured from in front of me while I struggled to keep myself from falling to pieces. I wanted to fold myself into his arms again. I wanted him to tell me everything would be okay even if I never believed him. Because I was right all along. It would never be okay.

He flipped the locket over and over again while his mind raced just like Vee would do. *Ross*, I corrected myself in my head. But then he did something different. He slipped a fingernail in the almost unnoticeable crack and the locket popped open in his palm. I gasped. All this time, I never even knew it opened. Vee had never opened it around me.

"I never knew he kept pictures in here," Rainer whispered, brushing his long fingers over the tiny windows. I couldn't see what was in them in the gloom surrounding us, but whatever it was caused Rainer to smile softly, then cock his head to one side and squint in confusion. After a beat, he spoke so softly I almost didn't catch it.

"Donnie." His voice sounded so much like Vee's when he said my name that my knees actually gave out and I collapsed back into the dirt beside him as I tried to force air back into my lungs. His eyes lifted from the open locket to meet mine and I prepared myself to see all the hurt from what I had just revealed. What I was *not* prepared to see was the same love he had been showing me for the past two months.

"You're Donnie," he finally said. I somehow managed to nod almost imperceptibly and Rainer reached out for my hand, brushing my fingers with his as he dropped the open locket into my waiting palm. I looked down and tried to see what had caused his epiphany through my tears. There, in the two tiny locket windows, were two miniscule pictures. One, an ultrasound image I was sure must be Viviana. The other was some sort of shirtless cartoon character.

I looked back at Rainer in confusion and his finger reached over to trace across the cartoon boy. "Donnie Thornberry, the wild child." What little composure I had been managing to cling on to was obliterated at his words. I could barely hear Rainer over the sound of my heart breaking even more than it already had. "He mentioned you. A lot actually. I just never knew Donnie was, well…you. He asked my parents if his friend Donnie could stay with us at the house for a while. They had already agreed. This whole time, you were supposed to be living with us."

I forced my eyes from the cartoon in the locket to meet his. "He wanted me to stay with you?" I croaked.

"You didn't know?" I shook my head, my throat too clogged with tears to respond. I wondered what my life would have looked like then. If that night had never happened. If I never missed our meeting time. If he hadn't driven to come check on me. If he hadn't *died*. Would I have still fallen for Rainer? Would Rachel still be the bitchy yet extremely caring and sensitive girl she is today? Would Ross be off living in the guest house raising his own daughter?

"Colt?" Rainer's hand reached out to take mine, folding the locket between both of our fingers and the tremors that wracked my body eased. For so long, touch from anyone had put me on edge. But here, now, I finally came to accept that Rainer's touch was the only thing that could calm me. "I'm trying really hard to be patient, because I can see this is destroying you right now even though you're still trying to pretend you're made of stone, but I need to know what happened. I need you to tell me what happened that night."

I clenched my hand in his even tighter, feeling the metal of the locket dig into my palm. "He had found out about my father. He was the first person I ever told. I tried to play it off like it wasn't a big deal, but he wouldn't believe me. He would come to my house when he worried I wasn't okay. I think that's what he was trying to do when he crashed," I said robotically.

"For a while after he found out, I managed to keep him calm. Everything was okay. But then I showed up to one bonfire with a nasty black eye and a concussion. My father had come home early one night that week and slammed me into a coffee table. That was the last straw for Vee. I mean Ross. He told me to pack a bag and bring it to the following week's bonfire. It was supposed to be so easy. It was something I did every week, go out to

Baker's Field on a Saturday night. It was so simple. It should have been the perfect plan."

"This was the night he died. That's why he begged me to go with him that night, isn't it? In case anything went wrong getting you back to our house?" Rainer asked softly, though neither of us would ever know the answer to that question for sure.

"Something went wrong," I said simply. I knew I had to tell him what happened that night, but I didn't want to. I had spent the last two years of my life doing everything in my power to force memories of that night from my mind, to pretend it never happened, yet here I was reliving it so clearly. Like not a single day had passed since that afternoon.

My stomach was in knots. Happy knots. Nervous knots. Was I really about to do this? Yes. Yes, I was.

I let the front door slam shut behind me because I knew no one else was home. By this point, I had pretty much perfected my timing. Get home late enough from the barn in the afternoon that my father had already left to go out drinking for the night but not so late that we would be getting in at the same time. That was never a good thing. On bonfire nights, like tonight, I could normally slip back in once he had already passed out in a drunken stupor. I don't think he ever even knew I was missing. If he did, he didn't seem to care. Not exactly the worrying type, my father. I actually laughed out loud at the thought before slapping a hand over my mouth. *What had gotten into me?* Even with my bruised face that had turned to a lovely shade of brownish-yellow at this point, I hadn't been able to wipe the smile from my face all week. Vee's promise was finally coming true. Tonight, I wouldn't have to sneak back into this house. Tonight, I would be free.

I tossed the duffle bag Jeremy had lent me on my bed happily and turned to my closet. Luckily, I didn't have much so I was able to easily fit in every piece of clothing I owned along with my sneakers and collection of makeup I had only ever used to cover up the countless cuts and bruises over the years. I guess I wouldn't have to keep doing that. Maybe I would actually get to learn how to use this stuff as more than just concealer.

I still wasn't entirely sure what Vee's plan was, but I knew he'd have something figured out. Oddly enough, I *did* trust him. As much as I had fought it, it was true. So I checked my watch again, just as I had been doing all day at the barn because tonight could not come soon enough. Seven o'clock. It was still too early for anyone to be there, but I'd rather wait for Vee at Baker's Field than in this house of horrors. I slung the bag over my shoulder and was halfway across the living room when I finally realized I wasn't alone like I thought I had been.

"What the hell are you so damn smiley about this week?" At the sound of his voice, my entire body tensed. Slowly, I turned to find my father lounging on the couch, an open bottle dangling from one hand. I could smell him from where I stood half a room away. Whiskey. The bottle in his hand was a few sips shy of being empty and those excited knots that had been in my stomach all week suddenly twisted into something sinister.

"I...uhm...nothing," I squeaked.

"Nothing, huh? You just feel like smiling for no goddamn reason then? Life is just that fucking great?

Sunshine and rainbows and butterflies all the damn time, that it?" he growled before tipping his head back and finishing what I had thought would be multiple drinks in a single swallow.

"No. No, sir. I didn't mean to be, I just-" The bottle slammed down on one of the end tables with a crack and I flinched. By the time I peeled my eyes open again, he was standing directly in front of me. His free hand wrapped around my bicep and he threw me back into the wall before I could even react. My head snapped back to crack against the drywall and I clenched my teeth tight against the sudden searing pain to keep from crying out. I knew from experience that only made things worse.

"You just what?" he snapped, the smell of whiskey on his breath so strong I could have gotten drunk just by standing near him. His fingers tightened their hold on my arm and with his other hand he smashed the now-empty bottle of Jack against the wall mere inches from my face. The shattered glass rained down on me and I felt a shard slice into my cheek, but other than that I was thankful for the long-sleeve shirt I was wearing for sparing me from the worst of it. My relief didn't last long, though.

"What's this?" The broken edge of his bottle slashed into my shoulder, the jagged glass easily cutting through the shirt I had just been praising and digging deep into my skin. I wanted so badly to scream but I couldn't. I refused to give him that satisfaction. With my free hand, I clutched my duffle bag tighter, pulling it free from my now-sliced-open shoulder that it had been resting on.

"Nothing," I managed to grit out. "It's nothing."

"Give it to me," he demanded. For the first time ever, I hesitated to obey one of his commands. I couldn't give him my bag. I needed it. It was the one thing Vee had told me to bring. My entire life was packed into it. "Did I fucking stutter? I said give it to me, bitch." The end of his sentence was punctuated by the blood-spattered end of the bottle being thrust into my stomach. Luckily, in his current state, his aim was poor and he only managed to graze my side instead of plunging it into my gut. Still, it was enough to have me doubling over at the stabbing pain, my duffle falling with a thud to the floor between us as I clutched my side.

My father wasted no time in falling to his knees to rip open the zipper. He looked back up at me from the floor once he had seen the heap of clothes packed away in in. "What the fuck is this?" he asked in a deadly calm voice.

I shook my head even though the motion sent pain shooting down my spine and began to back away from him as quickly as I could. I had seen him angry before. I had seen him belligerent. But I had *never* seen this look in his cold, grey eyes before. I needed to go. *Now.* I turned to make a break for it, but he was already a step ahead of me. His hand caught me around the waist, his fingers digging brutally into the brand-new wound there and I screamed in pain, unable to hold it in any longer. He threw me back against the wall so hard my vision swam and then landed a punch straight to my ribs before I could even catch my breath. I hunched over, trying and failing to suck in air until he was yanking me back upright by my hair.

"Have you told people about me?" he growled.

"No, sir," I coughed. My response was rewarded with a backhand across the face and the metallic taste of blood immediately filled my mouth.

"You think you can just pack up and run away from me then?"

"No, sir." Again, my answer was met with the smack of his hand against my jaw.

"You think it's that easy? That after all this, I'd just let you go?" He yanked my hair tighter and twisted the fingers of his free hand into my cut-open shoulder so that I cried out again. Before I could clamp my mouth shut, he landed yet another blow to my cheek. "You think you can run away and that would solve everything? Think again."

I didn't have time to think of what he could possibly do next but even if I had, I never would have guessed it. One second he had me pinned against the living room wall and in the next I was careening towards the sliding glass door. He whipped my body into the glass like it was nothing to him. My back hit first, the force of the impact cracking through my spine like nothing I had ever felt before and the sound of breaking glass came with it. My head slammed back from whiplash and the whole glass door shattered against my broken body, falling in huge shards just as quickly as I fell to the floor. I could feel pieces lodging into me from every angle as I came to rest amongst the ruins of the door.

"You think you can run from me?" I couldn't open my eyes. I couldn't move. Glass was stabbing into me in so many different places that I knew there was no way I could make it out of this alive. *Please just let me die,* I begged silently. *Please, just let this finally be over.* Everything felt wet, hot, and I realized that was blood slowly pooling beneath me. *My* blood. So much that I felt like I was floating in it. The crunch of glass under my father's boots came closer and *dear God, why can't this be over? Please let me die,* I pleaded. My body jerked from the impact of his steel-toe drilling into my ribs and I think I tried to scream but there was too much blood blocking my mouth. A sickening gurgle bubbled out instead and I heard him laugh at the sound of it. *Please,* I begged.

"You can *never* run from me. You hear that? I will *always* find you. Do you hear me? I will find you. You're *mine.* Your mother would just love to hear me say that after all these years, wouldn't she? You're mine, you fucking bitch, whether I ever wanted you or not." His boot landed against my sliced body once more and that was the last thing I remembered from that night before I finally blacked out.

"I've got you. I've got you, Colt. You're okay. It's okay. You're here now." Rainer's lips were kissing every inch of me he could reach. My hair, my cheek, the scar along my brow, and yet I was still as a statue. I was numb. I hadn't allowed myself to relive that night since it had happened. I never allowed myself to stop and look at that restored glass door every time I had to pass it when I walked through the living room.

"I woke up in the hospital wrapped in so many bandages I looked like a mummy," I continued in a dead voice. Rainer kept his lips pressed to my hair as he wrapped me tighter in his arms but I had no strength to return his embrace. "The nurses hadn't thought I would make it. I lost too much blood. And yet there I was...lucky me. The glass had cut all the way down to bone in some places. In others, it had to be surgically removed. They all told me how lucky I was to have survived such a bad fall through a second-story window. They had never heard of a pillow fight at a sleepover going so wrong before. Neither had I," I deadpanned. Rainer's whole body tensed around me and I could feel the anger pouring off him. Anger at what had happened to me. Anger at the pitiful cover story my mother had concocted for the hospital just so she could bring me there. And yet not one ounce of anger towards *me*. I didn't understand. He should be angry at me. Angry that I was the reason Ross was dead.

"When I finally recovered enough to leave the house, I snuck out to the bonfire one last time. I knew it was a huge risk, but I had to get to Vee. Except, he wasn't there. No one was there. I thought he had left me. He never came to check on me at the house, never worried if I was okay. I thought he forgot about his plan and just abandoned me. He had broken his promise. He couldn't get me out of that place after all." I lifted my head to look Rainer in the eyes and saw that tears were finally streaming down his cheeks. It wasn't right. Someone as beautiful as him should never cry. And it was my fault. I was the reason for it. I reached a shaky hand up to catch a tear as it dripped from his strong jaw and he turned his head in my grasp so he could press a kiss to my open palm.

"I was wrong," I whispered. "This whole time, I was wrong. He never abandoned me. He died trying to get to me. I'm so sorry, Rain. I'm *so, so* sorry."

His arms crushed me back into his chest and he rubbed circles over my back, over the ridges and valleys of scars and skin grafts I knew he could feel even through the cotton of my t-shirt. After all this time, he finally knew where most of them came from. "Shh, Colt. It's okay."

"It's not," I gasped through my tears. *How could he say that?*

"Do you remember the very first day you came here, to my house?" he asked while I sobbed into his chest. "Do you remember sitting and watching Viv play in the sprinklers when I first told you about the night Ross died?" I nodded my head against him. "I told you it was my fault he died and you said that sometimes, it's nobody's fault. Sometimes, things just happen. Even if we wish they never did."

Finally, I broke through the numb feeling in my body and latched on to him as tight as I could, wrapping my arms around his neck and locking my ankles around his waist as if I was some sort of spider monkey. I had never clung to someone before, had never wanted to hold onto someone as much as I wanted to hold onto him. "Rainer," I gasped, wanting so badly to say three little words I had never said before.

"I know," he murmured in my ear, tightening his hold on me even more than I thought was possible. "I know, baby. It's going to be okay. I promise. You know why?" I shook my head. "Because he *did* get you out of there. He brought you to me. He's here with us now and he always will be. You're right where you're supposed to be. *We're* right where we're supposed to be."

His hands came up to cup my face and tipped it back so he could look at me. Even in the dark, with tears brimming on his lashes, I could see the galaxy of colors hidden in his eyes. "I'm not going anywhere, Colt. Okay?

I promise. I love you…more than I know what to do with."

It was on the tip of my tongue. I wanted to say it, I really did. But I didn't know how. So instead, I did the only thing I could. I leaned forward, threaded my fingers through his hair, and pressed my lips to his, tasting the salt of our combined tears in the kiss.

Chapter Nineteen

"Boo."

"You want the blue one?" I asked, grabbing a puffy blue dress off its hanger from the closet.

"Lellow."

"So you don't want the blue then? You want this one?" I held up another dress, this one even poofier than the last one, if that was at all possible. At least Mrs. Ventrilla had branched out from pink, so I couldn't really complain all that much.

"Gween," Viviana squealed with a giggle.

I dropped my hands down to my sides and narrowed my eyes at her. "Okay, now you're just saying random colors." She giggled happily and clapped her hands from where she was sitting on the floor in just a diaper. I had been tasked with dressing her for her second birthday party. No big deal.

"If you're not careful, I'm going to put you in something pink just to spite you."

At the mention of pink, Viv shook her head of dark curls adamantly. "No!" she said with such conviction I couldn't help the laughter that bubbled from my chest.

"You do realize she has absolutely no clue what you're saying, right?" I looked up to see Rainer peeking his head in from the hall. Viviana jumped up at the sound of his voice and ran over to him, arms extended to be picked up.

"Of course she does," I scoffed as he lifted her into his arms. Her peals of laughter echoed in the room as Rainer covered her face in kisses while his long legs ate up the distance between us. When he got to my side, he shifted her to one hip in order to pull me in for a kiss as if it was the most natural thing in the world. Me, him, a baby, kisses. If someone had told me this would be my life four months ago, I would have called them certifiably insane. And yet here I was.

"Just shove her in a dress. Doesn't matter what one. You know it's going to be covered in cake within an hour anyway," he laughed.

"Hey, your mom trusted me to dress her and I-"

"Want it to be perfect," he finished for me with an endearing grin. "I know. But my mom loves you. She's not going to care if you picked a yellow dress or a blue dress."

I felt myself stiffen as his words washed over me. He said them so casually, like they weren't at all monumental. When he caught sight of my expression, though, his grin grew. He set Viv back down on the plush pink rug so he could cup my face in his palms. "You know she does, right? She loves you. And so do I."

He bent to press his mouth to mine once more and I felt myself rising on my tiptoes to meet him halfway. My heart beat double-time as his teeth lightly nipped my bottom lip before he pulled away again with a teasing glint in his eyes. "Now hurry up and throw her in a dress already and come downstairs. I want cake."

His hands grazed down my arms as he backed away like he never wanted to stop touching me. For the first time in my life, I understood that feeling. He bent and gave Viv's curls a quick tug, then tossed one more of his trademark smirks my way before disappearing back into the hall.

"Alright, tiny human," I sighed with a smile. "Get your little butt over here."

"She's so cute," Chelsea cooed from beside me as we watched Viviana attempt to eat her cake. Rainer had been right yet again. There was currently frosting all over the peach-colored dress I had finally settled on yanking over her head. Her hair looked more pink than brown at this point and her fingers were busy smooshing more cake into the tray of her highchair. "I think we should make one!" Chels said excitedly as she turned to her husband. Bless his soul, he appeared unfazed by this new desire of hers. Derek, on the other hand, was not so calm about the prospect.

"Oh, hell no," he coughed. I laughed at his response while Chelsea shot him a glare.

"What's that supposed to mean?"

He shoveled another bite of cake into his mouth, unperturbed by Chelsea's attempt at a withering stare. "You? Having a baby?" he mumbled around the cake before swallowing. "You would end up losing it because you somehow forgot where you left it. You would never remember to feed it. You would sign it up for some daycare or something, then never remember to get it there on time. You would-"

"Okay!" Chelsea cut him off. "Point made." Even Mr. Ventrilla was laughing from the opposite side of the massive table in the dining room where everyone was gathered.

It was quite the group we had assembled to celebrate Viv's birthday. Rachel had insisted we invite the barn family since they had all fallen in love with Viviana over the past weeks. Their casual clothes contrasted with the polished look some workers from the function hall were sporting. The bonfire group bridged the gap between the two, dressed nice like the golden children they were supposed to be and yet they were still as unruly as ever. Mrs. Ventrilla made sure to invite quite of few of the regulars from all those years ago, claiming Ross would have wanted them to know his daughter.

"Even if you did manage to raise a kid, what if it grew up to be like you? Can you even imagine trying to deal with *another* Chelsea?" Derek groaned.

Rachel elbowed me in the ribs. "See? He's not a fan of babies, either. I told you we're perfect for each other," she hissed in my ear. She had originally started taking riding lessons again from me but that all went out the window the first day she crossed paths with Derek.

I rubbed my ribs overdramatically and scowled in her direction. "He's too old for you," I reiterated for what had to be the sixtieth time.

Rainer's fingers twined with mine by my side and he brought our hands up to rest on my waist, pulling me back against his chest. "I thought I told you you're not allowed to date until you're eighteen."

In response, Rachel shot him one of her scathing looks before sauntering over to where Derek was standing. She didn't stop until she was directly in front of him.

"Hey, Derek. You've got a little frosting right...there." She stretched up on her tiptoes, chest out right in front of his face, and swiped frosting off the corner of his lip before popping that finger in her mouth to suck off the offending pink. I had to admit, she was *good*. I almost wanted to laugh at her little stunt. Until I heard Rainer legitimately growl from behind me, the vibration rumbling against my back.

"Oh, I'm gonna kill her," he seethed, stepping out from behind me to storm towards where Derek was now laughing at Rachel's antics. To his credit, he hadn't even glanced down at her chest when she all but thrust it into his face.

I wrapped my tiny hands around Rainer's thick forearm just before he was out of reach and tugged back. "Let her have her fun," I laughed. Rainer's feet stalled, not wanting to pull me further, but I could still feel the muscles of his forearm beneath my palms pulled taut from his anger. I let my thumbs ghost back and forth over his smooth skin. "You do know you can't control *everything*." He sighed at my words but eventually stepped back, tucking me into the crook of his arm and dropping a kiss into my hair.

"Presents!" Mrs. Ventrilla sang as she swooped back into the dining room with her arms full of perfectly wrapped gifts. Chelsea and Sander added their gift to the stack. Naturally, it looked as if a five-year-old had done the wrapping. I saw Jeremy stifle a laugh at the sight of it as he stepped forward to add his gift to the mix as well.

Soon, the stack was so big I couldn't even see Viviana behind it anymore. Not that she needed any more toys. She had enough to fill an entire guest room at this point. But it was fun to watch her tear into the wrapping paper and stick each and every bow to her forehead. In fact, she was more excited about the bows than any of the gifts she had opened so far, even if they did range from new play-doh sets (no pink included) to horse figurines and clothes in every color of the rainbow. She didn't care at all, until she ripped open the gift that happened to be from me.

"Foggie!"

"Frog," I corrected with a laugh as she squished the plush frog that was easily as big as her to her chest.

"Huh…my stuffed unicorn did not get nearly the same reaction," Seymour grumbled.

I smiled at him from across the table. "Yeah, well, unicorns are boring. Don't you know little girls like slimy frogs, not unicorns and daisies?" Seymour flipped me the middle finger in response which awarded him with a light smack on the back of his head from Mrs. Ventrilla.

"Hey! I didn't even say a bad word!" he complained while rubbing the back of his head. He had become a frequent visitor to The Mansion since the celebration of life Rainer had put on. However, he was having trouble remembering Mrs. Ventrilla's no swearing rule every time he was over.

Rachel snickered from her spot beside Derek, probably thrilled that it wasn't her being reprimanded for once. She had to have the worst potty-mouth out of any sixteen-year-old I had ever met and yet somehow it only made her more endearing.

"Words. Hand gestures. It doesn't matter, don't do it," Mrs. Ventrilla scolded. "Viviana is going to grow up to be a proper lady."

For a moment, everyone was silent. Rachel caught my eye over her mother's head and I saw Chelsea trading a look with Mr. Ventrilla across the table. Then all at once, the entire room burst into laughter.

"I'm gonna be honest, Mama V. The kid's favorite toy out of all that fluffy, girly shit was a stuffed frog," Seymour said, earning himself another glare for his word choice. "I don't think she's going to end up being a 'proper lady'. I think she's going to end up more like Donnie here."

My cheeks heated at his words and the attention suddenly being turned on me. Rainer's hand flexed on my waist lovingly. "There's nothing wrong with that," he laughed.

Mrs. Ventrilla smiled at me from across the room while she absentmindedly brushed back Viv's unruly curls. "No," she murmured. "There definitely is nothing wrong with that."

~

"Nose goes," Derek called out before slapping his index finger against his nose. Jeremy followed suit in a heartbeat.

"You are seriously children!" I exclaimed, clearly the loser of their little game.

"Nah, mate. You're just buggered because you lost," Jeremy chuckled.

"I'm not trailering to the show. Nope, you can't make me. Since when did I ever get roped into being an option to drive?"

Derek grinned at me devilishly, as if he wasn't a twenty-eight-year-old man who had just used "nose goes" to get out of doing a chore. Clearly, Rachel was rubbing off on him too much from all the time they had been spending together. He reached out and ruffled my hair until I batted his hand away. I noticed the barn family was becoming freer with their touches to me lately. It occurred to me that this was how they had always been with each other, but I was just now being included. I was *letting* them include me. "Aw, the little squirt's all grown up. Time to do the big girl stuff."

"Shotgun!" Jeremy called before shoving Derek out of the way and pulling open the passenger door of the stable's truck. *So much for being grown-ups*, I scoffed in my head.

"Derek, stop being a dick and drive. You always drive to the shows." Chelsea's voice echoed down the bay as she sashayed towards where we had been huddled around the truck, waiting for her so we could all leave together. Of course, she was the last one to be ready. She probably had forgotten we were even leaving at this time until five minutes ago. Derek wasn't wrong the other day. Her with a baby would be a nightmare. Luckily, she hadn't brought up that brilliant idea since the party.

"Oh, Colt! I keep meaning to give you this!" She slapped a hand to her forehead in frustration before reaching into her bag and pulling out an envelope.

I took it from her easily, thinking it was probably a note wishing us luck from Rainer, but then I recognized the handwriting on the front. My name in the neat writing became blurry as my hand holding the envelope began to shake. "Yeah, your mom dropped by really early this morning with it, but I keep forgetting to give it to you because I've been running around in circles trying to get everything together. You know how I get on show days. But anyway, there ya go. Are you riding with the boys? Or did you want to follow with me?"

I could barely hear her words as I tried to focus on the looping letters on the envelope. I didn't want to see what she had to say. I didn't want to read anything from her at all. It had been almost three months since she had come to the barn. Three months since she told me to never come back. I hadn't seen her since. She wasn't worried about where I was, how I was doing, if I had found a place to live. She didn't care about me at all. I was doing good. For the first time ever, things were okay. All she could do was ruin that. I had half a mind to just throw the damn letter in the nearest trash can.

"Colt, let's go! It's showtime!" Jeremy dramatically called from the open truck window. Derek was still grumbling but reluctantly followed Chelsea's instructions and climbed into the driver side. I tore my eyes from the envelope and found Chelsea staring at me with concern.

"Colt? You okay?" she asked as she hitched her bag higher on her shoulder.

"Yeah, uhm, yeah…" I stuttered. "I just have to…I just remembered I forgot to set up a bucket for Cinna's dinner meds. Let me just…I'll just meet you there in my own car," I rambled, trying to think up an excuse to escape from their scrutiny.

"You sure?" Chelsea took another step towards me and I immediately stumbled back, which only caused her eyes to grow wider in concern.

I waved a hand in front of me as if it was nothing, hoping to throw her off. "Yeah, no, it's fine. I have stuff in my car I need anyway. You all go ahead." Before any of them could question me further, I turned on my heel and headed towards the grain room. The least I could do was make my lie look convincing.

Once inside, I sat heavily on a bag of feed while the door fell shut behind me. I heard the roar of the stable truck's engine start and gently pull out of the barn, then Chelsea locking up the wide double doors we only opened to load up trailers. After that, the only thing I could hear was the shuffling of horses who were upset to be left behind and the deafening beat of my own heart. I looked down at the envelope I had balled in my fist and slowly pried my fingers open from their hold on it. My name on the front was crinkled now, but there was no denying the writing was my mother's. What could she possibly have to say after all these weeks? Did I really want to know?

My free hand reached into the pocket of my new riding pants and felt for the locket I still kept with me. For a brief second, I understood what Rainer meant when he said Vee would always be right here with me. *Ross*, I corrected myself again. *He was Ross*. My brain was still having a hard time processing that. The metal slipped between my fingers easily, giving me the strength I needed to pull myself together and ease my finger under the flap of the envelope to break it open. My hands were still shaking as I pulled two sheets of paper out and shook them open.

Colt, the letter read. The words continued far down the page, disappearing onto the next and I wondered how she could possibly have so much to say to me now when she had barely said three words to me before.

I know you're angry at me right now, and you have every right to be. I don't deserve anything else. But I need you to know that everything I did was because I love you. I know that by doing what I'm about to do, you're going to hate me even more. But I have to do it. You have to understand. Maybe not now, but one day.

I know you'll be okay. I want you to know, I never stopped caring. I never stopped worrying. I saw you. At Ventrilla Vineyards. I was delivering flowers for a wedding and I hardly recognized you. You looked amazing, Colt. You truly did. I had never seen you look so happy before. I'm so proud of you. I'm so, so proud that you got out. That you were so much stronger than me. That you didn't let him ruin you. I saw you with Mrs. Ventrilla and her daughter. You were laughing. You were all laughing together. I'm so sorry we could never have that mother-daughter relationship.

I tried to picture what my mother had seen. That night we had all gone to the wedding together and Rachel and

I had tried to sneak in unnoticed because we were late. I remember being worried Mrs. Ventrilla was going to be so mad at us, but instead we had all ended up laughing over her fashion sense, or lack thereof. I had no idea my mom had been there to witness that whole exchange. I can't even imagine what she must have thought, seeing me laughing and then holding a baby. Seeing me showing so much scarred skin as if I didn't have a care in the world.

It seemed like a lifetime ago. My life had changed so much just since that night. I had learned Vee had never abandoned me. Rainer and I had grown to be almost inseparable. I had come to accept that people could love me. I bit my lip to hold in my emotions as I kept reading.

I haven't been able to stop thinking about you since then. I stopped by the barn a few days ago because I needed to make sure you really were okay. You were out in the pasture and didn't see me, but that's okay. You were with a man and he was staring at you like you hung the moon and I could tell just from that one look, he's special. I could tell just from seeing the way he looks at you that he loves you. Please, Colt, I know you may not believe it because of what we've been through, but please let him love you. You deserve it. You deserve so much more than anything I've ever given you. That's why I'm trying to make it up to you now.

Please, Colt, one day forgive me for this. Forgive me for everything. Know it's all I have left to do. I'm sorry I never told you sooner.

Your father isn't actually your father. He's your uncle. I was young and stupid and in love. If I knew what it would have cost me, cost you, I never would have done it. Your father has a twin. His name is Scott.

My jaw dropped as I read her words. My father wasn't even my father? A twin? Is this why we never spoke of his family? Why I had never met anyone at all in his family? Why I could never even bring them up? Because my mother had cheated on him with his *twin brother*? How could she? How could she have ever been so stupid?

He had been away at college when I first met your father, but when he came home, we couldn't deny there was something between us. Something far stronger than what I ever felt for your father. We started sneaking around. It was stupid; I know it was. But I loved him so much. I was going to leave your father. Then I found out I was pregnant with you. Obviously, your father thought you were his. Only Scott and I assumed the truth. I secretly did a paternity test once you were born just to make sure. You were Scott's.

For the first few years, it was fine. There was no way your father could have known you were really his niece and not his daughter. And so Scott and I got to raise you almost together, though you only knew him as your uncle. Then one day, when you were almost three, I came home from meeting Scott at the park to find your father drunk with the paternity test in his hand. He had found it when he was looking for something in our room. That was the first night he ever hit me. And I deserved it. I know I did. Once he had passed out, I called Scott. I begged him to leave. I knew if he stayed around even one more day, your father would find him and hurt him. I told him we were happy and I couldn't let him keep hanging around our happy family. I made sure he believed me and he left. I haven't seen him since that day, but I found him recently. For you, Colt.

If I had known then what your father would become with us, I would have gone to Scott and begged him to take you with him when he left. I never could have imagined he would turn into the monster you know. I thought it would be enough to punish me for my mistake and I would *take it because I knew I deserved it for what I had done. But it wasn't long before he started to punish you, too. I swear, I tried so hard to keep you from it. I tried my best to hide you away when you were small, but as you grew it became harder and harder. You kept trying to intervene whenever he got violent. You didn't understand I was trying to shield you.*

I furiously swiped at the tears that were threatening to fall off my chin. I couldn't let them blur the words on this page. All that time I had tried to break up their fighting when I was little, I never knew it was me they were fighting over. I always thought I was the one trying to protect my mom from him because she just let him hit her, but it was *her* trying to protect *me*. All the times she had told me to go to my room when I was so little, I had only thought it was because she was mad at me. She had been trying to *protect* me. And as I got older, I refused to listen to her commands. I didn't understand why she didn't fight back. This whole time, it was because she thought she deserved it. She thought she deserved it and all she wanted was to keep me safe. And all I had done was left her there alone.

I felt like there was a hole ripping open in my stomach and my body doubled over in sobs, but I kept reading.

The older you got, the more you looked like Scott and not him. It got worse and worse. He completely turned his attention from me to you, no matter how hard I tried to keep it on me. I am so, so sorry, Colt. I wish more than anything I could have protected you better. I wish I had never had you so you never would have known this pain. All I can do now is free you from it.

I told you I found Scott recently. I've mailed him a package of all the evidence I've been collecting over the past few years. Ever since that horrible night he threw you through the glass door. I've been documenting everything. Pictures, letters, recordings, anything I could gather without him knowing. I vowed I would somehow set you free. Now I can. I sent it all to Scott so that your father wouldn't be able to find it and destroy it. I asked him to come and find you, to bring it to the authorities with you. I promised I would set you free one day, and that day is today.

Please don't be angry with what I'm about to do. I'm sorry I didn't do this sooner, but at least I know you're safe now. I know you're happy with this new life you have. Please know, that's all I wanted for you. I'm alright as long as you are safe. But I can't keep living with myself for all the pain I've put you through. I can't keep living with myself for the mistakes I've *made that could have cost you your life. I can't keep living.*

Just know,

I've always loved you. I will always love you.

—Mom

No. No, no, no. She couldn't be saying what I thought she was saying right now. Not when she had finally told me everything. Not when I finally knew the truth. She couldn't give up now. *No.*

I hastily crumpled the letter in my fist and I took off at a sprint with only one thought in my brain. I was going back to that place I swore I would never set foot in again.

The gravel of our driveway kicked up as I slammed on the brakes and threw open my car door, not even bothering to cut the engine. I sprinted around the back of the garage, feeling along the rain gutter there until my fingers met the spare key I had hidden years ago. Then I was running again, back up the front walk towards that faded red door I once prayed I would never have to see again. For the first time since I read the last line of the letter, I hesitated. My heartbeat echoed in my ears and I knew my entire body was shaking while I stood stupidly on our front step just staring at that damn door. I remembered all the nights I came home late from the bonfires and carefully tried to open it so it wouldn't make a sound. I remembered rushing out of it when I had gotten older as I tried to escape my father's drunken violence. I remembered leaning back against it while I held my broken ribs the night Vee had come here. I remembered the last time I had pulled it shut before I moved into the barn. My eyes squeezed shut in an effort to block out all the memories, almost all of them horrible. *God?* I thought. *If Rainer's right, and you are real? Please, please don't make this another bad memory. Please,* I begged silently.

I took a deep breath in, trying to steady my hand then inserted the rusted key into the lock and twisted until I heard the latch click open. I turned the knob and slowly pushed the door open, then waited with bated breath. The sounds of my footsteps echoed around the empty entryway as I stepped into the house for the first time in months. "Mom?" I called out hesitantly. Only silence answered me as I walked further in and then turned into the living room to see it was just as I had left it. Almost as if I had never left at all. As if I hadn't grown in the months since I walked out that door. Like I wasn't a completely different person now. I felt every bit the scared, unsure, eighteen-year-old girl who had run away that June morning.

"Mom, please," I begged, my voice breaking over the tears threatening to fall already. *Please, let her just be at work.* "Mom?"

My feet carried me across the living room while my stomach grew heavier with each step. Turn down the hall. Six steps forward. Turn to the right. Again I was reminded of just how normal this door appeared. Just another brown, bedroom door that could be found anywhere. The dented wall just to the right of the door handle was the only thing that reminded me otherwise. A small mark that would forever be a sign of what had happened here.

"Mom?" I whispered one last time, praying that she would somehow answer me this time. When there was still nothing, I lifted my hand and curled it around the doorknob.

It twisted easily under my touch and the door swung forward but I immediately wished I could take it back. The letter I had been clutching ever since I had finished reading it at the barn fluttered loose from my grasp as the first sob ripped through my body. I wanted to pull that door shut and never have it open again. I wanted to close it and back away and come back later, like this was all some horrible dream and the sight before me wasn't real. But I had learned long ago that my life wasn't a nightmare. Even when things were ugly, and painful, and traumatizing, I couldn't just wake up the next morning and push the images from my mind. There was no forgetting this scene. No erasing this from my memory.

"Mom," I sobbed, crashing forward into the room. The chair she had used was toppled over from where she had kicked it out from under her and I almost tripped over it in my rush to get to her. "Mom, no. Please, God, no," I screamed as I finally made it to her, wrapping my arms around her legs that dangled at chest level and clung to her desperately. "No, no, no, Mom." I was screaming incoherently, my throat already becoming raw from my wailing as I scrambled to pull her down even though I knew it was pointless. She was gone. She was already gone. "Mommy, please, no."

I wasn't sure how long I had been wailing alone in that room, but I finally managed to get her down to the floor and was cradling her lifeless body in my lap when I felt hands on my shoulders. "Colt, come on. You've got to let go. You've got to let her go, baby, please." They were gentle at first, trying to pull me off her, but I couldn't let go. I wouldn't let her go. I had given up on her once before. I wasn't going to now. "Colt, you can't help her now, she's already gone."

"I'm not leaving her!" I wailed, thrashing against the hands that were trying to pry me off. "I'm not leaving her here with him!" My endless tears poured down onto her face where her head rested in my lap and into her bulging eyes. My hands tried obsessively to smooth down her hair, tuck it behind her ears, as if it actually mattered. As if she could feel what I was doing.

"You have to. There's nothing we can do. Baby, please. You can't be here if he comes home."

I knew I continued to wail and fight, but I couldn't even tell what I was saying or what I was fighting for. Eventually, it could have been mere seconds or long minutes later, Rainer managed to pull me from her limp body and gathered me into his chest. I didn't have to look to know it was him. I could tell even in my blind panic. Of course he had found me here. Every time I ran, he somehow managed to follow.

I finally accepted it and turned in his lap to cling onto his t-shirt just as tightly as I had been trying to hold onto my mother's empty shell. He pulled me further into his chest and rocked us from side to side while his cheek pressed against the top of my head. "I've got you. I've got you, baby. We've got to go, though. You can't stay here."

"Please, no. I can't leave her, please," I sobbed, knowing my words were barely discernable through my sobs. "He can't have her. I won't let him take her. Please," I begged.

"I promise I won't let that happen." I felt us rising from the floor as Rainer stood with me in his arms but I couldn't even find the strength to lift my head from his chest.

"Please, Rainer," I whimpered.

"Trust me?" he asked as he turned to take us out of that horrible place, that house of horrors. I felt him carry me down the hall, across the living room and past the glass door from my nightmares, then finally out onto the front step. I heard the front door click shut behind me one final time and yet I still hadn't been able to give him an answer. I just sobbed into his chest even harder while the door to my old life finally closed for good.

Chapter Twenty

The rain beat down in my eyes any time I tried to glance up. So I just stopped trying. My eyes were riveted to the hole in the earth anyway. I wondered if it was okay for it to be raining so hard during a burial. Would it flood the casket? It's not like I had the money to buy one of those super nice ones. This one was probably more cardboard than wood. *Sorry, Mom.* I wondered if she could hear me wherever she was now. Probably not. And what did I care? Did it even matter if the casket flooded? I mean, she was dead already. Not much worse could happen from there.

"Colt, sweetheart? We're going to go. You sure you don't want to come with us?" Mrs. Ventrilla's soft voice shook me from my reverie.

"I just need a few more minutes," I whispered back, my voice thick with emotion. I couldn't look at her. Partly because of the damn rain beating down, but also because I didn't want to see her face. I didn't want to see her heart breaking for me when I wasn't even sure I felt anything. Did that make me an awful daughter? I couldn't tell if I was sad or mad or hurt or in disbelief. I had essentially been a robot since I found her hanging four days ago. I had the Ventrillas to thank for pulling this makeshift funeral together. For making sure I even had her body to do this.

Rainer kept his promise. I never asked how, or for any of the details, but he made sure my mother's body was taken from the house before my father returned home from whatever bar I'm sure he had been busy day-drinking in. I wasn't sure what would have happened if Chelsea hadn't called him that day and asked if he could check on me because she was worried about whatever that letter from my mom had said. I was lucky he had even thought enough to find our house after I wasn't at the barn. Because without him, I didn't know how long I would have sat there on the floor with her head in my lap. Probably until it was too late and my father really did stumble home. There's no telling what could have happened then. I guess it wasn't so bad to have people that cared about me after all.

I could fully admit the few people who were here today were more of a family than any people I was related to by blood. Mrs. Ventrilla had hugged me more than my mom ever had. Mr. Ventrilla gave me advice when my own father had only ever given me bruises. Rachel irritated me in the way only a little sister could do, but also loved me when I didn't deserve it. Chelsea had taken me in like a loving aunt who never asked too many questions and always let you have chocolate for dinner. I would always think of Jeremy as the brother I never had, though it had taken him a while to accept that as his role. And they were all here for *me*. It may have been a funeral for my mother, but I knew the real reason these people were standing out in the rain today and it wasn't for the woman being buried six feet in the ground.

My hand reached up and fingered the locket I now had on a chain around my neck. Rainer had given me the chain two days ago after we had turned in my mom's letter to the police and given our official statement. We had been sitting on the bench outside the conference room they had questioned us in when he pulled the gold chain from his pocket. Without him even having to ask, I had felt deep in my pocket and pulled out that golden locket I had clung on to since the first morning I had woken up in his bed. He threaded the locket onto the chain and then hesitated, reading the expression on my face, waiting to see my permission there just like he still did every time he touched me. And then he had reached around my neck and clicked the clasp closed for me. The gold weighed heavy against my breastbone, a constant reminder of Vee. Of Ross. I knew he was with us now as I felt Mrs. Ventrilla's arms wrap around me and hug me to her. Mr. Ventrilla's hand came to rest on my shoulder as I was wrapped in his wife's embrace and my skin didn't even crawl from all the contact. Instead, I felt warmed from it. *This* was my family. This was my *only* family.

I felt Rainer's arms snake around my waist and pull me back against his chest as I realized that my whole body was shaking, completely overcome with silent sobs. Just like the sky had decided to open up after so long without rain, I too was breaking open. As his parents walked away, back to their car, Rainer's lips pressed into my hair, murmuring words I couldn't possibly comprehend. Probably stuff about love. I wasn't sure I would ever fully know what love was. Was what my mother did out of love for me? Should I be thanking her? Of course. But how could I when I was the one left to bury her, left to find her hanging there? Who did that to their own daughter?

"Colt," a deep voice said in an almost reverent tone after what felt like an hour. Everyone else had left long ago. Only Rainer and I remained and I knew he would stay as long as I needed to, even if the rain had soaked us to the bone. I found myself finally pulling my arms from where I had them wrapped tight over my chest to find his hands over my stomach and twined my fingers through them. He squeezed back and held me tighter. Eventually, I looked up enough to figure out who was speaking to me now.

As soon as my eyes met his, I lost what little shred of control I had been managing to cling to. I tripped over my own feet while I attempted to back up even further, but Rainer's chest was at my back. He felt me growing frantic against him and tightened his hold even more while he stepped back with me in his arms. My head shook back and forth vehemently but no words passed my lips.

"It's not him. I'm not him. I promise you, Colt. He's gone. He's not coming back. I'm not him." The voice that spoke wasn't the one I had been expecting, so I knew his words were true. But I couldn't help my reaction. I knew my mom said in her letter that he had a twin, but I could have never imagined what looking at him would do to me. They had the same dark hair, though this man's was cut shorter than my father had always worn his. He had crinkles in the corners of his eyes as if he smiled too often and laughed even more. He was just as tall as my father, only not as bulky as him. He was more on the slim side, almost like me. But it was the eyes that truly did me in. They were *his* eyes. *No,* I thought. *They were* my *eyes.*

Tears poured freely down my cheeks now as I stared at him. And I knew. Everything my mom had written in the letter was true. I *knew* I had known him before. I *knew* we had spent time together. I remembered days spent at a lake I forgot existed, the last time I had ever gone swimming. It had been with this man, though he had grown so fuzzy in my memories over the years. I remembered him pushing me on park swings. Back when I was so young the memory of him and my father had simply blurred into one, he had been there. Before my father had started hitting us. Before the constant abuse. He had been around. I remembered it. But I remembered even more right now as I stared back at him in the rain in this empty cemetery. I remembered seeing him in passing at the barn over the years. He would meet with Chelsea and no one else. I had never gotten a good look at him, he was always turning away, but I knew he had been there. I remembered him.

"God, you're so beautiful," he finally whispered, unable to keep his eyes from roving over ever inch of me as if he would never get enough. Like he had been starved of the privilege for years. Rainer's grip around me tightened even more and I felt him tensing. He didn't know what was going on here. He didn't know how I was reacting. Hell, *I* didn't even know how I was reacting. But I squeezed his fingers back to reassure him all the same.

"Scott?" I finally croaked. It was all I could manage to say. Hearing my voice sent a jolt through him, as if he had been electrocuted, and his eyes welled with tears.

"Yeah, it's me. *I'm* your dad."

I felt Rainer's reaction to his words but neither of us said anything. I couldn't, and I knew Rainer enough to know that even though he was probably dying to say something, he was giving me the time I needed to come to my own senses. He wouldn't fight my battles for me. But he would fight alongside me if I needed him to.

I had known this moment was coming since I had first read through my mother's letter. And then when I reread it. And also when I reread it just before turning it over to the police two days ago because Rainer had been smart enough to pick it up from where I had dropped it on her bedroom floor. I just hadn't expected this moment of meeting him to come so soon. I hadn't expected it to be at a funeral I had invited zero people to for a person I wasn't sure I had ever truly known. I wasn't prepared for this. I didn't know what I was supposed to say to him. *Hi, Daddy?* In his dreams.

"Where have you been?" Scott flinched back from the venom in my words, clearly not what he had been expecting, and I got a sick satisfaction from seeing that reaction on him. While logically I knew he wasn't the man I wanted to take my anger out on, he looked so similar that for now it was enough. "All this time...where have you been?"

"Colt, I swear I-"

"No. Don't swear. Just tell me where the hell you've been my whole fucking life!" I stepped forward, breaking from Rainer's hold on me. I was strong enough to do this on my own. Scott stepped back in time with my steps forward. If he wasn't careful, he'd fall right into that grave.

"Look, Colt, I know you're upset right now. I have no clue what you must be feeling right now-"

"You're right, you don't. Because you weren't *here*! You have no clue what I could possibly be going through right now because you just left me!"

His eyes hardened at my last words and he stopped backing away from me. A part of me wanted to cower at the look in his eyes, so much like all I had known my whole life, but I would not back down. Not anymore. Not here. Not now. "You don't know what you're saying," Scott spat.

"I'm pretty sure I do." I folded my arms over my chest again, not even feeling the rain as it pounded down around us and plastered the black dress to my thin frame.

"I *never* left you," he growled.

I laughed without humor and turned my head to the side, refusing to look at him. "Right. And I grew up frolicking through the flowers with my daddy."

"Look at me." I felt his heat before he even touched me and his hands pulled my head up to look at those all-too-familiar grey eyes again. That's when I lost it.

"Don't touch me!" I screamed, clawing at his arms violently. Rainer was immediately there again, scooping me against him in an instant. "Don't you fucking touch me!" I continued to scream while my arms and legs thrashed as Rainer held me up.

Scott's hands instantly fell from me as if my skin burned him and the look of horror on his face was enough to shock me from my flashback. He wasn't *him*. He wasn't the one who had hit me and threw me against walls and sneered at me with whiskey breath. He wasn't here to hurt me. But it hurt all the same. "I had no idea," he was mumbling over and over while Rainer rocked me back and forth in his arms just like he had four days ago. Just like he had in the dirt of the vineyard. Always there to pick me up when I fell. "I had no idea. What did he do? What did he do to you, baby?" He kept repeating the same things until I finally lifted my head from Rainer's chest and looked back at him.

"Just tell me," I pleaded with tears clogging my throat. "Why did you leave me?"

"I didn't leave you, Colt. You have to believe me. I never would have left you if I had known what he was; what he had become. I thought I was doing the right thing. I thought I was doing what was best for you. And even then, I still couldn't leave you. I was never far. I had to see you, even if I knew I couldn't."

"The barn..." I whispered, knowing what he was talking about. He was always close. Chelsea had known him. I had caught glimpses of him every year and never known who he was. *My dad.* "You would come to the barn. You know Chelsea."

He nodded and shook his head all at once, water droplets gathering on his lashes as he stared at me with pain in his eyes. "She doesn't know who I really am. In the beginning, she used to comment how similar I looked to a guy from town, but she was easy enough to convince it was just a coincidence. She only knows me as a business man from Michigan who boarded a horse there."

My eyes widened and I finally was strong enough to disentangle myself from Rainer's arms and stand on my own again. "No..."

"He's yours, Colt."

"No…" I said again, my head swinging back and forth in denial.

"I bought him for you. When I first found out how much time you were spending at that barn. I researched for hours about horses, just so if one day I ever had the chance to spend time with you again, I would be able to connect with you. I wanted to give you the whole world, but I couldn't. So I did what I could. I bought a horse and left him in the one place I knew you would always be. It was selfish. If your mother ever found out, she would have been furious. But I was selfish. I wanted you to have a piece of me."

My tears were flowing unchecked now and my voice cracked when I spoke. "You bought me Gizmo. You gave me my best friend."

He nodded. "He's yours. He's in your name, you know. I had the title made up with your name as the owner. He's always been yours. It was the least I could do, Colt. If I had known what was really happening, I would have gotten you out of there. I would have found a way, I promise you. I swear, your mother never told me. She only told me to leave and never come back. That the three of you were happy and if I stayed, I would ruin it. So I did as she asked. I had no reason not to believe her. I only ever wanted to make the two of you happy. So I did the only thing I thought I could. I listened to her without arguing. I loved her. I loved her so much, I let her go. I didn't want to ruin your life. I swear, I never knew." He was shaking his head, like even now, seeing my mother in a casket in the ground and knowing what had led to it, he still couldn't believe it. And in those eyes that were so similar to my own, I saw the truth there. He truly had no clue what had been happening all those years. He would have come back for me if he did. He really thought I had been okay from the glimpses he caught of me each year at the barn. He really had never left.

"Okay," I croaked. I felt Rainer stiffen behind me in surprise.

"Okay?" Scott asked.

I lifted my shoulders in a shrug and for a minute I thought of Vee. *Ross,* I corrected in my head. I thought of how he would have playfully scolded me for not giving a definite answer. But I also thought he would be proud of me if he could see me now, see that I could do this on my own. I reached out for Rainer's hand and he immediately wrapped his fingers around mine. It didn't hurt to have a little help. "Okay," I repeated. "I believe you. That you didn't know. That you just found out somehow and came as soon as you could. I can see it's true. But I'm not ready for anything else." Rainer's fingers squeezed mine. He was proud of me. I could feel it even without his words. Just like I could feel myself loving him even if I couldn't say it.

Scott's shoulders slumped in what looked like both relief and defeat. I knew he wanted to say so much more. I could see everything there in his eyes. Those eyes that held so much more emotion than I had ever seen in my father's. Or my own. He was still drinking in the sight of me like he would never see me again, and I wondered just how cruel my mother was to send him away all those years ago. Maybe some day I would know. Maybe some day I would ask him. But not today. I had enough for today.

"Okay," Scott whispered.

Epilogue

Six Months Later

"It's not really a surprise if you can see where we're going," Rainer grumbled.

"If you honestly thought there was any way in hell I would agree to put on a blindfold, I would be breaking up with you," I deadpanned from the passenger seat of his truck. The trees were still bare even though most of the snow had melted at this point, making the woods look wide open as they blurred by my window. I pulled my sweater tighter around my shoulders. Rachel had given it to me for Christmas, so naturally it was a bit too tight and showed more skin than I would have ever picked out for myself. Of course, it looked great on me and Rainer made sure to let me know any time I put it on. Rachel had a devilish fashion sense. She seriously was going to drive men crazy as she got older, but I had a feeling she'd be able to handle it just fine. After all, she was worth far more than a million dollars.

"Oh, I'm sorry. What was that? Was that you finally admitting we have something that could be broken up?" His eyes flashed to meet mine for the briefest second before focusing back on the road in front of us. He never took his eyes from it for long and I loved him for that because I knew what had made him that way. I reached over the center console to capture his hand in mine, just because I could, and I saw his cocky smirk grow to the loving smile he reserved just for me. My heart stuttered in my chest and the butterflies took flight again. I had just learned to live with them, we were old pals now anyway. I had a feeling they weren't planning on going anywhere anytime soon.

"Yeah, maybe," I said coyly.

His thumb swiped over the back of my hand as he brought it up to his lips to give it a kiss. "About damn time," he grinned, ever the overconfident asshole, and I rolled my eyes but couldn't hide my grin.

"Yeah, yeah, yeah. So will you tell me now what the hell we're doing today?"

He released my hand to clutch his heart in mock pain. "You're just telling me what I want to hear so you can figure out my surprise, aren't you?" Another flick of his eyes over to my sly grin. "Colt Jefferson, you're a sneaky woman. But nope. You'll just have to wait and find out."

"Rainer," I whined. "You know I hate surprises." And I still did. That wasn't about to change anytime soon. Probably not ever. A lot had changed with me in the months since meeting Rainer, but some things never would. Rainer and his family, who had become my family as well, had come to know and accept that. When you spent eighteen years trying to anticipate every single thing that could go wrong, when you were scared to ever turn your back or close your eyes, it was no surprise I would have habits that couldn't be broken. I still had things I would never be comfortable with. Surprises and blindfolds were just two of the many.

His long fingers threaded through mine again and he made sure I was looking at him instead of out the passenger window when he spoke next. "Yeah, but Colt? This is a *good* surprise." I nodded and bit down on my lower lip, turning back to look out the window for the rest of the ride. I was still getting used to there being such things as good surprises.

It wasn't long before the truck was slowing down and then rolling to a stop in front of an old mill building. Rainer cut the ignition and smirked that stupid, cocky smirk at me before hopping down from the truck. I stayed put, watching as he ran around to my side and opened my door for me. I rolled my eyes and hopped down without taking his hand for help. He laughed and threw an arm easily over my shoulders, as if there wasn't a worry in the world that I may react badly to his touching me. I snuggled into his side deeper and wrapped my own arm around his waist. I was better at touching now. Especially with my home. *Rainer* had become my home. "What are we doing here?" I sighed against him.

"What do you think we're doing here?"

"Rainer Ventrilla, I hate riddles," I scolded.

A buzz sounded from the double glass doors ahead of us and he pushed them open, walking across a spacious lobby to the bank of elevators at the back. Naturally, he didn't wait to see if I was following. And of course, I was following. "You hate riddles. And you hate surprises.

And you hate touching. And you hate Chef Boyardee Ravioli. But you put up with my games. And you let me touch you. And you even let me make you raviolis sometimes."

"Yeah, well, you actually make them from some secret family recipe, not a can," I pointed out. He reached out to hook his arm back around my neck so he could reel me in to kiss my forehead, ensuring I shut up again.

"Just trust me on this one, Colt?" he asked as the elevator pinged its arrival at the fourth floor.

I looked up at him from under my lashes, about to give him something he'd been waiting on from me for a long time. "I trust you, Rainer." His eyes fluttered shut at my whispered words, his impossibly dark lashes brushing those high cheekbones that made him look so much like a Greek god. I felt his chest rise and fall against me as he breathed in a deep breath and pressed his lips to my forehead again. He was thanking me without words. Because it wasn't just this moment I was trusting him with. It was with *me*. I trusted him with all of me.

This time when he stepped forward, he tugged my hand in his and pulled me from the elevator with him. Right now, he looked exactly like he had on Christmas. It was as if my words just now were the best gift he could have ever received. I couldn't help but smile as he tugged us further down the hall so fast I was almost tripping over my feet.

"Rainer," I finally laughed. "Slow down, I'm going to fall."

He turned so he was walking backwards facing me, his hand still in mine tugging me forward, that cocky grin in place. "I'll catch you."

Suddenly he came to a stop and pulled me in front of him. We were facing a plain black door, just like every other one we had passed in this hall. I looked back over my shoulder at him, wondering what we were waiting for. Were we supposed to knock? Who lived here? Who was going to open this door and greet us? I wasn't entirely sure I wanted to know. Scott and I had been meeting up for coffee or lunch in the past months, getting to know each other, but I hadn't signed on for a meetup today. Was this Rainer's surprise? A visit with my real dad?

"Okay…close your eyes?" He grinned down at me, still with that energy as if it was Christmas morning.

"Fat chance," I muttered, but I couldn't even pretend anger with him. His enthusiasm for whatever was happening right now was contagious. His laughter rumbled through me as he reached around to insert a key into the door we were standing in front of, swinging it open. "Rainer…" I started, but didn't have any words to keep going with it.

He nudged me forward, holding my hips as he walked me into the now-open doorway. It was an apartment. A beautiful, amazing, stunning apartment. I had never known what kind of place I wanted to live in until now, because I felt like everything in this room fit me perfectly. There were exposed beams above us, worn wooden floors across the whole space, oversized furniture in the living room. Huge windows spread so much light over the open space and there were no frilly curtains hanging to block it out. It was dark, like Rainer's room back at The Mansion, but also light like the room that had been Ross's, *mine*, and yet through it all it was its own thing. Almost as if it was wild, *free*, if a room could ever feel that way. It reminded me of the barn, but with the elegance of The Mansion, only more understated here. Like it didn't have to show off, it just *was*. It was absolutely perfect.

I didn't realize my feet had carried me all the way into the apartment. I wasn't even sure how long I had been standing in the center of the room, taking it all in, when I finally turned back to find Rainer watching me from the doorway. He had that look of adoration on his face that I still didn't think I deserved. "Rain, this place is amazing. Whose is it?"

My favorite smirk came over his face, but he stayed at the door, not coming any closer to me. "It's ours," he whispered.

My head was shaking back and forth. "No," I said, even though I knew he wasn't lying.

His grin grew. "Yes, baby. It's ours."

"Rainer, I can't. No." There was no way I was accepting this. He knew I had wanted to leave his house for months now. I couldn't stay there. The only reason I was still there was because all my savings had gone to paying for my mother's pitiful funeral and I was back to square one when it came to saving money for a place of my own.

After the funeral, my father's case had gone to court. It had been messy. Brutal, really. All the evidence my mom had collected was brought to light. She had been collecting so much more than I ever knew and storing it away in the file she eventually mailed to Scott. There were more letters found that she had written documenting everything. Her affair with Scott. When I was born. How she had tried so hard to pretend I was my father's daughter, but he had found out when I was just a toddler.

How the abuse had started. How she believed she deserved it but I never had. The way she had forced Scott away, thinking if he wasn't around anymore my father would get over it eventually and somehow accept that I could be their daughter, even if I was really his niece. Everything he had done to us over the years, in brutal detail. I had to relive it all. Scott was given another paternity test to make sure this was all true, like the courts couldn't believe something so sordid had happened in their perfect, tiny town.

Scott was there the whole time, too. My real father. Not only had he brought most of the evidence in whatever my mother had mailed him, he also gave his side of it all. How he never knew. How he worried that his brother would have been mad but that my mom hadn't let on to anything every time he checked in. She had only begged him to stay away and yet he continued to check on me regardless.

At first, it was hard to even look at him in the courtroom because he just reminded me of my father. I never wanted to talk to him after the sessions let out even though I could see he was dying to get to know me. Lately, I was slowly warming up to the idea of him. I knew we still had a lot more talking to do in the future. And I was okay with that. Actually, I was starting to kind of look forward to it.

And of course, *he* was there throughout the trial. I had to see him for the first time since I had run away from our house. He looked the same even though he had been spending his days in a holding cell awaiting the outcome of the trail. Same boyish features. Same grey eyes. It had made me want to vomit just sitting in the same room as him each day. I hadn't been able to keep my eyes from darting around the room, marking each exit around us while my knee bounced up and down under the table restlessly. The attorney Mr. Ventrilla had hired for me had done his best to keep me calm, but his best was shit. Nothing could have kept me calm then. Not knowing that my father's ankles were shackled and hands in cuffs. Not seeing the guards shuffle in with him each day we reconvened. Not watching them guide him back out and knowing he would be in a cell each night. I still didn't feel safe. Not until I could leave the stand and the courtroom and collapse into Rainer's arms at the end of each day. Not until I could hear Mrs. Ventrilla cooing in my ear about how brave I was and how it would all be over soon.

Though it hadn't been soon like she said, it was finally all over. The judge had made his final decision thirty-seven days ago, not that I was counting or anything. My father was sentenced to life in prison without parole based on seven counts of first-degree assault, two counts second-degree assault, rape, and fifteen counts of child abuse and endangerment. He didn't even fight it. I had to give him that much. He accepted that the game was up. The charade he had played on this town was finally over. It should have been the best day of my life, watching him walk out of that courtroom for the last time. Knowing he would never again lay a finger on me or my mother. But I had been too numb to even react. And I hated him for that. Hated him for forcing me to become this cold, detached, shell of a human. But he no longer had that control. *I* did. And it was high time that I took control of my own life.

I knew I could never go back to that house. I never wanted to see it again. Not after everything that had happened behind its closed doors. So I asked Mr. Ventrilla if he could put it up for sale for me because I had no clue how to go about doing that. I told the Ventrillas I would be moving out. While they had been so much more helpful than I could have ever asked for, I couldn't keep staying there. It wasn't right. Especially now that most nights I wasn't even staying in my own room. But I left that part out when I talked to Mr. and Mrs. Ventrilla. All they needed to know was I simply needed to get a place of my own. I was just waiting for the house to sell so I would have enough money to somehow buy a place. I was hoping Mr. Ventrilla would be nice enough to help me figure all that out as well, seeing as I was still only eighteen. It was weird to look back and remember what my life was like at this time last year. How I had been unable to hope for anything, let alone something as big as a place of my own.

"Look, I know you're going to tell me I'm an overconfident ass, but I went out on a limb here and just assumed it would be okay with you if we could stay roommates. You know, now that you planned on moving out and all." Rainer was still standing in the doorway, holding his hands up with his palms facing me like he had that very first day on the back stairs, trying to show he wasn't a threat.

"I don't understand," I croaked, tears already clogging my throat. Because I think I did understand. I just couldn't believe it.

"I'm twenty-five, Colt. I can't still be living at my parents' house, either. I had moved back to help the whole family with the baby. And then I stayed because we all fell apart when Ross died. But you know as well as I do, they don't need me there anymore. They don't need me to try to keep everything in place and fix them. They can fix themselves. They *are* fixing themselves. You showed them that. *You* did, baby. Because that's how *you* are. You don't need me. I know that. You don't need me to fix you. You don't need me to save you. You never did. You were always your own hero, Colt." Tears streamed down my face uncontrollably at his words and dripped off my chin onto the beautiful wood floors of this apartment. *Our* apartment. He had found this apartment for me. For *us*. And he had made it ours. The first place I could ever call my own.

He was wrong; I *did* need him. So much.

"So this place is yours, Colt. The house sold. The realtor called my dad last week to tell him the news. He made you a bank account and transferred the money to it, except not all of it. It's up to you, but if you want it, this place is yours. Just say the word and I'll transfer the rest of the money to pay for this place. Because I knew you'd never let us buy you a place. So you can rest assured, you are doing this on your own. With your own money. And this is *your* place. Well, technically, it's in my name right now because I knew you'd love it so I just went ahead and bought it. I know you'll want to pay me back for it. Every last penny, I'm sure. But like I said, I'm an overconfident ass and was thinking maybe we could split it fifty-fifty? What do you say, Colt? Think you can put up with me for a bit longer?"

I shook my head at the man standing in the doorway in front of me, not bothering to wipe away any of my falling tears. "You're wrong," I said.

His face went blank at my words, but he hurried to fix it. "There are two bedrooms, Colt. I wasn't thinking you'd be ready for that yet, so I made sure to get a place with two bedrooms. I'm not pressuring you into anything, and if you never want to get to that point, I'll respect that, I will, I promise I won't ever hurt you or push you or-"

I kept shaking my head at him as I smiled through my tears before cutting off his panicked blabbering. Although, I had to admit, seeing Rainer Ventrilla's ever-present confidence falter for once was quite amusing. "You're wrong," I repeated. "I *do* need you, Rain. I've *always* needed you. I just didn't know how to say it. I love you," I confessed. "I love you, Rainer Ventrilla."

He straightened and I watched his eyes flood with tears. And then he was finally stepping into the room, into our apartment, letting the black door slam shut behind him as he took two long strides to reach me and scoop me into his arms. His lips met mine in the sweetest, most loving kiss I had ever felt in my life and I clung to him harder than I ever had. When we finally broke apart to breathe and his forehead rested against mine, his eyes flicked open to meet my grey ones. The ring of blue and the green that swirled in the deep brown held me captive as he stared at me so hard, I swear he was looking straight into my soul. And I let him. I would let him every single day of my life. Because he saved it. He really did save my life.

"Say it again," he whispered, his breath tickling against my lips.

I smiled and lifted up on my tiptoes to press my lips to his before whispering against him, "I love you."

His eyes fluttered closed and his mouth sealed over mine, but only for a second. "I love you. So much. God, I love you."

His hand dropped from cradling my cheek and his fingers found the locket that still rested against my collarbone. I never took it off. I never would. My eyes drifted down to watch his long fingers wrap around the gold, holding it just as Vee had so many times in my memories. *Hey, Vee?* I thought as I let my eyes drift closed and Rainer's lips found my forehead again. *I still don't know if I believe in God or angels or all that shit Rainer does, but if you're up there? If you did this? If you brought us together? Thank you.*

Colby Millsaps

Acknowledgements

First and foremost, I'd like to acknowledge the seriousness of domestic and child abuse in the United States. Each year, upwards of 4.1 million cases involving over 7.4 million children are reported to Child Protective Services due to child maltreatment. An estimate of 1,750 children die each year due to physical abuse in the home. In the tiny state of New Hampshire alone, where this novel was based, 16,822 reports were made of child abuse in the year of 2016. That averages to almost 65 children in 1,000 throughout the state (from National Child Abuse and Neglect Data System). This just goes to show that these horrors are happening in our own backyards. And these are only the cases that make it to Child Protective Services. An ongoing study that was conducted early in the 2000s until recently estimates that only 1 in 10 instances of abuse are actually brought forward, making it almost impossible to know how many kids are truly suffering (from medical journal *Lancet*). Further, on average, nearly 20 people per minute are physically abused by an intimate partner in the United States, just as Colt's mother was. During one year, this equates to more than 10 million women and men (from National Coalition Against Domestic Violence). These numbers are utterly heartbreaking. So please, please, I ask that if you see something that just doesn't seem right, or someone who looks like they could use a friend, to simply offer that support. You never know what life you could be saving.

1-800-422-4453 – National Child Abuse Hotline
1-800-799-7233 – National Domestic Abuse
Hotline

With all that to consider, this book was definitely my biggest challenge to date. I wanted to make sure I did the

Colby Millsaps

story justice while also creating a love story of hope. In one sense, I feel like this book has taken a lifetime to write. The idea for *Doors* came when I was working as a landscaper, delivering flowers to a vineyard for a wedding that night, and I saw the contrast between the dust-coated workers and the meticulous venue. I had the idea of a girl meeting a man who changed her life there with that same contrast but also coexistence between clean and dirty still present. I forgot about the idea for a long time. Long enough to dropout of college, finish a different novel and publish it, and work five other jobs after that landscaping gig. Since then, the story has evolved to so much more than just that. I've written parts of this novel in a desk in my English Lit class at Ohio State. I've written parts on rooftop patios and airport terminals of Guatemala. I've debated endings and pieced things together while walking to the "End of the Earth" in Finisterre, Spain. Maybe I've just lived a lifetime while writing this.

With that being said, I have a village to thank for supporting me while I wrote this. My family, of course, for allowing me to come home when I was at my worst and still treating me like I was worth it. Thank you for always showing me undying love even when, like Mrs. Ventrilla and Colt, I felt very unlovable. Thank you for waiting me out while I, like Colt, learned to start loving myself and to accept the love of those around me.

My amazing friend, Devon, who I trust so wholly, who was kind enough to beta read *Doors* to make sure it didn't completely suck. Who let me ask her endless questions of if this worked, or that, or if I wrote this well enough, or if I did this part justice. Thank you for being one of the strongest women I know even when life isn't pretty. I love you.

Deb Kneisley, for not only being such an amazing friend, mentor, and teacher but also for being the only editor I ever truly trust. Thank you for making time to read the sloppy versions of *Doors* even when you had 84 senior essays to be grading. Also, sorry for having more comma splices in one novel than you could possibly find in all those essays.

My colleagues in the two schools I've been lucky enough to work at, both Chester Academy and Pinkerton Academy. Thank you for supporting me, watching my writing progress from when I was a student at both these schools to when I work alongside you, and encouraging me to keep going.

And lastly, Paula Zofrea. I wish I could have been there to say goodbye this past summer. I wish you would have shared so much more with me than you did. I guess I never thought our time together would be gone so soon. Thank you for believing in my writing far before the rest of the world had ever seen it. Thank you for teaching me the foundations I needed to create every story I could ever dream up. Thank you for being the best teacher I've ever known, in far more than just English. Thank you for sharing your true self with me. I'm honored to have known you. I hope you're proud up there. I hope your crown is on straight and you're smiling down on us peasants in your kingdom. I love you.

**Enjoyed *Doors*? Continue reading for a look into
Colby's other novel, *Crossing Lines*!**

MAY – PRESENT DAY
Noah

I clenched my jaw tight and flicked my eyes to the clock on my computer when Grant strode into the room. 5:37. It was way too early to be dealing with this again. Especially after sitting awake all night wondering what the hell I had done. I was sure the dark circles under my eyes would alert him to the fact that I hadn't slept a wink, yet he had the audacity to walk in here looking as if nothing had changed. Looking as if my entire world hadn't blown up yesterday...or had been on the brink of blowing up. All because of him. Not that it was his fault. It was my own damn fault. But I was angry and hurt and it was easier to blame him.

"Look Grant, I don't want to hear it honestly. It's over. I kept my end of the deal, I need you to keep yours."

"Noah..."

"I don't need another lecture, okay?" I snapped. "If you're here about what I think you're here for, save it. I took care of it like I said I would. Just let it go, please. I'm begging you. You don't understand the circumstances."

"Noah, I didn't come to-"

The door swung open again and I inwardly groaned. If Carter walked in right now, Grant wouldn't believe a word I was saying. Everything I went through yesterday would have been pointless. I braced myself and turned to look at the door, but it wasn't Carter who stood there.

"Samantha," I said, surprise clear in my voice. She was one of Carter's friends. "Is there something I can help you with?" Anything that would end this conversation with Grant.

He wouldn't be deterred though. "Noah, I just need to talk to you for a minute," he hissed. "Miss Greene, could you please give me a moment with Mr. Sweeney?"

"Actually, it's kind of an emergency, Mr. Olsen." Her voice shook as she tore her eyes from me and glanced at Grant. Something was off about her. Her hair wasn't perfectly straight like it had been every other day this year. And she looked like she was wearing the same shirt from the day before. Her eyes looked smaller without their normal layer of makeup, and they were red and swollen.

"Mr. Olsen, I'm sorry but we'll have to discuss whatever it is you need at a later time. It was nice to see you," I lied. He gave me a pointed look, begging me to reconsider, but I didn't change my mind. After a tense silence passed between us, he finally backed out of the room without another word.

I turned to Samantha earnestly. "Samantha, what's wrong?"

She swallowed hard and glanced around as if to make sure no one else was here and my panic rose. "Sam..."

"Someone needed to tell you," she finally croaked out, her voice shaky. "You should know."

"No..." I was already shaking my head because there was only one reason for her being here, for her being a mess, and it wasn't good.

"It happened yesterday. She was on her way home."

"No." My stomach turned. On her way home. Her way home from talking to me. No. I screamed in my head, refusing to believe this was possible.

"They say it wasn't her fault. He was texting and swerved into her lane. There was nothing she could have done except maybe be driving slower. But you know, I guess that doesn't matter now. The car was a mess. They had to cut it open to get her out. They showed me the pictures and-" Her words started running together but I had tuned her out. I was just imagining the last time I had been in the car when Carter was driving.

"You drive too fast." I had finally told her as I eyed the speedometer inching towards twenty-five miles per hour over the limit. I had always wondered why there were so many handles in a car. Then, as I clutched one for dear life, I finally understood.

"But," she said earnestly, "I *want* to go faster."

"What does that have to do with anything?" I gasped as we whipped around another sharp corner.

"It's all relative. So I'm practicing some restraint in not going any faster."

"Oh good. That's great. That will help us so much when we get pulled over. Or die." I had added only half sarcastically. She looked over then and smiled at me and although I had the urge to yell at her to keep her eyes on the road, I knew it was okay. That it was alright so long as she was around.

Samantha was still talking when I finally focused back on her. Tears had started to fall down her face and I knew I needed to ask but I was having trouble forming words. I also wasn't sure I wanted to know the answer.

I forced my legs to bring me to stand directly in front of her and made her focus on me. "Is she… Samantha…did she…" I took a deep breath. "Is Carter dead?"

"No."

"No?" I repeated, not willing to get my hopes up. Sure I had misheard. "She isn't dead?"

"No. They flew her to Mass General."

"So she's still there? She's still alive?" Sam nodded. "I've got to go. I have to get there." Suddenly I was throwing random papers and folders back in my bag, rummaging for my keys.

"Wait, you can't go." I heard Samantha saying but I ignored her as I rushed towards the door. "Mr. Sweeney, stop."

"Look Sam, you can stay in this room or you can go, but I'm leaving."

She hurried after me as I practically sprinted down the hall and then took the stairs two at a time. "Mr. Sweeney! You have classes to teach!"

"Someone else can teach them."

"What are you going to tell the office? You can't just say you're going to see her. What are they going to think?"

"I don't give a damn what they think." I knew I was being harsh and that Samantha didn't deserve it. I knew I was supposed to be the rational one but all I could think about was Carter and how she looked when she was sad or scared. How she looked yesterday after everything that had happened between us. All I knew was that I needed to get to wherever she was.

I reached the front doors of the building and stopped before turning to face Samantha. "I need you to do something for me, okay? I need you to go to the office and say an emergency came up for me and I won't be able to teach today. Say I can explain it all later. Can you do that for me?"

Samantha nodded and swiped a stray tear away. "Mr. Sweeney," she called softly once I had turned to push open the doors. I paused with my hands on the door but didn't turn back to face her. "She loves you, you know."

The pounding of my heart echoed in my ears. "Mass General you said?"

"Mass General," she confirmed.

AUGUST – NINE MONTHS EARLIER
Carter

"Business or pleasure?" A guy's voice asked from above me. It wasn't some deep baritone or a voice that would cause me to melt in a puddle, but there was something different about it. Despite being low, there was an authoritative edge that made me look up. I slowly lowered my book, folding the corner of the page to hold my place, and took in the man behind the voice. It wasn't fair for guys to look like that. His hair was dark and fell in waves upon his forehead, almost too long but not quite. His eyes were deep set, impossible to decipher what color they were, and it bothered me that I wanted to know their color at all. He was older than me, that was for sure, but not by too much. And there was something about him, a certain air that he didn't belong on a beach full of sunbathing girls and boisterous teenagers. Somehow he just seemed more refined than any boy I knew.

I scrambled to remember his question and replied in a voice so calm I even surprised myself, "Pleasure."

"Huh," he muttered to himself as if he hadn't been expecting my response and was taken aback. "Ambitious."

"Yeah well, it's one of my life goals so…" I trailed off.

His head cocked to one side at that admission. "Your life goal is to read *The Complete Works of William Shakespeare*?" he asked, quoting the title of my volume. Instead of sounding turned off or confused as I assumed a guy like him would be, he sounded fascinated. Intrigued even.

"One of," I clarified. "I have a lot of life goals. But yes, it is."

"Huh," he repeated while running a hand through his hair. It was a simple enough gesture but it had me wanting things I had never wanted before. "There's a lot of tragedy," he noted.

"There's plenty of comedy," I countered. A smile lit his face and right then I knew if that was the only smile I saw for the rest of my life, I would be perfectly content.

Before he could respond again, a hand came down on my shoulder. I flinched at the contact and hoped he wouldn't notice. "Come on, C. It's the last day of summer. Stop reading and come swim with us." My friend Nate grabbed my hand and tugged me to my feet, causing my book to go tumbling to the sand. I bit my lip and shrugged my shoulders at the mystery man.

"Wait, aren't you going to tell me your name?" he asked as Nate relentlessly pulled me towards the water.

"I really don't see any point," I replied coyly over my shoulder.

A smile spread across his face and he chuckled at me. Then I saw him slowly bend down and carefully place my book back on the blanket right side up, his fingers gently skimming over the gold lettering. He looked back at me and shook his head, that perfect smile still on his lips. "Don't give us a story like Romeo and Juliet where I don't know your name until it's too late!" he called after me, but I only laughed and turned back to face the water. "My name's Noah! Just so you know. Noah Sweeney!"

I laughed at his effort but didn't look back again, only picked up my pace until I was running into the waves in an attempt to catch up with Nate. When I finally turned back to face the beach, my hair dripping salt water now, I expected him to still be there. I expected him to be standing there, still looking perfectly out of place on the hot sand watching me. But he wasn't. I frowned for a minute, disappointed.

"Noah Sweeney..." I whispered to myself. Then I smiled slowly. What I didn't know was that he was wrong. Knowing his name wouldn't change anything for us.

Noah

"Hey, where'd you go this afternoon? I must have fallen asleep for a bit but when I woke up you weren't there."

I thumbed through another folder, making sure I had the class list and a copy of the syllabus for this class. "Oh, I went for a walk down the beach. You know I don't like just sitting there." I replied distractedly while I placed the folder back in my bag and grabbed a second one. I began flipping through the pages of this one until Whitney suddenly snapped my bag closed on my hand as I reached for another folder.

"Noah!" she snapped, clearly exasperated with me.

"What are you doing?"

"What are *you* doing?" she fired back. "Relax. You're going to be fine. You're always fine."

"This isn't just going to a new class, Whitney. This is important."

"I know that," she huffed. "but Jesus, Noah. I haven't seen you smile or laugh in a week. Well, it's been even more than just a week. It's been months. I thought going to the beach would give you a break."

The beach was something she liked, not me. She hadn't thought it would help me. She had thought of herself, just like she always did. I only sighed and the girl with the book came to mind. I almost smiled just thinking about her. When I blinked, Whitney's defeated face came back into focus. She couldn't be more different from that girl; I could tell that from the few short moments I spent with Juliet. But I reminded myself that I loved Whitney, because I did. Right? I did love her. I had to after dating her for so long. She had dealt with my bullshit for so long. So I took a deep breath before replying, "It did. It was nice. But I need you to understand this is a big deal for me, Whit. This internship could be the difference between me actually getting a job to support us or not. A job that will allow me to get him back. I need this. *We* need this."

"What *we* are you even talking about, Noah?" she said angrily, her eyebrows raising in a challenge. "Because it seems to me that the only *we* you'll ever care about does not include me. It just includes him." I bit my lip in regret. I didn't want another fight. Since Keaton had left us I thought she would have been happier; that it would have relieved some part of the strain from her and put it squarely on my shoulders. Clearly, that wasn't the case. All it had done was make me miserable and her even more dissatisfied with me.

"I didn't mean it like that. I meant us...you and me. You know that."

"No, actually, I don't know that," she snapped.

"Whitney, come on. Can we not do this right now?" I pleaded. She rolled her eyes and swiveled away from me, quickly stalking out of the room. Her dark hair had only just disappeared around the doorway when the phone rang. Seconds later, she was back in front of me, thrusting the phone at my chest.

"It's for you," she hissed before turning on her heel. I rolled my eyes at her back and lifted the receiver to my ear.

"Hello?"

"Noah Sweeney?" A deep voice boomed back at me.

"Uhm, yes?" I stammered.

"This is Principal Goldsworth."

"Oh, right, of course. Hello, Sir." I squeezed my eyes shut and inwardly groaned at my lack of finesse.

"Yes, good evening. Well you see Mr. Sweeney, the reason I'm calling is because there has been an accident. With Mrs. Granger."

My breath caught. "What do you mean an accident?"

"She passed away last night. An unexpected heart failure."

"Oh my God," I gasped, "That's terrible."

"Yes. As you can assume, it has put us in a bit of a predicament. School opens tomorrow and it seems like our staff is one English teacher short. I, of course, could find a substitute in the interim. But then I realized we have you at our disposal."

"What do you mean exactly, Mr. Goldsworth?"

"If you want it, the position is yours for the year."

I sat down at the counter in shock. "I...I'm not sure what to say."

"Yes would be acceptable."

"Yes. Yes, of course I want the job, Sir."

"Wonderful," he said brusquely. "We'll go over the details tomorrow morning. Please arrive early to meet in my office. It is my understanding that you are prepared to begin tomorrow? Mrs. Granger had everything ready at school. Other than that, you should be prepared from the last week."

"Yes, Sir."

"Very well. I'll see you bright and early tomorrow, Mr. Sweeney." And with that, the line went dead.

***

I picked up the remaining syllabi and counted them out, making sure I had twenty-four to match this class roster. I was tired and more than a little overwhelmed. Most of all, I was sick of the sidelong glances and hurried whispers I got whenever I walked through the halls. For the last half of the day, I had stayed hidden in my room to avoid the throngs of high school girls. I kept reminding myself this was what I wanted, but more than that, this was what I *needed*. If this year went well, I could get Keaton back even sooner than I had anticipated.

There was a soft knock on my door and it was pushed open to reveal another teacher who looked only a few years older than me. "Hey, I'm Grant," he extended his hand and I shook it.

"Noah."

"Yeah, I heard." His smile was a more reserved one but one that exuded a sense of calm nonetheless. For some reason, he gave off a feeling of positivity. "It gets better you know."

"What?"

"This. All of it," he extended his arms to encompass the classroom around us. Then he smiled at me again. "It's overwhelming at first, trust me I remember it well. But it's great, you'll see. If you ever want to grab a beer some time, let me know. You'll probably need one after this week."

I gave him a small smile. "Thanks. I'll keep that in mind." I wondered what it would be like to go get a beer and take time to hang out with friends just for fun. It struck me just how much I had missed out on in the past years. Did I even know what a friend was at this point?

"Great! Well, it was nice meeting you, Noah. I'm sure I'll see you around."

"Yeah, yeah…Nice meeting you, too." He gave me one last reassuring smile before the door clicked shut behind him. Only seconds later, the bell rang and I took a deep breath in. *Almost over*, I repeated in my head for what had to be the tenth time this afternoon. The door swung open again and students began filing in. A pair of girls walked in and instantly blushed when I happened to glance their way. Their whispered giggles soon followed, and I inwardly groaned. *One more class.*

I uncapped my marker and turned my back to the classroom, meticulously spelling out my name on the board as the remaining kids found their seats. When the last bell rang, I turned to face my final class of the day. "As you can see, if you can read, my name is Mr. Sweeney. And I sure hope you can read seeing as this is senior English. Now, I know your schedules may say Mrs. Granger for this class, but she is no longer with us. So it'll just be me this year. And if you couldn't already tell by my lack of finesse, this is my first year teaching but I'm going to do the best I can."

I made my way around the desk and took a seat on the edge of it to survey this group of kids, half of which had their heads down. "I could lie and tell you that if I had known I was going to be your teacher today, I would have planned some fun activity. But even if I had time to plan, it probably still would have been less than exciting. So instead, I'll be cliché and we're just going to get to know each other today. I'll go around to everyone and you have to tell me your name and one thing about you. Then you can ask me any question you want and I have to answer honestly. Sound fair?"

There were a few groans, as I had been expecting, but for the most part the students nodded along. After teaching five different classes, I was pretty sick of this game myself but I didn't really have any other plan. Maybe this class would surprise me. I reached behind me for the class list to follow along with the new names and readied myself.

"Okay, so I guess we'll start here." I nodded my head to a girl with a pierced lip sitting in the first desk to my right. A lock of pitch black hair fell over one eye, a single purple streak capping off the look of teenage angst. "What's your name?"

She didn't even look up at me when she muttered, "Jade."

A pair of girls snickered from the back corner and I shot them a glare. "Okay, Jade. And something about you?"

She finally looked up from chipping off her own nail polish long enough to level me with the most bored expression I had ever seen. Her words came slow when she spoke. "I'm only here because I need this class to graduate. And no, I'm not asking you a question. Frankly, I don't give a damn about you."

I bit my lip to keep from laughing and attempted to regain my composure by checking her name off on my attendance list. I probably should be scolding her for her use of language or lack of participation. A real teacher probably wouldn't be on the verge of laughter from her response, but I couldn't help it. "Right then," I finally managed to get out. "Moving on." I focused on the girl to Jade's right. She couldn't be more opposite from the previous student. She sat with her back straight, hands folded before her. Her golden hair fell in perfect ringlets despite the heat of the late summer afternoon and it was neatly tucked into a ribbon tied with a bow.

"My name is Abigail. Something about me is that I've gone on three mission trips with my church to Ecuador, Haiti, and Guatemala." She proudly told me and beamed her blindingly white smile. I subconsciously blinked and flinched away from it in response and fought to give her a closed lip smile as a part of me struggled to picture this pastel-covered, prim and proper girl in a third world country.

"That's amazing Abigail." I replied politely, checking her name off and looking up again.

"So Mr. Sweeney, what do you do in your free time?"

I had answered this question in each one of my classes now but I continued to smile and paused as if to think of my answer. It wasn't a complete lie...it just wasn't the complete truth, either. That was the nice thing about being a teacher, though. No students would pry into your personal life. I could reveal as much or as little about myself as I wanted to. "I read a lot. Or I go for a run. I also play pick-up soccer if I have the time. So who's next?" I focused on the boy next to her. Max who raced motocross. I continued on, answering my favorite book, my favorite food, what music I liked, where I went to college. All the mundane questions.

I came to a girl in the back last who had an empty seat beside her even though she gave off the aura of popularity. Her dark hair was pin-straight and framed her face perfectly and her makeup gave her an intimidating, yet almost porcelain look. "I'm Samantha. Don't think of making it cute and calling me Sammie. It's just Samantha. I'm the class president. How old are you, Mr. Sweeney?" She said all this without pause, just calmly stared back at me, her eyes holding my own long after I had chuckled awkwardly at her forward question. Not one student had been so bold as to directly ask my age yet. Age seemed a taboo topic, but not to Samantha apparently. A few other girls began giggling yet again.

"Yeah Mr. Sweeney, how old are you?" One called out. Mariah I believed her name was.

I licked my lips and pushed off my perch on the desk to make my way behind it again. I stole a glance at the clock on the back wall while I fought back my initial response of *Too old for you*. Only three more minutes of class. I looked back to Samantha and she only folded her arms across her chest and raised one brow.

"Twenty-three." For the most part, the class remained silent, though I could hear some whispers rustling through the room, people calculating how many years older I was. Samantha for one, kept a perfect poker face as she gazed back at me until the door burst open and her eyes swiveled to see whoever had just walked in. I worried it would be Principal Goldsworth, already coming to check in. I straightened up in an effort to look more professional and turned to face him, but upon seeing the late arrival, my breath caught. Then, an uncontrollable smile spread across my face before I even had time to process.

"Juliet," I breathed.

Colby Millsaps

About the Author

At twenty-one years old, Colby Millsaps has done more than many have done in a lifetime. After spending two years at The Ohio State University, her battle with depression led her back home to New Hampshire where she struggled to get her feet back under her. In less than a year after leaving OSU, she had self-published her debut novel *Crossing Lines*. In the summer of 2018, she took off to France with just a backpack and her eleven-month-old German Shepherd Dog, Maverick, to walk El Camino de Santiago from St. Jean Pied de Port, France through Santiago de Compostela, Spain all the way to Finisterre which was once considered the end of the known world. For now, she spends her days teaching high schoolers and hiking mountains in her home state while she plans her next overseas trek with Maverick.

To follow her adventures and writing endeavors, check out her website www.colbymillsaps.com or follow her page on both Instagram and Facebook @cmillsapswrites.

Other Titles by Colby Millsaps

Crossing Lines